Acclaim for the work of Philip Luber

By Philip Luber:

DEADLY CONVICTIONS
FORGIVE US OUR SINS*
DELIVER US FROM EVIL*
PRAY FOR US SINNERS*

Published by Fawcett Books

PRAY FOR US SINNERS

Philip Luber

FAWCETT GOLD MEDAL • NEW YORK

A Fawcett Gold Medal Book
Published by The Ballantine Publishing Group
Copyright © 1997 by Philip Luber

Grateful acknowledgment is made to Jon Landau Management for permission to reprint excerpt from the lyrics of "For You" music and lyrics by Bruce Springsteen. Copyright © 1973 CBS Inc.

http://www.randomhouse.com

Library of Congress Catalog Card Number: 97-97040

ISBN 0-449-18329-7

Manufactured in the United States of America

First Edition: February 1998

10 9 8 7 6 5 4 3 2 1

ACKNOWLEDGMENTS

For her gentle encouragement and support, I am grateful beyond all measure to Barbara Pankau.

I thank Lawrence Block for the inspiration of his writing and for his sage advice.

At critical junctures, these friends provided important help: Paul O'Brien, Greg Adams, Tim Vaill, Rory Cowan, and Les Malkiewich.

I thank my wife, Cindy Mate; my daughter, Holly Mate-Luber; my agent, Alice Martell; and my editor, Susan Randol. Thanks go also to Joe Blades and Kristen Busch at Ballantine Books for their assistance.

I will not leave you orphaned; I am coming to you.
—JOHN 14:18

Where is your father?
Where is my mother?
Where will I find you?
In the house of prayer.

1: Rachel

Santa Claus lay hurt: cut and bleeding.

His Salvation Army kettle was tipped over, and scattered coins on the sidewalk reflected the light of a nearby street lamp.

The little girl and her mother chanced upon the scene when they emerged from the department store. The girl noticed the small cluster of bystanders, then the overturned kettle, and then the stretched-out figure of the man in the red costume. He was lying on the sidewalk, his head propped up against the lamppost. It was drizzling lightly, and the drops that had collected on the lamppost trickled down onto the man's head.

Santa Claus was black. She had seen black people before, of course. There was one in her fourth-grade class, and a few scattered through the other grades in her school. But she had never seen one bleed.

Blood dripped from the man's lower lip to his synthetic white beard. She thought: *It's the same color as mine.* It would have to be, of course; her brain told her that. After all, blood is blood. But seeing the red flow on the black face was jarring for a moment, nonetheless.

The half dozen bystanders stood quiet and still in the drizzle, none of them taking any action. The girl's mother stepped forward. "What happened?" she asked.

A woman in an expensive fur coat with an umbrella shrugged her shoulders and turned away, sniffing the chilly air as if she were trying to locate the source of an offensive odor.

A tall man said, "A couple of teenagers. They grabbed some dollar bills. When they started to run away they bumped into him and he fell. They ran off that way." He pointed down Washington Street toward the Town Hall area.

"This is Wellesley," said the woman in fur. "These things don't happen here."

The girl's mother said, "Apparently they do." She drew a handkerchief from her handbag and knelt next to the black man. "Has anyone called the police?" she asked the others.

The bystanders glanced back and forth at one another. No one spoke.

"No," she said, answering her own question. "I suppose not." She looked at her daughter. "Darling, there's a pay phone in the lobby. Dial the operator and tell her a man has been attacked outside Filene's. I'm sure one of these *nice* people will lend you a dime." She leaned sarcastically on the word *nice*.

"She won't need money to call the operator," huffed the woman in fur.

The girl's mother glared at the woman, then said to her daughter, "Go ahead, darling."

The girl took a step toward the revolving door. This apparently shamed the tall man into action. "I'll call," he said, and he disappeared inside.

Her mother leaned toward the black man and dabbed at his blood with her handkerchief. "You must be cold," she said. "Do you suppose you can stand and walk inside the store?"

He didn't respond at first; he looked at her without expression. Then he shuddered, closed his eyes for a moment, and nodded.

"Here. Let me help you." Her mother placed a hand under the man's arm and guided him to his feet.

The Santa rose slowly. He steadied himself and looked at the bloodstained cloth on the ground. "Sorry about your handkerchief."

"It's not a problem."

"What's your name, ma'am?"

"Rachel Pace."

"Is this your daughter?"

"Yes."

He glanced at the girl and smiled, then turned back to the girl's mother. "God bless you," he said. "God bless you, Rachel Pace."

Afterward the girl and her mother walked east on Washington Street. The drizzle began to fall more steadily as they walked.

"Mom, do you think they'll catch the people who did it?"

"I hope so, darling."

"Why would somebody steal money from the Salvation Army?"

Her mother sighed. "I don't know. But it makes me angry. That woman in the mink coat was right. This sort of thing isn't supposed to happen here."

The girl thought about that as they walked past the upscale gift shops and clothing stores. "How come there aren't many black people in Wellesley?"

"I suppose it's a matter of money. And of prejudice."

"That isn't right."

"No, darling. It isn't right."

They came to a gourmet shop, and her mother said she needed to do some last-minute Christmas shopping. She selected four bottles of wine and had them gift-wrapped.

Stepping outside, they noticed that the rain had turned to snow. By the time they reached their car, it was coming down heavily. They placed their packages in the trunk and worked together to brush the flakes from the windshield and windows.

The girl slid into the front passenger seat and secured her seat belt. She asked, "Who did you buy the wine for?"

"They're extra presents. Sometimes neighbors or people from your father's law firm stop by unexpectedly with gifts. If that happens, I'll have something to give them in return. I leave the name tags blank until I need them, then I fill them in at the last minute."

"But isn't that dishonest?"

Her mother paused, then said, "If you brought someone a gift and received nothing in return, how would that make you feel?"

"I don't know. I guess I'd feel sad."

"Of course you would. Anyone would." The woman turned the key in the ignition and pulled slowly away from the curb. "Sometimes it's all right to tell a small lie to avoid hurting someone's feelings."

The girl considered that for a few moments. "But it's still a lie, isn't it?"

Her mother smiled. "You have a strong sense of justice. I hope you hold on to it."

They drove east into Newton Lower Falls, where they enjoyed the Thursday-night pasta special at their favorite Italian restaurant. It was still snowing when they finished dinner; by then, two inches had fallen.

They drove back to Wellesley. It was about eight-thirty when Rachel Pace guided her car up the inclined driveway, slipping slightly in the rapidly accumulating cover of snow, and pulled into the garage.

They watched television together for a short while as the snow continued to blanket their quiet street. Then the girl showered and readied herself for bed, and she came downstairs to say good night. "Can I sleep in your bed with you?"

"Not tonight, darling. I'm very tired, and you always thrash around when you sleep. Besides, your father called this afternoon to say he may come home a day early. It wouldn't be fair to make him sleep on the sofa after such a long trip, would it?"

The girl's eyes opened wide with excitement. "You didn't tell me Daddy was coming home tonight."

"I said he *may* come home tonight. With this weather, it's difficult to know. I didn't want to give you false hopes." They kissed good night. "Love you, darling."

"Love you, Mom." She walked toward the stairs, then turned around. "Are you mad at Daddy?"

"Am I . . . No, of course not. Why do you ask?"

"You keep saying 'your father' instead of 'Dad.' I just thought maybe you're upset or something."

Her mother sighed. "I miss him, that's all. I don't like being alone at night."

"You still have me."

Rachel Pace smiled. "Yes, darling. We'll always have each other."

A noise—she didn't know what—roused the girl from a deep dreamless sleep.

Nothing seemed amiss. The radiator hissed, the clock ticked, and her aquarium bubbled softly in the far corner of the room: familiar and soothing sounds.

She rose—too quickly—and grew dizzy when the blood rushed from her head. She waited until she felt steady, then walked to her window and pulled her shade up. The snowfall had stopped, but only after laying a three- or four-inch cover of white on the houses, sidewalks, and trees.

She heard a man's voice from down the hall and thought, *He's finally home.* Then there was a single thumping noise, like something striking the wall that separated her parents' room from hers, and she realized that a similar noise seconds earlier must have awakened her. The noise came again moments later: louder this time, making the wall vibrate. She heard her mother's voice—a muffled groan—and wondered: *Why are they rearranging the furniture?*

She staggered into the hallway and walked toward her parents' door. It was open. Their room was illuminated only by the dim glow of a night-light. The girl thought she saw something move, and she heard a gasp or a wheeze—like a weak whooshing sound.

She flipped the wall switch. In a flash, bright light flooded the room. It threw everything into crisp, stark relief.

They were locked in an embrace against the wall, clutching one another. She thought, *He's happy to be home.* And then she understood: It was not her father, and the embrace was anything but loving.

The man had her mother pinned against the wall. He wore dark pants and sweater, gloves, and a ski mask. Everything about her mother registered instantly and indelibly: her throat in the clutch of one of the assailant's hands as she struggled for breath . . . her face being pummeled by the other hand . . . the trail of spattered blood droplets on the wall behind her.

Her mother's eyes widened when they met hers. The woman said nothing, could say nothing, and yet the girl knew what her mother was trying to tell her: *Run away! Run away!* But fear seized her. She stood as though glued in place, unable to turn away from the nightmare unfolding in front of her.

The attacker yanked Rachel's long hair, whipped her forward, then flung her skull against the wall. She crumpled to the floor.

The man turned. The girl stared at him for the briefest of moments. Then she looked at her mother: horrible as that sight was, she couldn't look away, even though she knew the attacker was moving toward her.

An ammonia-like odor enveloped her, a warm wetness spread down both legs, and she realized she had wet herself. She looked down at her pajama bottoms. And as she moved her gaze from her mother to herself, she saw it for the first time: the small handgun, lying on the corner of the bed, fallen there during her mother's futile struggle.

The man was almost upon her. She lunged for the pistol and grabbed it, falling to the floor as she did so. He stopped in his tracks and hovered near her, considering his next move.

He was panting; she felt his breath on her face. She aimed the barrel at the man's chest, the widest part of the target. She tried to pull the trigger, she wanted to pull the trigger, but fear kept her fingers frozen.

He dropped his hands to his sides. He slowly backed away. He fixed his eyes on her as he moved toward the door. She held the pistol in front of her as he backpedaled across the room.

He lingered briefly in the doorway. He hissed, "Until we meet again."

The man disappeared into the hallway, then ran down the steps and through the house and out the back door.

And when the intruder was gone, when all was silent, her fingers finally unlocked. She squeezed the trigger and fired wildly: once, twice, then two more times in rapid succession, until the gun was empty.

The words echoed inside her head: *Until we meet again.*

2: The Manner of Death

The body is opened with the usual Y-shaped thoracoabdominal incision. . . .

On a midwinter New England night, I sat alone in my den and paged through Rachel Pace's autopsy report. There were words and terms I hadn't read since my medical-school training almost twenty years earlier. *Sclerae . . . Sella turcica . . . Subconjunctival hemorrhage . . .*

I learned some personal details: Her daughter was born by C-section. A childhood fracture of Rachel's left tibia healed poorly, leaving a visible bump and, perhaps, a slight limp. She had had a hysterectomy. Her final meal—only partially digested at the time of death—included pasta, broccoli tips, and pieces of white meat chicken.

I learned things that weren't known until after her death: the thickness of the adipose tissue in her abdominal wall; the quantities of fluid in her bladder and pericardial sac; the weights of her heart, lungs, brain, liver, spleen, and kidneys.

And I learned that skull fracturing ran from the anterior cranial fossa to the right parietal-temporal region.

In his summary opinion, the medical examiner was unequivocal:

The decedent died from multiple blunt-force injuries to the head. These injuries involve the central forehead, nose, and right forehead and face.

7

These injuries caused skull fracture, facial fracture, bleeding within the brain, and bruising of the brain.

There were finger marks present on the neck, but there was no significant trauma to the neck muscles or other tissues, except for the skin.

There were no preexisting injuries or disease which may have contributed to death.

The manner of death is homicide.

I knew that the name Rachel meant "like a lamb." I thought: *A lamb to the slaughter.*

I tossed another log into the fireplace and stoked the embers. I looked outside; the light snowfall that had dropped an inch of fresh powder was winding down. In the distance, off by the wildlife refuge, I heard a few staccato beeps: hardy Canada geese whose winter migration had taken them no farther south than Concord, Massachusetts.

I returned the autopsy file to its folder and reviewed the crime-scene report and witness statements. I already knew the essential facts from conversations with Rachel's husband and daughter, although both of them were reluctant to talk very much about the murder. "I don't want to cry anymore," the daughter had told me.

It occurred to me that Rachel had unknowingly saved her daughter's life by not allowing the girl to share her bedroom that night. I wondered if her daughter ever considered that. If she did, the thought probably heaped a pile of survivor's guilt onto the normal terror and depression that someone who witnessed her mother's murder would feel.

Survivor's guilt: Someone in my field—some other psychiatrist, or maybe a psychologist or social worker—coined that expression to describe the depression experienced by people who come through accidents in which others were killed. They think: Why was I spared? I am no better than those who died. I do not deserve a fate better than theirs.

According to the police report, a neighbor heard the shots Rachel's daughter fired and telephoned the police.

She had told me that after firing the gun, she cowered on the floor, her eyes shut tight as if she were willing the horrible scene away. She didn't know how much time passed. She was aware of doorbells ringing, knocks on the front door, and people moving through the house and up the stairs to the second floor.

Two Wellesley police officers entered the bedroom: crouched, guns drawn. They saw two collapsed bodies on opposite sides of the bed: the inert form of a murdered woman, and a trembling nine-year-old girl. I supposed the acrid smell of cordite hung in the air; the police report said the girl was still holding the handgun when the officers got there.

By the time the police photographer arrived, Rachel Pace's skin had blanched and the streams of blood had clotted and dried on her face. Blood looks jet-black on monochromatic film; gazing at the crime-scene pictures, I was struck by the sharp contrast between the dark congealed liquid and Rachel's alabaster skin. Her head tilted toward the side at a most unusual angle; I was surprised the autopsy didn't list a broken neck in its catalog of injuries and insults.

I scanned the reports from the homicide investigation: the reconstruction of the victim's final hours, the interviews with friends and relatives, the questioning and requestioning of the young girl. But I already knew the bottom line: No one had any idea who the murderer was, and no one had a clue about identifying him. Rachel Pace's killer was still at large.

Forensic evidence was sparse. There were fibers underneath Rachel's fingernails: fibers consistent with the ski mask her daughter said the killer wore. There were no unexplained fingerprints: not at the point of break-in, or in the bedroom, or on the kitchen telephone that the killer lifted from its hook.

I put all the documents back into the folder, pausing over one of the crime-scene pictures: a close-up of Rachel's face. Her lifeless eyes were open. I wondered: What if her retina could retain the last image cast upon it before death, her killer's ski-masked visage? Would we be any closer to knowing who had snatched her life away?

"Hi, Dad."

My daughter startled me. Lost in thought, I hadn't heard her enter the den. I hurriedly slipped the photograph into the folder. Melissa saw me do that. She said, "Let me guess. You're looking at something you think I'm not old enough to understand."

I avoided the question. "It's a school night, sweetheart. Don't you think you should be in bed?"

Melissa shrugged. "Usually the geese help me fall asleep. Tonight they're keeping me up. What's in the folder?"

"Nothing, really. Just some reports."

"About one of your patients?"

I shook my head. "No, it's something Veronica brought home for me to review."

"An FBI case?" The thought clearly excited her.

"Not exactly. But something like that." I glanced at my watch. "I really think you should get into bed."

"Yeah, I guess so." She yawned. "Where are you sleeping tonight—your room, or Veronica's room?"

I nodded toward the window, in the direction of the barn that was converted into an apartment years earlier. "I think I'll walk over to see Veronica. Is that all right with you?"

"Sure."

"If you need me, just use the intercom."

"Uh-huh. And remind her she's supposed to come talk to my class tomorrow, okay? I think the other fifth-grade class is joining us."

"I'll remind her. But I'm sure she hasn't forgotten."

"Thanks." She walked toward the door, then turned back toward me. "What should I call her?"

"What do you mean?"

"When Veronica comes to my school tomorrow. I could say she's my father's friend, but that sounds so weird. And I can't say the two of you are boyfriend and girlfriend."

"Why not?"

"*Dad*-dee. You're too, uh . . ."

"Too what?"

"You're too, you know—too *old* to be somebody's boyfriend."

I thought for a moment. "Why don't you just introduce Veronica as *your* friend?"

Melissa considered that. "Yeah. That'll be okay. Thanks, Dad. G'night."

She turned away again. I called after her. "Melissa?"

"Huh?"

"Nolan Ryan pitched a no-hitter when he was about a year older than me. He threw another one a year later."

"Nolan who?"

"You know who Nolan Ryan is."

She smiled. "G'night, Dad."

"Good night, sweetheart. I love you."

"Uh-huh." She yawned once more, then went upstairs.

I used the intercom to call over to Veronica in the barn apartment. "It's me," I said. "I'll be there in a few minutes."

"All right, Harry."

I grabbed the folder with the autopsy and police reports. I put on an overcoat and stepped outside, locking the door behind me. I looked up at the second story; Melissa's room was dark. I walked the thirty yards to the barn, my footsteps scattering the thin layer of freshly fallen powder.

My wife and I bought the property almost a dozen years earlier, when she was pregnant with Melissa. The old Concord farmhouse was built around 1800, and it sat on two acres of land near North Bridge, where colonial Minutemen returned British fire for the first time. We converted the barn into an apartment, complete with an intercom setup to communicate with the house, and a live-in housekeeper stayed there for many years, until the previous July. After she retired, Veronica moved in.

My wife had been dead for almost seven years. Janet lay buried a mile down the road in Sleepy Hollow Cemetery, the resting place of the Emersons, Alcotts, and Thoreaus. There was snow on the ground when she died. And now, whenever it snowed, I remembered what Melissa said the day Janet was buried: "I don't want Mommy to be cold."

I looked at the snow-covered field next to the barn. When Melissa was a toddler, Janet took her into the field and taught her how to make snow angels. But Melissa stopped making snow angels after her mother died.

I let myself into the barn. When I flipped the switch for the stairwell light, the bulb blew. I pulled my key chain out and used the small flashlight on it to light my way.

I climbed the stairs to Veronica's apartment. I walked through the living room and into the bedroom.

Veronica was sitting on the edge of the bed, toweling herself dry from her shower. She watched me set the folder with the murder materials on her dresser. "Put it in the safe," she said. "Melissa may come over in the morning. It's not a healthy thing for an eleven-year-old to see."

I thought: *It's not a healthy thing for anyone to see.* I opened the small safe that doubled as a nightstand. I placed the folder on top of Veronica's service revolver. Then I shut the door and spun the dial.

I said, "The light on the stairs needs a new bulb."

"I'll tell the landlord."

"Very funny. I'll replace the bulb for you in the morning."

"Thanks." She yawned. "Are you staying here tonight?"

"Yes," I replied.

"Did you remember to leave a note for Melissa?"

"She was still awake a few minutes ago. She knows I'm here."

She nodded toward the bed. "I don't think I feel like . . . you know, doing anything."

"That's okay." I kicked off my shoes and began to get undressed.

She asked, "What did you think of the materials?"

I hesitated. "It's sad beyond words."

She sighed. "I couldn't bring myself to look at the pictures. I had a hard enough time just reading the reports." She looked at the floor for several seconds. "What do you think I should do, Harry?"

I didn't know what to say. "Let me take a shower first. Then we can talk about it." I grabbed a towel from the linen closet, walked into the bathroom, and turned the water on full force.

I was worried about Veronica. Her depression had ripened

for several weeks. I knew it was related to the murder I had spent the previous hour reading about.

I couldn't bring myself to look at the pictures. Before she moved over to the FBI, Veronica prosecuted homicide cases. Over the years she had visited dozens of murder scenes. So she was no stranger to scenes of utter depravity: She walked in them, studied them, sifted through the evidence . . . all in the name of justice, and all without blinking an eye.

But Rachel Pace's murder was different. And Veronica couldn't bring herself to look at the pictures.

I crawled into bed and made sure the covers on my side were tucked firmly in place, lest Veronica pull them off of me during the night. *You always thrash around when you sleep.* I moved toward her. Her back was toward me; I placed an arm around her waist and kissed her lightly on the neck. The fire glow reflected off her cheek.

She said, "I've never had a fireplace in my bedroom before. It soothes me."

"It was Janet's idea. She thought that when Melissa grew up we would give the house to her, and we'd move over here. She had it all planned out. I guess things have a way of not working out like we plan them."

"I know." She brushed her dark curls off of her face. "It still bothers me sometimes when you talk about your wife. Maybe someday it won't." She turned around. "Harry, please tell me. What do you think I should do?"

I knew she was talking about Rachel's murder again. "Any reasonable person in your situation would have a hard time deciding."

"Don't talk to me like I'm one of your patients. I need to know what's on your mind. What do you think I should do?"

I held her in my arms and said, "I think you should let it be."

She pressed her cheek hard against my chest and wrapped her arms tightly around me. "I guess I should," she said. "But I can't." She trembled silently, and I felt her tears dropping onto me. In our year and a half together, I had seldom seen her cry.

Veronica turned away again and stared at the fading fire. She said, "When I was in school I read a play about a man whose spirit was forced to wander in limbo until the person who killed him was brought to justice. And that's how I think of her. She's out there, somewhere . . . wandering . . . and I have to do something to help her rest in peace."

Nothing is worse than having to watch helplessly while someone you love suffers. I went through it with Janet when the cancer devoured her. I had done it with Melissa countless times, over sorrows large and small. When the only thing you can do is love someone, love never seems enough.

I rested my hand on Veronica's side. "Whatever you decide to do, I'll help you any way I can."

She clasped her hand over mine: tightly at first, then more weakly as she drifted off to sleep. She said, "Her last words to me were, 'We'll always have each other.' "

And as the flames died and the embers cooled, just before she fell into a fitful slumber, Veronica Pace murmured, "I have to know. . . . Who killed my mother?"

3: A Movie of My Life

Bobby Beck handed his breakfast menu to the Colonial Inn waitress and lifted the cup of decaf to his lips. He sipped, considered the taste for a few seconds, then set the cup down.

"How is it?" I asked.

"How is what?"

"Your coffee."

"You don't like coffee, Harry."

"So?"

"So why do you care how my coffee is if you don't drink coffee?"

"Geez, why are you so cranked up?"

Bobby paused. "Sorry, pal of mine." He sighed. "I'm preoccupied by the deposition I have to take this morning. A special-education teacher in Chelmsford is suing the school system. She objects to the education plan her supervisors wrote for one of her students. The boy is mentally retarded, he has seizures, he has trouble controlling his movements, he drools all the time—the poor kid has lots of problems. And he has a tendency to gag on his own saliva. The education plan says the teacher shouldn't try to intercede if that happens."

"Why?"

"The parents are single-minded when it comes to all that 'may God's will be done' stuff. They figure if a glob of saliva gets stuck in the kid's windpipe and he can't dislodge it on his

15

own, then that must be God's way of calling him home. And they don't want anyone standing in God's way."

"And the school system is going along with that?"

"The superintendent is afraid the parents will take him to court if he doesn't go along. What he didn't count on was the teacher making such a fuss. She has this crazy idea that it might be bad for the other children's welfare if they have to watch this kid choke on his own sputum. She says if she can't help the kid in an emergency, the other kids won't feel safe in her room."

"Hell of a nerve she has."

"Yeah," Bobby said, echoing my sarcasm. "Hell of a nerve."

I buttered a slice of toast. "What does she want?"

"She just wants the court to invalidate the kid's education plan."

"She's not looking for any money? Claiming emotional distress, that sort of thing?"

"No. She just doesn't want to have to stand by if he starts to choke. She's a very impressive woman. I like her. I think you would, too, Harry."

Our waitress brought Bobby's French toast and my bowl of cereal. "What are the teacher's chances?"

He shrugged. "Fifty-fifty for a temporary injunction. Maybe a twenty-percent likelihood of prevailing in the end."

"That's all?"

"Her only real chance is if the court appoints an outside guardian to represent the kid's interests, which it may or may not do—and then the guardian joins in the teacher's suit, which *he* may or may not do."

I poured milk into my bowl and sprinkled sugar over the cereal. "Sounds like your kind of odds."

"What do you mean?"

"Twenty percent. You're a four-to-one underdog on the side of justice and mercy. You've always liked that sort of fight."

He frowned. "Yeah, well, my firm is representing the school officials."

"You're *kidding* me. Why?"

"Because that's how the system . . . C'mon, Harry, you don't need me to explain that to you. You can't always handpick your clients." Bobby speared a piece of French toast with his fork. "It's giving me a headache. And speaking of headache, or maybe I should say pain in the ass, here comes Lower Case *b*."

Alfred Korvich, Concord's police chief, approached us. Bobby called him Lower Case *b*—behind his back—because of his unusual shape: a prodigious potbelly hanging off an otherwise skinny frame.

"Well, well," Korvich said. "Ever since they changed management, I guess they let anyone eat here."

Bobby said, "Nice seeing you, too, Chief."

"Last week I saved one of your legal brethren from drowning."

"That's nice."

"Ask me how."

"Excuse me?"

"Ask me how I stopped him from drowning."

Bobby sighed. "All right, Chief. How did you save a lawyer from drowning?"

"I took my foot off his neck." Korvich beamed. "Well, I'd love to sit down, fellas, but duty calls."

"That's redundant," Bobby said.

"Huh?"

" 'Sit down' is redundant, like 'stand up' or 'fall down.' 'Redundant' means needlessly repetitious. Really. You could look it up."

"I *know* what 'redundant' means." Korvich was no longer smiling. "And you could look up 'schmuck.' "

I jumped in, trying to defuse the situation. "I think he'd need a Yiddish dictionary for that, Chief."

He turned on me. "Don't condescend me, Harry. I've told you that before."

Bobby said, "I think you mean, 'Don't condescend *to* me.' "

Korvich muttered something, then left.

I said, "You shouldn't bait him like that. No need going out of your way to get on his bad side."

"He started it."

" 'He started it.' What are you—eight years old? Anyway,

Korvich would probably say you started it with the statue thing."

At North Bridge, just down the road from my house, was a famous statue of a colonial Minuteman. It was sculpted by Daniel Chester French, a Concord resident best known for the huge statue of Lincoln at the Lincoln Memorial. A few years earlier the National Guard had asked the town for permission to make a copy of the statue for their national headquarters. I thought it was a reasonable request, but most Concordians opposed it: Yankee parochialism at its worst.

For reasons I never quite understood, Bobby Beck led the fight to deny the statue to the National Guard. He prevailed.

Chief Alfred Korvich was in the National Guard. He remembered.

Bobby said, "I don't think he's terribly fond of you, either."

"It's because of last spring," I replied.

The previous year I had killed a man in self-defense. I was cleared of any wrongdoing, but Korvich didn't like having to process the matter. It upset his concept of what a small-town police chief should have to deal with.

Bobby said, "Murders aren't supposed to happen in Concord."

"Or Wellesley."

"Wellesley?"

I told him about Veronica's intention to investigate her mother's long-ago murder. She had given me permission to tell Bobby; she knew I kept few things secret from him.

He said, "I hope your girlfriend knows what she's getting herself into, opening up that can of worms."

"Melissa says I'm too old to call Veronica my girlfriend."

"Smart kid. She has a point."

"Thanks a lot."

"Don't mention it." He swirled his French toast in the blueberry syrup.

"I tried to talk her out of it, but I couldn't. She's meeting with her boss this afternoon. She may ask for a month off."

"How old was she when it happened?"

"Almost ten."

"And she saw the whole thing," he said. "Christ. How do people get over something like that?"

"I don't think they do."

"No, I guess not. How long ago was it? Twenty years?"

"Twenty-one years ago last month. A few days before Christmas."

Bobby did the arithmetic in his head. "That was our senior year at Tufts," he said. "It must have made the news. I wonder if you or I read about it back then."

"Maybe. I don't remember. Unless you were personally connected to the case, it probably wouldn't catch your attention more than any other homicide. Just an attempted burglary gone wrong. The only thing noteworthy was that it happened in Wellesley instead of Dorchester or Roxbury."

Like our town of Concord, Wellesley is an enclave for the wealthy and privileged, a place where homicides are extremely rare.

I said, "I tried to talk her out of pursuing this. I don't think anything good will come of it. I figure the trail is too cold, and she won't be able to do anything the police didn't do, and she'll end up more forlorn when she comes up empty at the end."

"You're probably right. Still, some investigators specialize in things like this. A lot of big cities have what they call a cold-case squad—detectives who take a fresh look at old unsolved murders."

"How do they solve them?"

"They don't, usually. But if the physical evidence has been preserved, sometimes they can analyze it with new technologies—DNA testing, or specialized methods for lifting fingerprints. Or sometimes someone who kept silent about what he knows has a pang of conscience years later. And sometimes just bringing a fresh perspective to old evidence breathes new life into it, like spotting a line of inquiry that was somehow overlooked years earlier."

"Even so, I wish she would just drop it."

"Maybe she can't."

"Maybe not." I swallowed a couple of spoonfuls of cereal.

"Is she still staying in the apartment in your barn? She hasn't moved back into the house?"

"She was never officially *in* the house. She just used to spend most of her time there."

"But she's officially *in* the barn, right?"

I nodded. "She sold her condo and moved in after Mrs. Winnicot retired." Mrs. Winnicot was my live-in housekeeper for many years.

"You and Veronica have a strange arrangement."

"It's just the way things have worked out. Maybe it'll change. Maybe it won't. I asked her dozens of times to move into the house. I began asking her to do that last year, before she even moved into the barn. Finally, I stopped asking."

"But you love her."

"Yes."

"As much as you loved Janet?"

"It's different. I try not to compare them."

"And you go along with this strange arrangement because you love her." Bobby beckoned to our waitress for a refill on his decaf. "Let me tell you about a case I handled when I was a criminal lawyer, way back when."

"I've always liked that expression. 'Criminal lawyer.' "

He ignored my gibe. "A very attractive woman in her thirties, divorced—we'll call her Bonnie—she asks her boyfriend to kill another woman in the neighborhood. So the boyfriend—we'll call him Clyde—"

"That's cute."

"So Clyde engages in the obligatory five minutes of soul-searching, then agrees to do it. But he botches the job, ends up shooting himself in the ankle, and goes to the emergency room to get patched up. The doctor there calls the police, which they always do when someone shows up with an inconveniently placed bullet hole. The police come, they question the fellow, and he folds like the legendary house of cards, tells them the whole story."

"Which you will now tell me, even if I don't want you to."

"It turns out Bonnie's teenage daughter was trying to become a high-school cheerleader. There was one opening on the squad, and there was one other girl in the running. That other girl's mother was the woman Clyde was supposed to kill."

"I don't get it."

"Bonnie thought the other girl would be so overcome with grief after her mother was killed, she'd drop out of the competition."

"And Bonnie's daughter would win by default."

"Exactly. Bonnie was willing to plan a murder in order to help her daughter get what she wanted. And Clyde was willing to do the killing to help Bonnie get what *she* wanted." He pushed his plate away, leaned back in his chair, and wiped his lips with his napkin. "I'm sure you understand my point."

"I'm not even sure *you* understand your point."

"The point is—when it comes to love, there's no telling what some people will do."

A blinding snow squall, wet and wind-driven, welled up in the middle of the afternoon. When it hit I was on my way into Bedford, the next town over from Concord. As the flakes fell on my windshield they melted and turned to ice. I ran my defroster on high blast, crossed through the center of town, and drove toward the Veterans Administration Hospital where I had worked several years earlier.

The lot next to the administration building was slick with snow. Visibility was poor, and as I pulled slowly into a parking space I was barely able to make out a dark object amid the swirling flakes. Only when I stopped directly in front of the object did I realize it was a person: a tall, razor-thin man in a hooded sweatshirt. He was underdressed for the weather, yet he stood mute and motionless, not shivering. His skin tone and facial features suggested a Middle Eastern ancestry. The man gazed at me through the car window, expressionless.

I took my eyes off of him for a moment as I stepped out of my car; by the time I looked up again, he was gone. I assumed he was a patient. I wondered if the staff on his ward knew he was wandering in the snow.

The lobby of the administration building was deserted. The odor I used to smell in my sleep at the end of a hard day washed over me: a mixture of mildew and ammonia. The buildings at the Bedford VA always reminded me of the patients on the chronic wards: clean and well tended on a day-to-day basis, but decaying and in desperate need of repair.

No one was in the receptionist's area of the hospital director's office. Someone heard me arrive and called from the inner office. "I'm in here. Please come in."

Dr. Greta Anselm sat behind her desk. "Dr. Kline, isn't it?" she said.

"Yes."

"Sit down, please. Forgive me for not getting up."

She gestured in a downward motion, and I noticed that she was in a wheelchair. I had met her briefly near the end of my tenure at the hospital, shortly after she joined the staff as chief of radiology. Now I remembered that she relied heavily on a cane back then, and I assumed that whatever condition she suffered from had taken a degenerative course.

She wasn't one for small talk. After a brief question about the driving conditions, she flipped open a folder on her desk. "I pulled your old personnel file after you made this appointment with my secretary. I understand you want to come back to work at the VA. You used to direct one of the psychiatric wards, am I correct?"

"Yes."

"Both psychiatric wards have full-time directors now. I don't anticipate either doctor leaving in the foreseeable future."

Her tone was neither unkind nor solicitous. She was merely providing information and waiting for my reaction.

I said, "I'm looking for a part-time position, perhaps one or two mornings, nothing more."

"I understand. Something predictable to supplement your income. I know managed care has really put private practitioners into something of a tailspin. Am I correct?"

"In a way." She was right about the general decline of the private practice of psychiatry. She was dead wrong about my reasons for wanting to return to the hospital.

She shuffled the papers in my personnel folder. "You first came here directly after your residency at McLean Hospital."

"Yes." McLean Hospital was a prestigious psychiatric facility on a rolling hill outside Boston.

"I know from your file that your skills are considerable. Did they offer you a position at McLean when your residency was completed?"

"They did."

"Those positions carry appointments to the faculty at Harvard Medical School. Am I correct?"

I nodded.

"Yet you came here instead, even though you had the opportunity for something more prestigious, more remunerative. Why was that?"

By the end of my residency, I was weary of the patients—and their families—who believed their names, wealth, or position entitled them to more consideration than people who weren't as privileged. Back then I assumed that VA patients were grappling with problems far weightier than trying to figure out the family time-sharing arrangements at summer estates in Bar Harbor and Martha's Vineyard. I was right.

I thought about all this, but said only, "I came here because the work suited me."

"I see." She paused. "But then you resigned about seven years ago, after working here for . . ." She glanced at the folder. "You resigned after five and a half years. May I ask why you left?"

"I wanted to spend more time at home."

She raised an eyebrow. She didn't say anything.

"My wife passed away shortly before I resigned. My daughter was only four years old. I wanted to spend more time with her."

"Oh." She closed the file and folded her hands on top of it. "I'm sorry. I didn't know. I didn't mean to intrude."

"No offense taken."

She sat quietly for several moments. "I may be able to use you for a few hours per week to do some supervision and training. I can't promise anything just yet. Would you be interested if something like that were available?"

"Very much."

"As I said, it would only be for a few hours, and at a rather low rate, I'm afraid."

"Dr. Anselm, just to let you know, I'm well situated. The work always interested me. That's why I'd like to come back part-time. Money isn't a big issue."

"Well, that's good, considering what we can afford to pay you." She gestured toward her window, in the direction of the lot, and smiled for the first time. "Of course, the parking is free."

"What more could a fellow ask for?"

She looked out the window and pointed. "Perhaps you can help us solve the mystery of Caleb Wilson."

I looked outside. The tall, thin man was standing motionless in the parking lot again.

"Is he a psychiatric patient?"

She nodded. "He was transferred from Walter Reed Hospital two weeks ago. His psychiatrist says he has post-traumatic stress disorder, and he may also be psychotic. He won't talk to us, and we can't learn anything about him. Whole portions of his record have been expunged. The Department of Defense isn't saying anything, but we're assuming he had a breakdown while he was working on an intelligence mission, perhaps in the Gulf War."

Caleb Wilson turned his face slowly toward the sky. Snow pelted him. He seemed oblivious.

"You and he have something in common, Dr. Kline."

"Oh?"

"The army offered to transfer him to any hospital of his choosing, no matter how expensive. He could have selected McLean or some other private facility. Instead he chose this hospital."

The man was facing the administration building now. I wondered if he saw us watching him.

Greta Anselm placed my personnel folder in her desk drawer. "The other day I found Mr. Wilson sitting in an empty room in the basement of this building. He was facing a bare wall. I asked him what he was doing. He told me he was watching a movie of his life, and that he had to stay there until the movie was over. Later I thought, what a terrible thing it would be—to be forced to watch a movie of your entire life."

"We've all gone through terrible times," I said.

"Yes. And we've all done terrible things."

I thought about a friend of mine, a Catholic priest. He would have you believe that God is with each of us in all the moments of our lives. I had my doubts.

The hospital director gestured toward the window again. "I wonder what goes on in his head. I'm a radiologist. We have CAT scans. We have PET scans. We have X-rays, EEGs, and MRIs. Not to mention evoked potentials." She sighed. "We can map a person's brain, but we can't fathom the human mind."

I looked out the window again. Caleb Wilson was nowhere in sight.

Shortly after I returned to my car the snow stopped as suddenly as it had begun. I drove through the center of Bedford and past the trailer park and defense contractors that ringed the north side of Hanscom Air Force Base.

As I approached the Concord town line my cellular phone rang.

"Harry, it's Martin Baines."

I had given very few people my cellular-phone number. Martin Baines wasn't one of them. He was Veronica's boss, the Special Agent in Charge at the Boston office of the FBI.

He said, "What's the story with Veronica?"

"Did she give you this phone number?"

"Of course not. Harry, what's going on? She met with me a little while ago and requested a leave of absence. Announced she's taking a leave would be a more accurate statement. Are you aware of this?"

"She told me she would be meeting with you."

"Did she tell you why she wants a leave?"

"Didn't she tell you?"

He hesitated. "No, and you know how stubborn she can be

when she wants to. But I assume you know what this is all
about. I'd like you to get her to change her mind."

Martin Baines joined the FBI right after college. So although he was only a few years older than me, his term at the
Bureau went back to the Nixon administration and the last days
of J. Edgar Hoover. He liked Veronica, and I'm sure he was
concerned about her. But he was from the old school: He
probably thought a man should be able to keep his woman under control.

"I'm not a happy camper, Harry. And when I'm not happy, I
get very . . . well, unhappy. See what you can do about this.
Please."

He hung up before I could learn how he got the phone
number—and before I could say, "Veronica will have a cow
when she learns you called me about her."

Ingrid was loading the dishwasher when I entered the house
through the kitchen door. She was the part-time housekeeper I
had hired the previous fall, primarily to watch my daughter
after school.

She said, "Melissa is upstairs with her friend Emily. I was
hoping I could leave early. I need to study for an exam tonight.
I made a casserole. All you need to do is heat it up for dinner."

"Sure. No problem."

She gathered her coat and gloves and headed for the door.

"Ingrid, did a fellow named Martin Baines call while I was
out?"

"There was one call while I was in the basement doing laundry. Melissa wrote down the message." She pointed at a note
on the table, then left.

The note was indecipherable. The previous year Melissa had
experimented with hairstyles, switching several times each
week in a symbolic quest to define herself. Now it was handwriting: constant changes in another mode of self-expression.
Today's choice was especially exasperating: convoluted curls
and waves that doubled and tripled back upon themselves, impossible to decode.

I took the note and walked upstairs to Melissa's room. The
door was open. She and Emily were sitting on the floor.

Melissa had taken her guitar from its case and was showing Emily the chords her music teacher had taught her.

It was her mother's guitar, actually: a steel-string Martin that Janet had since college. I gave it to Melissa after Janet died. I also gave her Janet's collection of folk-music records, which now occupied a shelf in Melissa's bookcase. When she first saw them, at age four, she said, "Gosh, they're so much bigger than CDs."

I stepped into her room. "I have your note here," I said. "It looks like my choices are either 'chill under water' or 'climb on an otter.' "

Melissa looked at Emily and started to laugh. "It says, 'Call Uncle Donald.' "

Donald Pace was Veronica's father. My daughter was the closest thing to a grandchild that Donald had. Veronica and I had been together for more than a year and a half—mostly on, sometimes off—and somewhere along the way Melissa began calling him Uncle Donald.

"Did he say what he wanted?"

"Just for you to call him. He said he'll be at his office until four-thirty."

"All right." I wondered if Veronica had told him about her intention to look into her mother's death. Perhaps that was what he wanted to talk about with me. I checked my watch, then asked, "How was Veronica's talk at school today?"

Melissa looked at her friend as if they were sharing a secret. "It was okay."

"Just okay?"

Emily said, "You should tell him, Melissa."

"Tell me what?"

"Go ahead, Melissa."

My daughter furrowed her brow. "She talked about the FBI, what she does and stuff like that, and then she let us ask questions. And Billy Spires, who is *such* a butthole—"

"Melissa!"

"I'm sorry, Dad, but he really is. Anyway, Billy asked her what it feels like to kill somebody. And everybody got really quiet, and Veronica just sat there for the longest time. And then she said she had to get into town for a meeting, and she left. And it looked like she was crying when she left."

I looked at Emily. The girl nodded, agreeing with Melissa's description of events.

"What's wrong with her, Dad?"

"I guess she just didn't want to talk about it." Melissa knew that Veronica once killed someone in the course of her job. I let her assume that Veronica was reacting to that memory; but I knew she was probably remembering the time she trained a gun on her mother's killer and didn't pull the trigger.

I heard the high-pitched hum of Veronica's Honda as it came up the long driveway and stopped between the house and the barn. I looked outside and saw her walking into the house. "I'll talk to her," I said. "By the way, did a man call here a little while ago and ask for my cellular-phone number?"

"Huh? No. Why? Was someone supposed to do that? I thought you told me never to give that number out to anyone."

"Just checking," I replied, and then I returned downstairs.

Veronica was hunched over on the couch in the den. I sat next to her. She leaned against me and put her head on my shoulder.

"Rough day?" I asked.

"I told Martin I needed to take some time off. It made him angry."

"I know."

She sat up and looked at me with a quizzical expression.

"He called me. He said you didn't tell him why you were taking a leave. And he asked me to try talking you out of it."

"He had no right to call you about me."

"That's true. But he was concerned about you."

"Well, I hate it when you men get that condescending attitude. Like women are mindless children who can't be trusted to make decisions for ourselves."

We sat quietly for a minute or two. I held her hand in mine.

She said, "Are you going to do what he asked? Are you going to try to talk me out of it?"

"Do you want me to?"

She paused. "If I get in over my head, you can tell me."

"How will I recognize if you are?"

She shrugged. "You're the doctor, Harry. You'll have to figure out if I'm falling to pieces. And then you'll have to put me together again. It's written in your job description." She clasped my hand with both of hers and pressed it to her heart. "Speaking of jobs, how did your meeting turn out?"

"Nothing definite yet, but I think it went well."

"I'm glad." She glanced at the paper I was holding in my hand, the note Melissa had written. "When did my father call?"

"I can't believe you can read that handwriting."

"It's not that difficult. Did you call him back yet?"

"I'm going to try now. Would you like to say hello?"

"No. I'll just sit here by myself for a little while if that's all right with you."

"Sure." I stood and walked toward the kitchen.

"Harry, please don't tell him about this. Don't tell him I'm trying to do something about my mother."

"All right."

"I'm not ready yet to talk about it with him. I'm not sure why. Do you promise?"

"I promise."

When I reached the doorway I turned back for a moment. Veronica was staring at the blank television screen. I thought: *She's watching a movie of her life*. And I ached for her.

4: Nightingale

When I spoke with Donald Pace he invited me for lunch the next day at his firm's private dining room. Donald was a senior attorney in the corporate-law division at Putnam & Blaine, one of Boston's most prestigious old-line law partnerships. Donald said we would be joined by a friend of his who needed some advice on how to find a psychiatrist. I accepted his invitation.

The wind cut through me when I emerged from the underground parking lot at Post Office Square, midmorning on Thursday. It was one of those winter blasts that roll off the ocean, then seem to gather strength as they squeeze through the city streets.

The NYNEX building loomed behind me. To my right was the segmented facade of the State Street Bank, its various portions jutting out and receding from view. Since my last visit to that area, several years earlier, a park had replaced an ugly three-story parking garage. I walked along its pathways toward the corner of Pearl and Milk streets.

I passed the Hotel Le Meridien. Its cardinal red awnings were rolled away for the winter. Chiseled into its stone facade were the words: FEDERAL RESERVE BANK BLDG #30. As I approached the building where Donald Pace's office was located, I saw that it, too, had an inscription from another era: MASSACHUSETTS BONDING AND INSURANCE CO. I was certain those words from yesteryear hadn't been left behind carelessly or casually by the buildings' developers. No doubt they were left—

perhaps even refurbished—as an homage to another time, an example of Boston's self-congratulatory veneration of its own upper-crust traditions.

The reception area of Donald's law firm was uncluttered and elegant. Visitors to Putnam & Blaine would immediately intuit that money was being made and important agreements were being brokered in every office that lined every hallway.

The receptionist took my overcoat and showed me into Donald's office. He greeted me warmly, and we sat in two leather chairs near the window. Two flights below lay the block-long park I had just walked through.

I said, "The city did a nice job improving the area."

"The city had very little to do with it. The old parking garage was a terrible eyesore. Some of the property owners in the area bought it and tore it down. Then they put in the park and the underground lot. They maintain the park, too. You should see it in the summer, Harry. It's quite a sight."

"I guess altruism survives."

"Perhaps." He shrugged. "But the truth is, property values shot up because of the improvements to the square, so everyone came out ahead. The people got a park, the city doesn't have to maintain it, and some very wealthy people became even wealthier."

We made some small talk about the Celtics, politics, and our daughters. Because I was twelve years older than his daughter, I was closer to Donald's age than most men are with the fathers of their partners. Talking with him had always come easy.

Donald said, "I'm glad you could come here on such short notice. I hope it's all right with you that someone will be joining us."

"You said she was a family friend."

"She is, but she's also a client. Marilyn Levine. I'm worried about her. I'd like her to see a psychiatrist."

I hesitated. "That would be awkward."

"Pardon? Oh—no, I'm not asking *you* to be her psychiatrist. I know you can't treat someone so close to me and my family. I'm just looking for help persuading her to go for a consultation. I think she needs to see a doctor, but she resists the idea."

"Why do you think she needs help?"

Donald reached toward a pile of neatly arrayed periodicals on a nearby table. He selected one and handed it to me. "You've probably heard of this company," he said.

It was a mail-order catalog for the M. L. Nightingale Company. They manufactured and distributed a line of casual wear. "Preppie clothes," I said. "I think my wife used to order from them. I recall her getting catalogs in the mail several times a year."

"Marilyn Levine started the company from scratch. She's the M. L. in M. L. Nightingale."

"Who's the nightingale?"

"Actually, she's the nightingale, too. Perhaps she'll tell you about that part over lunch. Marilyn has been with me for almost twenty-five years. When she started the company, she didn't have any business background at all. Before long she was in way over her head. She was a friend of my wife—my first wife, Rachel—and so she came to me for help. And she became my friend, too. A friend of the family. Ronnie used to call her Aunt Marilyn."

Ronnie was the nickname Donald sometimes used when he talked about Veronica.

According to Donald, Marilyn Levine was a talented and capable woman. But there was a dark side to her story, too. Marilyn Levine was high-strung and moody, subject to bouts of erratic behavior and deep despair. There were suicide attempts and psychiatric hospitalizations.

Donald said, "I'm uncomfortable revealing my friend's problems to you, someone she's never even met. But I know you'll be discreet with this information."

"Of course."

He continued. "After she went in and out of the hospital a few times, she was finally diagnosed as manic-depressive. Her psychiatrist prescribed medication, and he kept her on a fairly even keel for many years."

"Was it lithium?"

He nodded. "Unfortunately, her doctor retired three months ago. And Marilyn refuses to start treatment with another one."

"Did she say why?"

"She said she doesn't think she needs it. I'm hoping that you can help me persuade her to make an appointment with a doctor now, while she's doing well, so she'll have someone to rely on if things take a turn for the worse."

"Makes sense."

"Marilyn and I scheduled today's lunch meeting several days ago. I went back and forth deciding whether to tell her that I planned to invite you. I decided not to tell her. I was afraid she'd find an excuse to cancel. Does that cause a problem?"

"Not for me. It may cause one for her. She may feel ambushed."

"I know. It's hard to decide how to play a situation like this."

"Is she still taking medication? Maybe her family doctor is prescribing it for her."

"No, she stopped a couple of months ago. This isn't the first time she's stopped her medicine. But before it was always under the care of her doctor. And she always went back to the medicine eventually."

"You said you were worried about her."

"We've entered negotiations to sell a major part of her holdings. But Marilyn wants to retain some operational control after the sale goes through. So I expect the prospective buyers to investigate her thoroughly, because it will be their money at risk if she stays with the company. I can't let her get into a situation that may blow up in everyone's face. I want her to line up some professional help now, before there's a crisis." He paused. "With Marilyn Levine, crisis is always a viable option."

Just then the door to Donald's office burst open with such force that the papers on his desk flew to the floor. A thin woman with a gray ponytail bounded in. She dropped the large shopping bag she was carrying—from Louis, a men's clothing store on Berkeley Street—then dashed across the room and wrapped her arms around Donald. "It's *so* good to see you, Donny!"

Skillfully, Donald returned the embrace while simultaneously disengaging from it. "Marilyn, I'd like you to meet Harry Kline. He's—"

"Hello, Larry." She pumped my hand, then walked past me to retrieve the shopping bag. "I have a surprise for you, Donny. I'm sorry I didn't get this to you in time for Christmas, but I'm running a little behind this year. I didn't even have time to wrap it."

She reached into the bag and pulled out a burgundy sweater. She walked over to Donald. "Feel it, Donny. Isn't it *wonderful*?"

He touched the fabric. "It's very nice."

She turned around. "Would you like to feel this, Larry?"

"I'm Harry."

"Of course you are. Let me show you how this feels on a man's face. Close your eyes."

I did as she asked. The soft material rubbed against my cheek. "It feels like cashmere."

"It *is* cashmere," she replied.

I opened my eyes and found myself gazing into hers: deep blue, surrounded by an expressive smile. There was something familiar about that smile, as if I'd seen her before in some other circumstance, long ago and long forgotten. I smiled back, a spontaneous reaction.

She said, "I like giving presents *so* much, especially when it comes as a surprise. Are you new with the firm, Harry? Donny never mentioned you before."

"I've mentioned him to you, Marilyn, but not in this context. He's Veronica's friend. He's joining us for lunch."

She looked puzzled. "Veronica's friend," she repeated to herself. "Veronica's friend. Oh!" Her face lit up: a look of recognition. "Of *course*. Veronica's *friend*! I really *am* glad to meet you, Harry." She shook my hand again. "Are you a lawyer?"

"No, I'm a doctor. A psychiatrist."

She stepped back and eyed me. She looked confused, or maybe perturbed; I couldn't tell which.

Donald said, "I've asked Harry to help us sort things out."

"You mean, sort *me* out, don't you?" Marilyn frowned and

stepped away from Donald and me, clutching the cashmere sweater. She sat down on the windowsill, like a cat looking for a safe perch. "Well, now, Donny. I guess I'm not the only one who likes to surprise people."

Donald spent a few minutes explaining his concerns and intentions to Marilyn. I could tell they had been through variations of this conversation before. Marilyn listened quietly, wriggling her fingers and tapping one of her heels in rapid-fire motion.

Donald said, "This is a big decision you're considering, the sale of your company. We need to make certain you're doing what's best."

She said, "I think you mean, you need to make certain I'm not looney tunes. Three cards short of a full deck. Cruising on only one cylinder."

Marilyn's body tensed. She turned to the window and gazed at the park. "You treat me like a child sometimes, Donny."

"I treat you like a friend. A very valued friend."

She cleared her throat and turned around. "No offense, Donald—or to you, Harry. But I don't think I want Harry to have lunch with us."

"For goodness' sake, Marilyn. He's Veronica's *boyfriend*."

She stared impassively at me. "He's too old to be called someone's boyfriend."

I said, "You're the third person to tell me that this week. I'm beginning to feel a little paranoid."

A very slight smile flickered across her face for a moment. She checked her watch and said, "I left some matters dangling at my office. I think I should get back to work. We can have lunch another time, Donny."

I said, "I can give you a ride, if you'd like. Where is your office?"

She stood and walked toward the door. "My driver is waiting for me downstairs. And the whole world is my office." She flung her arm toward the window, gesturing expansively toward the outdoors.

"You must run up one hell of a heating bill," I said.

"I'm sure you must be a nice person, Harry, or Veronica

wouldn't be involved with you. But I'm not in the mood for a conversation about psychiatrists. I just finished with one. I'm not looking for another. And I've never felt better than I do right now. What? Why are you raising your eyebrows like that? You see what I mean?" She smiled. "You psychiatrists are enough to drive a person crazy. Donny, walk me to the elevator, please."

She left the room without waiting for Donald. He followed quickly behind. As he passed me he mumbled, "That went really well, didn't it?"

I walked over to the window and surveyed the scene two flights below. The benches and footpaths in the small park were all completely cleared of snow, but no one tarried in the winter cold. There were a few evergreens, but most of the trees were deciduous; their bare branches lent a forlorn look to the scene.

Directly below, on Milk Street, an MBTA bus tried to navigate the narrow passage that was made even more constricted by several illegally parked cars. It got stuck momentarily on the curb, then spun off wildly, nearly clipping a pedestrian and the rear end of a luxury automobile. Horns blared and the pedestrian flashed his middle finger at the bus.

Donald had blundered by inviting me to lunch without first clearing it with Marilyn Levine. He wasn't the sort to make a mistake like that, and I took it as a sign of his deep concern about the woman: affection overcoming judgment.

Marilyn was buoyant, bold, and bright—qualities that no doubt served her well in her work, and qualities that often make manic-depressive people hard to manage when they begin a manic episode.

Turning away from the window, I noticed three pictures on Donald's desk. The first was the fifth-grade portrait that Melissa had sent him a few months earlier. Then there was a large color photo of Donald and Shana, his second wife, on a warm-weather cruise. Finally, there was a small black-and-white picture of Veronica and a young girl of eight or nine; the girl looked familiar to me.

I picked up the framed picture. Veronica and the girl were

seated side by side on a park bench. Both were smiling. They were leaning against each other, the girl's head resting on Veronica's shoulder. Veronica's hair was pulled back and tied, a style I'd never seen her wear. Her arm was draped over the girl's shoulder—a caring and protective pose I'd seen her take with Melissa a few times, but with less naturalness than she showed to the girl in the picture.

Donald returned to the office and closed the door. He sat in his chair near the window. "I guess I miscalculated. I hope that scene didn't make you feel too uncomfortable."

"Don't worry about it."

He slouched in his chair and rubbed his eyes. "I think I managed to calm her down in the hallway. I took the liberty of giving her your phone number. I asked her to call you for a referral to a new doctor. She didn't say if she would. She told me again that she's never felt better."

"Which always puts me on alert when I hear it from a bipolar person."

"Bipolar?"

"Bipolar affective disorder," I said. "That's my profession's fancy name for manic-depressive illness. When bipolar people are at the beginning of a manic episode, sometimes it actually feels good. That extra rush of energy excites them and makes them more exciting to the people around them. By the time things get out of hand, they usually need hospitalization to get them back on track."

Donald considered that for a moment, then pointed toward the picture in my hand. "The resemblance is uncanny, isn't it? She looks so much like her mother did at her age."

Like her mother. Of course, I thought. That's why the girl in the photo looked familiar. The *girl* was Veronica, and the woman was Rachel Pace.

Donald said, "I took that picture in the fall of 1972. It was one of the last shots of the two of them together. I almost put it away after Rachel died, and again after I married Shana. But I didn't."

"Has Shana seen it?"

He nodded. "I considered placing it in my drawer the first

time Shana visited me here, just for that day. But if I did that, I would have to remember to do it every time she came. I decided not to get started down that track."

"I'm surprised you don't have a picture of Veronica as an adult."

He laughed. "I've been after her for years to give me one for my office. She hates having her picture taken. Perhaps you've noticed that."

"I have."

"Do you still keep pictures of your wife?"

"Melissa has a picture on her nightstand. All the others are put away in albums."

"Do you ever look at them?"

"I used to. They're in the attic. Melissa goes up there sometimes to look at them."

Donald took a deep breath and exhaled slowly. "What to keep, what to throw away. The calculus of arranging your life after your spouse dies. It's hard to explain it to someone who hasn't experienced it."

I said, "It took me until last spring, six years after Janet died, to take her clothes from the attic and give them to Goodwill." I placed the framed black-and-white photo back on Donald's desktop. "It's a nice shot. I've never seen a picture of your first wife before. Veronica seldom talks about her."

"I know. It was so terrible. And to actually watch it unfold in front of you . . ." He didn't complete his thought. He stared out the window for a few seconds.

"You were out of town when it happened, weren't you?"

"On my way back from a business trip. I had hoped to get home earlier, but the snow delayed me." He furrowed his brow. "I've always felt guilty about that, Harry. I used to dwell on it, along with other things. I've always assumed that it never would have happened if I had been there to protect her."

"You don't know that."

He grunted. "Come on, Harry—a burglar breaks in looking for something to steal. He thinks no one is home, he panics when he finds a woman holding a gun on him, they struggle, he beats her. Do you think he would have tried to beat two people, a man and a woman, if I had been there? More likely he would have just run."

"It was your gun, wasn't it?"

He nodded. "Did Ronnie tell you that?"

I hesitated for just a moment. "Yes," I lied. Actually, I had learned that detail from the police report. But Veronica didn't want her father to know of her interest in reopening the case, and I had promised to keep it secret. So I couldn't say anything about reviewing the report.

"I purchased the gun because I was spending so much time away from home."

"Whose idea was it—yours or Rachel's?"

"Mine. She was wary of having it in the house, especially with a child there. But I insisted. We kept it locked in the night-table drawer, with the key on the top shelf of the closet, out of Veronica's reach. Rachel went along with me, reluctantly. I should have listened to her."

"What do you mean?"

"I assume the burglar panicked when he saw the gun. Perhaps things wouldn't have gotten out of hand if the gun hadn't been there."

"You don't know that, either. Besides, if the gun hadn't been there for Veronica to grab, she would, you know. . . ."

My words trailed off. For some reason I didn't want to give voice to my complete thought: *She would have been murdered, too.*

There was a knock on the door. "Come in," Donald said, standing up.

A man about Donald's age walked in carrying a large manila envelope. I had seen him before, but I couldn't remember where until Donald introduced us. "Harry, this is Oliver Gray, one of my partners."

"We've met, Oliver," I said, rising to shake his hand. "At the party Donald and Shana held on Patriots' Day last April."

Oliver's handshake was limp: the kind that feels like air and gives you no clue regarding the substance of the man offering it. He said, "Of course. You're the Jewish fellow, Veronica's boyfriend. Donny, here are the documents you asked me to review."

"Thanks." Donald took the envelope and placed it on his desk. The black-and-white snapshot caught his attention. "Harry and I were just talking about Rachel."

Oliver looked down at the floor. "They broke the mold, Donny," he muttered. "Broke the mold." He left the room and closed the door behind him.

Donald said, "He knew Rachel for many years. He took her death quite hard."

"He thinks it's important to highlight the fact that I'm Jewish."

"I could tell that made you uncomfortable. I'm afraid he sometimes makes a poor first impression."

"Second impression. He did the same thing at your house last April."

"I see. I don't know what to say about that, Harry. Sometimes our friends embarrass us, and the longer someone has been your friend, the more you'll overlook. I'm willing to overlook a lot with Oliver."

I changed the subject. "What else did you dwell on?"

"Pardon?"

"You said you dwelled on other things, in addition to the fact that you weren't home that night."

He paused and drew a deep breath. "I used to wonder about the end all the time. It must have taken Rachel several seconds to produce the gun, because—as I said—it was locked in a drawer and the key was in the closet. Since she was able to get it, I assume that she must have heard the burglar before he got to our bedroom, must have had time to contemplate what was happening. I used to go over that again and again—wonder how much time she had, wonder what was going through her mind, imagine how frightened she must have been."

Donald lapsed into silence. In the time I had known him—a few months shy of two years—he had spoken very little about his first wife, and not at all about the murder. I wanted to know more—about Rachel, about her death, about the life as a mother and wife that was ended so quickly and cruelly. I wanted to know anything and everything that could help me aid Veronica. She wanted my help in her search for her mother's killer. And she would need my help when that search failed, as I knew it inevitably would.

I said, "That must have been the worst night of your life."

He looked off into space, focusing his eyes on nothing in particular, as if he were replaying a scene in his mind.

Donald told me he arrived home at around midnight. As soon as he turned off of Pilgrim Street onto Rutgers Street, he saw that the lights in every room of his house were on, and he knew that something was very wrong. Then he saw the four police cruisers, and the Channel 5 station wagon, and the same yellow tape he'd seen countless times in movies and on television programs when fictional police mark the fictional perimeters of fictional crime scenes.

He jammed on his brakes and slipped into a skid. His car glanced off the front bumper of one of the cruisers and came to a stop. Donald flung open the door without bothering to pull into the driveway—he didn't remember if he shut it behind him or turned the motor off—and ran across the snow-covered lawn.

The front door was unlocked. He burst into the foyer and rushed for the stairs, oblivious to the two police officers standing there. They reached out and held on to him, halting his forward progress. "Whoa, brother, whoa! What do we have here?"

Oliver Gray and two more police officers stepped into the foyer from the living room. Oliver was wearing pajamas underneath his overcoat, and he looked haggard and drawn. "Donald . . ." he said, his voice fading in a hoarse whisper.

"Rachel," replied Donald, the unspoken question forming in his eyes.

Oliver shuddered and shook his head.

Donald tried once more to rush for the stairs, but again the police officers held him back.

"Rachel isn't there anymore, Donny," said Oliver. "They've already taken her."

"Veronica!"

A voice behind him said, "Your daughter is safe, Mr. Pace. I'm Detective Branson. Let's sit down, please. I'll explain everything to you."

As they walked into the den Oliver said, "The firm's answering service called me, Donny. They knew I lived close by."

The detective's words seemed to dance in and out of the cascade of internal noise: the quickened beating of Donald's heart, the blood rushing in his veins, the breathing so shallow and rapid that he thought he might hyperventilate. *Burglary. Rachel. Gun. Struggle. Dead. Dead. Dead.*

"When?" Donald asked.

"Around ten-fifteen."

Donald stood, unsteady on his feet. "I want my daughter."

"We'll bring you to her shortly. Mr. Gray here tells us you were away on business. Where were you?"

Oliver placed a hand on Donald's shoulder and guided him back down onto the chair.

"I was in Chicago."

"Yes, that's what Mr. Gray told us. What airline did you use?"

"TWA."

"Do you remember your flight number?"

"My flight number?"

"Yes, your flight number."

"I don't understand. Why—"

"Perhaps you can check your ticket."

Donald ran his hands through his pockets. He pulled the ticket from his suit jacket. "Flight 187."

"May I see it, please?"

Still uncomprehending, Donald handed the ticket to the detective.

"It says you were scheduled to land at eight-ten."

"We were delayed. We arrived around ten-thirty."

"I see." The detective nodded to one of the police officers. The officer stepped out of the den and headed toward the kitchen.

Oliver went to the bar and poured two drinks, one for Donald and one for himself. Donald set his on a table without drinking from it. The detective asked more questions; Donald didn't remember the conversation afterward.

The police officer returned from the kitchen. "Flight 187 landed at ten-thirty-three. They confirm that Mr. Pace was on board."

And now, twenty-one years and one month later in his office on Post Office Square, Donald looked as lost and bewildered as I imagined he looked on that long-ago December night.

He said, "It's true what they say, Harry. The husband is always the first suspect. The police wouldn't let me see Ronnie until they determined that I had an alibi for the time of Rachel's death." He grunted. "An alibi, for God's sake. I had to give them an alibi for the murder of my own wife."

I shook my head in disbelief.

"I lost her a long time ago. And for sixteen years I've been with Shana, whom I love and who loves me, and I know I'm very fortunate." He sighed. "But there are certain things one can never forget."

Donald sat up straight in his chair, as if snapping out of a dream. "Ronnie is fortunate, too," he said. "She has you. When the two of you had problems last year, it saddened me. I was pleased that you worked things out."

Veronica and I had separated from each other the previous spring. Eventually we reconciled, and then she sold her condo and moved into the barn. But while we were apart Veronica went gallivanting with a high-profile district attorney from another part of the state; she met him while they were working together on an interstate murder case. I had an affair with a Concord woman named Marjorie Morris. Both situations ended poorly.

I said, "When your daughter and I had those problems, you were a big help."

"Oh? In what way?"

"By offering to help."

"But you never took me up on that."

"The offer itself was helpful."

He thought about that, then said, "It's unusual to get credit for doing the job when all I did was offer to do the job. If I could bottle that and sell it, I'd be a wealthy man."

"You *are* a wealthy man."

"Yes," he said, a dull monotone. "I am a wealthy man." He looked out the window at the picture-perfect park below.

I said, "I know they never caught your wife's attacker. I imagine that only makes things worse."

He faced me again. He looked at me for several seconds without speaking. Then he said, "You've never asked me about Rachel's death before. Yet today you have many questions about it."

He delivered that in a neutral tone: a mere statement of fact, not an accusation, not even a direct question. Still, it seemed to call for a response. But I couldn't tell him the true reason for my questions without breaking my promise to Veronica.

I said, "I love your daughter. I know the murder haunts her, even though she rarely mentions it. I want to understand what she went through."

It was a true statement, but not a truthful response to Donald's remark. He watched me without comment for several seconds more. I wondered if he believed me.

5: Danger in the Games We Play

At six-thirty my last Thursday patient arrived.

Richie Conover was in no great despair. There were no cataclysmic stressors in his life. And if he was a little short on plans for his future at the end of college, he had so much money coming to him that he would never have to worry about finding work. Everything had always been provided for him: a life arranged to minimize want, need, and effort. So it was little wonder that he had no constructive blueprint for his life; for without need, there often is no incentive.

His gangly form filled the chair across from me. "I've been thinking some more about the sort of book I want to write after I graduate, Doc. I'd like to run some ideas by you."

Richie attended Brandeis. It was a matter of convenience. His parents' mansion near the center of town was a five-minute walk to the train station, and the train from Concord to Boston stopped at the Brandeis campus, just fifteen minutes down the line. He could roll out of a bed he would never have to make, eat a hot breakfast, and be in class—all within an hour.

He had the home to himself. His parents were spending the winter in Palm Beach. They had, of course, left a maid behind to tend to Richie's needs.

"It's another travel book," he said, "but I think it's better than the last two I talked about."

Six or seven weeks earlier—during our second session—Richie Conover glanced at my bookcase and saw a copy of the book I had written about my work with Vietnam War veterans. Almost immediately, like a formless gel taking the shape of the nearest container, he decided he would become an author after he graduated. And now every week he came in with another book proposal.

Two weeks earlier he talked about visiting and photographing post offices across the country, then writing some text about each one and publishing a coffee-table book. The next week he made a similar proposal regarding cemeteries for a book he planned to call *The Tombstone Tour*.

"This is how I see it," he said. "It's a whirlwind two-to-three-week cross-country travelogue. I start out in Memphis in the middle of August."

"Why Memphis?"

"The candlelight vigil at Graceland. This year will be the seventeenth anniversary of Elvis's death. By the way, you know how he died, don't you?"

"How?" I knew, but I wanted to hear how it was relevant to him. This was the first time I had ever seen him so animated.

"He was constipated from all those drugs he was taking. He had a heart attack on the toilet while he was trying really hard to, uh, to . . ."

"To relieve himself."

He smiled. "Yeah. To relieve himself. I always got a kick out of that, you know? The King died while he was sitting on the throne."

He waited to see if I would laugh. I gave him a noncommittal smile and a nod of the head, encouraging him to continue.

"So I start in Memphis, and I head generally west. I still have to fill in the middle of my itinerary. But I finish up on the West Coast on Labor Day, where I sit in the audience and watch the entire Jerry Lewis telethon for muscular dystrophy." He looked at me. "What? You never heard of the telethon?"

"I've heard of it. But I read that they clear the room out every hour so as many people as possible can have a chance to sit in the audience."

He furrowed his brow. "Oh." He paused. "Well, that's just a detail. I'll donate ten or twenty thousand, and maybe they'll let me do it. Anyway, I write the whole trip up as a real slice of Americana. And the title would be *The American Dream Tour.*" He leaned back in his chair. "So—what do you think?"

I thought: *Sounds more like the American nightmare tour.* I said, "I can tell you've put some thought into this."

He smiled, satisfied with my comment.

Richie Conover was desperate for some form of validation by me; once I found a way to provide it, we could move beyond the superficial book discussions to a serious consideration of his life.

He told me he would have to cancel our appointment for the following Thursday; he and his sister, who had her own home in town, were flying to Atlanta to meet their parents for the Super Bowl. I offered him a Wednesday appointment, but he declined.

It was almost seven-thirty when his session ended. After he left, I walked along the passageway that connected my office to the house.

I supposed Richie's latest proposal could be considered an improvement. His first idea, several weeks earlier, had seemed unusually bizarre. He wanted to contact death-row inmates and ask each one what he would like for his final meal. Richie planned to come up with a recipe for each meal, then pair it with a short biographical blurb about the inmate who requested it, including a description of his crime.

"It would go something like this," he had told me. "Joe Schmo is currently awaiting execution in Florida for the rape and ax murder of his five-year-old nephew. For his last meal, he plans on asking for 'some kind of fish, preferably freshwater.' We suggest poached salmon in a cream-and-dill sauce. Here's our special recipe."

He thought the book would make a lovely Christmas gift. He proposed putting a print of da Vinci's *Last Supper* on the cover. He would call it *The I-Hate-to-Eat-and-Die Cookbook.*

Compared with that, even *The American Dream Tour* sounded good.

When I stepped into the kitchen, I heard the faint, distant sounds of a guitar and a woman singing.

The music was coming from upstairs, and I assumed Melissa was listening again to one of Janet's old folk-music records. I couldn't make out the words, but the tune was familiar. Perhaps I had heard the record before, or maybe Janet had sung the song for me.

I walked to the steps and headed upstairs. The closer I drew to Melissa's room, the richer and clearer the music sounded. The voice was a rich, expressive alto. She sang about the pain of loving in a troubled world—a personal protest song, with vague allusions to political themes from the 1960s. There were no rumbles or cracks in the noise, which seemed odd for a record so old. And there was a fullness to the sound that made it seem urgent and alive.

The door was open. From the hallway I could see them, Melissa and Veronica, sitting on the floor with their backs against Melissa's bed. Their eyes were closed. They were leaning against one another, and Melissa's head was resting on Veronica's shoulder. Veronica had an arm wrapped around my daughter, a replay of the pose I saw that morning in the picture on Donald Pace's desk: first Rachel shielding Veronica, and now Rachel's grown daughter shielding my child.

I stepped into the room, and I saw her: a familiar-looking woman standing with Janet's old guitar, playing it and singing. Her thin frame seemed too insubstantial to support her deep alto voice.

When I saw her earlier that day, she wore a ponytail. Now Marilyn Levine's long, gray hair flowed over her shoulders. She smiled at me and continued her song:

> There's danger in the world today
> Danger in these games we play
> All the things we do and say
> Or so it always seems
>
> If your song should ever fail
> I will be your nightingale
> You will hear me in your dreams

A record album was lying on the floor. It was called *Nightingale*, and the artist was named Mara Lee. But the woman smiling up at me from the cover was a younger, dark-haired Marilyn Levine.

Marilyn's song had lulled Melissa and Veronica to sleep. When the song ended they didn't stir. Marilyn placed the guitar in its case. She picked up her handbag, coat, and scarf. She looked at the scarf for a moment, then walked over to me and draped it around my neck.

"It's cashmere," she whispered, and left it there.

"Thank you."

Marilyn Levine stood on her toes and spoke into my ear. "There *is* danger in the world, Harry. You have a lovely family. Keep them safe."

She kissed my cheek, and then she was gone.

6: Showeth No Mercy

I was hunched over the morning paper when Melissa walked into the den. "You're maturing," I said.

"What do you mean?"

"You had time for a full breakfast, you already have your coat on, and your school bus isn't even due for another four minutes."

She laughed. "Are you waiting for Uncle Bobby?"

"Uh-huh." Every Friday morning Bobby Beck and I took a brisk walk to North Bridge before he drove into Boston.

"Say hi for me. And don't forget—I'm going to Emily's house after school. Maybe you want to write that down so you don't forget."

"I think I can remember that without writing it down."

My daughter laughed again, and then she was out the door. I watched through the window as she raced down the long driveway to Monument Street.

Melissa was eleven years old, growing a bit further from me every day. I knew that was normal and healthy, but I was ambivalent about it nevertheless. Neither her mother nor I enjoyed close relationships with our parents once we reached adulthood; I hoped—for my own sake—that Melissa didn't follow the same path.

50

I finished the sports page and was halfway through the news section when the front doorbell rang. Bobby always walked in without knocking or ringing, so I knew it wasn't him. I opened the door and found Father John Fitzpatrick standing there.

"Harry, my boy—top of this somewhat chilly morning to you." His breath turned into puffs of visible vapor as he spoke.

I ushered him inside and took his coat. He was casually dressed, without his collar. Father John was pastor of St. Bernard's, the Catholic church on Monument Square. We became friends several months earlier. He had been to my house on three or four occasions, but never uninvited. "You're up and about early, John. Can I get you some coffee?"

"In other words, why has this man arrived at my home unexpectedly so early in the morning? And no, thanks—I've had my morning cup already. Has Melissa left for school?"

"Yes."

"And Veronica? Is she here?"

"She's on her morning run. Through the center of town and out to Merriam's Corner." Veronica made the round-trip run to that Revolutionary War site several times each week. She covered the distance, not quite five miles, in about thirty-five minutes. "She should be back soon."

"Perhaps you and I can go to your office, then. I was hoping we could talk privately for a short while."

I hesitated. "Well, I was planning to walk over to North Bridge and—"

"Splendid. A walk it is, then." He took his coat back from me. "Better dress warmly, Harry. It's cold out, but if you bundle up well, it's absolutely beautiful today."

"Are you always so cheerful this early in the morning?"

"I suppose I am."

"It's a good thing you're not married. Your wife would probably kill you."

He chuckled at that thought. I debated how to tell him that we wouldn't be alone on the walk without making him feel that his presence would represent an unintended intrusion. Then I heard a car door slam shut, and a few seconds later Bobby's voice sounded from the kitchen door.

"Harry?" His voice came nearer as he walked through the house looking for me. "Get your ass in gear, pal of mine. It's goddamn cold out there."

"I'm by the front door, Bobby."

"Oh," he said when he found me. "I didn't know you had company."

Father John said, "And I didn't know you were expecting company. If this is a bad time, perhaps we can talk later."

The two of them had never met, so I introduced them to each other: my best friend for more than twenty years, and the older clergyman. I told Bobby that Father John was going to walk with us. Then I grabbed my coat, and we stepped outside and headed for Minuteman National Park.

After a few minutes of walking we came to the visitors' center, a three-story brick building that was once the home of a prominent Concord family. The building sat on the crest of a gently sloping hill, overlooking a bend in the Concord River.

We stood near the building and took in the view. At the foot of the hill and off to the right was North Bridge, an arched wooden footbridge that marked the site of the first pitched battle of the Revolutionary War. On an April morning in 1775, in the nearby town of Lexington, British soldiers fired on colonial Minutemen for the first time. Their shots went unanswered. Later that same day four hundred Minutemen gathered near the very spot where the three of us now stood. The Redcoats fired from the other side of North Bridge. This time the colonists returned the enemy's fire: the first forcible resistance to the British invasion.

"Battlefields," said Father John. "Many of them are so beautiful. It's ironic, isn't it?"

"This is one of the prettiest," I replied. Bobby nodded in agreement.

The landscaped garden area next to the old mansion had been put to bed for the winter. Where flowers once bloomed, now there were only patches of frozen soil peeking through the light snow cover, like a brown-and-white checkerboard.

The stone path that led down the hill to the river was bare, already worn clear of the last snowfall. Father John did a brief stretching exercise. "If it's all right with you lads, I think I'll put on a little speed and run ahead."

Bobby shrugged. "Sure, Father."

I said, "We'll meet you down by the bridge, John."

With that, Father John Fitzpatrick kicked into a sprint, leaving Bobby and me near the flagpole in front of the mansion.

"You call him by his first name?"

"Uh-huh," I said. "That seems to be his preference with friends."

"And you consider yourself his friend?"

"Sure. I've told you about him before. What's the problem?"

"I don't have a problem."

"I can hear it in your tone of voice, Bobby."

"Well, I just think it's a little strange. You never go to synagogue, and now you're getting chummy with a Catholic priest. What kind of message are you giving to Melissa?"

It was a sore point between us: Bobby was my daughter's godfather, and he was a founding member of the Jewish temple on Elm Street. For some time he'd been after me to enroll Melissa in Hebrew school so she could be bat mitzvahed when she turned thirteen. I hadn't ruled it out, but time was growing short.

Bobby said, "Why did you invite him, anyway?"

"He invited himself. He arrived a few minutes before you did. I wasn't expecting him. He said he needed to talk with me. You showed up before he had a chance to tell me what he wanted. I guess I'll find out after you leave."

We headed down the sloping path to the footbridge. A huge, gnarled tree spread in all directions to our right. I said, *"Fagus sylvatica fagaceae."*

"Come again?"

"It's the Latin name for that particular beech tree."

"Oh." Bobby thought for a moment. *"In canis corporate transmuto."*

"I give up. What's that?"

"A line from one of the classics."

"Which one?" I asked.

"The Shaggy Dog."

Two joggers coming uphill passed us and mumbled an out-of-breath greeting to us.

"So he just came to your house unannounced at eight-thirty in the morning?"

I nodded. "It's been that sort of week. I had another unexpected visitor last night. A woman named Marilyn Levine."

"Who's she?"

"You probably know her as Mara Lee. Used to be popular as a singer."

He nodded. "She gives me fever."

"That was *Peggy* Lee."

"Oh, right." He paused. "Wait a minute—funny-looking hat, checkered suit, used to do kids' TV shows when we were little?"

"That was *Pinky* Lee, you idiot."

Bobby began to laugh. "I know it's Pinky Lee. I just like giving you a hard time. And I know who Mara Lee is. The *Nightingale* album. The only one she made before she freaked out. What was she doing at your house?"

"Visiting Veronica. She's an old friend of the family. What do you mean, 'freaked out'?"

"I don't remember the details. Cracked up on stage. Got into a fight with someone. Took up with some sort of cult. Some or all of the above. I didn't even know she was still alive."

Up ahead, Father John reached the bottom of the hill near the bridge and continued running in place. Bobby said, "He's in pretty good shape for someone his age."

"He used to be a boxer. Almost turned pro, then he decided to join the priesthood."

"That's a hell of a career change."

"I'm sure he had his reasons." The switch, I knew, came after he killed a sparring partner in the ring. Revealed to me in private conversation, it was a secret I decided to keep.

I said, "Marilyn Levine made an interesting career change, too." I told him about the M. L. Nightingale Company.

Bobby checked the tag on his gloves. "These are from Nightingale's. A Hanukkah present from my sister."

"Veronica was very happy to see Marilyn. And right now I'm thankful for anything that makes her even a little happy."

"Is she still going through with her plan?"

"Yes. She took a month's leave of absence. And she's meeting with the Wellesley police chief later to review the case. I'm going with her."

Father John was standing alongside the Minuteman statue when we caught up with him. He said, "I understand there was some controversy about this statue a few years ago, before I moved to Concord."

I briefed him on the town's refusal to let the National Guard make a replica. I didn't mention Bobby's role in spearheading the town's opposition.

Father John said, "I find that very curious—the notion that the value of something intangible would somehow be diminished by letting others share in it."

Bobby looked away, saying nothing. He took a few steps toward the bridge.

"I was a diocesan priest in Waltham before I came here. When I announced that I was moving to Concord, one of my parishioners said, 'They have a lot of smart dead people there.' He was referring, of course, to the ones who were actually deceased."

The morning sun reflected off the life-size figure that grasped the handle of a plow in one hand and a musket in the other. I pointed to the words chiseled into the plinth that supported the statue.

> By the rude bridge that arched the flood,
> Their flag to April's breeze unfurled,
> Here once the embattled farmers stood,
> And fired the shot heard 'round the world.

"I've always liked that poem," I said.

"Who wrote it?" asked Father John.

"Longfellow. It's from his poem about Paul Revere."

Bobby spoke up from several feet behind us. "Emerson wrote it."

"No," I said, "it was Henry Wadsworth Longfellow."

Bobby sighed and rolled his eyes. "Ralph Waldo Emerson wrote it in 1836. I was *born* in this town. I've lived here my whole life. I know what I'm talking about, goddammit." He paused. "Sorry, Father."

Father John smiled at both of us. "Boys, boys. Longfellow, Emerson—what difference, really? Two very smart dead people."

We crossed North Bridge, a span of perhaps fifty paces. We passed the obelisk monument and the common grave of three British soldiers who died in battle that long-ago April morning. I always felt sad about the plight of the nameless men buried there: stuck forever in an alien, distant place, far removed from their homes and their loved ones.

We continued on the path, past Nathaniel Hawthorne's home, and back out to Monument Street. We turned left and walked the final leg of our circular route from my house and back.

When we reached my house, Bobby got into his car for the drive into Boston. Father John said, "It was nice meeting you."

"The same here, Father. Harry, call me later so I can find out how your meeting in Wellesley went."

On our way inside, Father John said, "You and your friend seemed a little upset with one another."

"It's not a big deal. We go back a long way. We'll go on a long way."

Veronica wasn't in the house. I assumed she was in her apartment showering after her run, getting ready for our drive to Wellesley.

Father John and I sat in the kitchen. "Your daughter came to see me at the rectory yesterday," he said.

"Oh?" Melissa had met Father John in my presence on two or three occasions. And I knew she liked him. But learning she had gone to visit him surprised me.

He said, "She had a couple of things on her mind. First and foremost was Veronica. Melissa is worried about her."

"Did she say why?"

"It was difficult for her to talk about it. She said Veronica is taking time off from work, and that she seems to get upset easily." He paused. "It was my sense that she's worried Veronica might be ill."

"Ill?"

"You seem surprised."

"Veronica isn't sick. She's been worried and distracted lately, but that's no reason to . . . Oh . . ."

"What is it, Harry? What are you thinking?"

"It just occurred to me. We're in the sickness season."

"I don't understand."

I checked the wall calendar. "It's January twenty-first. Seven years ago Melissa's mother was dying. She was diagnosed in early January, and we knew that it was probably terminal. She died February fourth. It doesn't surprise me that Melissa noticed that something was bothering Veronica, and that she would jump to the conclusion that she was sick, especially at this time of year."

"Ah. Perhaps she just needs to be reassured."

"Yes, of course."

Father John walked to the cupboard and got a glass, then poured tap water into it and sat down with it. He took a sip, then said, "She asked me if I could lend her a book that would help her learn more about Catholicism. She also had questions about how one converts."

"Why?" I asked, as much to myself as to my friend.

"She remembered the time last year when the three of you came to one of my Masses. She seemed particularly interested in our emphasis on the afterlife. Perhaps this, too, has something to do with her mother."

"What did you tell her?"

"I said I wanted to talk with her father first."

"Did she know you would come this morning?"

"No."

"I see. Do you have any advice for me?"

He sighed. "Talk to her, Harry. Pray for help in finding out what she needs, and then pray for a way to help her get it."

"I'm not big on praying."

"I know. But it might surprise you to learn that she is."

He let that sink in for a minute, then continued. "If you want me to respond to her, I will. If you don't, I'll encourage her to approach you with her concerns. She may not realize how difficult it is for a parent when a child talks about turning away from her own religion."

"I haven't given her enough to turn away from, let alone to hold on to."

"So you've told me. Perhaps this, too, has something to do with Janet."

I shrugged. "Probably."

My wife's death shook whatever faith I may have had—which made it difficult for me to bring faith into Melissa's life.

"How can I tell my child that God is just? Your mother dies, and everything changes forever."

He thought for a moment, then said, "On my way down the hill a little while ago, I saw a large European beech tree."

I thought, *Fagus sylvatica fagaceae.*

"A very broad tree," he said, "sprawling all over the place. I looked at its trunk and I noticed that it was split into huge limbs near the base. I suspect lightning struck it when it was quite young."

"I've always been curious about that tree. Never thought about lightning hitting it."

He said, "If a tree survives being struck by lightning, its growth pattern is changed. The shape is altered. One side may grow more quickly or more slowly than it would have under ordinary circumstances. It's still just as beautiful. But it's different forever from the way it would have been if it hadn't been struck." He sipped from his glass. "Is that a useful comparison?"

"More than you realize. It certainly applies to my daughter." I hesitated. "It also applies to Veronica."

"In what way?"

Veronica was very fond of Father John; I didn't think she would be angry if I told him about her decision to search for her mother's killer. I talked to him. He listened quietly: nodding, considering.

"And what will she do if she succeeds?"

His question caught me by surprise. "I've been worrying

about what *I'll* do when she *doesn't* succeed. It never occurred to me that this would prove to be anything other than a wild-goose chase."

"I don't know Veronica well, but I know she is very clever. You shouldn't underestimate her."

His question put a new spin on everything. "I don't know. I assume she'll turn her findings over to the police."

He put his glass in the sink, then sat down again and asked, "Is she merciful?"

"Merciful?" I echoed, uncertain of how to respond.

"There's a passage in the Apocrypha I'm fond of. 'One man beareth hatred against another—and doth he seek pardon from the Lord? He showeth no mercy to a man, which is like himself—and doth he ask forgiveness of his own sins?' "

Veronica was a former homicide prosecutor. When she graduated from Harvard Law School, she could have had any of a number of high-status or well-paying jobs. But she went instead into the trenches. When I first met her, she told me that she became a prosecutor because she had a mission when she decided to study law: She wanted to hurt people who hurt other people. Later, when I learned about her mother's murder, I understood why she thought that way.

I looked outside at the cold, bleak morning. "No," I said. "Veronica is not that way at all. She showeth no mercy."

7: An Open Wound

The Wellesley police station was a nondescript two-story brick building. The only thing striking about it was location: directly next door to a funeral parlor. I thought it an ironic juxtaposition, and said so to Veronica as we walked toward the building. I thought it might help break the tension, but she was too edgy to appreciate the odd pairing. "I don't get it," she said.

"It's just a funny combination. I can't put it into words."

"Uh-huh." She bowed her head and took a deep breath as I held open the front door for her.

The interior had a faded, aged quality: dingy and stale. It was the sort of place that would still look dirty after several washings and a repainting. Just inside the front door was a display of an artist's renderings for a new building. I looked at them and noticed that the anticipated date of occupancy was two years away.

There were only two people in the lobby. A young uniformed officer sat behind a desk. A casually dressed man with a broom and dustpan was sweeping something off the floor, paying no attention to us.

The officer saw me eyeing the drawings of the new police station. He said, "Looks pretty nice, doesn't it?"

"Where are they going to build it?"

"Right here. Same spot as this one."

"When are they going to raze this one?"

"They're not raising this one. They're going to demolish it."

"Of course. My mistake."

Veronica said, "I have an appointment with Chief Amory."

He yelled across the room. "Hey, Chief—someone here to see you."

The casually dressed man with the broom turned to face us. He looked a little older than me. He was tall, and he had the broad build of a linebacker. His reddish brown hair was thinning and flecked with gray. He walked toward us and held his hand out to Veronica. "You must be Veronica Pace. I'm Charles Amory. People call me Charlie."

Veronica returned his handshake and nodded at the broom in his other hand. "Your disguise fooled me."

"Pardon me? Oh, the broom." He laughed. "I dropped my three-hole puncher while I was walking through the lobby. About a year's worth of little paper circles flew all over the place."

"No janitor?"

He shrugged his shoulders. "It's my mess." He glanced my way, which Veronica took as a cue to introduce me. We shook hands and then he said, "What kind of doctor are you?"

"I'm a psychiatrist."

Veronica said, "Harry is a friend. I asked him to come for moral support. And please—call me Veronica."

He led us upstairs. Chief Amory's oddly angled office was large, but it felt cramped: Two desks, a long conference table, and several file cabinets and storage cartons were packed into it. On his wall were a bachelor's diploma from Boston University, a master's diploma from Northeastern's criminal justice program, and an enlarged snapshot of him surrounded by Little Leaguers. There were some photos on the desk. I presumed they were family pictures, but I could see only their backs because they were turned to face his chair. I liked that; I've always been wary of people who turn their family pictures outward to display them for visitors.

The table was overrun with stacks of paper; he cleared a small area and the three of us sat in mismatched chairs.

Veronica said, "I brought the case file you sent me." She handed it to him.

He placed it on the table and said, "It's a duplicate file. You can hold on to it for now, if you'd like."

She hesitated, then pulled the file closer to her. "Yes, that would be helpful." She was staring at him, as if trying to fix his image for future reference.

He was conscious of her gaze, and he looked away from her and addressed me. "Have you looked at the file, too, Harry?"

"Yes."

"A very sad situation. I'm sorry for your loss, Veronica." He drew a deep breath. "I knew the detective who handled the original investigation. Joe Branson. I want you to know he never closed the book on it. Up until his retirement a few years ago he talked to your father once or twice a year to review it. But I suppose you know that already."

She nodded slightly, but I saw from the trace of puzzlement on her face that this was news to her. I couldn't tell if Charlie Amory picked up on that.

"Your father lives over near the college, doesn't he?"

"Yes. We moved away from the Rutgers Street house in 1974, a year or so after my mother died. How long have you been police chief?"

"About three years."

"Have you read the file?"

"Yes."

"What do you think?"

He stood and walked to one of the desks. He reached into a pile of papers and located a large packet, then returned to the table. "My copy of the file," he said. He looked through it.

He said, "Your mother . . . the break-in at your house occurred on December twentieth, 1972. It was one of four break-ins that Detective Branson believed were committed by the same person. Branson thought burglary was the motive, and he concluded the thief was either an amateur or just pretty bad at what he did."

"Why was that?" Veronica asked.

"Things that would be of obvious value to an experienced thief were left behind, and other things—less valuable, and harder to carry—were taken."

Veronica asked him about burglar alarms. None of the four houses were equipped with systems in 1972. Then she asked what similarities existed in the four break-ins, what facts led the police to conclude that they were related.

The police chief said, "They occurred on four consecutive Thursday nights, beginning on November twenty-third, which was Thanksgiving. All after dark in the same general area of town. Which suggests some regularity of habit or circumstance that put the perpetrator in the same area on a predictable basis. And all four had the same point of entry, broken basement windows in the rear of the house."

Veronica said, "Was there any specific evidence that tied the break-ins to one perpetrator?"

"At all four houses, we found linen napkins just inside the points of entry. They appeared to be from a matched set. They had glass slivers in their folds. The burglar apparently wrapped them around his fist, then punched the windows in. And there's more."

He placed two pictures on the table. They were images of shoe prints: one set on some sort of smooth surface, the other in mud. Veronica pointed to the first one. "This was in the file you sent me. A notation said it was found on the top of the dryer in the basement of my house, near the window he used to gain access."

He nodded. "The other one came from the first break-in. I didn't send the materials from the other crime scenes to you." He tapped the two pictures. "Detective Branson was able to match these up. The same size and model men's boot, with an apparent irregularity in the tread, right over here."

I couldn't see what he was showing us, but it seemed to satisfy Veronica. She said, "This is a pretty clear indication that break-in number four at my house is connected to number one. What about the others? Do you have anything else to tie them together?"

"Gastric distress, believe it or not."

"Huh?" That was my only contribution to the conversation.

"Di-Gel," he said. "We found an antacid tablet on the floor

at house number two. None of the occupants there used Di-Gel."

I thought: *Must have been a Tums sort of family.*

He continued. "The occupants of house number three didn't use the stuff, either. Which made it seem pretty significant when we saw an empty Di-Gel box in one of their trash cans."

Charlie Amory leaned back in his chair. He folded his hands behind his head and pointed his elbows outward, his thick upper arm muscles straining against his shirtsleeve. He said, "We found one fingerprint. He must have taken one of his gloves off so he could open the box. Then he tossed the box away when he was finished with it."

Veronica was visibly surprised. "Were you able to match it?"

He shook his head. "No, unfortunately. We checked it against every breaking-and-entering suspect for the previous five years. Not only Wellesley, but Natick and the other surrounding towns. And Branson kept checking against new arrests for years afterward. When we switched to a computerized retrieval system, we plugged that print into the database. We've never had a hit."

Veronica ran her hand through her hair and sighed. "I guess the department did as much as could be expected."

"I wouldn't know where to look for something new, twenty-one years later."

"There were just these four break-ins?" she asked. "Nothing afterward?"

"Nothing that would obviously point to the same perpetrator. Branson's guess was a teenager out for some easy holiday money, things got out of hand at your house, and it probably scared him away from doing any more."

"Can I get copies of the files on the other three break-ins?"

He thought for a moment, then said, "It's a little irregular, but what the hell. They're old cases. I don't see any harm in doing that. I'll make copies for you."

Though only a few feet from me, Veronica looked distant and small. It was an optical illusion brought on by the odd shape of the room and the cluttered sight lines, and her stooped, defeated posture.

Charlie Amory said, "I know your reputation as a prosecutor," and he rattled off the names of some of her more publicized murder trials. "And I'm familiar with your work with the FBI, read some of the monographs you wrote for the Behavioral Science Unit. It's not entirely impossible that you might be able to unearth something, even at this late date."

"But."

"But?"

"But," she repeated. "I can tell from your tone of voice that there's an implied 'but.' 'It's not entirely impossible'—but what?"

"But I think it's very, very unlikely." He hesitated for a few seconds. "And I think you're the wrong person for the job. If you're intent on taking a fresh look, hire an investigator. I'm sure you know a number of competent people. If you don't, I can help you find one. And this is still an open case for us—so anyone you hire, we'll work with that person. I can assign someone new to the case, work it for a little while to see if it can go anywhere. You handle it yourself, you open an old wound, and where would that leave you?"

She looked at him again with the determined gaze of someone trying to remember something she wasn't even sure she ever knew. She said, "My mother was thirty years old when she died. I turned thirty-one earlier this month. I couldn't take care of her then, that night, when I was younger. But for the past couple of weeks—ever since I turned thirty-one and realized I'm older than she ever was—I've been thinking that I need to take care of her now. Maybe later I'll take your advice. But not now. And as for reopening an old wound—who said it ever closed in the first place?"

She slouched forward and brought her hand up to her face, covering her eyes. I moved closer and touched her arm lightly.

The police chief lowered his voice almost to a whisper. "What happened to your mother that night was horrible. What happened to *you* was horrible. I believe you when you say it still haunts you. I know it must, because it still haunts . . . I'm sure it still haunts everyone who was part of it."

There was a delay of two or three seconds, and then she looked directly at him with unnerving intensity. "You said you would assign someone to help. Well, I want you."

"I don't know if—"

"I want *you*," she said once more, "because I just remembered who you are."

He sighed and said nothing.

"You were very good to me, Chuck. I always remembered that."

"And I've always remembered you, Ronnie."

I thought: *Chuck. Ronnie.* There was a history here I knew nothing about. I felt as though I had walked into a movie after it started.

Charlie Amory reached across the table and touched Veronica's hand. "But if I had my way," he said, his voice faltering, "you wouldn't have remembered me—or anything else about that night."

8: Homicide

On a Thursday evening twenty-one years earlier, the dispatcher's call crackled over the radio shortly after Patrolman Charlie Amory's shift began. "Car six, where are you?"

Charlie was behind the wheel. His partner, Gus Slattery, answered the dispatcher. "Heading west on Washington Street, just coming up to the Town Hall area."

"Perfect," the voice responded through the static. "Two kids just stole some money from a Salvation Army Santa Claus outside Filene's. We think they ran into the park area near you. One in a hooded green coat, the other in bright blue."

They were coming up fast on an entrance to the park. Charlie hit his brakes hard. The street was slick from a light rain. The cruiser fishtailed just a little, and then Charlie cut a sharp right off the street and into the park near the duck pond.

Two figures were running parallel to them, about fifty yards away. In the darkness and the drizzle, Charlie couldn't tell for sure if their coats matched the dispatcher's descriptions. The figures were scampering up the rise toward the old Town Hall. Charlie drove along the serpentine path to the top of the hill. When he reached the crest he cut off his engine and his lights, and he and Slattery stepped out of the vehicle. They had, in effect, circled around the figures, and two teenagers were now puffing up the hill with their heads down, heading directly toward the police officers.

Their clothing matched the description; the officers could

see that now as the boys came closer. When they were twenty yards from the crest, the boy in green looked up and saw the cruiser. He stopped in his tracks, pivoted, and darted off to his left. Slattery ran after him.

The boy in bright blue was out of breath when he reached the top of the hill. He was too busy looking for the other boy to notice Charlie standing directly in front of him.

"Did you lose something, son?"

"Huh?" Spooked by Charlie's voice, the boy spun around and saw the young police officer standing with arms folded, leaning against his cruiser. "Oh, shit." His breath came in rapid, shallow spurts. "Can't run . . . anymore . . . too tired."

Charlie opened the rear door of the cruiser. "Relax, kid. Take a load off. Get dry."

The boy sat inside the car. He had long, unkempt curls, and he was so thin that he almost looked sickly. Charlie kept the door partially open and stood next to him. In the distance they heard Slattery yell, "Where are you, you little dipshit?" Charlie and the boy looked at each other, and they both broke into laughter at the same moment. But after several seconds the boy's laughter turned to tears, and he buried his face in his hands.

"Hey, hey," Charlie said. "It's not that bad."

"I'm not crying for me. I'm crying for my friend. His father is gonna beat the living crap out of him if the other cop catches him."

"How do you know that?"

"His father is *always* beating the living crap out of him."

"How old are you, kid?"

"Fifteen."

"And your friend?"

"Sixteen."

"What's your name?"

"Jonas. Jonas Cavaleri."

"And will *your* father beat the living crap out of *you*?"

The boy shook his head. "I don't have a father." He started crying again.

"Do you have anything with your name on it, Jonas?"

"My library card."

"Let me see it."

The boy produced the card. Charlie wrote down his address, then handed the card back.

Charlie looked down the hill. Slattery was at the bottom, alone, beginning the trudge to the crest.

He turned to the boy and asked, "Do you have a juvenile record? Ever been pulled in by the police before? Don't lie to me, now, because I can find out the truth really easy."

"No."

"My partner is a pretty hard guy. He's going to lean on you for your friend's name. Maybe you want to keep it to yourself."

The boy stared at him, incredulous. "Huh?"

"You heard me right. Don't give up your friend's name. Do you think you can do that?"

"I . . . I guess. But I don't . . . why are you . . ."

"Christmas is five days from now, Jonas. Maybe we can spare your friend at least this one beating."

Slattery was within earshot now, muttering and cursing. He was looking down, trying not to trip in the darkness. He was too far away to get a good look at what Charlie was doing.

Charlie turned to the boy and held the car door wide open. "On second thought, kid—get the hell out of here."

"What?"

"Come on, now. Get out of here before my partner gets back. And before I change my mind."

The boy stared at him for another second, then stepped out of the car quickly. As he started to move away Charlie grabbed his arm. "One more thing, Jonas. Tell me your friend's name and address."

"But you said . . ."

"I won't go after him for this. But in a couple of days I may pay a little visit to his father, check out the situation. Maybe your buddy doesn't deserve to get beat all the time."

Jonas Cavaleri gave the information to Charlie, then bolted. After he was gone, Charlie mumbled, "Merry Christmas, kid."

The rain began turning over to a wet snow.

Slattery returned a minute later. "The little fucker was too fast," he said. "Hey—what happened to *your* little fucker?"

"My little fucker was too fast, too."

The other man groaned. "Goddamn kids."

"Yeah," Charlie replied. "Goddamn kids."

They drove over to Filene's, where two other officers were taking statements from the Salvation Army Santa and a few witnesses. Charlie knew nothing would come of it, and he had second thoughts about letting Jonas Cavaleri go when he saw blood on the Santa Claus outfit. But the victim seemed none the worse for wear. No one had actually hit him; he got cut when the teenagers knocked him over by accident as they made their escape.

Thursday was always a busy night for the stores in town, and this last one before Christmas was especially active. But dangerous things seldom occurred in Wellesley, and this night was no exception. Charlie and his partner were called to the scene of a shoplifting. Then they drove a prominent citizen home who was too drunk to drive himself and too embarrassed to call his wife. They visited a loud party at the request of the party giver's elderly neighbor and negotiated a decibel-level reduction.

At around ten-fifteen Slattery said, "Looks like there's a break in the excitement. What say we grab some coffee?"

The snow stopped falling on their way to a nearby doughnut shop; the heavy but brief storm had left a three- or four-inch coat of white.

The dispatcher interrupted their break at around ten-twenty. In the ensuing years Charlie would sometimes think about the clichéd nature of things: that the most memorable call in his career would come as he sat in a doughnut shop, hunched over a decaf and a jelly-filled cruller.

"Multiple gunshots reported at thirty-five Rutgers Street," sparked the dispatcher. "All available units report."

They were just a few blocks away from that address; they could cover it in two minutes, maybe a little longer because of the snow. They dashed out of the doughnut shop and jumped into their cruiser. This time Slattery drove. "Jesus Christ," he muttered, sweating profusely as he hit the accelerator. "Jesus H. Christ."

It was an average Wellesley neighborhood: richer than some, less rich than others. But because Wellesley was Wellesley, the residents of even an average neighborhood were well off. Clapboard houses sat on quarter-acre lots. It was a district of successful professionals: some on their way to grander stations, others comfortably settled at a level to which most people only aspire.

They drove with lights flashing but no siren: standard procedure for getting someplace quickly without alerting or panicking any perpetrators.

The house was dark except for one second-story window. Next door a man and woman stood in their driveway; the man approached the officers when they arrived. "I'm the one who called about the gunshots."

"How many people live here?" asked Slattery, pointing to the house.

"Three. Donald and Rachel Pace, and their little girl. I think the husband is out of town. I tried to call them as soon as the shots went off, but the phone was busy."

"Did you see anyone going in or leaving the house?"

The man shook his head.

Charlie said, "What's the girl's name?"

"Ronnie."

A second cruiser pulled up and two more police officers stepped out. Slattery directed one to watch the rear of the house, and the other to remain alert in front. Then he and Charlie approached the house with service pistols drawn.

The front door was locked. They peered inside a front window but were unable to see much of anything. It was a judgment call: ring the bell and wait several seconds, giving whoever was armed time to take a hostage; or break into the house—possibly triggering an alarm—and frighten the armed person into action.

Slattery shielded his face and hurled himself through the living-room window. No alarm sounded. Charlie jumped in after him. They stood inside, listening. A soft sound—some sort of whimpering or moaning—came from upstairs. A ray of light shone down the stairwell. The two men bounded up and headed for the room the light was coming from. They could smell the recent discharge of a firearm.

Charlie stepped first through the open door; his partner came in behind. To their left was the inert crumpled heap of a woman's body. Across the room a young girl sat on the floor, dazed and whimpering, still holding the gun with two hands.

Slattery muttered, "Jesus H. Christ. She shot her mother." His fear made his voice turn harsh. "Drop the gun! Drop it now!"

Charlie saw the woman's battered face, the pattern of blood smears on the wall, and the lamp that had been knocked from the night table. He knew instinctively that there had been a struggle between the woman and a man.

"Drop it, goddammit!" Slattery shouted. The girl, her eyes unfocused, twisted her body toward them—her hands moving with her body, the gun moving with her hands. In a moment it would be pointed at them. Slattery trained his pistol on the girl.

"No!" Charlie shouted. He pushed his partner out into the hallway. Then he holstered his own pistol. He dropped slowly to his knees, eye level with the girl who sat ten feet away. "Ronnie—it's okay, little darling. Everything is okay." He began to inch closer to her.

"I wet myself," the girl said.

He spoke in a loud whisper. "Shh. Don't say anything. Just take a real deep breath. . . . That's good. . . . Take another deep breath. . . . That's very good." He was five feet away from her.

"I wet myself," the girl repeated. "I'm all wet. I'm sorry, Mommy."

"It's okay, Ronnie. Your mommy's not mad at you. Now, I'm going to reach my hand out, very, very slowly. Don't move. That's good. That's very good."

He extended his arm toward her so slowly that he seemed to be moving a millimeter at a time. As his hand reached the barrel of the gun, he grasped it and turned it away from himself. In the same moment the girl went limp, crumbling against him. He pulled the pistol from her fingers and placed it on the floor. Then he held the girl in his arms. The pungent odor enveloped Charlie as she pressed against him, the urine moving osmotically from her pajamas and through his uniform, down to his skin.

The whimpering turned into a choked, truncated cry, and she began to gag. He held her against one shoulder and stood up, lightly patting her shoulder: like a new father instinctively but awkwardly cradling a baby for the first time.

He carried her into her bedroom and sat on the edge of her bed, still holding her. "My name is Chuck, and everything is going to be okay."

He knew it was the biggest lie he had ever uttered.

As difficult as it was for Veronica and me to listen to Charlie Amory's story, it was just as difficult for him to tell it. And now he lapsed into silence as he stood by his window and looked out at Washington Street.

"I remember that," Veronica said. "I remember you sitting with me in my room while all sorts of people walked in and out of my house. I remember feeling like you were my friend."

"You had a hard time getting the story out. When the detective, Joe Branson, showed up, he couldn't get you to tell him anything. You just sat there in my lap, clutching me. Branson told me to leave the room, and you just grabbed on tighter. So finally he just stood in the doorway while I asked the questions."

"You and your partner both wrote reports because you were the first officers on the scene. Neither one of you put in the fact that I wet myself."

"There would be no purpose served in mentioning it, so I left it out. Maybe my partner didn't notice." He smiled. "Or maybe he thought it was me."

"I don't remember being there when my father got home."

Charlie nodded. "You weren't. At first we didn't know where he was. Then your neighbor gave us the name of your father's law firm. We called and reached the answering service. They gave us the name and phone number of one of your father's partners who lived in Weston, right across the town line, and he came over to your house. He said your father was due back the next day. He offered to keep you overnight at his house. Then a friend of your parents showed up, and she and your father's partner argued over who would watch you that night."

Veronica closed her eyes for a moment, as if trying to visualize the long-ago and long-forgotten scene. "Of course. I went with my Aunt Marilyn," she said.

"I don't remember her name," said Charlie, "and for some reason it's not mentioned in the police report. I guess things were pretty chaotic, and some parts didn't get written down."

I thought that was pretty sloppy work, but I said nothing.

Charlie continued. "You told me you wanted to go with her, so I told Branson, and he saw to it that you did. I was glad they got you out of there before you knew just how bad things were. You kept asking me if your mother would be okay, and I lied and said I hoped so, because I didn't know what else to do. I knew your mother was dead, but I thought you should hear it first from your father."

There was another reason they took her from the house, I realized. Donald told me two days earlier that he wasn't permitted to see his daughter until the police were satisfied that he had an alibi for the time of the murder. I saw no purpose in mentioning that now, so I kept silent.

Charlie said, "You heard more than I wanted you to hear, though—because you said something very sad just before you left."

"What did I say?"

He paused. "It was a question. You asked, 'What does homicide mean?' I never forgot that."

"What did you tell me?"

"I don't remember my answer. I only remember your question."

Charlie sat down again. He looked at Veronica and said, "I wondered about you now and then when you were growing up. How you were doing, what you were doing, whether what I did that night helped or made things worse. It was my first and only time at a murder scene. Such things don't happen here very often."

"Did you ever see me again?"

"No. I called your father a couple of times, checked up on you that way. I have a younger sister a little older than you. When she heard about you she wanted me to give you one of her stuffed animals. I asked your father if I could bring it over. He said he'd ask your psychiatrist if that would be okay, but I never heard back from him after that, so that was that."

Veronica had never mentioned anything about seeing a psychiatrist. She didn't say anything about it now.

"It's funny, in a way," Charlie said, "thinking about the things you remember and the things you forget. I remember telling Branson you were very brave. And I remember him saying you were very lucky. Lucky that the pistol was a trigger-cocking model. A Smith & Wesson number ten. Otherwise you wouldn't have known how to discharge it."

"What happened to the gun?"

"We held on to it for a little while, and then Branson brought it to your father. Your father asked him to dispose of it, said he never wanted to see it again."

An awkward silence prevailed for several seconds. There was a link between them, forged long ago in a horrible moment that had reverberated throughout both their lives.

Veronica said, "I never got the chance to thank you, and here I am asking you to help me again."

"Yes. Well." Charlie cleared his throat. He gathered together his copy of the file. "I'm not really an investigator anymore. But I have someone who is. He's very loyal to me. I trust him completely." He grabbed his phone receiver, punched in a couple of numbers, and then spoke into the mouthpiece. "Hey, kid. You got a couple of minutes for me?"

Charlie hung the phone up. He turned to Veronica and asked, "How old were you? Eight? Nine?"

"Nine. Just shy of my tenth birthday."

"I'm forty-six, and I've never fired a gun anywhere but the practice range. And you were only nine." There was a syncopated rapping of knuckles on the door. "C'mon in, kid."

The door opened, and into the office stepped a beefy young

man with shaved head and a goatee. He smiled broadly at Charlie. "What's up, boss?"

"I'd like you to meet a couple of visitors. I've been telling them a little bit about you. Harry Kline, Veronica Pace—meet Detective Jonas Cavaleri."

That was certainly a surprise; Charlie Amory obviously had a sense of the dramatic. As Jonas Cavaleri and I shook hands, I tried to connect his hulking cue-ball appearance to the skinny, curly-haired boy Charlie had told us about. It was a long stretch—and, I suspected, a long story.

"Jonas, Veronica is a special agent with the FBI. Harry is a psychiatrist. They're here about a murder that happened in town in 1972. An unsolved murder. I want you to help them look into things."

Jonas arched his eyebrows. "Long time ago, boss." To Veronica he said, "How'd the Bureau get interested?"

"Her interest is personal," said Charlie. "The victim was her mother."

"Oh, shit. Excuse me. I just, well, Jesus God, I'm really sorry, ma'am."

"Jonas, she's younger than you."

"So?"

"So, maybe you can call her Veronica, instead of 'ma'am.' "

"Okay, boss."

"I want you to read this case file." Charlie handed the packet to him. "Then the two of you can decide how you want to proceed. I've told Veronica I think chances are slim to none that anything can come of this. But I want you to give it a try. Give it a read-through now, then call Veronica at home when you're done."

Veronica scribbled her phone number on a piece of paper. "Here's where you can reach me, detective."

"Call me Jonas."

He took the file and turned toward the door. "Wait," Charlie called out. "I left something in the file."

Jonas handed the packet back, and Charlie retrieved a few pages of lined yellow notepad paper. "Just some notes on the case I might need," he said.

The detective told Veronica he would call her later, and then he left.

I said to Charlie, "You made a real difference in his life, didn't you?"

He shrugged. "He always had it in him to do something good. I just helped out a little bit."

"It's funny how the circle comes back around."

Veronica said, "What do you mean, Harry?"

"None of the witnesses outside of Filene's that night called the police until your mother entered the picture. If she hadn't been there, if the police hadn't been called at that specific moment, Charlie and Jonas would never have met and Jonas wouldn't have become a police detective. And now Jonas is going to try to help you find out the truth about what happened to your mother."

We were quiet most of the way home from Wellesley. We crossed through Weston into Lincoln, and through Lincoln into Concord. When we were just a mile or two from home, I said, "The picture is more complicated than I realized. Four crimes instead of one."

"That makes it simpler, not more complicated."

"How do you figure that?"

"It's four puzzles with one solution. If any one of them is solved, then all of them are solved, and then I know who killed my mother."

"Maybe Charlie Amory can help you get in touch with the detective who used to handle the case. Charlie said his name was Branson."

She shook her head. "It sounds like he developed some sort of relationship with my father. I don't want to take a chance on him telling my father what I'm doing."

"Why not?"

"I'm not sure. It's always been hard for us to talk about what happened. I just don't want that pressure now."

We crossed Route 2 and headed for the center of town. I said, "Tell me something about your mother."

"What?"

"Something. Anything. I know about her death, but I know next to nothing about her life. The sort of person she was, her influence on you."

Veronica thought for a couple of minutes. "She was the fairest person I ever knew. She judged people on what they did, not who they were—which didn't always make her popular in a town like Wellesley. Are you familiar with the METCO program?"

"Sure." It was a voluntary school busing program that for almost thirty years had been taking children from Boston—mostly black—out to the schools of mostly white suburbs like Concord.

"My mother helped make Wellesley one of the first towns to participate in METCO, back in 1966. One of the earliest memories I have—I was about three and a half at the time—was the opening day of school that year, when the buses from Boston were due for the first time. Someone called on the phone that morning, and my mother became very upset. I remember her taking me and rushing outside to the car, driving over to one of the schools. Someone had spray-painted the words 'Niggers go home' on the schoolyard wall. My mother explained what it meant. And then she said to me—and I remember it so clearly—she said, 'This is what hatred looks like.' "

I turned left where Main Street came to a dead end by the flagpole in the center of town. We passed Father John's church, St. Bernard's, and headed up Monument Street.

Veronica continued. "There was no way to erase the message on the wall in time for the arrival of the METCO bus. I guess eventually they sandblasted it off. But whoever vandalized the wall had left a can of spray paint on the ground. My mother picked it up. And with dozens of people watching, she walked up to the graffiti and sprayed over it, aimed the can at it and obliterated it."

It was nearing sunset when we reached my house. All was quiet; Melissa was at her friend Emily's house for dinner and a sleep-over.

We walked into the den and I checked the answering machine. Bobby had called wanting to know about our visit with the Wellesley police chief. "I told him you're looking into your mother's death."

"That's okay. I said you could. I know you tell him things."

I paused. "There's someone else I told, too."

She bit her lip. "Please, God—don't let it be my father."

"No, not him. I told John Fitzpatrick."

"You told Father John? I guess that's all right, but why did you do that?"

"It just sort of came out in conversation."

"It must have been an interesting conversation."

Veronica went to her apartment for a while, then came back to the house for dinner. "Jonas Cavaleri called," she said. "We're going to visit the scenes of the other three break-ins tomorrow."

"Should I come?"

"I wish you would."

We had a pizza delivered from Papa Gino's, then clicked through the cable stations in search of an old movie. We hit on the beginning of a black-and-white movie with a film-noir look about it, and I realized I had seen it before and that it wasn't a good one for us to watch under the current circumstances. I reached for the clicker, but Veronica stopped me cold. "I've always wanted to watch this," she said, and so we did.

In *Laura*, Dana Andrews is a detective investigating the murder of a beautiful young woman. Midway through the movie, she shows up very much alive, miraculously and unexpectedly.

Afterward Veronica said, "I used to think my mother would come through the door one day, and everything would seem like a bad dream that was finally over. Isn't that strange?"

"No, I don't think it's strange." I thought, but did not say, that after Janet died—even three or four years later—I sometimes found myself thinking of her in the present tense.

We locked up the house and walked together to her apartment. I built a fire in her bedroom while she showered, then I showered and joined her in bed.

She said, "I just want to lie here, if that's okay. I'm not . . . I'm not in the mood to do anything."

I was getting used to hearing that. "Sure," I replied.

We lay on our backs underneath the covers and watched the flames' flickering reflections on the ceiling.

I said, "Charlie Amory mentioned you saw a psychiatrist when you were little."

"My father thought I should probably talk to someone about what I saw that night."

"Did it help?"

"I don't know. It was so long ago. Why?"

"I was thinking, maybe it would help you to have someone to talk to now."

She touched my side lightly with her hand. "I have you for that, Harry. I can talk to you."

"I mean—well, you know what I mean. An objective listener. A professional relationship. Someone you could talk with about things you may want kept private. Someone you could even talk to about you and me."

"Why would I want to talk to a therapist about my relationship with you?"

I shrugged. "Maybe, you know, someone to help you sort out why we seem so distant lately."

"Distant?" She pondered that for a few moments. And then, struck by a sudden realization, she said, "Sex. You're talking about the sex, aren't you? I can't believe this."

"Listen, I wasn't—"

"I'm halfway to falling apart, and you're worried that you're not getting enough. I can't believe this."

There was an awkward silence. Then she flung the covers off, revealing herself: naked and defenseless. Her voice trembled. "Do whatever the hell you want to."

"It isn't that import—"

"Go *ahead*, goddammit! You want to fuck me, then go ahead and fuck me! Pretend I'm your precious little friend, Marjorie Morris."

I felt small for my selfishness, ashamed of having added to her worries. I held out my hand to touch her cheek. She slapped at it, hard. She grabbed the covers, pulled them onto herself, and turned away from me.

"I think you should go," she said.

"You don't mean that."

"Don't *ever* tell me what I mean and what I don't mean. I want you to go. Now."

And so I left.

9: Scene of the Crime

Bobby said, "That wasn't very tactful, pal of mine. No wonder she's pissed."

"I know." I leaned my head to one side, clutching the phone between my ear and shoulder as I pulled myself into a sitting position in my bed.

"You're hereby disqualified from the running for this year's 'Sensitive New Age Male' award. Does Veronica still want you to go back to Wellesley with her today?"

"I don't know. I hope so. I'd like to keep track of what's going on."

"For what it's worth, it sounds like the wildest of wild-goose chases. Even with Batman and Robin helping out."

"Batman and Robin?"

"The police chief you were telling me about, and his trusty sidekick. Hey—what's that noise?"

"I'm on the portable phone," I said. "I walked into the bathroom and I'm running water in the sink."

"If I hear a toilet flush, I'm hanging up."

"Thanks for the warning."

"Do you think they're gay?"

"Who?"

"Batman and Robin."

"How the hell would I know? I just met them yesterday."

"Not the police chief and his sidekick. Batman and Robin. The real ones."

"Bobby, let me break this to you gently. Batman and Robin aren't real. They're cartoon characters."

"You know what I mean. The real cartoon characters. Do you think they're gay? I seem to recall there was a lot of speculation about that when we were kids. Only back then we said 'homo' instead of 'gay.' "

"Maybe there was speculation in your neighborhood. Not mine."

"Something about Alfred the butler," he continued. "It'll come back to me if I think about it long enough."

"I can tell you've already devoted a lot of thought to this very important matter."

"Yeah, well—anyway, as far as *your* sex life goes, in all your years with Janet, I don't remember you having complaints."

"That's because I never had any. Nothing we couldn't work out. It was always pretty good between us."

"But not with Veronica, I gather."

"It's uneven. She blows hot and cold."

"Uh-huh. You know, that's not a very politically correct way of characterizing things."

I ignored his comment. "Things were great for the first year. They've been up and down since she moved in last spring."

"Up and down," he repeated. "Another piquant image. Have you considered a career as a country-music songwriter? Oh—speaking of songwriters, I asked my wife about your friend Mara Lee. Seems like I was right."

"Right about what?"

"Right about her freaking out. The story is she smashed a guitar over Dave Van Ronk's head backstage at the Newport Folk Festival in the sixties. And there was some incident at the Chelsea Hotel in New York, either an accidental overdose or a suicide attempt. Her record company sued her when she failed to put out a second album, and then she joined up with some sort of religious commune and was never heard from, musically, again."

I heard the front door open and shut, followed by footsteps running up the stairs. "I think Melissa is home. I'll talk to you later."

I put on a robe and walked down the hall to my daughter's room. She was unpacking her overnight bag. I hadn't seen her since she left for school the previous morning. We engaged in the ritual father-daughter small talk about her school day and her sleep-over at Emily's house. I told her I might be tied up most of the day helping Veronica take care of some personal business. This didn't particularly move her one way or the other.

I said, "Father John paid a visit yesterday morning."

She stopped what she was doing. "Oh" was all she said.

"Can I sit down?"

She nodded. "You can toss that stuff on the floor." She pointed to the papers, clothes, and heaven knows what else that were piled high on her chair. I made a space for myself there, and she sat across from me on the edge of her bed.

"Father John says you've been wondering—about God, things like that." I wondered: Could I possibly feel or sound more stupid than I do right now?

She rubbed her hands against her knees, a small discharge of nervous energy, and waited for more.

I continued. "This isn't something we've ever really talked about. Not as grown-up to almost-grown-up, anyway."

"No."

"You probably have a lot of questions."

She shrugged.

I said, "I'm not sure I have any answers for you."

She turned her eyes toward the floor and dug her toes into her carpet. Then she looked at me and said, "How come we never go to temple?"

"Your mom and I took you a few times when you were little. When she left us, I guess I didn't want to go anymore."

"Why? Did you stop believing in God when she died?"

My first thought, which I didn't share, was that I wasn't sure I had believed in the first place. I said, "Perhaps I stopped believing in a God that cared."

"But everybody dies."

"Of course."

"And everybody has problems."

"Yes."

"So if everyone who had problems stopped believing in God, then no one would believe."

"I . . . guess so." It was a nifty little syllogism: Everyone has troubles, troubled people no longer believe in God, no one believes in God. The logic was unassailable; I wondered where she was going with this.

"But Father John believes. And Uncle Bobby believes. Lots of people believe."

"I think I probably believe in something, too. I'm just not sure what that something is."

She thought about that for a moment. "Jews don't believe in Jesus."

"No."

"What would happen to us if I decided to believe something you don't believe?"

I wondered if this was a forerunner of adolescent battles in the future: the struggle to be autonomous while maintaining the connection.

I said, "When I was a few years older than you, I heard a song I really liked. It ended like this: 'I believe I believe in nothing, if I cannot believe in you.' "

She furrowed her brow. "I don't understand. What are you saying?"

"I'm saying that my love for you is the one thing I'm certain will always be there. There's nothing you can ever do that will change that, and there's no way you can get out of it, even if you try."

"What if I wanted to talk to Father John some more?"

"Do you think you need my permission?"

"I don't know. Do I?"

"You don't need my permission to talk with him. But you have it, anyway. If you want to talk with him, then that's what you should do."

This seemed to satisfy her for the moment, and I was thankful—because in conversations like that, I was just treading water, trying to stay afloat until the tide went out again.

* * *

John and Gertrude Tinsley were the victims of the first break-in, three weeks before the murder of Rachel Pace. Gertrude Tinsley was elderly now, and a widow. She grudgingly let Jonas, Veronica, and me into her home.

"I told you when you called, detective—I don't believe I can do anything to help you. It was such a long time ago. I have come to recognize time as a most valuable commodity. I suspect you're wasting your time with this conversation. As am I."

Jonas Cavaleri said, "We just want to go over the old police report with you, Mrs. Tinsley, and maybe take a look around if it's not inconvenient for you."

He told her that Veronica and I were assisting him on the case, allowing an impression to develop—without stating in as many words—that Veronica was present in an official FBI capacity. It was a deniable deception: If called on it, he could insist it was an unintended misunderstanding.

We settled in the old woman's den. She poured herself some tea; she didn't offer us any. Jonas asked her what she remembered about the break-in.

"One felt as though one had been invaded in a very personal way. That is what I recall most vividly. Arriving home after a lovely Thanksgiving dinner at my nephew's home in Dover, and finding that an intruder had rummaged through our belongings while we were out. It was not a violent act, but it had a profound effect on us nevertheless. To feel unsafe in one's own home is . . . well, it is most inconvenient."

The dour woman's deep wrinkles looked as though they had been steam-ironed into permanent residence in her forehead: etched there from dozens of years spent frowning disdainfully at people and things that offended her conservative sense of propriety.

Jonas looked through the file from the original police investigation. "The burglar did some minor property damage, is that right? Broke the basement window to get in, knocked over and broke a ceramic object and a vase? That's what you told us in 1972, I believe."

"I'm certain we didn't tell *you* anything, young man, since at that time you were likely not even shaving yet." She stated this as cold fact, not as good-natured kidding. "But, yes—that was the damage he did. And he absconded with very little. A bit of cash that was lying about, some watches and rings. He took items that tended toward the gaudy—gifts I had accumulated over the years—and left my more tasteful items that would have been worth much more money to him. He surely must have been quite stupid."

Gertrude Tinsley uttered the word *stupid* with contempt, practically spitting it out of her mouth, as if somehow the burglar's incompetence were a personal affront. Apparently she thought she was entitled to a higher class of criminal.

She said, "The investigating officer didn't hold out much hope for solving the burglary. My late husband speculated that the police wouldn't put much effort into the case. Not long afterward a woman was murdered a mile or two away from here. This served to focus the police department's attention remarkably well. They believed the same person was responsible for both crimes. They returned here for a more studied look at the situation. Ultimately they had no success." There was an unmistakable smirk on her face as she continued. "Perhaps if the police had devoted sufficient resources to capturing the person who robbed me, the murder would not have occurred."

Veronica tensed slightly upon hearing those words, then said, "I'm sure it won't surprise you—being an intelligent person as you are—that the murder is the real focus of our concern right now."

"Don't patronize me, young lady. Of course I realize that. No one would do a follow-up investigation of a simple burglary twenty years after the fact, would they? Nor does it surprise me that the police have found it necessary to ask the FBI for assistance."

Veronica said, "I think the Wellesley police conducted very thorough investigations, Mrs. Tinsley. Of the murder, and of your situation."

The woman addressed Jonas Cavaleri. "This all transpired more than twenty years ago. Why are you suddenly interested in that old murder case? If you ask me, this is just a waste of local tax dollars. Federal, too," she said, looking at Veronica.

"You were barely out of diapers at the time, young lady. You don't know anything about this."

Jonas jumped in to deflect the woman's attention away from Veronica. "Mrs. Tinsley, how many people other than you and your husband had a key to the house at that time?"

She shot him a withering glance. "The intruder broke into my house. He did not use a key. Your question is irrelevant."

She grudgingly sat through Jonas's recitation of the original investigation, confirming the essential details, changing one or two unimportant ones. She let escape no opportunity to remind us how fruitless the endeavor was, and how irritated she was at having to participate in it. She allowed us to inspect the corner of the basement where the intruder gained access, and the two rooms—and only those rooms—from which items were stolen; she insisted on being present the whole time.

After our selective tour of the site of that first burglary, she brought us back to the front foyer. She said, "The town manager is a good friend. I'm certain he'll be interested to learn how the police department is using its budgeted funds."

We headed for the door. Then Jonas turned to the woman and said, "By any chance, did you know the woman who was murdered?"

"No, I did not. I recall reading that the intruder shot her with her own pistol. She was foolish to have a gun in the house."

At that remark, Veronica walked outside. When Jonas and I caught up with her she was standing by the curb, staring at the sidewalk.

I held her hand. "She had no business saying those things."

Veronica nodded and squeezed my hand. She said nothing.

Jonas said, "I hope I never have to come back here."

"Actually," I said, "I *do* need to go back. I left one of my gloves in her house. Give me a minute."

I returned to the house. The woman offered no pretense of civility when she answered the door. "What is it this time?"

"Sorry to trouble you, Mrs. Tinsley, but I believe I left a glove inside. Brown leather, looks like this one." I held the other glove up for her inspection.

She sighed, clearly annoyed, and went to retrieve my glove. A minute later she returned with it. She tossed it at me and began to close the door.

I blocked the door with my foot. Her eyes opened wide, a look of fear. And though that was not my intent, I confess I took some pleasure from it.

"Why are you so unpleasant?" I asked.

"Why are you bothering me? Remove your foot at once or I shall scream for help."

"The woman who was murdered never had time to scream. And she wasn't shot to death with her own gun. The killer beat her to a bloody pulp and fractured her skull with his bare hands. Her daughter was nine years old, and she witnessed the entire thing. Can you imagine what that must have been like for that little girl?"

I had her attention now. She released her pressure on the door, and I removed my foot. I said, "Take a good look at the woman standing by the curb. Twenty-one years ago that woman was the little girl who watched her mother get killed."

If I expected that to elicit some glimmer of human compassion on the old woman's face, I was sorely mistaken. "Good day," she said, and she slammed the door in my face.

"You're a horse's ass," I muttered under my breath.

"I heard that, young man!" she yelled from behind the closed door.

Good, I thought.

I returned to Jonas's car and we continued on our way.

Our hosts at the second and third homes were more welcoming than Gertrude Tinsley was. But we didn't learn anything new. I hadn't thought that we would and, I sensed, neither had Jonas. At both houses, residents had changed since 1972. A young Asian couple owned the second home; they had resided in the United States only five years and knew nothing of the murder or break-ins from so many years earlier. At the third home, a middle-aged college administrator had a dim recollection of the murder, but had no idea—until Jonas told him the day before—that the house he now lived in had been burglarized shortly before that murder.

We left the third house and climbed back into Jonas's car. He and Veronica sat in the front seat; I was in the back. Jonas put his key in the ignition but did not turn it. He sighed, turned to Veronica, and said, "Should we continue down this track? The house you grew up in has changed hands three times since your father sold it. It's owned now by a man named Alan Hurwitz. I wasn't able to reach him to make an appointment. Do you want to go by there anyway?"

Veronica shook her head and said, "No, thank you. That's not necessary. I think I've had enough for today."

We returned to the police station. Jonas said, "The chief said I should give these to you." He gave Veronica copies of the files from the three other break-ins. He and Veronica made plans to meet on Monday, two days later, to review the files together and decide how to proceed.

We stepped out of his car. Jonas said to her, "Why don't you let me look into things on my own for a little while. If anything turns up, I'll call you right away."

"Monday, Jonas. I'll be here at nine o'clock. Let's go home, Harry." She headed toward my car.

Jonas looked at me, shrugged his shoulders as if to say, "I tried," then went inside the station.

I pulled out of the parking lot and headed west on Route 16. We passed a park on our right. She said, "This is where Charlie Amory first met Jonas. I wonder how things would have turned out for Jonas if that hadn't happened." A short while later Veronica pointed to a building on our left. "Once upon a time, that was Filene's."

I knew she was thinking about her mother, and the act of kindness Rachel Pace performed that long-ago December evening on that very corner, and of the tragedy that followed on the heels of that Filene's incident.

I turned onto Weston Road and headed north toward Concord. We drove in silence for several minutes.

Without warning Veronica said, "Make a right turn here, Harry. I changed my mind."

I hit my brakes just in time to make the right turn onto Pilgrim Street. A minute later she directed another right turn.

We were on a quiet residential street. The houses were large without being ostentatious. Shrubs were wrapped expertly to ward off the blows of winter. Everything was in order, not a hint of disarray.

"Park here," she said, and I pulled the car to the curb and stopped the motor. She stared out her window at the three-story clapboard house next to us. "This is it, Harry. This is where we lived."

I asked, "How long has it been since you saw it?"

She didn't reply. She just repeated, "This is it." She opened the car door, and then she stepped outside.

10: Angie and Frankie

The house was set twenty-five yards from the street. We walked up the curving brick pathway to the front door. Veronica rang the bell. A minute later we were greeted by a diminutive woman in her fifties, with large gold earrings and hair that looked lacquered into place.

She smiled broadly at us, and when she spoke it was with the unmistakable accent of working-class Boston. "Hiya. Sorry I took so long. I was in the cellar, trying to get my new washer started." When she pronounced the words, it sounded as though she had been trying to *staht* her *warshar* in the *celluh.* "What can I do for you kids?"

"Are you Mrs. Hurwitz?" asked Veronica.

"Hurwitz? No, hon. I'm Angela Cirone. Angie." She held her hand out, and Veronica returned the handshake awkwardly. "You kids want to step inside?"

We followed her across the threshold. She pointed at the cartons piled up in the front hallway. "Sorry the place is such a mess. We just moved from East Boston a little before Christmas. Still getting organized. You kids want some coffee? Which house is yours?"

"Which house?" Veronica appeared confused. "Oh, we're not your neighbors. I *used* to live in Wellesley, but not any longer." She introduced herself and me to Angie Cirone.

"So, I guess you came to the wrong house. You want I should try to find your Mrs. Hurwitz in the local phone book?"

"No, that's not necessary. I asked if you were Mrs. Hurwitz because the town records show this house belonging to an Alan Hurwitz."

The woman furrowed her brow and thought for a moment. "No, I don't know anyone . . . Oh, wait—sure. Al Hurwitz. I don't know him real well. He's one of Frankie's associates. I don't know nothing about his name on the deed. That must be a business thing. I don't ask Frankie much about his business. Oh, gee, hon—I think Al and his wife live in Chelsea. You want to talk with them, I'm afraid you came all the way out here for nothing. How about that coffee? It'll have to be instant. You can be drinking that while I see if I can find Al Hurwitz's number in the Boston book. Or I can call Frankie. He's visiting his sister in the old neighborhood, and he'll know the number. Here, let me take your coats."

Before I realized it she was heading for the foyer closet with our coats. Somehow she had peeled them from us so naturally and effortlessly that we had no time to realize it was happening, let alone to protest it. She ushered us into the kitchen and we all sat at the table.

Veronica replied, "There's no need to trouble yourself looking up the Hurwitzes' number. We didn't come to talk with either of them. As I said, I used to live in Wellesley. In this very house, until I was eleven years old."

I said, "We were in the neighborhood, and Veronica decided she wanted me to see the house she grew up in."

Angie Cirone smiled and patted Veronica's hand. "Oh, that's so sweet. Are you kids married?"

In unison, we replied, "No."

"Well, why not?" She laughed, then walked to the stove to tend to the boiling water pot. She returned to the table with three steaming cups. "If you came here to look at your old house, I guess you must be feeling sort of homesick. That's it, isn't it, hon?"

"I don't know."

"Listen." She patted the back of Veronica's hand. "I know how it is. I never been away from East Boston before, suddenly Frankie and me in this big house, and all I can think of is I want to have all the old neighborhood over for dinner. Believe me, hon, I know how it is. And I know why you came here."

"Oh?"

"Why, to look at your old house, of course. Maybe something happened recently to make you want to do it. No—you don't have to tell me. Frankie always tells me I talk so much that people tell me things that are none of my business just to shut me up."

"Frankie is your husband?"

"Thirty years, hon. And five kids."

"Do they live here, too?"

"What?" She laughed. "No, no—grown and gone, hon. Grown and gone. But the house is big enough. Room for my kids and their kids when they visit. A happy house, I hope. Well—would you like to walk Harry and me down memory lane? Take a look at your old house?"

Our cordial and talkative hostess guided us through the ground floor rooms. At another time they may have held some interest for Veronica. But I could tell from her casual and quick attitude that she hadn't come just to soak in nostalgic ambience.

"Would you like to see your old room, hon?"

"May I see the basement first?"

"The basement?" Angie Cirone shrugged. "If that's what you want, then—sure. You remember the way, I bet. Go on down while I check on the sausage lasagna I'm making for Frankie."

Veronica opened the door to the basement and flipped on the light switch. We descended the stairway. "Someone carpeted the steps," she said, more to herself than to me.

The basement was finished with pine paneling. Cartons and file cabinets lined the walls. There was no furniture. The area was partitioned: a large room that I imagined could serve as an informal den, a smaller room that could serve as a study, and an unfinished utility room.

We stood in the doorway of the utility room. Veronica pointed to a window high on the wall above the dryer. She said, "This is where he entered." I required no explanation; I knew what she was referring to. "He stepped onto the dryer, which was a different dryer, of course, from the one here now."

I said, "We saw the footprint in the police report."

She nodded. Then she directed her gaze toward the window, and then again at the dryer. She repeated this several times.

"What are you looking at?"

"I don't know," she said. "Something doesn't seem right, but I can't put my finger on it. Something about the police report." She continued to stand there.

"Maybe it'll come to you. Perhaps if you read the report again after we leave."

"Perhaps." She turned around, and I followed her across the large finished room to the stairwell.

Angie Cirone was checking something in the oven when we returned to the kitchen. A light odor of garlic prevailed. "We haven't done much with the basement yet," she said with an apologetic tone. "I bet you'd like to see your room now. Do you want to go upstairs?"

Veronica glanced my way quickly, and I could read the panic in her eyes. But she stayed in control, and she forced a smile onto her face. The three of us proceeded to the stairway leading from the front foyer to the second floor. Angie led the way, with Veronica next, then me. I reached for Veronica's hand, but I slipped on the new carpeting and missed.

It occurred to me that we were retracing the killer's path: up from the basement, through the kitchen, across the foyer, and up to the family quarters. And I wondered: What did Rachel Pace hear sometime between ten o'clock and ten-fifteen on that long-ago, godforsaken night? Was it the sound of the window breaking in the laundry room on the far side of the house? Or was it footsteps in the kitchen—where the phone was taken off the hook—or on the stairwell or in the hallway outside her door? I knew she heard something—something that frightened her—because she took her husband's small-caliber handgun from the locked box in her closet.

Rachel's little girl lay in her own room that night, dejected that Rachel wouldn't allow her to stay in the master bedroom, not knowing then that being sent away had probably saved her life. By nine-thirty she was fast asleep.

And that girl, now grown, was standing before the doorway of her old bedroom once again.

The door was shut. Angie said, "This is Frankie's room. He keeps it locked." She smiled and produced the key. "I think we can let in the girl who used to sleep here." She unlocked the door and pushed it open.

It was no longer a bedroom. There was a long desk covered with notebooks and packets of paper, each packet held together with a large butterfly clip. On the floor were unopened cartons containing computer components, a photocopier, and a fax machine.

Angie said, "I tell him it's his *Star Wars* room. But Frankie, he don't think that's funny."

Veronica pointed across the room. "I had a fish tank over there. I got rid of it after my mother died. I didn't feel like feeding them anymore."

This was the first mention Veronica had made of her mother. Angie turned toward her, alert and curious, but Veronica said nothing more.

"Maybe you want to see your parents' bedroom, hon."

Angie led us down the hallway toward the master bedroom. When we were halfway there Veronica said, "I don't feel well. Harry, you can look. I'll wait in the car."

"I'll get your coat, hon," Angie said, and she followed Veronica down the stairwell. A few moments later I heard the front door open and shut.

I stepped into the bedroom. The furniture was different, of course, and there was nothing to directly connect the room I was standing in to the one I had seen in the crime-scene photos. Still, the position of the closet and the bathroom doorway helped me orient myself. And thus I was able to pick out the wall against which Rachel Pace's body was pummeled, and the corner where Veronica cowered in fear after firing off four rounds.

I heard Angie climbing the stairs again, and I wondered for the first time whether she and her husband knew about the room's horrid past. Three other families had lived there since Veronica moved away. Did the house's macabre history get passed along from owner to owner? I doubted it would be much of a selling point, and therefore gathered that the last owners may well have kept the information to themselves—if, indeed, they even knew about it. The Cirones could have learned about it from neighbors, but Angie's greeting when we arrived made me think she and her husband had little contact with them.

"What is it, Harry?"

I snapped out of my reverie. "Pardon?"

"You seem interested in this room."

I thought: *It's a long story.* I said, "I admire what you've done with it."

The front door open and shut again. A man called, "Hey, Angie. What the fuck. Who's that girl in the car outside, crying?"

"I'm upstairs, dear. We have company." She went to the top of the stairway. I followed her.

Frankie Cirone looked about sixty. He was tall and thin. His gray-black hair was slicked back with some sort of pomade. He looked at me with dark, recessed eyes. "Who the hell is he?" He started to walk upstairs.

Angie wrung her hands. "Dear, this is Harry—"

Frankie saw the open door of his *Star Wars* room. "What the *fuck* are you doing in there?" Enraged, he bounded quickly up the steps. "I told you. No one goes in there." His face was inches from mine. "Who the fuck are you?"

"These nice people came to look at the house, dear." Angie's voice quivered slightly as she spoke.

"Why? It's not for sale. You—I want you to leave. Now!" He grabbed me by the elbow and began to forcibly escort me down the stairs.

"Frankie, don't—"

He turned back to his wife, who was still at the top of the stairwell. "I'll deal with you in a minute."

I didn't like the sound of that. When we reached the bottom

of the stairs I pulled loose and said, "Listen, your wife has been very—"

"Oh. Now *you're* telling *me* about my wife, huh? Just who the fuck are you?"

"My name is Harry Kline. I'm a doctor—"

He snickered. "And you decided to make a house call. Well, no one here is sick." He tried to grab my arm again, but I pulled it away. "You son of a—"

"Frankie! No!" Angie ran down the stairs. "They're good people. His friend grew up here. Tell him, Harry."

"Oh, yeah?" he snarled. "Is she a doctor, too?"

"No. She's a lawyer. She works for the FBI and—"

"The FBI?! She works for the F-fucking-BI?" He faced his wife. "Are you fucking crazy, letting them in here?" To me he said, "You got a warrant?"

"Like your wife said—my girlfriend just got a little nostalgic."

"Yeah, well, tell her to take a walk around the block. Talk to all the old neighbors. Get yourself a soda pop at the corner store and talk about old times. But stay the *fuck* away from here."

He spun me around by my shoulder, turning me toward the door. I tucked my shoulder in and turned farther than he expected me to turn, making use of his own weight and momentum to bring him forward. The move brought me to one knee; it brought him onto all fours. I heard Angie Cirone gasp in the background.

He was between me and the door. I stood and stepped back so I could keep both of them in sight, lest Angie decide to curry her husband's favor by incapacitating me. I was breathing rapidly.

I said, "This is silly. Just move away from the door and I'll leave. No harm, no foul."

"Please, Frankie. We don't want no trouble. Our beautiful new house."

Cirone stood up. He blocked my way for several seconds, the two of us standing just a few feet apart, neither one giving away anything. Then he slowly stepped sideways, giving access to the door.

I moved slowly toward the door, eyeing him the whole time.

He sneered and said, "Don't come back, Kane."

"Kline."

"Whatever the fuck your name is. Don't come back. Do you know who I am? Do you know who you been fucking with?"

I opened the door and put one foot out. "Sure. You're the asshole who lives in the house where my girlfriend's mother was murdered."

Angie shuddered. "Mary, mother of God," she mumbled as she crossed herself.

I stepped outside. As I pulled the door shut I heard Frankie Cirone yell, "You're too fucking *old* to have a girlfriend."

Cirone was right: Veronica had been crying. I could tell from the redness in her eyes and the crumpled tissue she was absent-mindedly tearing into a hundred pieces as we drove toward Weston.

We drove in silence. I tried to draw her out, but she was deep in her depressive shell. I didn't see any reason to add to her distress by telling her about Frank Cirone.

We were all the way to Wayland when Veronica finally spoke. "Did you see the alarm panels?"

"Burglar alarm?"

She nodded. "I wonder how long it's been there." She gazed out the window. "I guess back then people didn't see the need."

She was no doubt thinking about the different outcome that might have ensued if her parents had installed an alarm before that fateful December night.

We followed the serpentine way of Route 126 into and through Lincoln. Crossing over into Concord, we passed the eastern edge of Walden Pond on our left. Almost a hundred and fifty years earlier, Thoreau's cabin stood on the northwestern rim, not far from the path now taken by the commuter rail line.

Veronica said, "Think how different things would be if I had been able to pull the trigger sooner that night. I would have killed the man who murdered my mother. We wouldn't be on this search now. We might not even be together now. Change a major life event like that, and everything that flows from it changes. I would have led a very different life. I don't know how it would have been different, but it would have."

"I suppose that's true."

"But there's one thing that would be exactly the same."

"What's that?"

"My mother would still be dead."

After dinner I drove Melissa to a friend's house. I returned home and started a fire in the den. Veronica and I sat there quietly with CNN for background sound. Even though she often waxed taciturn, she still liked having noise in the background for distraction. She once told me it was a natural outgrowth of the fear of the dark she had for many months after her mother died.

After a while she stood and yawned. It was still early, especially for a Saturday night, but she was ready for bed.

"Do you want me to come with you?"

"No."

"Do you want to stay in the house with me?"

"No, not tonight."

I hesitated. "Is it because of what I said last night?"

She sighed, exasperated. "Why do you always assume that everything is somehow related to what you do?" She paused. "I'm sorry. That was unfair of me to say. I know you're trying to help."

"It's all right. I shouldn't have said what I said last night."

She shrugged, then left, without a kiss or a touch of the hand.

I channel-surfed for a while, settling finally on a re-rebroadcast of a Channel 38 tribute to Ted Williams. I watched the compendium of interviews and old film clips that I had seen before, and my mind began to wander. I thought about the incident at the Cirone house. I considered calling Frankie Cirone to apologize for shoving him, but I couldn't think of anything I might have done differently that afternoon, under the circumstances that had been present. Cirone had acted; I had reacted.

Just as Ted Williams was about to win the 1941 all-star game with a home run off of Claude Passeau, the phone rang. I hit the mute button on the TV remote control and took the call myself.

"Harry? Harry Kline?"

"This is he."

"This is Charlie Amory. From the Wellesley Police Department." There was a very brief silence, and then: "I need to meet with you as soon as possible."

11: Burial Ground

Watertown has a less genteel feel than either Wellesley or Concord. It is closer to the city, almost part of it. The town is on the western side of the Boston-Cambridge urban plane, and close in toward its center.

Two- and three-family homes prevail. They look like large single-family houses but are, in fact, apartment buildings or condominiums: one apartment or residence per story, or two of them set side by side. The plots are small, and the homes stand close to one another, like the houses that sit four abreast on the narrow, crowded spaces of Monopoly board properties.

Charlie Amory lived in a two-family home, the side-by-side type, off of Belmont Street near the Cambridge border. Indeed, the Mt. Auburn Cemetery, which was just over the Cambridge town line, was within walking distance. They buried Rachel Pace there; I had no reason to think Charlie knew that.

I arrived at the tail end of the family's Sunday breakfast. Charlie offered to make up another batch of pancakes, but I had already eaten. He introduced me to his wife and his teenage son. His daughter was there as well. She appeared to be in her early twenties, and she was with her husband and their infant. As the conversation progressed I realized that Charlie's daughter and her family lived in the other half of the two-residence building.

Charlie and I withdrew to a small area off the living room. It appeared to double as a computer room and a sewing

102

room. The space was cramped, but the chairs were comfortable. "Do you have children, Harry?"

"A daughter."

"If you're only going to have one, a daughter is the way to go. All other things being equal, boys leave, but girls stay. My two older boys, California and New Mexico. But my daughter moved directly from this side of the building to the other side, right after she got married. Do you have grandchildren?"

I laughed. "My daughter is only eleven."

"Terri and I figured kids would be our main business in life, so we started early. Different strokes, I guess. How about you and your wife? Do you want any more?"

"My wife passed away seven years ago."

"Oh." He paused. "Sorry. You and Veronica, then. You're . . ."

"Yes, we are."

"Uh-huh." He rubbed his chin for a moment.

His questions, though direct, weren't offensive or unwelcome. But I knew he had something more important to talk about from the urgency of his invitation the previous evening. I asked him what was on his mind.

"Well, a couple of things. First of all, did you really call Gertrude Tinsley a horse's behind?"

"Not exactly."

"Oh." He looked puzzled.

"She overheard me muttering something to myself. It wasn't intended for her ears. And I didn't say she was a horse's behind."

"What did you say?"

"I said she was a horse's ass."

He winced, shook his head, and then almost in spite of himself began to chuckle. "Well, she does create an impression, that's for sure. Would you mind telling me why you did that?"

I gave him a rundown of the old woman's boorish behavior, then said, "Frankly, it wouldn't surprise me if she knew all along who Veronica was and intentionally decided to torment her."

"Well, now, that sounds a little farfetched, don't you think?"

"Not at all. She remembered the murder. It's not unlikely she would remember the murder victim's last name." I realized I was sounding defensive. "Anyway, why did she call you? Did she think you would arrest me?"

"No, of course not. She just felt obligated—I believe she used the words 'civic duty'—to inform me how wasteful it is to reinvestigate the case, and how terrible it is when law-abiding citizens like herself are subjected to such vicious abuse." He scratched his cheek. "Yeah, I think that's a pretty fair characterization of what she stated." He thought about that for a moment, then said, "You know what? She *is* a horse's ass." We both laughed at that.

The baby wailed in the kitchen. Charlie smiled. "After four of my own, I never thought I'd enjoy a baby fussing as much as I do with this one."

He stood and shut the door to block out his grandchild's cries. He was only a couple of years older than me, but in an entirely different phase of family life.

He sat again and asked, "What do you think of your police chief, Alfred Korvich?"

He caught me by surprise with that one. I wondered why he was asking and what, if anything, he was hoping to hear. "I suppose he's competent at what he does, although I wouldn't know for certain how to judge that." I realized how lukewarm that sounded.

"Personally, I mean. How does he come across to you?"

I wondered why he assumed I knew Korvich. "Our relationship is not a warm one."

"Not exactly a ringing endorsement. Then again, he gives you a pretty mixed review, too."

"You spoke to him about me?"

He nodded. "On the one hand, he says you helped solve a hit-and-run homicide in Concord last year. You persuaded one of your patients to turn the perpetrator in. But on the other hand, I got the sense that he just doesn't know what to make of you. Says you hold your cards close to your chest."

"That's all he said?"

"That was pretty much it. Why? Is there more?"

There was a lot more Korvich could have said about my

own involvement in that homicide case, but if he hadn't mentioned it, I wasn't going to. I said, "Why did you ask him about me?"

"A couple of reasons. First of all, Gertrude Tinsley is definitely not one of my favorite people. But she has the ability to make my job difficult, tie me up explaining myself to the town manager. After she told me about your confrontation with her, I wanted to check you out a little bit, see if I had to worry about a loose cannon going off."

He apparently hadn't been contacted by Frankie Cirone. I wondered if I should bring the incident up, make a preemptive strike by getting my version of events on record first. I decided to hold back on that.

"What did Korvich say?"

"He said you're unpredictable, but probably not reckless. But that wasn't the main reason I called him, although I guess it's related to that reason. I wanted to know if he thought you could be trusted with sensitive information about a police matter."

"What did he say?"

"He said he wasn't certain, but that you probably could." Charlie smiled. "I don't think he enjoyed acknowledging that."

Charlie reached for an envelope on a nearby table and produced a few pages of lined yellow notepad paper. He studied them for several moments. "These are some notes from the original case file on Rachel Pace's murder."

"I saw you take them out of the file before you handed it to Jonas."

He nodded and put the papers back in the envelope. He shut the envelope in a drawer. Then he turned to me and said, "Okay with you if we take a walk?"

We put on our coats. Charlie went to the kitchen to tell his wife we were going out for a while. We walked to the corner and then turned onto Belmont Street, heading east.

He said, "You're in the business of listening to other people's secrets."

"I suppose you could say that."

"I guess a lot of people, married people, talk about being unfaithful."

"Some do."

"Do you think it goes on more now than it used to, say, twenty years ago?"

"Divorce is more common. I don't know about infidelity. And I wasn't practicing back then, so I don't know if people talk about it more in therapy than they used to. Why do you ask?"

He avoided the question. "Do you think a man can cheat on his wife and still love her?"

"Yes."

"And suppose they have a child. How would it affect a child if the cheating was revealed?"

We stopped for a traffic light, then continued along the avenue past the storefronts. I said, "Please don't take this the wrong way, but is this a personal matter you're referring to?"

"A personal matter?" He looked confused for a moment, and then understood the nature of my question. "Oh—no, of course not. Not even close."

"I see. What, then?"

"Rachel Pace was murdered on a Thursday night. Joe Branson, the detective on the case, talked a little bit that night with Donald Pace, but everyone realized we had to get him to his daughter as soon as possible. The next day Donald wasn't very available, which these days would probably mark him up as a prime suspect, but back then seemed perfectly understandable. That Saturday, Branson asked me to join him at the Pace home, where he was scheduled to conduct a formal interview of the deceased's husband."

Just as Charlie and the detective were getting ready to leave the police station and drive to Donald Pace's house, Donald walked into the building. He addressed Charlie first. "I appreciate your helping my daughter the night before last. Thank you."

"You're welcome, sir."

Donald spoke to Branson. "You said you wanted to talk with me about Rachel."

Branson took Donald to an interview room and asked Charlie to join them.

Donald's mood was somber. His eyes were red from crying. His perfectly pressed expensive suit seemed to hang loosely on him, as if he had lost ten pounds overnight. He said to Branson, "I want you to find my wife's killer."

"Of course. This is our absolute top priority. Isn't that right, Amory?"

"Yes, sir," Charlie replied.

There was a brief silence. Branson seemed to be waiting to see where Donald Pace would lead him. The detective waited with his pen poised over a yellow notepad.

Donald stared at his hands folded in front of him and mumbled, "They never show you anything about the cleanup."

"What was that?" asked Branson.

"The cleanup. The police shows on television never show you what happens afterward. Somehow you assume that the mess gets cleaned up. Until it happens to you, you don't realize that you're the one who has to do it. The bloodstains on the wall. The carpet. The broken lamp. They don't magically disappear as they do on television."

"No, I guess not."

Donald looked directly across the table at the detective. "No offense, detective, but how many murder investigations have you handled before?"

"Only two, although they do send us into Boston sometimes, attach us to homicide investigations there to keep us up to date on techniques. As I'm sure you know, we don't have many homicides in Wellesley. Another few days and this would have been our ninth complete calendar year in a row without one."

"Well, I'm sorry my wife had to go and ruin your record." Donald sighed. "Pardon me. I don't mean to give you a hard time. I'm upset. I'm angry. And I don't have a clue what to tell my daughter about this, or how to get her to stop shaking."

Charlie said, "You have a brave little girl, Mr. Pace." Then he saw Branson motion him to stop talking, and he understood that he was there to help by observing, not to take part in the questioning.

"Yes, I do."

Branson said, "You remember, of course, that I was going to come to your home today to talk with you."

"Certainly."

"And yet you came here instead."

"I wanted to spare my daughter the sight of the police coming into our home again. And I wanted to be certain I could speak with you in private, and candidly, away from her."

"I see."

Donald sat quietly and folded and unfolded his hands several times. "Recently I was involved in an indiscretion."

"Indiscretion?"

"An affair." He shifted uncomfortably in his chair. "It was unplanned, and it was very, very brief. And it's over."

"Did your wife know?"

Donald shrugged. "Are you married, detective?"

"I am."

"Then I'm sure you've discovered—sometimes wives seem to know things you would think they have no way of knowing. I'll never know now."

"Who was the woman?"

"Someone I met through my work. She used to be a client."

Branson leaned back in his chair and exhaled slowly. "I'm sure you realize that by telling me about the affair, you raise the possibility of a motive on your part for harm to come to your wife."

Donald nodded. "If you are as thorough in your work as I hope you are, then you might have learned about it without me telling you. And were I not to tell you about it now, if you came to suspect the affair later, then you would come to suspect me as the killer. Frankly, I'm not personally concerned if you suspect me. But every minute you would spend investigating me would be a minute taken away from the real task."

"And of course," Branson said, "this also raises the possibility of a motive on this other woman's part."

"I spoke with her this morning. She's willing to meet with you to answer your questions. We both hope you'll be discreet—for her sake, and for my daughter's sake."

"And for your sake, no doubt."

"At the moment I have other things to worry about."

"Why did you end the relationship, Mr. Pace?"

"I was . . . uncomfortable with it. Uncomfortable with the image of myself as an unfaithful husband."

"And are there other, uh, indiscretions we should be informed of?"

There was a derisive edge in Branson's voice when he pronounced the word *indiscretions*. Charlie could tell it was there, and he assumed that Donald picked up on it, too.

Donald sighed. "Listen, detective. Normally I take care to create a good impression on people. It's the way I was raised. It's also good business. But right now I don't care how you judge me. I don't give a damn whether you like me, pity me, or find me utterly distasteful. All that concerns me is that you find my wife's killer. Until you do, I'll worry that he may try to harm Veronica. She is, after all, the only witness. She's the only source of information you have, and he must know it."

Branson finished writing something on the yellow pad. He rubbed his chin and stared at Donald for several seconds, as if he were considering his next move. Charlie knew that Branson already had information about the perpetrator, information that would likely eliminate Donald as a potential suspect.

Branson said, "Ah, what the hell. There's no good reason not to tell you this. Your daughter isn't the only source of information we have."

Donald considered that for several seconds. "You mean there's another witness?"

"No. But in the past few weeks there were three other break-ins in your part of town. I'm almost positive they were committed by the same person who . . . who was in your house. This gives us some additional information to work with." He paused. "For example, we have a fingerprint from one of the other break-ins. Once we have a suspect, that print should help us rule him in or out pretty quickly."

Branson let that information sit with Donald. After several seconds Donald understood that Branson was giving him an opportunity to make the suggestion himself. Donald said, "I want you to take my fingerprints."

Charlie thought, *I was hoping you would say that.*

"As you wish," said Branson. "Officer Amory here can take care of that."

And now, twenty-one years later, Charlie Amory still remembered fingerprinting Donald Pace. "Harry," he said as we continued on our walk, "I never felt so embarrassed taking someone's prints. And I never felt more relieved when they checked out negative. Because when I took his prints, I kept thinking, 'If they come up positive, what can I possibly say to that little girl of his?' "

"But you knew it wouldn't be positive, because whoever left the fingerprint at break-in number three also killed Rachel, and Donald was on an airplane when his wife was killed."

Charlie nodded. "His former client—the one he had the affair with—came up clean, too. Not that Branson actually had any real doubt. He told me that later on when I asked him. And in case you're wondering, he never told me the name of the woman. He never wrote it up formally, just left those yellow note pages without her name lying in the case folder."

Belmont Street merged into Mt. Auburn Street, and now we were walking alongside the cemetery. Charlie Amory stopped and said, "It's pretty here in the spring. A very posh place, with lots of well-known Boston families represented. They have a lot of unusual trees that attract different types of birds. A lot of bird-watchers."

"I know. I did my psychiatric residency at McLean Hospital. There used to be a joke that the life goal of certain upper-crust Bostonians was to graduate Harvard, live at McLean Hospital, and get buried at Mt. Auburn Cemetery."

We came to the main entrance. Charlie stopped walking and stared at the wrought-iron gate. He said, "Rachel Pace is buried here."

"Yes, I know."

"Joe Branson and I were here the day they laid her to rest."

"I've heard that the police do that when it's a murder case.

You want to see who's in the crowd, because it may include the murderer."

"That's why Branson came."

"And you?"

"Well, I came because he asked me to. But I wanted to be there for Veronica's sake. I knew I had helped her the night of the murder. I had this idea that my being there might make things easier for her."

I tried to visualize that nine-year-old child at the funeral, but the image was too painful to contemplate. "Veronica brought me and my daughter here last Mother's Day to visit her mother's grave. It was her first time here since the funeral."

"Do you remember where it is?"

"I believe so."

"Maybe we should go and pay our respects."

The grave was easy to find, set on a hillside with a commanding view of the city, underneath two distinctive cherry trees that had been in full bloom on my earlier visit.

On that day eight months earlier Melissa asked Veronica how her mother died. Veronica said, "She was killed by a man who broke into our house to rob us. My father wasn't home. She died trying to protect me."

A look of utter despair flashed across Melissa's face. "You were there?"

"Yes."

"And you saw it happen?"

"Yes."

"Oh, no! That is so awful!" She fell into Veronica's arms and cried. "Did they put the man in jail?"

"No, honey. They never caught him."

Melissa stepped back. "But they *have* to catch him! *You* have to catch him! Can't you get the FBI to help you? *I'll* help you if you want."

And now, standing near the simple granite marker, I wondered if that conversation had helped set in motion the events that had brought me there once again.

Charlie Amory took a step closer to the grave. He sighed and said, "Such a pity."

"Yes," I said.

We turned around and looked out over the city. Charlie said, "A city cop gets to see death a lot more than a cop in Concord or Wellesley. I'll never forget that night. I'll never forget how awful I felt for your friend Veronica. She was, what—ten years old?"

"Not quite."

"I remember thinking, if she was younger, she might not remember. And if she was older, maybe it would be easier to handle."

Charlie looked at the grave site once more.

I said, "Those pages of notes you took out of the file before you handed it to Jonas—those were Branson's notes about Donald Pace's affair."

"Yes."

"Why did you tell me about it?"

"I assume Veronica doesn't know anything about it. And I assume she might somehow figure it out if she continues to pursue things. I'm hoping you can persuade her to stop. She's not going to uncover the killer's identity. She's just going to uncover more unhappiness for herself, and revisit old misery. If you care about her, Harry, tell her to let it go."

I called Bobby that night and gave him a rundown of the weekend's events. In my description of my conversation with Charlie Amory, I left out mention of Donald's infidelity. I saw no reason to reveal it.

Bobby was most interested in the visit to Veronica's childhood house. "So—Frank Cirone is living in Wellesley. I wonder what Wellesley's rich and famous think of that."

"You know him?"

"Well, not personally. Only by reputation." He paused. "You mean, you *don't* know him?"

"No."

"Tsk, tsk. Like I always tell you, pal of mine. Stop reading the *Boston Globe* and get a subscription to the *Herald* instead. You can hold it in one hand, you don't have to think when you read it, and you can learn all about the latest exploits of the

Boston mob, including one Frank 'the Blade' Cirone. How do they come up with those idiotic nicknames, anyway? They should hire a media consultant."

" 'Boston mob.' You mean . . ."

"Yeah, I do. Congratulations, Harry. You've managed to piss off the Mafia."

Bobby gave me a rapid-fire rundown of Frank Cirone's alleged felonious exploits. It was an impressive résumé. I said, "Thanks for sharing that with me. Should I be concerned?"

"Let me see. . . . A Jew from the suburbs intrudes on a gangster's lair and assaults him in front of his woman. Why, no, why should you be concerned?"

"Well, he knows how to find me if he wants me."

"Whoa. Who are you—John Wayne?" Bobby chuckled. "Relax, pal of mine. I'm sure Frank the Blade has more important fish to fry. Or skewer."

I thought about what Bobby said after I hung up, and I decided he was right. I couldn't see Cirone wasting his time on me. Earlier in the day I had again considered calling him to apologize, and again had decided not to do it. I saw no reason to change my mind now.

The three of us went to Chang An for dinner. Afterward Melissa retreated to her room to do homework. Once again Veronica expressed a preference for sleeping alone. This was the third night in a row, if I counted Friday night when she asked me to leave her place. I couldn't recall such a streak occurring since she moved into the barn the previous summer.

I was in the den reading the Sunday *Times* when the phone rang.

"Is this Harold Kline?"

"Yes."

"You and me. We need to talk."

"Who is this?"

"Who *is* this?" he repeated. "This is the asshole who lives in the house where your girlfriend's mother was murdered."

12:
That Which Does Not Kill Me

We woke up in separate beds for the third straight morning. Veronica walked over to the house for breakfast. There was a palpable tension in the silence between us.

Finally, I said, "How did you sleep?"

"So-so," she replied as she buttered her toast. "My father called. He wants the three of us to come for dinner tomorrow night. I told him I'd check with you."

"That's fine with me."

"Uh-huh." That was all she said.

"Do you want me to call him back to tell him?"

"No, that's all right. I'll do it." She poured coffee and lapsed back into silence.

I went to the refrigerator for more juice. "I'm seeing patients this morning. Then I have some errands to run at lunchtime."

Had she asked about the errands, I would have avoided the question or made something up. I saw no reason to tell her I was invited—perhaps summoned was a better word—to a meeting in Boston's North End with my mafioso friend, Frank the Blade. But she didn't ask.

I said, "If I have time this afternoon, I'll swim some laps at the club."

"Maybe I'll meet you there."

"I'd like that." I checked the clock. "I'd better get a move on."

I brushed her shoulder with my hand as I walked past her.

"Harry," she called as I was on my way out of the kitchen.

I turned to face her. She looked at me for several seconds, unable to decide what she wanted to say. "I don't know. Nothing." She paused. "My washing machine is making a funny noise when the water drains out."

"I'll take a look at it. If not today, then tomorrow."

"Are we still going to the PTA meeting tonight?"

"If you want to."

"It's important to me."

"All right. By the way, in Concord they call it the PTG. The Parent-Teacher Group. If you call it PTA tonight, you'll stamp yourself as an outsider."

"Why don't they call it the PTA?"

I shrugged. "It's Concord. Folks like to think they're special." I thought about Father John's comment and said, "They have a lot of smart dead people here."

Frank Cirone sent a car for me at midday. It was a burgundy Ford station wagon, and that made me laugh. The driver got flustered and said, "Did I do something wrong, Doctor?"

"No, no. I was surprised by the type of car, that's all. I guess I expected a black limousine."

He laughed. "Too many movies, Doctor. You see too many."

The North End has a closed-in feeling: old buildings on narrow streets, the streets arranged at odd angles to one another. Once a Jewish shtetl, then an Irish ghetto, now it was a predominantly Italian neighborhood and work district.

The driver pointed out the window. "That old Prince Spaghetti commercial? The kid running home? Right there."

He parked in front of a dry-cleaning store. We walked through the store to a back hallway that led to a stairwell. Alone in a room on the second floor, Frank Cirone sat behind a desk and reviewed a ledger.

He peered over his wire-rim reading glasses when I entered the room. His hair was neatly slicked back. He looked more like an accountant than whatever it is that he was.

He made a slight movement with his right hand, and I understood that he meant for me to sit down. Then he had a small wave with his other hand, and the driver understood that he was expected to leave. Both the driver and I did as we presumed we were being told to do. I didn't bother to take off my coat.

He closed the ledger. "Monday. A lot of catching up to do." He took his glasses off. "I'll ask you again. Do you know who I am?"

"Yes."

"Good," he replied. "You see now why strangers in my house bother me. Especially the FBI."

I nodded.

Cirone said, "How did you find out about me?"

"I asked a friend."

"Someone you trust?"

"Yes."

"It's hard to know who to trust," Cirone said.

"No, not for me. I'm pretty good at knowing whether I can trust someone."

"Maybe that's because of your training." He paused. "You look surprised."

"How do you know what I do for a living? For that matter, how did you know where to find me?"

"I wrote down your license-plate number the day before yesterday. I have to pay attention to things like that. With your license number, I got your address and phone number, and other information."

He provided no more detail on what he knew or how he had learned it, and I didn't ask.

Cirone leaned back in his chair. I noticed for the first time how thin he was. I wondered if his nickname—the Blade— came from his appearance or from something more sinister.

He said, "Someone once gave me a hard time. Then he learned who I am. He called me to apologize."

"I thought of apologizing, but that was before I learned about you. After I learned, I changed my mind."

"Why?"

"You might think I was only apologizing because I feared you. And that would make the apology meaningless." I hesitated. "Also, I thought I was the one more deserving of an apology."

He considered that for a moment. "Interesting," he said. "Were you nervous coming here?"

"A little."

"Uh-huh. I have that effect. I know it. And I use it. Not my intention to use it now." He stood and reached for his coat. "Come. We'll eat."

I followed him down the stairs and out a rear door, different from the door through which I had entered the building. His driver and another man saw us and silently followed behind.

We were in an alley. The driver and the other man walked about fifteen yards behind us. The end of the alley opened up onto a narrow street. People milled about: women hurrying in and out of the stores, men walking slowly with cigarettes in their hands or mouths.

"Hungry?" asked Cirone.

"I could eat."

"You like Italian?"

"Yes."

"You're in luck."

He opened the door of an unmarked dark storefront. The driver and the other man remained outside in the January chill. Once inside, I realized that it was a restaurant, although I saw no menus, no waiters or waitresses, and no cash register. There were about a dozen tables. Four tables near the front were occupied by old men, singly and in pairs, sitting silently.

Cirone led me to a table at the back. He sat against the wall, giving himself a view of the entire room. A man and a woman appeared at the table with a pitcher of water, a basket of bread, and a bottle of red wine. Cirone gestured at me and then at himself, and then he nodded to the man. The man said something in Italian, and I realized that Cirone had just silently ordered our meal. Obviously they knew him well enough to know what he wanted.

He pushed the basket toward me. "Bread?"

I tore off a piece. "Do they have butter?"

He pointed to a small bowl with some sort of textured

spread. "Try it. Minced garlic in a little bit of oil, a few other seasonings mixed in."

He watched me bite into the bread. He said, "You killed a man last year. Hey—take it easy. You all right? Here, take some water." He poured it into my glass.

I took a sip. "Sorry. You caught me by surprise."

He waited until I composed myself. "Like I said. You killed someone. I bet that doesn't happen often in Concord. But you weren't indicted. The Middlesex DA didn't even bring it to the grand jury."

"It was self-defense," I said. "He was trying to kill me."

"You use a weapon?"

"No."

"Your bare hands?"

"Not exactly. I hit him. He fell. He died from the fall, not from being hit. I wasn't trying to kill him."

He raised his eyebrows. "A man tries to kill you and you don't try to kill him first? If you weren't trying to kill him, what did you think you were doing when you hit him?" He paused. "Bare hands, huh? You got one on me with that. How did it feel?"

"Terrible. It wasn't what I wanted to happen. It wasn't something I planned."

"Uh-huh." He reached for the bottle of wine. I didn't want any; he poured a small amount for himself. "Your friend. The one who was with you on Saturday. She wasn't always FBI."

"No," I said.

"She used to be a Rhode Island ADA out of Bristol County. Prosecuted murder cases. I personally know two people serving life sentences because of her." He sipped his wine. "But this is not a concern today. I understand the difference between business and personal. And that was business." He looked beyond me for a moment. "How much Italian can you speak?"

"Not a word."

A young man with a stiletto-shaped mustache approached our table and knelt down. He glanced at me. Cirone said something to him in Italian, probably, "Don't worry, the idiot won't understand if we speak our language." He and the man talked briefly, and then the man bowed deferentially and left. The same ritual occurred with two other visitors during our meal.

The lunch entrée was a boneless chicken breast covered with mozzarella and topped with slices of a spicy sausage. There was a side dish of linguine in marinara sauce.

Cirone ate in silence; I followed suit. The meeting was his idea. If there was some purpose, I was still waiting to hear it.

The waiter cleared our plates and brought coffee. Cirone gestured toward the front of the room. "The table by the window, on the left over there. You see it?"

I turned to look. "Yes."

"How old are you?"

"Forty-two."

He thought for a second. "That table, maybe a year before you were born. I was sixteen. My father and I sat there one day for lunch. I went to the bathroom downstairs. Someone was already in there, so I came back upstairs. I was standing right there, next to where you're sitting. I got back just in time to see someone approach that table and put two bullets into my father. One in the head. One in the chest. He dropped the gun and walked out, very calm. Planned, not like your situation. He had waited until I went downstairs, which is the way these things are done. He didn't expect me back so quick." Cirone looked at the corner table for several seconds.

"I don't know what to say."

For the briefest instant his expression softened. And then the moment was gone.

"People wonder why I still come here, how I could do that. I tell them, what doesn't kill me makes me stronger. I think some German guy said that."

"Nietzsche. *'Was mich nicht umbringt, macht mich starker.'* I had a gym teacher who always used to say that."

Cirone sipped his coffee. "The story goes, my father died in my arms. But I think he was already dead when I got to him. It was the first time I saw someone die."

Cirone's implication was clear: He had seen others die, too.

He looked at me and said, "You being a psychiatrist, you're probably wondering how that affected me. I would say it influenced my choice of career. There was unfinished business, and I thought it was my job to finish it. I imagine the same was true for your friend Veronica."

I remembered what Veronica once told me about her decision to become a prosecutor: *I wanted to hurt people who hurt other people.*

Cirone said, "So you see—I have some sympathy for your friend Veronica. Some understanding of her situation. Maybe even more than most people."

"I don't think you need to say 'maybe.' "

"This is why you are here. So I could tell you that story. So you would see that I appreciate your situation and have no ill will." He paused. "I don't do good with apologies. Instead, I offer to help. So maybe I can help you and your friend."

"In what way?"

"From what I hear, the murder was unplanned, a burglary gone wrong. Not likely that anything can be done at this point. But I could ask around. Sometimes people talk about what they do, what they know. Word gets out. Like I say, it's probably too late. But do you want me to see if I can find out anything?"

"Why are you asking me? Wouldn't it make more sense to ask Veronica?"

He furrowed his brow. "Think what you're saying. How would it look for her if she took help from me?"

I gathered his meaning. "You're right. It might appear that she had compromised herself. But why are you offering?"

He shrugged. "Like I said, I have some sympathy for the situation. And I should have done different at my house the day before yesterday."

"If I accept the offer, what will I owe you in return?"

"What will you . . ." He looked confused for a few seconds, and then he started to laugh. I hadn't seen him so much as smile until that moment. "What will he owe me, he wants to know. That's terrific. This isn't *The Godfather.* If you *ask* for a favor and I give it, *then* you owe me. But if I offer and you accept, then nothing is owed." He laughed again.

We left the restaurant and took a different route back, winding up next to the burgundy Ford station wagon that was parked in front of the dry cleaner. The driver stepped into the car. Frank and I talked for a few minutes more.

He said, "Lunch was good."

"It was," I replied. "So was the company. Reputation doesn't always tell the story."

He sighed. "Reputation. It works both ways. You, for example. The man you killed. You say it was self-defense, right?"

"Yes."

"No witnesses."

"No," I said.

"You're a doctor. Respected in your town. No criminal history. If the known facts of the situation fit your story, you escape being charged—even if the facts could also fit another version in the hands of a sharp DA. But not with me. The same facts, and I would be indicted." He opened the car door for me. "If you led my life, you would have been indicted."

"I never looked at it that way."

"No. You would have no reason to." He shook my hand. "Some other time, Harry. Do you like going to the movies?"

"Sure."

"Maybe a movie sometime. My wife, she hates to go, so I like having company." He smiled. "Cops and robbers, that's what I like best. *Bonnie and Clyde*, things like that."

"Which side do you root for?"

"Depends on who's right."

He stepped away from the car and I stepped inside. He said, "You didn't answer. Do you want me to see if I can find out anything about the murder of your friend's mother?"

I considered the offer for a moment. I doubted there was anything he could do to help this late in the game. And if I accepted his offer, I would have to keep it secret from Veronica, and I was a little uncomfortable with that. But I remembered what they say about gift horses. "Yes," I said. "I would appreciate the kindness."

"One should never mistake a kindness for a weakness," he said, and walked away.

I thought: *Only a fool would make that mistake with you.*

13: The Swimmer

On a wooded site in West Concord, they cut down dozens of trees, put in three swimming pools and eight tennis courts, and named the private club after the godfather of the environmental awareness movement. Being the sometime misanthrope that he was, local son Henry David Thoreau would have appreciated the irony.

The lap pool was enclosed for winter use. The smell of chlorine hung in the moist air. I was backstroking my way along the twenty-five-yard length, thinking about my lunch that day with Frank Cirone, when Veronica arrived. She slipped into the lane next to mine, and waited for me to reach that end of the pool.

"How did things go with Jonas?"

She wet herself down with the lukewarm pool water. "He gave me cartons of old files to look over. Break-ins in Wellesley and the surrounding towns from the fall and winter of 1972. I focused on the ones that were cleared."

"Cleared?"

"Cases that resulted in an arrest. It's too late to learn anything from the ones that were never solved. Charlie Amory stopped in while I was looking at the files. He assured me that back then, Joe Branson looked at those cases for possible links to my mother's case. Anyway, I didn't find anything terribly promising. I may try to track down two of the burglars just to satisfy my own curiosity—two whose crimes were somewhat similar to the four in Wellesley that ended with the one at my house."

I remembered Charlie's advice: *She's just going to uncover more unhappiness. If you care about her, tell her to let it go.*

I said, "I've been hoping you might reconsider, perhaps take my advice not to do this to yourself."

"Save it, Harry. I'm not in the mood." She positioned herself into a racer's start along the wall. "Four pool lengths, freestyle. Are you ready?"

"Can we just do a leisurely swim, side by side, instead of racing?"

"Are you *ready*?" she demanded.

"You don't have to do this, you know. *We* don't have to do this."

"Don't give me a hard time." She called the pool attendant over and directed him to give us a three-count start. "And stay around to judge the winner, please," she added.

I assumed the position. She always came close, but she had never beaten me freestyle.

"Ready."

She always got angry afterward.

"Set."

And she wouldn t be satisfied until she won.

"Go!"

As always, I got off to a strong lead. I had power; she had endurance. I relied on building an insurmountable lead; she counted on closing the gap as my energy faded.

When I made the turn after the first length, she was five yards behind me. I was into my rhythm, still racing hard. *Extension, kick. Extension, kick.* For a moment I was back on my college swim team.

Two lengths down, two to go: At the halfway point my lead had increased another yard. It wasn't my longest lead ever, but it wasn't the shortest. I figured to beat her a few minutes later by two or three yards.

Veronica's intensity was part of her appeal. But it's hard getting close to someone who treats everything like a contest, and who can't tolerate being bested.

Midway down the third length, I hit my fatigue point. I could hear her now, her sleek form cutting through the water like a switchblade knife. I made the last turn; heading into the final pool length, my lead had been cut to two yards.

Tiring, I was taking in water. I tasted the chemicals. My thighs began to ache. Veronica would make it close—closer than I had expected—but she wouldn't catch me. I would win again, and then we would both walk away feeling like losers.

And then it hit me: I could let her win.

I *should* let her win.

She deserved to feel good about something.

I cut back on my leg action and shortened up on the arc of my arms for three strokes. Veronica caught up with me five yards from the wall. She eked out a half-stroke victory.

I was out of breath; that part I didn't have to fake. "I started to cramp up. I guess you finally beat me."

Veronica glared at me. She climbed out of the pool and headed for the women's locker room.

I followed her. "Hey," I said in a joking tone of voice, "I thought you'd be more magnanimous in victory."

Ahead of me and facing forward, she muttered, "You let me win."

"I let you . . . ? I told you, I started to cramp—"

She whirled around. "You *let* me win," she hissed. She stepped forward, her face inches from mine. "Don't do that again. Don't ever let me win. *Ever.*"

The Alcott School's Parent-Teacher Group—the PTG—meets once a month in the school library. Fund-raising efforts are reviewed: the sweatshirt sales and cake bakes that provide money for small items not covered by the town's budget. Information about school activities is disseminated. Parental input is sought on a variety of mundane matters.

The meetings are, in a word, boring. The items for discussion vary little from meeting to meeting. And thus very few people attend. I tried to show up a few times each year; I saw it as a civic duty, like voting at the annual town meeting and donating to the community chest.

A couple of weeks earlier Veronica asked if she could come to the January PTG meeting with me. It didn't take a psychiatrist to see a relationship between her interest in parenting-like behavior and her attempt to lay the unresolved matters about her own mother to rest. But I didn't offer that interpretation to her.

About twenty other people turned out that night: the principal and her assistant, three teachers, and fifteen parents (all but three of them women). I introduced Veronica to a lifelong Concordian named Katherine Carter. Katherine was president of the PTG. She had attended the Alcott School herself, and now her youngest son was in Melissa's class.

Veronica said, "Louisa May Alcott was my favorite author when I was growing up. I think it's wonderful to have a school named after her."

Katherine tilted her head and literally looked down her nose. "Actually, the school was named after her father, *Bronson* Alcott."

Veronica said, "You would think there would be a plaque somewhere to let people know."

"People already know, my dear." Her tone of voice made clear her irritation with Veronica's comment.

I said, "It's a common misconception. Actually, Katherine," I continued, trying to change the subject, "I need you to clear something up for me. The inscription on the base of the Minuteman—I have a friend who insists it was written by Longfellow."

Katherine clucked disapprovingly. "No, no. Let him know it was written by Emerson."

"Right. Emerson. That's what I keep telling him."

So Bobby was right on that point, and I was wrong.

We sat in a circle and Katherine called the meeting to order. Minutes were read. Committee reports were detailed and discussed. The old business seemed very old, indeed; and the new business seemed almost as old as soon as it was raised.

Near the end of the meeting, the principal spoke about METCO, the voluntary busing program that brought inner-city children to schools in Concord and other mostly white suburbs of Boston. "Many of you know that METCO was level-funded again this year, and the program is cutting back on expenditures. They're canceling the late bus for the rest of the semester. I'm hoping the Alcott PTG can contribute money toward reinstating it. The principals at the Thoreau and Willard schools are making the same proposal to their PTGs, as are the middle-school and high-school principals."

Someone asked what the late bus was. The principal explained. "The METCO students sacrifice a lot to come here. They return to Boston too late to play with other children in their neighborhood. And they can't stay to socialize with their Alcott friends because they have to take the bus right after school. Until now, METCO has always provided an extra late-afternoon bus once each month. That way the Boston students can have play dates with their Concord friends."

If anyone was against the idea, they kept it to themselves. There were a half-dozen testimonials to the value of the METCO program, most of them laced with subtle condescension.

A third-grade teacher said, "We need to do everything we can to give these disadvantaged kids some real advantages. The METCO boy in my class and another child got into a fight last week. I told the other child I was ashamed of him for acting that way."

Katherine Carter said, "Well, I certainly favor funding the late bus. We can't do things halfway. If we're going to let these people into our town, then we should be as gracious as we can be toward them."

A few unassertive parents nodded with sycophantic approval when Katherine said that. Veronica didn't. Flushed with anger, Veronica said, "You talk about the Boston kids as if they were little black Sambos."

The third-grade teacher pointed at Veronica. "Now, just who do—"

"And why did you only reprimand the white boy for fighting? Do you think the black child is genetically incapable of understanding you? Why do you have lower expectations of him?"

Yvette Mason, one of the other parents, began writing quickly on a notepad.

Veronica glared across the circle at Katherine Carter. "And you, with your talk about 'letting' people into 'your' town. Do you have any idea how incredibly racist that statement is? How incredibly racist *you* are?"

Except for Yvette Mason's scribbling, the room was silent. An image flashed through my mind: Rachel Pace spray-painting over the racist graffiti in Wellesley.

Katherine Carter sighed deeply, taking great pains to display her indifference to the confrontation. "I'm sorry, dear—I didn't catch your name."

"Veronica Pace."

"Of course. Veronica. Tell me, dear—what class is *your* child in?"

Veronica was momentarily rattled. "I don't have a child in this school."

"I see. You don't *have* a child in this school. Nevertheless, you've come to share your wisdom with us on this important matter, for which I'm certain we are all very grateful."

That remark, dripping with condescension, took *me* over the top. "She's with me, Katherine, and you know that. And she's correct in her assessment of the situation." I turned to Veronica. "Let's leave."

"Gladly." ·

We strode out of the library. When we reached the hallway, Veronica said, "Thanks for sticking up for me."

"Listen to me. I don't care how much this thing with your mother is tearing at you. What you did in there was wrong."

"Jesus, Harry—you heard them."

"Yes, I heard them. And, yes—there are plenty of petty, prejudiced, self-centered people in this town. But it's *my* town. I live here. My daughter lives here. How others view me in my own backyard matters to me. And I don't want to bring embarrassment to Melissa."

"I live here now, too, Harry. Or have you forgotten that? And I'm concerned about Melissa, too." She spied something behind me, down the hall. "What the hell are *you* looking at?"

I turned and saw Yvette Mason. She was still scribbling, no doubt writing down what she was witnessing. And then I remembered: Although Yvette came to the meetings in her capacity as parent, she was also one of only two full-time reporters for the local paper.

"What are you doing, Yvette?" I asked.

She shrugged. "You never know where you're going to find news."

"The *Journal* doesn't cover PTG meetings."

"It would if something interesting ever happened." She smiled. "Interesting, like what happened tonight."

"You have an opportunity not to be a jerk, Yvette. This isn't news."

"That's what editors are for, Harry. I just write it. The editor decides whether it's news or not."

I paused. "This is payback time. That's what you're thinking, isn't it?"

"I think the psychiatrist is getting paranoid," she said, and then she returned to the meeting.

"Shit," I muttered.

"Who is she?"

"Yvette Mason. She writes for the *Concord Journal*."

"What did you mean by 'payback time'?"

"The fight over the Minuteman statue. I've told you about that."

"When the National Guard wanted to copy it?"

I nodded. "Yvette's husband was dead set against it. He and I got into an argument at a town meeting. Voices rose. Intelligence was questioned. Motives were impugned. His side won the vote, but he was made to look foolish in the process." I sighed. "I think we'll soon be hearing more about your little performance tonight."

Alone once more in my bedroom—for the fourth consecutive night—I thought about Janet and Veronica, the two loves of my life.

Janet and I met in college. We got married four years later, near the end of my medical-school studies. We had been married less than ten years when she passed away.

I was smitten when we met. I remained smitten until she died, and beyond. Our connection was so strong that I felt as if I had been with her always: as if the power of our love had taken us back in time to our childhood, linking us together from the earliest parts of our lives. I still carried images of events in her life that, in fact, happened long before we met. We were the truest of companions.

After she died, the rooms of our house echoed as I walked through them. I could hear Janet in those echoes, and I yearned for her. It was, of course, like trying to capture the wind: You feel it as it brushes against you, yet you cannot hold on to it.

I went five years without a woman in my life. The dull ache that Janet's death placed in my heart never completely faded.

And then I met Veronica. Circumstances brought us together to work on a criminal investigation. During its course we each faced danger, and we each rescued the other from danger. The intensity of the shared experience spilled over into our relationship.

Over the next year I came to love her tenacity, her seriousness of purpose in everything she did. I wanted her to live with me. And although she was spending nearly every night in my bed, she didn't want to move into the home I had shared with Janet. Her father had moved after his wife died, she said, so why wouldn't I?

The impasse drove us apart; and then the sadness of not having one another drove us together again. So when my housekeeper retired, Veronica moved into the barn apartment. It was a compromise, though we never spoke of it directly in those terms.

Loving Veronica was more of a struggle than it ever had been with Janet. Whenever I came to a gate along the path to Janet's heart, she threw it open willingly to me. But Veronica kept herself shut away. Doors stayed closed. Her intensity masked inner terrors I could not get near.

And now she was involved in a futile pursuit of tragic proportion. I didn't like what it was doing to her. I didn't like what it was doing to us. I had to find a way to get her to give up the battle.

I thought: *I've had enough of sleeping alone to last a lifetime.*

Just then the intercom sounded near my bed. "I'm coming over," Veronica said. She didn't wait for a reply. I checked the clock; it was almost midnight.

A few minutes later she walked into my room. I heard her throw off her coat. She climbed roughly into the bed and pulled the covers over herself. "Too many bad dreams," she mumbled, and then she fell into a fitful sleep.

The room was pitch-black in the middle of the night. Something startled me awake. It was Veronica, thrashing restlessly underneath the covers. She made muffled noises, as if she were yelling at someone or something in her dreams.

She lay on her side facing away from me. I rested a hand on her shoulder to let her know I was there. She reached back and covered my hand with hers, and she was still for a moment.

"I'm afraid," she said.

"Of what?"

"I don't know. I just know that I am. I need you to hold me."

I rolled onto my side and folded my body into hers, my front to her back. We were like two spoons, one cradled in the other. I wrapped my arm around her, bringing my hand to rest on the side of her face, caressing her hair lightly.

As my face brushed against her back I felt this sudden urge to taste her body, to lick her shoulders, to run my tongue in broad strokes against the natural salty essence of her skin. But she wanted to be held, so that was what I did. Something was troubling her, and I wished I could crawl inside her and chase that something away, whatever it was.

I felt myself growing hard where I lay nestled against her. "Sorry," I said, and I backed away.

"Don't pull away. I need you near me."

I moved next to her again. She backed up against me. Slowly, by achingly small degrees, we began to rub against one another.

My hand dropped down, brushing against her breast. I caught her nipple in the middle of my open palm and moved in small, slow circles with my hand. I showered the back of her neck and her shoulders with soft kisses.

She reached back and pulled me harder against herself, digging her fingernails into the backs of my thighs. I moved my hand between her legs and parted them slightly.

I entered her from behind, slowly, centimeter by centimeter. I brought my fingers around her front, sliding them lightly across her pubic mound, and then along the folds of her lips. She let out a tiny gasp.

The pace quickened, both of us moving on automatic pilot through the motions we had come to know so well. In the darkened room I couldn't see her. I was lost in the compelling sensations of touch, sound, and smell. We reached a satisfactory rhythm, softly pounding, and held on to it.

Suddenly she reached down and guided my fingers, helping me find the right pace, intensity, and position. She began to buck wildly, and I knew I wouldn't be able to hold out much longer. I strained to rein myself in, to prolong, but soon it became too much to contain. I pushed into her as deeply as I could, not too hard, then slowly pulled almost all the way out until just the tip was in her. Then I plunged: once, twice, a half-dozen times. We grabbed tightly onto one another as I exploded: cascade and release.

We lay there for several moments, my cock still inside her as it softened, surrounded by the moistness from our fusion.

She said, "I almost came with you inside me."

And then she began to cry: long and deep sobs, heartbreaking sounds.

I didn't understand what was happening. I wrapped my arms around her, still front to back, and I held her close and tight.

She said, "I know what I'm afraid of. I'm afraid of you."

"Why on earth would you be afraid of me?"

"I'm afraid of my feelings for you. I'm always afraid of things I can't control. It's very dangerous—because if I love you completely, and then if *you* leave me, where will I be?"

I reached for her hand. She grasped it with uncommon intensity. She started to shiver. I pulled the covers over us and held on to her for dear life. Eventually her breathing took on a regularity that connoted sleep.

I whispered, "I'm not leaving."

14: Calls

Bobby called the next morning, Tuesday, shortly after Veronica went back to her apartment to shower and dress. He asked, "Do you remember the story I told you at breakfast last Wednesday?"

"Sure. Bonnie and Clyde. They tried to kill someone so the victim's daughter would be too grief-stricken to become a cheerleader."

"Not that story, you idiot. I'm talking about the mentally retarded kid from Chelmsford. His teacher sued the school system because they wanted her to let him choke without intervention."

"I remember. You're representing the school system in the case."

He paused. "I *was* representing the school system."

"You quit?"

"No." Bobby was silent for several seconds. When he spoke again, I could hear the weariness in his voice. "The kid died last night. He choked in his sleep. The superintendent just called me to review the statement he plans to make to the press. He's going to say all the things you'd expect him to say. Terrible loss, hard on the other students, heart goes out to the parents. But it's total unadulterated bullshit. If you ask me, he's glad to be rid of the problem. And he's especially pleased that the kid died at home, not at school." He sighed. "*Shit*. Sometimes this job makes me take the side of people I really don't like."

"Speaking of taking sides, I had a run-in last night with someone who was on your side in the fight over the Minuteman statue."

I told him about Yvette Mason, and the scene that Veronica created at the PTG meeting. "I think she's going to put it in the *Journal*. I tried to talk her out of it."

"You're one of the last people she'd go out of her way to help. You rubbed her husband the wrong way, embarrassed him in front of a lot of people."

"Alex Mason had it coming."

"Maybe so. One thing is certain. I'm sure they'd both love to have a chance to return the favor."

Veronica returned to Wellesley that afternoon. I went to her apartment to investigate the noise in the washing machine. A moment after I arrived, her phone rang. My first inclination was to pick it up. But then I would have had to take a message, so I figured I would let her answering machine handle that. Besides, that way I could get a voyeuristic surge from listening as the caller—who would not suspect my presence—left a message for her. Perhaps it would be someone I knew. Maybe it would be a friend I had never met, and I would get a glimpse into a part of her life I didn't know. Psychiatrists are, after all, voyeurs by profession.

Perhaps it would be that slime-bucket district attorney from Berkshire County with whom she went on a fucking binge the previous spring. *That* would be an interesting message to eavesdrop on. I always told myself I had nothing against the guy, wouldn't know him if I tripped over him, didn't give a damn about him, and—other than hoping he would rot in hell and that I might get a chance to slug him just once before I died—had absolutely no feelings toward him at all.

Yeah, right.

Ashamed by my baser instincts, I grabbed the phone after the fourth ring, just as the answering machine was about to kick in.

The caller, no doubt surprised when a male voice answered,

hesitated for a moment or two. "Harry? Is that you? This is Martin Baines. Is Veronica there?"

I wondered what Veronica's boss wanted. "I think she'll be back by dinnertime. Do you want to leave a message?"

"No, not really. I just wanted to see how she's doing."

He wasn't a touchy-feely sort of guy, so that surprised me. "I'll let her know you called, Martin."

"I'd appreciate that." But he didn't hang up right away. He was silent for a few seconds, and then he said, "I know why she decided to take a leave of absence, and it troubles me. A surgeon shouldn't operate on family members. And a Special Agent of the FBI shouldn't be investigating the murder of her own mother."

"I agree."

"Well, that's good. Can you do anything about it?"

"She knows how I feel. It hasn't dissuaded her so far. How did you learn what she's been doing? When you called on my cell phone last week, you didn't know why she was taking time off."

"A woman named Gertrude Tinsley called our public-affairs office yesterday. She wanted to know why the FBI is bothering her. We get calls all the time from people who think we're harassing them. Often they also complain about the CIA. Or the post office is reading their mail or NYNEX is tapping their phone lines. Every once in a while they talk about the ghost of J. Edgar Hoover speaking to them through the transistor in their head, urging them to use force against communists."

"Which category would you put her in?"

"The category of a pain-in-the-butt citizen with an exaggerated but legitimate concern. That's what the public-affairs fellow thought, and I trust his judgment. The woman made special mention of you, Harry. She said that you accompanied Veronica to her house, and that you were . . . I think her words were, 'uncommonly rude.' "

"I'm glad she didn't find me to be common."

"I don't see any realistic chance for Veronica to succeed at what she's trying to do. And I can't help her. I can't get the Bureau involved unless the Wellesley police make a formal request. And they would need something substantial to justify our getting into it after so many years."

"Substantial?"

"New evidence they want us to look at, or some sort of old evidence that we can analyze with new techniques. It doesn't sound as though this is that sort of a case. I don't think there's anything we can do."

I thought: *Not to worry. I've got the Mafia working on it.*

Martin said, "Are you going to tell Veronica about our conversation?"

"I think she has the right to know that you know what she's up to."

"Did you tell her I called you last week to find out why she was taking a leave?"

"Yes."

"Was she pissed off?"

"I think that's a fair assessment." I thought for a second. "By the way, how did you get my cell-phone number last week?"

"Give me *some* credit, Harry. I'm the head of the Boston field office. If I really needed to, I could find out your underwear size." He laughed at that, as did I. "Well, I probably couldn't do *that*. I'll tell you what I *can* do. I'll try to figure out a way to mollify this Tinsley woman, give her a response that she finds satisfactory. Stop her from doing anything else to stir up a hornet's nest."

"I'd appreciate that, Martin."

The woman was a pest. She already had complained to Charlie Amory and to the FBI. I wondered if she had called anyone else.

I would have my answer soon enough.

15: Don't Make Waves

Donald Pace owned several acres in Wellesley. The Georgian home had a square main body, with latter-day additions spreading out from its sides like bookends. A tennis court, horse barn, and riding corral dotted the heavily wooded property.

Donald and Veronica moved there about a year and a half after Rachel died. A few years later, when Veronica was fifteen, Donald remarried. Shana was younger than me, and she was only ten years older than Veronica. She was descended from royalty of both European and Asian lines, and her accent and appearance were correspondingly exotic. I had known Donald and Shana for more than a year and a half, and they both had been unfailingly—and genuinely—gracious and kind toward Melissa and me.

For the entire time I had known them, there was a palpable uneasiness between Veronica and this woman who was, after all, her stepmother. Veronica never really accepted her in that role: Shana came into her life too late in her childhood for that, and they were too close in age. And less than three years after Shana became part of her family, Veronica was off to college, never to live in Wellesley again except during school vacations.

But there was more to the awkwardness between them than age considerations. The violent loss of her mother left Veronica wary of attachment to new people. I saw it sometimes with me; I didn't doubt that it had been that way with Shana. Perhaps in reaction to that, Shana—who had no children of her own—had a very tentative approach to Veronica.

In conversation with me, Veronica referred to the woman by her first name. I never heard her address Shana directly, either by name or as her mother. She couldn't decide how to relate to the woman. This made perfect sense, of course. Never having closed the book on her mother's death, she had been unable to accommodate herself to her father's second wife.

The five of us enjoyed a simple dinner that night: boneless chicken breasts, skewered, grilled, and served with a lime sauce. Shana prepared the meal herself. The cook and the maid had the night off.

Afterward Melissa went off to watch a TV program. Donald said he needed to speak with me about a private matter. When Veronica realized she would be left alone with Shana, she flashed a beseeching expression in my direction. It was clear she felt trapped. I let her know with a shrug of my shoulders that there was nothing I could do to rescue her.

I followed Donald into the library. He shut the door. We sat facing each other in matching leather chairs. He said, "I hope you're coming to our Super Bowl party on Sunday."

It was an annual occurrence at the Pace home. The previous year almost a hundred people had showed up to watch Dallas beat Buffalo on the large-screen television in the party room.

I said, "We'll be here. I figure the Cowboys can't win forever."

"No. And the Bills can't lose forever, either."

I said, "Marilyn Levine came to see me the same night I met her in your office, last Thursday."

"I didn't know that."

"Actually, she came to see Veronica. By the time I returned, the visit was just about over."

"Well, they were once very close. More so when Rachel was still alive, less so afterward. Rachel and Marilyn were friends before I knew either one." He paused. "Was there more you wanted to say about her, before we move on to something else?"

"Oh. When you said you wanted to talk privately, I assumed you wanted to talk about Marilyn."

"No. I want to speak with you about my daughter."

We had discussions like this every few months. He was never so crass as to ask what my intentions toward Veronica were. But he was always gently, subtly prodding me to marry her. I think he felt more comfortable pitching the idea to me, another man, than to his sometimes rebellious and oppositional daughter.

I never took offense. I realized he was doing it because he thought Veronica and I were well-suited for one another. And he was very fond of Melissa, who was the closest thing to a grandchild he had ever had.

I thought I was in for another conversation like that, but then he said, "I received a call yesterday afternoon from the governor's chief of staff. He's an old family friend. It seems the governor got a call from one of *his* old family friends, a woman named Gertrude Tinsley."

"Damn it. Is there anyone in Massachusetts she *hasn't* called?"

"Excuse me?"

"Sorry. It's a long story. But I am *definitely* not liking that woman. She and the governor deserve one another. It was good of him to interrupt his squash game to take her call."

Donald knew of my distaste for our patrician Republican governor, a man who never missed an opportunity to find scapegoats for the state's problems amongst the downtrodden and disenfranchised.

"Be that as it may, Harry, it's not the politics of the situation that concern me."

"No. Of course not. I'm sorry."

"My concern is for my daughter. Apparently she has the idea that she's going to solve the mystery of her mother's murder. I'm intimately familiar with the case. The detective who used to handle it reviewed it with me on several occasions. Short of the killer making a deathbed confession, I don't think there's any chance of solving that mystery now. I worry that Veronica will only make matters worse for herself by pursuing it."

"Why are you bringing this up with me? Why not talk to Veronica about it?"

"She undertook this task without telling me. I presume she prefers that I not know about it. I don't want to force her into a discussion about it until she's ready to bring it up. Of course, you will have to use your own judgment regarding whether to tell her about this conversation."

It was ironic: Veronica had asked me to keep the matter secret from Donald, and now he was hoping I would keep his knowledge of it secret from her.

I said, "I think you're right. She shouldn't be forced to talk about it with you until she thinks the time is right."

"When she does—if she does bring it up, I will do my best to dissuade her from what she's doing."

"Maybe she just needs to try, and then afterward she can say she did all that she could. Maybe that would make it easier for her to put it in the past."

"It's not in my daughter's nature to tolerate failure, especially in herself. Even though she doesn't discuss it with me, I know she already has such feelings about herself because of what happened that night. I think she blames herself for not rescuing her mother. This will just compound matters. I hope I can bring you around to my way of thinking."

"You're preaching to the already converted, Donald. I've tried to persuade her to let it be ever since she raised the subject, a week ago."

"Oh? I heard you were at the Tinsley home, too. I just assumed you were encouraging Veronica."

I shook my head. "I couldn't persuade her not to go, so I thought it would be a good idea to be there with her, just in case she needed someone. But I wish she would drop it. Your police chief, Charlie Amory—he wants her to drop it, too."

This clearly interested him. "You've talked with Amory?"

"Yes."

He stared at me for several seconds, then said, "And what have you learned?"

I returned his gaze. "Quite a bit."

He considered that for several seconds, wondering whether

to ask about something he was hoping I knew nothing about. He spoke softly now, almost in a whisper. "Did he tell you about . . ." His voice trailed off.

"He told me you had an involvement with another woman shortly before your wife died."

He winced. Then he stood and walked to the far side of the room. He fiddled with a lamp shade, changing the angle several times until it was back in its starting position.

He said, "Did Amory mention the woman's name?"

"He said only that she was a former client. He never knew her name. Branson apparently kept that information out of his formal report."

He nodded slowly. "Branson promised he would do that. I'm glad he kept his word." He sat again. "Did Amory tell my daughter about this?"

"No. He told me in a private conversation."

He paused. "And did you tell her?"

"No. It wouldn't be my place to tell her something like that."

"You're not saying you think *I* should tell her, are you?"

"It's not my place to say something like that, either."

"You sound like you're talking to one of your patients."

"I'm sorry. I don't mean to sound that way. I'm just trying not to be judgmental."

He sighed. "Well, I'm glad Veronica doesn't know. I would like to keep it that way. I'm not thinking of myself as much as I'm thinking of her. She lost too much already because of what happened that night. I wouldn't want her to lose the image she had of me. I don't think she would understand."

"Seems to me it's a pretty straightforward concept to grasp." I regretted the words the moment they were out of my mouth.

"So much for not being judgmental." His eyes flashed, a momentary burst of anger. "Do you think I'm proud of myself? Don't you think I've regretted it for twenty years? And can you afford to cast stones, Harry? Can you?"

I had never cheated on my wife. It was a different matter with Veronica. I decided to treat his question as a rhetorical one. After all, what could I say? *While your daughter was*

*banging the Berkshire County DA, I was plowing the lovely
and sexually talented Marjorie Morris?*

Just then there was a loud rapping at the library door. In unison we both yelled, "Come in!"

Shana opened the door. She was alone. "Veronica and Melissa are watching *Jeopardy!* How are you fellows doing?" I wondered if our voices had carried beyond the shut door.

Donald said, "We're doing fine. Aren't we, Harry?" His tone was ice-cold.

Shana regarded us for several seconds, then walked out of the room. She left the door open. Donald and I took our seats once more. He pressed his thumbs against his temples, as if warding off a headache. I felt like telling him I was sorry for what I had said, and he may have felt like doing the same. But neither of us spoke, and eventually Veronica and Melissa came to gather me up.

Melissa sat in the backseat on the way home, plugged into her Walkman CD player.

Veronica said, "What was that movie with Donald Sutherland? You know the one I mean. He plays a restaurant inspector. Aliens are replacing humans, one by one, but they look identical to the people they're replacing. Or maybe they were taking over their bodies. I don't remember which."

"*Invasion of the Body Snatchers.* It was a remake. The aliens were called pod people, I believe. Why do you ask?"

"Because I think one of them got Shana."

"What are you talking about?"

"She was very nice to me tonight. She talked to me about her childhood and her family. She said she was sorry she never had a baby, but that she was glad she had me as her stepdaughter. At one point she even gave my arm a little squeeze. She's never done that before."

"Would you have let her?"

She thought about that. "I don't know."

"But you let her do it tonight."

"Yes. Tonight I thought she liked me."

"I've always thought she liked you."

"Really?"

"Of course. It's just that there was an awkwardness between you."

Melissa piped up from the backseat. "She likes you, Veronica. She told me she hoped I would be as nice a stepdaughter as you were."

Veronica and I both did a double take at that. Then she touched my knee, and I drove across the Concord town line and on toward home.

Melissa went upstairs as soon as we got home. It was a school night, and by the time she showered it would be her bedtime.

It was the first time Veronica and I had been alone for more than a few seconds since the morning. She had nothing new to report. I told her about Martin Baines trying to call her, and about my conversation with him. She wasn't upset that he called this time because he had called her directly, rather than calling me to suggest that I keep her in line.

We went into the den. I noticed the blinking light on the answering machine and walked over to play the message. The voice was male, and it cracked: perhaps a young teenager still getting used to his lower registers. "Oh, I'm sorry," his recorded words began. He hesitated for a moment, then continued. "I must have the wrong number. I was looking for the home of . . ." His voice trailed off, and then he shouted the rest of the message. ". . . the nigger lovers!" He and one or two other people broke into hysterical laughter, and then he hung up.

"Charming," Veronica said. She reached for the remote and clicked on the television.

"The *Journal* comes out on Thursday. I wonder if we'll have more of the same when that happens."

"I hope not." She flipped stations until she settled on CNN. Larry King was interviewing Clint Eastwood. "I love that man," she said.

"Which one?"

"Which one?" she repeated. "Clint Eastwood, of course. A girl could feel safe with him."

The phone rang. When I answered I heard a great deal of background noise and someone saying something about being wet. I made a gesture indicating that I needed Veronica to turn the volume down.

I said hello again and asked the caller to repeat himself.

The voice had an exaggerated rasping quality, like someone faking a cold when he called into his office and pretended to be too sick to come into work. "Tell your friend not to make waves. You make waves, you get wet."

I slammed the phone down.

This drew Veronica's attention away from Clint Eastwood. "What was *that* all about?" she asked.

"That, I believe, is trouble."

16: Forgiveness

I had been in the police chief's office a couple of times the previous year. It was still a Naugahyde nightmare.

Alfred Korvich leaned back in his chair and yawned. "Let me see if I have this straight, Doc. Your girlfriend mouths off at the PTG meeting at Alcott School on Monday night, pisses off a few people who are, shall we say, set in their ways. And on Tuesday night—last night—you get two crank calls."

"One was a crank call. The second one sounded more like a threat."

"He said you'd get wet."

" 'Don't make waves. You make waves, you get wet.' Those were his words. I hung up before he could say any more."

"Why?"

"I don't know. I didn't think it was wise to get into a debate with him. I didn't want to encourage him. It was instinct."

"Uh-huh. Instinct." He cracked his knuckles. "Was this your office phone or home phone? You do have two lines, right?"

I nodded. "Home phone."

"Listed?"

"Yes."

He thought for a moment. "How many people showed up at that PTG meeting?"

"About twenty."

He frowned. "That's all? Geez, in my town at least half the

parents show up. I guess you Concord folks must be very busy."

"I guess."

He took a few seconds to let his put-down sink in. Then he said, "Sounds like a hell of a meeting."

"You can probably read about it in the *Concord Journal* tomorrow. One of the other parents at the meeting is a reporter."

He made a note to himself, then said, "Whoever called you was probably at the meeting, or knows someone who was there, or maybe knows somebody who knows somebody who was there—"

"I get your point," I said. "The first call sounded like a high-school kid and his friends. Maybe one of them had a parent at the meeting."

"And the second call?"

"He was an adult, I believe."

I supposed Alex Mason was an odds-on favorite to be the caller, after Yvette told him what happened. But I held back from giving the police chief the name of one of the town's wealthiest citizens, since all I had to go on was supposition.

Korvich said, "They keep attendance? Did you sign any kind of sheet?"

"Yes."

"Well, that would be a place to start. Assuming."

"Assuming what?"

"Assuming that the second caller, the one who you think was threatening you, was calling about the stuff that came up at the PTG meeting."

"I think that's a pretty fair bet."

"I guess so," Korvich said. "Although after what happened last year, I would never underestimate your ability to piss off all sorts of people. Which reminds me—did you kill someone in Wellesley?"

"What are you talking about?"

"The Wellesley police chief called me. Fellow named Charles Amory, asked all sorts of questions."

"What did you tell him?"

"I told him the truth, which means you're fucked." He

laughed hard at his joke. "Seriously, though—why is he so interested in you?"

"Didn't he tell you?"

"No."

"Isn't that against the rules?"

He furrowed his brow. "What rules?"

"Don't all of you police chiefs belong to some sort of secret society? Don't you tell each other everything about everything?"

His intercom buzzed. The voice on the other end told him his wife was on the phone for him. As he reached for the phone he said to me, "I better take that. She Who Must Be Obeyed."

Alfred Korvich was still disturbed about the self-defense homicide I was involved in the previous spring. It caused a lot of publicity: something that small-town police chiefs don't relish. I think he almost wished I had been indicted.

He finished his call and said, "Concord doesn't have caller ID yet."

"Caller what?"

"Caller ID. This device you can attach to your phone, like an answering machine, that records the telephone numbers of your incoming calls. Boston has it. It won't be available here for a year or two. The phone company can arrange for something like it on a case-by-case basis if it's part of a criminal investigation. Aggravating to set up, not always successful, and an inconvenience to you, too. If you get another threatening call, we can talk about doing it."

"What about the attendance sheet from the PTG meeting?"

"It's a place to start. But then you're calling even more attention to yourself. Frankly, my advice to you is to just blow it off. Concord people like to think this town is special. But the truth is, it's just like anyplace else. No matter where you go, there's nice guys and assholes on every street corner. Sooner or later you're bound to run into some of the assholes."

On my way home through the center of town, I parked in one of the diagonal spaces outside Town Hall and walked across the street to the rectory for St. Bernard's Catholic church. It was frigid outside; I was shivering by the time I arrived on Father John Fitzpatrick's doorstep. It was an impromptu, unannounced visit, but he invited me in warmly.

"Harry, my boy. It's chilly in here, too. You may want to keep your coat on. Tell me—who do you like in the Super Bowl?"

"I like Dallas's chances, but I'd rather see Buffalo win."

"Aha. Rooting for the underdog. A very Christian thing to do," he said, laughing.

We sat in his kitchen. He poured me a glass of orange juice and put up some water for tea for himself. He said, "I hope you're not too cold. I keep the heat on low to hold the bills for the parish down. The place is too big, if you ask me."

It was a three-story brick building that once upon a time had been a small hotel. Most of it went unused now: underutilized space in an untaxed property on one of the prime parcels of land in town.

"So, tell me. To what do I owe the pleasure of this visit?"

"I'm not sure, John. I guess the weight of things is getting to me."

"The weight of things?"

"This whole matter with Veronica and her mother's murder that I mentioned to you last Friday."

"I see." His water pot boiled, and he went to the stove to pour it into his teacup. "Did something in particular happen that bothers you?"

"Last night I had an uneasy conversation with someone I care about."

"Veronica?"

I shook my head. "No. Her father. I was less than sympathetic regarding something he did years before I knew him. Something he shouldn't have done. Something I myself did recently. Something that he already feels bad about."

"This thing that he and you have done—is it something illegal?"

"No."

"Physically harmful to another person?"

"No, of course not."

"A moral failing, then. A betrayal of some sort of trust or obligation."

"Nicely phrased," I replied.

He sipped his tea, then held the cup between both hands, warming himself. "Why do you suppose you did that?"

"Why do I suppose I had the moral failing?"

He laughed. "No, no—unless that's what you want to talk about. Why do you suppose you had words with Veronica's father last night?"

"I have no idea."

"Might it have something to do with the sickness season? That was the phrase you used last week to describe the anniversary of your wife's final illness."

It was pancreatic cancer: almost always fatal by the time it's diagnosed. The victim's suffering is intense, but often—as it was in Janet's case—mercifully short. She was vibrant at the turn of the new year in 1987, and gone five weeks later.

I said, "She died February fourth, almost seven years ago."

He looked at a wall calendar. "That's nine days from now. A week from Friday. Do you observe the day in the customary way? Do you light a . . . what do you call those candles?"

"A Yahrzeit candle. No, I don't."

"I see. Do you go to temple and recite the Kaddish?"

I hadn't recited that traditional Jewish prayer for the dead since the week after Janet's funeral. "No. And you're supposed to do those things on the anniversary of the Hebrew date on which the person died, which changes on our calendar from year to year. I don't even remember what the Hebrew date is, let alone keep track of it. For me, the day was February fourth. It will always be February fourth."

"Do you do anything to observe it?"

I shrugged my shoulders. "I keep my calendar free from patients and other commitments, because I don't know ahead of time if I'm going to feel up to concentrating on anything. I usually wind up sitting around the house, depressed."

"Where is she buried?"

"Sleepy Hollow. You can walk there from my house in about twenty minutes."

"Do you visit her grave?"

"Not on February fourth. Melissa and I visit together on Janet's birthday and on Mother's Day weekend. And I go by myself in April, on our wedding anniversary."

"Does Veronica know this?"

"Yes."

"How does she feel about it? What? Why does that make you laugh?"

"Well, that's a long story. Last year I went to the cemetery on my anniversary without telling Veronica. She found out. Things were already rough between us at that point. She walked out on me."

The argument about my visit to the grave drove Veronica into another man's arms, which in turn delivered me to Marjorie Morris's bed. I still felt terrible about the whole thing.

I said, "I don't know what troubled her more—the fact that I visited the cemetery, or the fact that I tried to conceal it from her. We were apart for about a month. We both did some hurtful things."

My priest friend tapped his fingers against his teacup, lost in his thoughts for a moment. He said, "You say the falling-out was triggered by your visit to your wife's grave."

"Yes."

"But if Veronica wants to be with you, she'll have to make space in her life for the memory of this woman she never knew. Tell me—have you ever apologized to her for these hurtful things you say you did?"

"Not in so many words."

"When we hurt someone, an apology is the greatest gift we can offer. An apology helps the other person to forgive. And when a person forgives, he grows closer to God. So by offering an apology, you enable the person to grow closer to God." He paused, then smiled. "You have that same glazed expression I see on the faces of some of my parishioners during my homilies."

"I'm sorry, John. I'm not used to thinking about such things."

"I understand. Let me try another angle. Do you ever pray

for Janet's soul? Do you ever pray that she be in heaven with God?"

"No. What's the purpose of praying for someone who's already dead?"

He took my empty glass and his teacup and placed them in the sink. He returned to the kitchen table, sat across from me, and leaned forward. He spoke quietly, gently. "Each of us is connected to everyone else, living and dead, because we are all alive in God. That means the souls of the departed can intercede with God on our behalf. And it means we can ask God to have mercy upon those souls. When we pray for someone it always brings us and the other person closer to God, which is the ultimate good. The purpose of everything we do should be to bring us closer to the presence of God."

I had no idea what he was talking about, but I couldn't help being moved by the man's sincerity.

He said, "All right, let's forget all that for now. Let me just give you some advice. Next Friday, on the seventh anniversary of your wife's death, go to the cemetery. Take Melissa with you. Take Veronica with you—no, don't interrupt—take Veronica with you. And in the presence of your daughter and your woman, say a prayer for your wife. Open your heart to God, and see what happens."

I sat quietly for several seconds. Finally I said, "I don't know any prayers."

The priest placed his hand on my shoulder. "Whatever comes from the heart, my boy, that is something God hears as a prayer. If you don't know any prayers, try telling Him what is in your heart."

The house was empty when I returned home. Melissa was in school. Ingrid wasn't due until the afternoon. Veronica had left before I awoke, leaving a note that said she had business to tend to in Boston. I didn't know what the business was; I imagined she might be meeting with Martin Baines, either to ask for help, or to tell him to butt out of her affairs.

I received a call from Richie Conover, the Brandeis student who had canceled his appointment for the next day. He still planned to leave for the Super Bowl the next morning, but he said he needed to meet with me before he departed. I offered him an afternoon time. He said he couldn't get to my office until eight that night. I rarely see patients that late, but he said it was very important, so I agreed.

I went to my office and saw two patients. I finished at two o'clock. Ingrid was vacuuming upstairs. Veronica's car was parked next to the barn. I called her on the intercom.

"Can I come over?"

"I guess so," she replied, sounding weary.

I found her lying fully clothed on top of her bedspread, shielding her eyes with her hand. "Headache?"

"No. Just tense."

"Should I start a fire?"

She nodded.

I lit the kindling, then sat next to her on the bed. I rolled her onto her side, her back toward me, and I began to massage the muscles in her neck and shoulders. "Maybe this will help."

After a couple of minutes she inhaled deeply, then let her breath out slowly. I said, "What are you thinking about?"

"Mitochondria."

"Mitochondria?"

"Mitochondria," she repeated. "Microscopic bodies that live in the cells of all living organisms. They help convert food to—"

"I *know* what mitochondria are. What I don't know is why you would find yourself thinking about them."

"*Oh!* That feels good. Keep rubbing right there." She repositioned herself slightly. "Mitochondrial DNA testing is the best form of DNA testing. Even identical twins have different mitochondrial DNA. I was just thinking that I wished there had been some more physical evidence—fingernail scrapings, blood from the assailant, semen—"

"You should be thankful your mother didn't suffer that indignity."

"I know. And I am." She pulled her blouse out of her skirt. "There have been a lot of advances in forensic techniques since she died, but there's no evidence in this case to subject to those techniques. Even if we had DNA material, we'd be no better off than we are with the fingerprint that we already have. Because we would still need a suspect to match the DNA against."

"You said there were two burglars whose crimes were similar to the ones in Wellesley."

She said, "I learned that one was shot to death by a home owner in Natick a couple of years later. If he killed my mother, I guess I should be pleased with the end of his story. The other one was on parole when last heard of ten years ago. I don't think it's worth hiring an investigator to track him down."

"Do you have any other ideas?"

"If the crimes were recent, I'd be looking at the stores and restaurants in the area to see who worked on Thursday nights, what time they got off from work, which ones had criminal records. Check the AA directory to see which ones had Thursday-night meetings in the area, and then drop in on them. Check and recheck the acquaintances of all the burglary victims, on the chance that someone was working with prior knowledge of the victims' possessions. Walk the neighborhood streets on Thursday nights on the chance that I would see something unusual. But none of these approaches are realistic twenty-one years after the fact."

I stopped rubbing her back and lay down next to her.

She said, "I hate feeling powerless. I hate feeling weak. It brings back too many bad memories." She turned to face me. "And I hate not being in control. I lost control the night my mother was killed."

"What do you mean?"

"When I wet myself. I told you about that, I think."

She rested her head on my shoulder. She partially unbuttoned my shirt and began to run her hand lightly across my chest. "Did I ever tell you I used to be afraid of Roy Rogers and Dale Evans?"

"I find them pretty scary myself."

"I'm serious. I saw them on some TV show a few months after my mother died. They sang that theme song of theirs."

" 'Happy Trails to You.' "

"Right. And when they reached the part that goes 'until we meet again,' I freaked out. Because that was what the man who killed my mother said to me just before he left. 'Until we meet again.' "

We lay there quietly for several minutes. I thought about the girl, and I thought about the woman: the girl that Donald kept a picture of on his desk, and the woman she had become—the woman lying in my arms. I wished I could reach back into time and stand by the girl in the moment of her greatest suffering. And I wished that now I could suck the hurt out of her and take it into myself.

"I love you," I said.

"I know it may not seem so at times, but I love you, too. But that isn't always enough, is it?"

I knew that she would never completely open herself to me; the damage and loss she suffered so many years ago precluded that. She always held part of herself back. Even when we made fantastic love, there was never the complete melting together of souls that I had known with Janet. I could always comfort Janet with a touch, but I never knew for certain what it would take to comfort Veronica. And so I always held part of myself back, too, and in that we were a perfect match.

She said, "I'm out of ideas, Harry. I guess I never really had any in the first place." She closed her eyes and lay still.

I said, "How about this? I can take next week off. I'll call my patients and cancel all my appointments, and then you and I can go somewhere, just the two of us. Melissa can stay with Ingrid, or with one of her friends. I'll take you anywhere you want to go. Rome. Paris. Newark."

"Newark?" She smiled. "That's very tempting. And that's very sweet. But I can't do that."

"Why not?"

She rolled onto her back and sighed. "I made some arrangements in Boston this morning. I pulled some strings with the phone company. Then I called in an IOU. I have to stay here to see what happens next." She took my hand and placed it on her stomach, underneath her blouse. "I obtained a second phone number for myself. I got a Boston exchange, and it's being patched through to my phone here. Usually it takes a few days to set that up, but I knew who to call."

"Why did you do that?"

She hesitated for a few seconds. "I'm going public, Harry."

"I have a feeling I'm not going to like what you're about to tell me."

"I have a feeling you're right." She paused. "I told you I called in an IOU. I helped a *Globe* reporter on a story a few months ago. I called her today. I told her my story. My mother's story. It will be in tomorrow's paper."

"Why in the world—"

"I'm offering two hundred and fifty thousand dollars for any information that leads to the identity of my mother's killer, whether or not he's still alive."

I bolted into a sitting position. "Are you out of your mind? You're going to get calls from every crank and everyone with a score to settle in the greater Boston area."

She sat up slowly, brought her eyes level with mine, and said, "Desperate circumstances breed desperate measures."

"I hope you know what you're doing."

"I can't guarantee that I do." She lay down again. "Martin will be pissed. I'm going to call him in a little while to let him know what to expect."

"You should call Charlie Amory, too."

She nodded. "I don't know how this will affect him, but I owe him that courtesy. The people who live in the four houses in Wellesley may be inconvenienced. I'll call that nice woman who lives in my old house, Angie Cirone, and I'll call the people who live in two of the other houses. As for that prune-faced old biddy in the first house . . ."

"Gertrude Tinsley."

"Right. Well, Gertrude Tinsley can go screw herself."

"Amen, sister." We both laughed.

Veronica's grandfather—her mother's father—had left a significant portion of his estate to her a few years earlier. I knew she had the quarter-million dollars she was proposing to spend for the information she sought.

I got off the bed and began to stoke the embers. "There's

something you should know. I would have told you sooner if I had known you were considering talking to the press." I tossed another quarter log on the fire, then turned to face her. "Angie Cirone's husband, Frank, is in the Mafia."

She looked puzzled. "I don't understand. How do you know that?"

"Bobby told me."

"What does Bobby have to do with this?"

"Remember when we visited your old house, and you went outside to wait for me while I looked at your parents' old bedroom?"

She sat up. "Uh-huh," she said, a wary, tentative expression on her face.

"Frank Cirone came home right after that. He had a fit when he saw his wife had let strangers in the house. He had an even bigger fit when he learned one of the strangers was an FBI agent. We had a physical confrontation."

"Harry—"

"A minor one. No one got hurt. I saw no reason at the time to upset you further by telling you about it. When I told Bobby about it, he recognized Cirone's name."

"Why didn't you tell me at that point?"

I sighed. "Because right after I talked to Bobby, Frank Cirone called me. He wanted to meet with me. We had lunch together Monday afternoon. He had done some research. He knew what happened to your mother. And it turns out that he witnessed his own father's murder when he was a teenager. He felt bad for you. He felt badly for the way he treated me. He offered to check his sources to see if he could get any ideas on who may have killed your mother."

Her eyes widened. "And you, of course, declined the offer." When my silence gave her an answer different from the one she wanted, she threw herself back down on the bed and slapped her forehead. "I can't believe this. I'm a federal agent, and I have the goddamn Mafia doing me a favor."

"He's doing *me* the favor. I thought it was a nice offer. He'll make a couple of phone calls, find out nothing you don't already know, then call me back and say there isn't anything he can do. It's not a big deal." I sat on the edge of the bed. "Your father is the big deal."

"You told my *father*!"

"No, I didn't tell your father." That was true enough, because Donald learned from the governor's chief of staff, who learned from the prune-faced old biddy. "But you're going to have to tell him now, before he reads about it in the *Boston Globe*."

"Yes. I know. I spoke with Shana before you came over. I'm going to tell both of them tonight. I was hoping you would come."

"I can't. I have a patient with an emergency who I promised to see at eight. You can take Melissa for company. Come to think of it, you're going to have to tell her, too."

I lay next to her once again. I said, "I just wish . . ."

"What?"

"Nothing. It's not important."

"You wish I had taken your advice to just let this whole thing be."

I never wanted her to start down this path. And just when it appeared that she was ready to get off, instead she was hurling herself farther along. I said, "I read something a long time ago. 'Vengeance is in some sense a magic act. By destroying the one who committed the atrocity his deed is magically undone.'"

"What does that mean?"

"It means even if you find the killer, it may not help you feel better."

"I have to try, Harry." She held my hand. "I don't remember anymore what I was like before my mother died. Was I less introverted? Was I more trusting? I think so, but I don't know. Did I feel more often? Did I feel more deeply? Would it be easier for me to love you now if that man hadn't stolen my childhood away? I don't know. You're the psychiatrist, Harry. I'm not. I'll tell you what I do know." She turned toward me. "I know I won't be able to handle it if you're angry at me for this. I need you on my side."

"I'm always on your side. And I'm not angry." I kissed her: softly, gently probing. "Now there's something *I* want to say.

Something I should have said long ago." I hesitated, uncertain how to proceed. "I'm sorry about last year. I'm sorry about my relationship with Marjorie, and how much that hurt you."

I thought I saw a tear form in the corner of her eye. She said, "Yes, well, it's all over now. I don't think you did it to hurt me." She snuggled closer. "And I'm sorry, too, Harry. For everything. All the times I've closed myself off, become irritable, been less loving than I should have been."

"I don't care about that. None of it is important in the long run. I don't even care anymore about what's-his-name."

She pulled back a few inches. "What's-*whose*-name?"

"You know. That fellow you were with when I was with Marjorie. Galloway. The district attorney."

She pulled farther back. "Andrew Galloway? What about him?"

"Well, you know. You slept with him."

She stared at me, dumbfounded. "Is that what you think? Honestly, Harry. I don't know where you get some of your ideas. He and I worked on a case together. Period."

"Well, that's how you and I got together," I said.

"Aagghh!" She clenched a pillow and grimaced. "What is it with you men? When you get an erection, does it drain the blood directly from your brain? You and I were having problems at the time. Why would I want to make things worse by immediately jumping into bed with someone else?"

"Well, why not? *I* did."

She sighed. "I know that, Harry. *You* did. I'm not you."

I was speechless.

"Go back home, Harry. I need to rest. I'll talk to you later, before I go to my father's house."

Well, that's a kick in the ass, I thought as I stepped outside. For nine months I apparently had been stewing about something that was a figment of my imagination, and misjudging Veronica all the while.

I thought about what Father John had said about forgiving others and coming closer to the presence of God. Well, I couldn't forgive Veronica for something she hadn't done, so coming closer to God would have to wait for a while.

I walked back to the house. Just before I reached the kitchen door, I heard the squeal of rubber against asphalt, and then the steady low-pitched hum of a powerful engine. I looked down the long driveway toward Monument Street. A jet-black sports car was zipping toward the house, spitting gravel to the brush on either side of the driveway.

The car came to a halt five yards in front of me. The driver's door opened and a woman with shoulder-length wavy black-and-gray hair stepped out. She was wearing sunglasses and a full-length gray fur coat. She lifted the sunglasses onto her hair. Her eyes were cobalt blue. She smiled at me.

"Hello, Marilyn." I looked at her coat. "Don't tell me that came from the Nightingale catalog."

"I know, I know—*c'est très* politically incorrect. But it is exquisite, *n'est-ce pas*? And so very, very warm. It's chinchilla. Here—feel how soft it is." She walked over to me and rubbed her sleeve against my face. "Besides, it belonged to my mother when breeding, killing, and wearing furry rodents were still considered honorable endeavors."

I pointed toward the barn. "Veronica's apartment is up top. I'm sure she'll be glad to see you."

"Harry, my darling. I didn't come for Veronica today. I came for you."

"For me?"

She began to sing. " 'I came for you, for you, I came for you, but you did not need my urgency.' "

"I think I've heard that somewhere."

She stretched her arms out. " 'I came for you, for you, I came for you, but your life was one long emergency.' I always liked that line."

"What is it from?"

"A Bruce Springsteen song. I came for you, Harry. Donny called me this morning and said if I didn't come to see you, then my ass is grass and he's the lawn mower."

"That doesn't sound like something Donald would say."

"It's a paraphrase," she replied, and then she began to laugh. "You know, that Springsteen song is perfect for the occasion."

"And why is that?"

She slid her sunglasses down, covering her eyes again. "Because it's about a woman who commits suicide at the Chelsea Hotel. And that just happens to be where I made my first suicide attempt."

She removed a small object from her coat pocket, turned around, and pointed it at her Porsche. The passenger door sprang open.

"Climb in, my darling. Come and listen to the nightingale's story."

17: The Bad Gene

Marilyn Levine pulled her Porsche out of my driveway and onto Monument Street, heading away from the center of town, north toward Carlisle. She took the turns hard; she drove the straightaways fast. She maneuvered with one hand on the wheel, the other constantly fidgeting with the dials and buttons in front of her when it wasn't shifting gears. Steppenwolf's "Born to Be Wild" would have been a more fitting accompaniment than the old Broadway show tunes playing on her tape deck.

"You should dress more warmly in the winter, Harry. It's like the old saying. 'There is no such thing as bad weather. Only bad clothing.' "

"You could use that as an advertising slogan for M. L. Nightingale."

She laughed. "Poor form, my darling. Nothing with the word 'bad' should go into my catalog."

"I didn't think I'd need anything more than a sweater. I was only walking between the house and the barn. I didn't plan on being kidnapped."

She laughed again, and when she did the laughter came from deep within her, rippling through her whole body. I liked her laughter. It fit with her frenetic manner and a mind that always seemed in motion.

"Kidnapped," she said. "I like that. I know someone else who will like that, too."

162

She reached over and punched numbers into her car phone. After one ring a familiar-sounding male voice answered. Whenever I called Donald's office I went through his secretary; Marilyn apparently had a number that went directly to his desk.

"Donny, I'm in deep, deep trouble."

"What is it now, Marilyn?"

"Is kidnapping still considered a major felony? Do you know any decent criminal attorneys?"

"What are you talking about?"

"I'm in my Porsche, and I have absconded with your daughter's boyfriend."

"Harry? Are you there?"

"Hello, Donald."

"Marilyn, I thought we agreed that you would take a holiday from driving. Where's your town car and your driver?"

"Oh, Donny. I love it when you try to take care of me like that. Anyway, I thought you'd be happy I finally came to see your shrink friend. 'Bye-'bye, my darling."

The Porsche hugged the winding country road as we passed the horse farms and huge estates on the outskirts of Concord. We crossed the town line into Carlisle, and Monument Street became River Road.

Marilyn said, "I met Donny through his first wife. Rachel and I were friends at Radcliffe. We met at a civil-rights demonstration our freshman year. Rachel was a very solid person. Very firm in her beliefs about right and wrong. She stayed that way right up to the end. I always admired her for that. Even envied her a little."

"But you were very active in protest movements back then, too, weren't you?"

"I wanted to play my music. That's all I wanted. It was the only thing that made me happy. It was the only thing that had *ever* made me happy. And the people in the movement liked hearing me sing. If the Daughters of the American Revolution had given folk-music concerts, I probably would have found *their* politics appealing."

She downshifted and turned sharply around a bend in the

road. She said, "Anyway, neither one of us graduated. I dropped out to make a name for myself. Rachel dropped out to make a baby."

The road came to an end at Bedford Road. Marilyn sat for several seconds at the stop sign. "I never know which way to go," she said.

"We can go either way. We can circle back to Concord through Bedford, or through the center of Carlisle."

"Which way is prettier?"

"Carlisle. Turn left."

We headed toward the small town center. The late-afternoon sun was directly in front of us.

I said, "A lot of people go through their entire lives without finding something they love as much as you loved playing music."

She smiled when I said that: a quiet look, a mixture of longing and contentment. She said, "I have something I want you to hear."

She put a cassette in her tape deck in place of the one that was already there. "The sound is a little rough," she said. "I made the tape from old records my parents left me."

The music had a slightly jazzy big-band feel. The syncopated rhythm evoked hustle-and-bustle images of city streets. "I *like* that," I said. "Is it Gershwin?"

"No, but his influence is certainly there. It's the overture from the cast recording of *On the Town*. Leonard Bernstein wrote the music. It was his first Broadway show. It opened in 1944." She smiled. "My mother was in the chorus."

"Hey, no kidding?"

She beamed. "I was two years old when the show opened. I never saw it, but I remember Lenny. That's what everyone called him. Lenny Bernstein and my mother were good friends for many years. I can still remember the way he looked—a skinny man, always puffing on a cigarette, with these big, black, soulful eyes. He used to come to our town house on the East Side and play my mother's baby grand. Sometimes I sat next to him. To me he was just this nice man who made pretty music. I knew who he was, but I didn't know *who he was*, if you understand what I mean. But I'm sure I took something in from that whole experience, something that came back out of me years later."

She told me her father made a fortune in the garment district. Her mother was much younger than him, a trophy wife whom he met at a cast party for the first show she was in. "I got my drive from him, as well as whatever business skills I have. And from her I got my love of music. And the bad gene."

"Bad gene?"

"Mother was very moody, and very, very erratic. Sometimes she stayed in the town house with the shades drawn for weeks at a stretch. Other times she walked around the city for hours, handing out dollars to children passing by, buying things she didn't really want or need. One day she took me from store to store, Bloomingdale's to Bonwit's to Bendel's, buying every blouse they had in her size. She was manic-depressive long before they had the name or the treatment for it. Eventually she drank herself to death when she was only fifty."

We passed the Bates Farm ice cream stand, one of Melissa's favorite spots. It was closed for the winter. The cows and sheep and the lone goat were nowhere to be seen.

Marilyn said, "Well, that was a long time ago. Mother did get to see me play professionally a few times, and I think that gave her pleasure. I brought her to Club 47 the first time I performed there. I opened up for Pete Seeger."

"You knew Pete Seeger?"

"Honey, I knew *everyone*. Many of them in the biblical sense of the word."

The Carlisle town center was marked by a general store, a gas station, and not much of anything else.

"Damn it," she said. "Which way should I go? I *never* know which way to go."

"It's okay. Turn left. It'll bring us back into the center of Concord. Would you like me to drive?"

She didn't reply to my question. She shifted gears and made the turn.

I enjoyed listening to the Bernstein music as we cruised down Lowell Road. When she told me the story line of the play, I realized that I once saw the film version that featured Gene Kelly and Frank Sinatra.

After a few miles we came to the Middlesex School, one of Concord's prestigious private high schools. I said, "A few years ago two Hollywood production companies came to Concord at the same time. One of them filmed *Housesitter* at various places in town."

"I saw that. Steve Martin and Goldie Hawn."

"Right. And over here, at the Middlesex School, they made *School Ties*. Did you see it?"

"Was that the one about the college football star who has to pretend he's not Jewish in order to keep his scholarship?"

"Something like that."

"People always assumed I took the name Mara Lee to hide the fact that I'm Jewish. The truth is, I was just looking for something that belonged to me and nobody else. I got into a fight over it once with Dave Van Ronk."

Bobby had mentioned that to me. "I heard that there was some sort of incident at a folk festival."

"That's the popular version, but that's not what happened. It was at Gerde's Folk City, a coffeehouse in Greenwich Village. Dylan was beginning to make it big, and he was performing there on this particular night. Several of us went to see him and hang around with him after the show. Me, Van Ronk, Phil Ochs, and Jack Elliott."

"Ramblin' Jack Elliott?"

She nodded. "His real name is Elliott Adnopoz, and he's the son of a Jewish dentist from New Jersey. Which is relevant to the rest of the story. I drank a lot, and so did Van Ronk. I had been going with very little sleep for several days, and I was using the alcohol to bring myself down. I didn't realize it then, but I was in the middle of a mild manic episode, one of my first ones."

Her thoughts wandered off somewhere for a few moments.

"Anyway, after the show we were sitting backstage, Dylan and the four of us. Van Ronk pointed at me and he pointed at Jack Elliott, and he cursed us and called us fakers. Middle-class Jews who thought they could become working-class heroes by changing their names and strumming a few chords on a Gibson guitar. That really ticked me off, for several reasons. First of all, I was upper-class. Second, my guitar was a Martin. Third, I really didn't give a crap about the political stuff. I just wanted to sing. And fourth, he was just a mean son of a bitch."

"But Dylan did the same thing, didn't he? He changed his name from something that sounded obviously Jewish."

"Yes, but Van Ronk didn't have the nerve to go after him. Anyway—I picked up Van Ronk's Gibson guitar and smashed it against the wall. He staggered to his feet and came at me, but someone jumped on his back, and besides—he was too drunk to do much harm. I was drunk, too, but that didn't prevent me from driving a very hard punch right into that big belly of his."

She grew quiet. I couldn't tell from her expression whether the memory she had related brought her pleasure or pain.

Marilyn said, "Say—that road looks pretty. Where will it take us?"

"Out to Route 2, by the state prison."

She made a sharp right onto Barrett's Mill Road. "Over the years the story took on a life of its own and got blown up into something it wasn't. I read once that I smashed a guitar over Dave Van Ronk's head at the Newport Folk Festival. That didn't happen. What *did* happen was this . . . I was placed in restraints, and I spent about three weeks getting pumped full of Thorazine. My first psychiatric hospitalization. And when I came out, I sank into a terrible depression, and one night in the Chelsea Hotel I scored fifty Seconal and swallowed them all at once." She paused. "But you probably hear stories like this all the time."

"Not exactly."

"Variations on a theme, then. We're all just variations on a theme." She laughed. "I still don't know why the others changed their names, but my decision had nothing to do with hiding anything. Hell, if anything, being Jewish back then was a plus. It's always been a plus in my business career, too. And I'm sure it hasn't hindered you in your medical career."

"No."

"Now, Donald Pace—*there's* someone who can be thankful he's a white Episcopalian male. When he started his career, law firms like his probably required blood tests to make certain you were one hundred percent WASP. And I'm sure there's still a current of that thinking in his firm today."

"Well, he has one particular partner whom I've met twice, and both times he found it very important to let me know that he knows I'm Jewish."

"That sounds like Oliver Gray."

"Do you know him?"

She laughed. "That's a story for another time."

We were at the left-then-right curves near the intersection with College Road, very sharp and poorly banked. Marilyn made the turn to the left without any problem, but her speed took her partway into the oncoming traffic lane when she tried to make the second turn. Fortunately, there were no cars coming in the opposite direction. She slowed down and continued down Barrett's Mill Road.

She said, "I know some people envy me my money and the things I can do with it. But there's also been a lot of loss. My father was already an old man when I was born, and my mother had her problems, so I grew up lonely. And I lost both of them early. And when Phil Ochs killed himself . . . Are you familiar with him?"

"Protest songs. Pretty strong stuff."

"You would never think that someone who wrote so angrily could be such a sweet and gentle man. Anyway, when he killed himself it really ripped me apart. But the worst, absolute worst thing that ever happened to me was Rachel's murder. So many times she was an anchor for me. She saved my life once, found me unconscious and got me to the hospital before the pills I had taken could kill me. She was there for me, always. And then she was gone."

We passed the minimum-security state prison, a working farm without watchtowers or fences.

I said, "You were there right after she was killed, weren't you?"

She nodded. "I brought Ronnie home with me until Donald

came for her. Oliver Gray was there, too. He was my lawyer at the time."

"I thought Donald was always your lawyer."

"It's a long story, Harry. Hey—what the *fuck* is *this*?"

In front of us was the rotary at Route 2. That highway fed into the rotary from two directions, east and west; three other roads, including the one we were on, connected to it as well.

She sat at the stop sign, panic-stricken, for a few seconds.

"You didn't *tell* me it was going to be a rotary! I can't *do* rotaries in this car!"

A pickup truck pulled to a stop directly behind us. When the driver saw that Marilyn wasn't moving, he began to lean on his horn.

I said, "Do you want me to—"

Marilyn hit the gas pedal and lurched awkwardly into the stream of traffic. She moved quickly through first and second gears. She hit third, and her knuckles turned white as she grasped the steering wheel tightly with both hands.

She hugged the inside of the rotary, curling counter-clockwise, not making an effort to move toward any of the roads spinning away from the hub. She made a complete circle, continued past the spot we had entered from, and began her second trip around the rotary. And then she passed Barrett's Mill Road again, and we were on our third go-round.

She was stuck in a circuit, like a nerve triggered by a random electrical charge, firing again and again toward no purposeful end. Talking to her would be too much stimulation for her to handle: It would either prove fruitless, or it would distract her and perhaps cause her to do something sudden and unsafe.

We passed Barrett's Mill Road again and entered the least heavily traveled segment of the circle. I pulled clockwise on the steering wheel. The car jerked to the right, away from the rotary, onto Great Road. "That's good," I said. "You're doing fine. I'm going to ease up now and let go of the wheel."

She exhaled hard and twitched, like someone shaking off the effect of a drink that was too strong.

I said, "We're coming into Acton. There's a Burger King just over the town line. Pull in there."

She parked the sports car and we walked inside. It was four-thirty, coming up on sunset, and there were about a dozen people there.

Marilyn sat while I got a couple of Cokes. When I brought them to the table she said, "I think people are staring at me."

"Well, at this particular Burger King, in the average day they probably only get three or four chinchilla coats."

It took a couple of seconds for that to sink in. When it did she smiled, and then her laughter built up slowly, until she was laughing so hard that she almost sent her Coke flying.

She said, "You're a good man, Harry. Rachel is lucky to have you."

I knew she meant to say "Veronica." She was still thinking about her lost friend. I didn't call the slip of the tongue to her attention.

"She looks so much like her mother," Marilyn said. "It's almost painful for me to look at her. I guess that's why I haven't spent much time with her in recent years."

"What was she like that night, after you took her home with you?"

"Grateful, for one thing. Oliver got there first. He wanted to bring her to his mother's home. Veronica barely knew him. She didn't know his mother at all. He and I had a small argument about it. There was a young police officer, very helpful. He asked Veronica what she wanted, she told him, and he told me I should take her. She didn't talk at all on the way to Dover, and I didn't know what to say, so we were very quiet. But Veronica has always been very focused, just like both her parents. As soon as we stepped into my house she said, 'Tell me the truth. Will my mother be all right?' "

"What did you say?"

" 'No.' And then she asked, 'Is she already dead?' "

Marilyn sipped her Coke. Her hand began to quiver slightly; she put the drink down so it wouldn't spill. She looked at me and said, "I assume you were the one who told your daughter that her mother had died."

"I was."

"Then you know what it's like."

"I do."

"She asked me that question, 'Is she already dead?' And I said, 'Yes,' and I started to cry. And I laid my head in her lap, and she stroked my forehead, just like her mother used to do when I was sad and lonely. It is a permanent ache, Harry. A permanent ache."

Marilyn didn't let herself stay in that moment. She downed her Coke, smiled, and said, "Is there a way back to your home that doesn't involve going around that fucking rotary?"

There was: down Pope Road, then Strawberry Hill Road, and across the town line into Concord.

Veronica's car was gone when the Porsche came to a stop outside the house. As I stepped out of the car Marilyn said, "So much for the story of Mara Lee. Tomorrow I can tell you the story of Marilyn Levine and M. L. Nightingale. And then you can decide if I'm a brick or two shy of a full load."

I knew that the next day, Thursday, would bring the *Globe* story about the murder of Rachel Pace. It would probably bring a story in the weekly *Concord Journal* about our PTG adventure. I said, "Friday would be better for me. I'll be free by three o'clock."

"Then Friday it shall be. *À bientôt*, my darling."

Inside I found a note from Veronica informing me that Melissa had gone with her to Wellesley. There was a note from Ingrid telling me about a dinner I could warm in the microwave. And there was a flashing light on the answering machine in the den.

I walked over to the machine and pressed the play button. Background noise, like traffic or airplanes, sounded on the speaker. And then there was that voice again: rasping, chilling, almost metallic in its scraping sound. "You hung up on me last night," it said. "I want to make certain you understand me. Both of you. Tell your lady friend to stop making waves. You make waves, you get wet."

18: The Last Appointment

I called Bobby to discuss the phone message I had received. He said, "I wonder why he keeps calling you, rather than calling Veronica."

"Both of my numbers are listed. Veronica's phone isn't."

"I thought only your office line was listed in the directory."

"That's the way it used to be. Then Melissa asked for her own phone number. I thought she was too young for that. But she complained that her friends couldn't look up our phone number because it was unlisted. So as a compromise, I began listing it. I'm glad I did, because some of her friends had begun calling for her on my office line."

"Do you think Melissa put them up to it?"

"Huh. I never thought of that."

"That's because you don't have the mind of an eleven-year-old girl. Or the mind of a lawyer."

"Whereas you have both," I said.

"Are you going to take Korvich up on his offer to have the phone company trace the calls to your number?"

"I saved the tape for Veronica to hear. I want to discuss it with her first before I decide whether to accept Korvich's offer, but I don't see any reason not to do it. Do you?"

"None that I can think of, other than being beholden to him."

I thought about what Frank Cirone had said: *If you ask for a favor and I give it, then you owe me. But if I offer and you accept, then nothing is owed.*

I said, "I wouldn't be beholden to him for something he did as part of his job description."

"He might not see it the same way."

"Sometimes I think you're paranoid, Bobby."

"Well, you're the shrink."

Richie Conover arrived a few minutes late for his eight-o'clock appointment. Barring an emergency, we would still finish at eight-fifty. Psychiatry is the only medical specialty where patients know exactly how long they'll be in the office and when they'll be finished with their appointments.

"Well, I'm all packed," he said. "I like visiting Atlanta. Have you ever been to the Super Bowl?"

"No."

"I've been to every one for the past five years."

He gave me a rundown of each of those games, ending with the Cowboys' romp over the Bills in Pasadena the previous January.

"Aikman was fantastic," he said, referring to the Dallas quarterback. "Who do you think will win on Sunday?"

I replied, "It should be an interesting game."

"Who are you rooting for?"

I paused. "You have more questions than usual."

"Yeah, well, I guess so." He had taken my comment as a put-down, which wasn't my intent. But it's generally unproductive for a therapist to talk about his own likes and dislikes with a patient.

He sat quietly for a few seconds, and then grew suddenly animated. "I think I've come up with a good one this time, Doc. An idea for the book I want to write after I graduate."

This was, of course, his usual way of proceeding.

He said, "The prologue would describe my graduation. After the ceremony I walk over to the viewers' area to show my diploma to my family. They congratulate me. They tell me how proud they are. My mother hugs me. My father aims the video camera at me and says, 'Well, Richie Conover, you have your degree, you have your considerable trust fund, you've got a good life and the whole world in front of you. What are you going to do now?' "

He paused, waiting for my response. I said, "And what do you imagine yourself answering?"

He grinned. "I take off my graduation cap and fling it into the air. I smile at the camera and say, 'I'm going to Disney World.' "

"Disney World?"

"Right. You know, just like those commercials where they interview the Super Bowl quarterback as he's walking off the field. They ask him what he's going to do next now that he's had this great success, and he says he's going to Disney World."

"I've seen the commercial. But I wonder why you want to go there."

"Because I think it'll make a great book." He leaned forward in his chair, more excited than I had ever seen him in the two months he had been my patient. "This is how I see it. I spend a year at Disney World. I live a few weeks in each hotel. And I mean, I really live there. That's the gimmick—I never leave the grounds, not once during the entire year. I do everything there is to do. Ride every ride, visit every attraction, eat at every restaurant. I interview the people who work there and the people who come for vacation. And at the end of the year I write a book about my experience. Sort of a combination guidebook and personal journal." His eyes widened. "Hey—I could do it in diary form, a day at a time. It would practically write itself. What do you think, Doc?"

"It sounds like an expensive proposition."

He shrugged. "I figure an average of two hundred and twenty-five dollars a day—more when I'm staying at the Floridian or the Polynesian, less at the other places. Multiply that out, add on airfare, and I can do it for about eighty-five thousand."

We both knew he could afford that figure. He did shift in his seat when he spoke the number, perhaps a little embarrassed to be contemplating spending so much money on a lark.

I wondered how many books earn back that amount of money. I assumed that not many of them did.

He said, "I even have an idea for the title. I'm going to call it *The Year of the Mouse*." He leaned forward: waiting, not knowing what to anticipate. "What do you think?"

The truth was, it was the first book he had mentioned that I could actually imagine another person wanting to read. I said, "You've put more of yourself into this idea than into any of the others."

He leaned back in his chair, looking quite content. He let a minute or two go by without speaking, then looked at his watch and said, "I've got a long day ahead of me. I think I'll go home and get to bed early."

"You have almost a half hour left."

"I know, Doc. But I'm really tired."

"When you called you said you had something important you wanted to talk about."

He looked confused. "I did. The book."

"The *book*? That was *it*?" I was surprised by the stridency in my own voice.

"Well, uh . . . yeah. What did you think?"

I thought: *You could talk about the absence in your life of close friendships and romantic relationships. You could talk about the fact that everything is given to you, you want for nothing, and yet you're floundering around, with no future plan other than your latest pie-in-the-sky book fantasy.*

But I said none of that, even though those things were true. I didn't think he was ready for a direct confrontation. Besides, I didn't trust my motivation, because I was irritated at him for wasting my time. But Richie Conover was paying for my time. He had the right, within reason, to use it in whatever way made the most sense to him. Expressing my irritation might help me feel better, but that wasn't the object of the game.

I said, "I'll see you Thursday at our usual time."

After he left I started to make a few notes. I was still seated behind my desk, looking for some soft rock on the radio dial, when I heard shouting from outside my office entrance.

"Hey, you—stop that!" It sounded like Richie Conover's voice.

I heard something banging, like a metal object being dropped to the ground, and then someone running away from the building, down the long gravel driveway.

I sprang to my feet and dashed outside. Without so much as a sweater, I began to shiver in the cold January night.

Richie Conover's car was still parked there. I saw something shining in the reflected light of the spotlight near the office door. I walked over and picked it up. I held it up to the light and saw that it was a can of black spray paint. And then I saw the words that were inscribed on the white wall in foot-high black letters:

JEWS AND NIGERS GO HOME

Nice spelling, you jerk, I thought. *How the* fuck *am I going to get rid of that?*

The cold silence was shattered by the sound of breaking glass. I whirled around. Forty yards away, in the wooded area to the side of the driveway, two figures appeared to be struggling with one another. A third figure moved nearby.

I ran toward them. The night was too dark for me to see exactly what was happening. Just before I reached the three figures, one of the two that had been struggling disappeared from view.

The struggling figure that was left standing said, "Oh, fuck. Here comes another one." It was a male voice, youthful, perhaps high-school or college age.

The third person, also a male voice, nervous, said, "Come on, Tommy. Let's go."

"Just a second."

I was directly in front of them now. "Hey, wait a min—"

I never saw his fist in the darkness. The one called Tommy caught me squarely on the side of my face. The gloves he wore to shield him from the cold softened the blow, but only slightly. I wasn't down, but I was staggering.

"Tommy, let's get out of here, Jesus Christ."

My attacker reared back, then swung at me with full force. Just before he connected I fell: a delayed effect of the first punch. His fist continued past the space where my head had been; it smashed flush against a red maple tree.

The other fellow grabbed my attacker from behind. "Goddammit, we've gotta leave now!"

"My hand is broke! My fucking hand is broke!"

"It's my goddamn car and I'm getting out of here!"

One or both of them reeked of beer.

The accomplice dashed into the driveway and made a bee-line toward Monument Street. The attacker stood there for a moment, cursing under his breath and clutching his injured hand with his other one. Then he stumbled onto the driveway and followed the other figure.

Two car doors opened and shut from the direction of Monument Street. The ignition turned and the motor revved; then the tires screeched as the car accelerated quickly toward the center of town.

I lay on my back, shivering. My vision in one eye was blurred; I assumed that either I had a slight concussion or that blood was dripping into my eye. I felt myself grow faint. Even if I felt well enough to call for help, there was no one to hear me; the nearest house was almost a hundred yards away.

I knew that if I didn't keep moving I would pass out. And in the cold night, without even a sweater, I knew that passing out would put me at very real risk for hypothermia. I thought about what Marilyn Levine had said that afternoon: *There is no such thing as bad weather. Only bad clothing.*

I rolled onto my stomach, then pushed against the ground with my hands. I caught my breath as I rested for a moment on my hands and knees.

There was a sudden brief rustling on the ground just a few yards away. Then I heard a strange and sickening sound: like someone choking and wheezing at the same time. And then all was still.

I reached into my pants pocket and pulled out my key chain. I aimed the weak beam of the small flashlight in the direction of the noises I had just heard.

Richie Conover lay motionless on his back. His eyes stared upward, unblinking.

I crawled toward him on all fours. Just before I reached him I felt a sharp pain in my hand. I shone the light on the ground. I saw a beer bottle with the top broken off. I had cut myself on the jagged edge.

Blood poured from a wide gash in the jugular area of Richie Conover's neck. I ripped my shirt off and pressed it against the hideous wound. Holding the shirt in place, I was able to feel a weak but steady pulse. Seconds later the weak pulse became irregular. And after a half minute his pulse was no more.

On a cloud-darkened frigid winter night, with his blood and my blood dripping on the hard ground, Richie Conover died in my arms.

19: Shooting Arrows

Somehow I made it back to the house without passing out or vomiting. I called the police. When I said the word *murder* the dispatcher became nervous; homicides were rare in Concord, and she likely had never received such a call before.

I telephoned Donald's house. Shana answered. She was clearly upset from the conversation with Veronica, but I didn't have time to listen to any of that. I asked to speak with Veronica; Shana heard the urgency in my voice and asked no questions.

Veronica came to the phone. "I'm sorry we're here so late, Harry. We'll leave as soon as I—"

"Stay there!"

"Stay here?"

"Stay there," I repeated.

"Why? What's wrong?"

"Somebody murdered my patient outside my office after he left our session."

"Somebody did *what*?"

"I can't talk now. Stay in Wellesley tonight. I don't want Melissa to come home to police cruisers and a corpse."

"What should I tell her?"

"Make something up. Tell her the furnace is broken and it'll take all night to repair. I don't know. Think of something. Bring her home in the morning. Don't listen to the news or let her watch TV until you get here. I'll figure out what to tell her by then. Oh—and make sure you don't let her see the south side of the house, by my office door."

"Why?"

I told her about the racist and anti-Semitic graffiti. "Drunken school kids. I think my patient tried to stop them, and they panicked and accidentally killed him."

She thought for a moment, then said, "This is my fault, isn't it?"

"What are you talking about?"

"My tirade about the METCO program at the PTG meeting. The crank phone calls. And now the graffiti, and this."

"I really need to get off the phone. I have to go patch myself up and wait for the police."

"Patch yourself up?"

"I cut myself. It's not a big deal. Call me in the morning before you leave Wellesley."

It was about eight forty-five. I went into the bathroom to check out my wounds. My left palm had a puncture wound from the broken beer bottle—the bottle that likely had been used to slash Richie Conover's neck. I placed my hand in warm water to encourage the flow of blood, then squeezed it to get it to bleed. I wanted any debris and bacteria to get washed out from the inside. After a couple of minutes of forcing my hand to bleed, I put antibiotic ointment on it and placed a bandage over the hole.

The hairs on my arms were matted with Richie Conover's blood. I scrubbed myself clean.

The left side of my face had begun to swell, but there were no abrasions and no apparent bone damage. My vision had already returned to normal. I went to the kitchen, wrapped ice cubes in a hand towel, and fashioned a cold compress for my face.

The doorbell rang. As I invited the uniformed police officer in I noticed the flashing lights of an ambulance near the spot where Richie Conover's body lay. I said, "He's already dead."

"Yes, sir. I know that. But we always have an ambulance on hand to bring the body in. They know how to preserve evidence, prevent contamination, things like that."

He was methodical and thorough in his approach. He knew when to ask questions and when to let me talk, and within a matter of minutes he had elicited everything I knew about the killing.

He said, "My partner has a photographer taking shots of the murder scene. When he's finished I'll have him take pictures of the graffiti. You said it was on the south side?"

"Yes. There's a parking area there for my patients. His car is still there."

"You're referring to the victim's car."

"Yes."

"You might want to put some more ice on your face." He stood and walked toward the door. "I'm afraid we're blocking your driveway. Us and the ambulance."

"That's all right. I'm not going anywhere."

"Good. Because a detective will be along in a short while. He'll probably bring the chief with him. You know Chief Korvich, I believe."

"Yes. How did you know that?"

"I called him at home and notified him that someone phoned in a homicide. When I mentioned your name, he said he wanted to come out here himself. I got the feeling he knew you."

"Did he say anything else?"

"Yeah." The officer smiled. "He said, 'Make sure you block the guy's driveway.' "

I went into the den and stretched out on the sofa. My head hurt. My hand was throbbing from the puncture wound.

Richie Conover had come to me for help, and he had died trying to help me. The killing had occurred on my property, an intrusion into my safe space and my daughter's safe space. On the morrow there would be more questions to answer, more details to contend with. There would also be reaction to the article about Veronica that was scheduled to appear in the morning *Globe*, and fallout from the article about Monday night's PTG meeting that I presumed would appear in the weekly *Concord Journal*.

I spent the next fifteen minutes canceling my appointments

for the rest of the week, Thursday and Friday. I would need all my time and energy for the other things.

Alfred Korvich arrived a few minutes later with a detective named Kay Wheaton, who Korvich said had recently come to Concord from the Cambridge Police Department.

I led them into the den. Korvich looked at my swollen face and said, "You look lousy."

"Then I look better than I feel, because I feel like shit." I turned to Kay Wheaton and said, "Pardon my language."

She said, "Would you be apologizing to me if I were a man?"

I thought about that. "Good question. Probably not."

"Then perhaps you owe me an apology for that, instead."

If this detective wanted to start the interview by putting me on the defensive, she succeeded.

She began to lead me through another rendition of the night's events. I said, "I already went through this with the other police officer. Can't you get the information from him?"

She said, "You're calmer now. You may recall something you didn't remember then. Or I may ask something that he didn't think of asking."

"And of course, there's always the possibility that there might be an inconsistency between my two stories. Something you can pounce on me for."

"Is there some reason we should want to pounce on you? Come on, Dr. Kline. Let's just go through it one more time. Shall we?"

I described the events of the evening once again. I included all the details I could remember. She took notes. Korvich sat quietly and listened.

Kay Wheaton said, "You come up short on a physical description of the two assailants."

"Two graffiti artists, perhaps, but only one assailant. Only the one named Tommy fought with Richie Conover and attacked me."

"You were close enough to get hit, and yet all you can tell me about him was that he sounded young and appeared to be a little shorter than you."

"It was dark."

"It's a full moon tonight."

"Then there must have been cloud cover when it happened."

She said, "You couldn't see what he looked like when you were next to him because it was too dark, and yet you had enough light to see from several yards away that only one of them was grappling with your patient."

From the corner of my eye I saw Korvich smiling, enjoying my discomfort. I said, "That's the way I remember it."

"I see." She checked her notes. "So we're looking for a teenager or young adult named Tommy who may have a broken hand. And that's all you can tell me about him."

"That, and the fact that he's not exactly a Rhodes scholar."

"What do you mean?"

"They misspelled the word 'nigger' with the spray paint. And he said his hand was 'broke,' rather than 'broken.' "

She wrote a note to herself, saying the words out loud as she transcribed them. " 'Not a Rhodes scholar.' "

Korvich spoke up. "We probably won't find prints on the spray paint or the beer bottle, since the doc here says Tommy was wearing gloves."

Kay Wheaton said, "By any chance did you touch those items, Dr. Kline?"

"Uh, I guess I did. I picked up the can of spray paint to see what it was."

"Well, there," she said. "I told you I might come up with a question you hadn't already answered. Well, maybe the killer's accomplice was the one to use the spray paint. If he didn't wear gloves, maybe we can lift his prints from it. That is, if you didn't obliterate them."

Korvich chuckled.

The detective said, "You said they drove off toward the center of town. Are you positive about the direction?"

"Pretty certain," I replied. "Of course, I was lying on my back and my head was ringing."

She thought for a moment. "Chief Korvich told me that you were in his office this morning to complain about threatening phone calls. Did this Tommy sound like one of your callers?"

I tried to remember what the first caller sounded like. "The one who called me a nigger lover sounded like a teenager. And I think he had a friend in the background, laughing. Maybe that was him. I don't know."

"What about the second caller?"

"I don't think that was Tommy. The second caller sounded a little more sophisticated. 'If you make waves, you get wet.' Tommy didn't seem like the sort who would deal with metaphors or analogies."

"And you didn't recognize that caller's voice."

"No."

"What did it sound like?"

"Well, it was—" I smacked my forehead with my hand.

"What? What is it?"

"I can't believe I didn't think of this before. He called again this afternoon. He left a message on my answering machine. I saved the tape."

I placed the tape back into my answering machine and played it for them. First there came the background noise, and then his cold voice. "You hung up on me last night. I want to make certain you understand me. Both of you. You and your lady friend. Stop making waves. You make waves, you get wet."

Detective Wheaton said, "That doesn't sound like a teenager."

Korvich said, "Sounds like he called from a pay phone. All that noise in the background."

She said, "And his voice sounds unnatural, as if he intended to disguise it. That could mean he's worried about the possibility that you might recognize him—which, of course, would mean he knows you. On the other hand, maybe he just disguised his voice to make it sound more frightening. I'm going to need to take that tape, Dr. Kline. It's evidence in a homicide now."

"Of course." I pulled the tape from the answering machine and gave it to the detective.

"Chief Korvich told me about the meeting at the Alcott

School the night before last. Do you know who I can call to get a list of the people who attended?"

"Katherine Carter is the president of the PTG."

"PTG?"

"Parent-Teacher Group."

"Why don't they call it the PTA, like other towns?"

Veronica had asked me that same question. "Because Concord is Concord. Don't get me started on that."

She sat quietly for a minute and considered everything she had been told. "Was there any preexisting friction between you and anyone else at the meeting?"

Korvich said, "Just get the list from Katherine Carter and assume that everyone on it fits into that category."

I ignored his gibe. "There was one person there who doesn't exactly count me as one of her favorite people. Yvette Mason."

Korvich's eyes lit up. "Alex Mason's wife?"

Kay Wheaton said, "Is this someone I should know about?"

Korvich said, "The Masons are one of the wealthiest families in town. Even their money has money."

"Where did they get their wealth?"

I said, "They don't get money. They have money." I said to Korvich, "You remember them from the Minuteman controversy."

"What is that?" asked Kay Wheaton. Korvich and I filled her in on that point.

Korvich said, "You and Alex Mason exchanged some angry words over that. You made him look like a fool."

"That wasn't hard to do."

Kay Wheaton turned to a new page in her notepad. "Who else lives here, Dr. Kline?"

"My daughter and my girlfriend. Why are you smiling?"

"Oh, it's just that the word 'girlfriend' sounds a little funny coming from someone your age. What are you—forty-three, forty-four?"

"I'm forty-two. Ted Williams had twenty-nine home runs when he was my age. And you would prefer that I use 'significant other,' or 'partner,' or some desexualized term like that, I suppose."

She said, "How about, simply, womanfriend. I think that has a nice ring to it, don't you?"

I shrugged. "I never thought of that one."

"No, I don't suppose you have. I'll pretend to be surprised. Where are they? I'd like to speak with them. Perhaps they heard or saw something tonight that can help us piece things together."

"They're not here. They left four or five hours ago."

"How old is your daughter?"

"Eleven."

She checked her watch. "It's a school night. Is she often out this late?"

"Why does that concern *you*?"

"I'm just shooting arrows into the air, Dr. Kline. I don't always know where they'll land. But that arrow certainly seems to have hit something. Is there any reason why tonight, of all nights, you find yourself alone in the house?"

"Coincidence. My girlfriend is visiting her parents. My daughter went with her because I had a late patient." I paused. "A late patient. God, that sounds terrible, doesn't it?"

"When will they be getting home?"

"Tomorrow. I called my girlfriend—all right, my woman-friend—and told her what happened. They're staying in Welles-ley with her parents tonight. I didn't want my daughter to come home to all of this. Is that *acceptable* to you, detective?"

"Relax, Dr. Kline. I'm just trying to do my job."

Korvich said, "Well, I know you didn't have anything to do with killing him, Doc. Because if you did, that lawyer friend of yours would already be here."

As if on cue, the front door opened, and Bobby's voice carried through the house. "Harry—where are you? Are you all right?"

"I'm in the den, Bobby."

He walked into the room. He hesitated for a moment when he saw Korvich, not one of his favorite people, and a woman whom he had never met. He said, "Veronica called me and asked me to come over here. She told me what happened, and she said you might be hurt. Christ, you look like shit. Pardon me, ma'am."

Korvich and I started to laugh.

"What? Did I say something funny?"

"It's a long story," I replied. I introduced him to Kay Wheaton.

The detective gathered up her notepad and the answering-machine tape and put them in her coat pocket. She said, "I want to take a look at the graffiti. Where is it?"

I asked Bobby to take her to the south side of the house, near the entrance to my office.

After we were alone, Alfred Korvich said, "What was it Yogi Berra said? 'It looks like déjà vu all over again.' It seems like every time someone gets killed in Concord, you wind up in the middle of it. Tell me, Doc—have you ever considered moving?"

"Go screw yourself, Chief. I'm not in the mood for fun and games tonight."

He furrowed his brow. "Well, well. *You're* sure on edge tonight. And that's the second time you've done that, by the way."

"The second time I've done what?"

"The second time you've told me to go fuck myself. You had the same kind wish last year. Old Uncle Al remembers things like that."

I sighed. "Yeah, well, it's been a long day."

He nodded. "It seems to me that if we're going to be that intimate, we should at least be on a first-name basis. How would you feel about me calling you Harry?"

"I don't care. What do your friends call you? Assuming, of course, that you have friends."

"You can call me Al."

"Sounds like a song."

"Yeah, I guess it does." He looked at the bandage on my hand. "You must have gotten a lot of his blood on you, including on your cut hand. We'll be checking him for the AIDS virus. We'll get the results to you."

"Richie Conover wasn't involved in any high-risk activities. I don't think I have anything to worry about."

"Yeah, well, just the same. Old Uncle Al is always looking out for his friends."

He went outside to join Detective Wheaton.

Bobby came inside again a few minutes later. "They left," he said. "So—how are you feeling, pal of mine?"

I thought: *He wants to know how I'm feeling. My girlfriend is still depressed, my wife is still dead, my daughter is thinking of becoming Catholic, and I'm making friends with the Mafia. Today I almost got killed going around the Route 2 rotary, I got the crap pounded out of me, and I watched someone bleed to death. And he wants to know how I'm feeling.*

I said, "Have you ever watched somebody die?"

He shook his head. "No."

"I have. Too many times."

I thought about the person I had killed several months earlier. I thought about a suicide I once came upon: in time to watch the person die, too late to change the course she was on. I thought about the three people who died in my presence a couple of years earlier, when Veronica and I were on the trail of a serial killer. I thought about Richie Conover, alive and hopeful ninety minutes earlier, now an inert, lifeless mass en route to a coroner's metal table.

I thought about Janet taking her last breath in my presence nearly seven years earlier.

And I thought about another death, one I had seen only in my mind's eye: Rachel Pace being pounded until her face split and her skull caved in. And I thought about the little girl who watched it happen.

I thought and I thought, and then I thought some more. But none of it made any sense.

20: Taboo Subjects

There was nothing in the Thursday-morning *Boston Globe* about Richie Conover's killing; nighttime incidents in the suburbs sometimes didn't make the Boston papers until the second day. The *Concord Journal* wouldn't have it, either; it was printed on Wednesday for mail delivery on Thursday afternoon.

The story about Veronica ran on the first page of the paper, below the fold. The murder itself, horrible though it was, didn't warrant the prominence of the article; after all, that was old news. What made the story newsworthy was the here-and-now human-interest aspect, succinctly captured in the headline:

FBI AGENT OFFERS $250K TO SOLVE MOTHER'S MURDER

The article started with a focus on Veronica: hard-hitting murder prosecutor turned FBI agent, stymied on the most important case she had ever faced—her mother's murder, which she herself witnessed as a young child.

The three burglaries leading up to the murder were described. The fingerprint was mentioned. The article implied, but did not directly state, that the fingerprint had been recovered from the murder scene, rather than from an earlier break-in. I didn't know whether that misinformation represented incomplete reporting, sloppy editing, or a clever ploy to make the story seem even more dramatic.

There was information about the reward money. Veronica's

newly acquired phone number with the Boston exchange was listed. And in the only part of the story that was not likely to irritate Martin Baines, care was taken to point out that Veronica was looking into this case on her own time.

Veronica called from her father's house at eight o'clock. "We're getting ready to leave. We should be home in about half an hour. Did you see the *Globe*?"

"I'm reading it now."

"What do you think?"

"I think a quarter-million dollars is a lot of money."

"That's the whole idea."

"Have you told Melissa about this?"

"No. I thought you would want to be present when I did that."

"I think it would be better if you would tell her on the way home. Give her a chance to absorb that before I tell her what happened here last night."

"What should I tell her?"

"Just tell her the truth. She'll understand. When you told her about your mother's death at the cemetery last year, her first reaction was to tell you that you should try to discover who the killer was."

"That's right. I had forgotten."

As I showered I thought about something Dr. Greta Anselm said when I met with her at the VA the previous week. She had found her mysterious patient, a traumatized war veteran, sitting in an empty room staring at a bare wall. She told me, *I asked him what he was doing. He told me he was watching a movie of his life, and that he had to stay there until the movie was over.*

I wondered how many times the replay of Rachel Pace's murder had forced its way onto the screen in Veronica's mind. I wondered if she would ever be able to let go of it. And I wondered if I would be able to help her pick up the pieces once this fruitless search for her mother's killer was finished.

I got dressed and went downstairs just in time to greet Veronica and Melissa in the kitchen.

"Dad, what happened to your *face*?"

I could tell from her fidgeting that she was made anxious by what she saw, so I moved to calm her as quickly as I could. I said, "I'm all right. My face looks worse than it feels. It's just a bruise, and it'll be fine in a couple of days. I didn't even need to see a doctor."

"What's that yellow tape doing near the driveway?"

"The police put it there, honey. We had a problem here last night. Some older kids—"

"*Police!* Veronica told me the furnace was broken." She was never one to tolerate being lied to, and she glared angrily at Veronica.

Veronica said, "I'm sorry, Melissa."

"I told Veronica to make up a story, honey. I didn't want you to worry about me. But now I want to tell you the truth, what really happened."

"Go ahead," she replied. Now she was glaring at me.

"You know what the METCO program is."

"Of course I do," she said. "Everyone knows that."

I summarized the discussion at the PTG, and Veronica's role in it. "People got angry with one another. It shouldn't have happened, but sometimes it does happen. Just like the town meeting I took you to a few years ago, where Mr. Mason and I got angry with one another."

"I remember that. It was about the statue. He called you a communist, and people laughed at him. And you said he had no idea what America was supposed to stand for, and people applauded."

"That's right. Well, sometimes people do foolish things when they get angry. And that's what happened here last night."

I told her about the phone calls we had received the previous two days. I told her about the graffiti on the side of the house.

"When my patient left the office last night, he ran after the two kids—older kids—who sprayed the paint. They got into a fight, and he got cut very badly, and he died."

"They *killed* him?"

"Yes. I'm sure they didn't intend to do it. They probably don't even realize he's dead. They came here to drink beer and vandalize the side of the house. But my patient surprised them and tried to stop them, and they had a fight that killed him."

I paused to let that sink in. I wanted to see how she reacted before telling her anything else.

She said, "Your face . . ."

"I heard the noise. I ran outside. One of them hit me before they ran off."

Her eyes grew wide with fear. "Daddy! You could have been killed, too! Then what would happen to me?" She stood up. "Why are you always doing these things? Like when you killed that person last year."

Before I could think of a response, she turned and walked quickly toward the front foyer. "Where are you going?"

"To get my books. I'm late for school."

"I'd like you to stay home today. You're very upset."

"I *know* I'm upset. And I want to go to *school*!"

She stomped out of the room.

Veronica said, "I'll drive her. She's frightened. She wants to keep busy at school, rather than sit home and realize how scared she is." She looked at my face. "I hated not being able to be with you last night." She put her coat on and went off to take Melissa to school.

After they left I drove into town to pick up a copy of the *Concord Journal* at Snow's Pharmacy. I didn't want to wait until the afternoon mail delivery to read Yvette Mason's article.

An acquaintance and his young daughter were there. The little girl, Holly, smiled when she saw me. But when she saw my bruised face she shied away and grabbed her father's coat-sleeve. Phil looked at me and said, "You okay?"

I nodded, then scanned the paper quickly, cover to cover. I couldn't find the article. I turned the pages a second time, more slowly, and found nothing. Apparently I had misjudged Yvette Mason: Her byline was on articles about the zoning-board meeting and a new exhibit at the Concord Museum, but I saw no story about the PTG meeting.

I decided humility and a thank-you were in order. I said good-bye to Phil and Holly and drove home. I looked up the Masons' phone number and called their house. A woman's voice answered, with a French accent. "This is the Mason residence."

"This is Harry Kline. May I speak with Yvette Mason, please?"

"One moment."

Several seconds later Alex Mason's gruff voice came booming across the phone line. "What do *you* want, Kline?"

"Hello, Alex. Is Yvette at home?"

"She went to the doctor. What do you want with my wife?"

"She and I were at the PTG meeting on Monday night, and I—"

"I know about the meeting."

"Right. Well, she was planning to write about it for the *Journal*. I just wanted to thank her for changing her mind."

"She wrote the article."

"But I just looked through the—"

"She wrote the fucking article, you dipshit. How did you manage to keep it out?"

"How did I . . . I don't get it."

"Her dickhead editor decided to print it, and then the cocksucker pulled the story just as they were going to press."

"I have no idea—"

"Yeah, well, fuck you, and fuck you again."

I thought: *Keep buying those word-a-day calendars, Alex. I can already see an improvement in your vocabulary. Dipshit, dickhead, and cocksucker are all compound words.*

"Nice language," I said.

"Yeah, well, my language is as good as, like, whatever."

The next thing I knew, I was listening to a dial tone.

I called Will Dellums, the editor of the *Journal*. I had never met him, but he greeted me like an old friend when I identified myself.

"Why, hello, Harry. I hear you had some trouble at your place last night. Been a hell of a week for you, hasn't it?"

"I'm calling to thank you for making it a little easier. I appreciate your keeping Yvette Mason's story about the Alcott PTG out of the paper. I know you pulled it out at the last minute, which I'm sure must have been inconvenient."

"It's a small town, Harry. When the police chief asks a favor of you, it's usually for a good reason."

"The police chief? Why did *he* intervene?"

"Oh," Dellums said, and then he was quiet for a several seconds. "He told me not to let anyone know he had asked me to pull the story. I just assumed you already knew."

"No, I didn't. And I didn't mean to put you in a compromised position. I just wanted you to know I appreciated your killing the story."

He paused again. "I'll tell you what, Harry. Maybe you can do *me* a favor. I'd like to send Yvette out to talk to you about the homicide at your place. She was really upset when I killed the PTG story, especially when I couldn't give her a good reason. Hell, I didn't have a good reason. My only reason was the police chief asked me to, and he didn't want anyone else to know about his role. If you give her an interview, it would help me make things up to her."

The last thing I felt like doing was talking to Yvette Mason about Richie Conover's killing. I said, "Let me think about it," and I ended the call.

The police dispatcher put through my call to Alfred Korvich. "Harry, my pal, my buddy, my amigo. How's your head?"

I thought: *Perhaps we should return to a last-name basis.* "I'm all right," I said. "Did you ask Will Dellums to pull the article about the PTG meeting?"

He sighed. "Hell, he kept that secret for an entire twenty-four hours, didn't he?"

"Why did you do it?"

"Are you complaining?"

"No, of course not. I just want to know why you did it."

"I told you. Old Uncle Al is always looking out for his friends."

"But why?"

"I didn't want the word to spread too fast about the PTG meeting. I wanted to limit the number of people who knew about it—limit the number of possible suspects—in case you kept getting threatening calls. Of course, we're way beyond phone calls now, aren't we?"

"What happens next?"

"These guys weren't exactly criminal masterminds. I think

we'll find them pretty easily. Kay Wheaton is checking with paramedics at hospitals in the area, looking for anyone who showed up at an emergency room last night with an injured hand."

"So much for patient confidentiality."

"Doctors usually won't cough up a name. Some ER nurses will, some won't. But we work with the paramedics all the time at accident scenes. If we ask for information off the record, they'll usually help us out. We're also compiling a list of Toms."

"A list of Toms?"

He said, "We're checking the high schools in town for kids named Tommy."

There were three such schools: the public high school, and the two private schools—Concord Academy and the Middlesex School. I said, "What will you do then?"

"Shake hands with them all, squeezing very hard. The one who cries out the loudest is the guy who tenderized your face and broke his hand on your tree."

Veronica returned shortly after I spoke with Korvich. She said, "There's nothing to do now except sit tight and wait for someone to call the number that was in the *Globe*." She draped her coat over a kitchen chair and put water up for coffee.

"How did things go last night at your father's house?"

"Shana was good about the whole thing. She was like you—worried about me, wondering if it was a wise thing to do, but willing to do anything she could to help. Of course, there isn't anything she can do, but the offer was sweet."

"And your father?"

She shook her head. "You have to understand, Harry. This is the ultimate taboo subject between my father and me. He wasn't there that night. And he can't bear to live it through my eyes. And therefore he wants me to put it out of my mind. But I *can't* put it out of my mind. And I can't forget that he wasn't there to help us. When I think of that I get angry. I know it isn't logical. And it makes me feel guilty. But it's always been that way."

The water boiled. She made her coffee and sat down again.

I said, "You remind me of Melissa. The day after Janet died, Melissa said to me, 'You're a doctor. Why didn't you help her?' "

"Poor Melissa." She touched my hand for an instant, then pulled away. "And poor you."

"And poor Janet," I said, the sadness welling up inside me. I was accustomed to the dull, chronic ache of her absence from my life: the background noise of my day-to-day existence. But it had been a long time since I was seized by a sharp, cutting pang of grief like the one I felt in that moment. I was definitely in the sickness season.

"And that, Harry, is the ultimate taboo subject between you and me."

"Why is that?"

"I'm sure it's complicated beyond words. And I'm not in the mood today for self-analysis. I can tolerate you talking about her, usually. But I can't engage in the conversation with you."

I remembered what Father John said the previous day: *If Veronica wants to be with you, she'll have to make space in her life for the memory of this woman she never knew.* But this was not the time to press the issue.

She said, "I'm going over to my apartment. I want to be there if anyone calls about the *Globe* story. Will you keep me company?"

"I'll be there in a little while. I just want to take care of some odds and ends."

I called my insurance agent to see if I was covered for the spray-painting vandalism. I was.

I called a painter to see if there was something I could do, short of repainting the side of my house, to rid myself of the graffiti. There wasn't. And since January wasn't a good time for house painting, I might have to choose between covering the wall with a temporary tarp, or leaving the message for all my patients to read as they entered my office.

Detective Kay Wheaton called. "What do you have on your schedule for today?" she asked.

"I don't have anything planned. I canceled all my appointments for today and tomorrow."

"I would appreciate it if you would stay close to the phone. We may be ready to do a lineup sometime this afternoon."

"*That* was quick."

"We aim to please. It was easy to get a handle on this case. It's not often that you get the first name of someone stupid enough to break his hand during the crime."

"Do you know who it was?"

"I've suspected for a couple of hours. I've known for a half hour. I don't have enough evidence for an arrest yet, but I expect to get it soon. And then I want to see if you can identify them."

"I doubt that I'll be much help on a lineup. It was too dark to see much of anything."

"It was a full moon."

"Then it must have been cloudy. And didn't we already have this conversation?"

"I was feeling nostalgic. Seriously—please try to stay available."

"I'm going to be at Veronica's place. I'll forward my calls to her number."

"Last night you said she lived with you."

"In a manner of speaking. She has the apartment above my barn."

"But you said she's your womanfriend."

"No, you said she's my womanfriend. I used another word."

"Let me see if I understand this. The two of you are a couple, and you live at the same address, but you don't really live together."

"It's a complicated situation," I said. "My wife and I used to have a housekeeper—"

She cut me off. "Do I need to know what you're about to tell me?"

"No, I suppose not."

"Good. I want to get back to work. I want to wrap things up as soon as possible, or I'll wind up working on Super Bowl Sunday."

I called Richie Conover's sister to offer my sympathies. I

could tell from her quavering voice that she was on the verge of losing control.

She said, "The detective who talked with me said you tried to help Richie. She said you got hurt."

"I wasn't hurt badly. I'm just very sorry I wasn't able to stop what happened. And I want to let you and your parents know that you have my sympathy."

She snickered: a bitter laugh. "Daddy is very upset, you know, because . . ." She started to cry, and it took several seconds for her to finish her thought between sobs. "Because now he'll have to miss the Super Bowl." She sobbed more loudly, and then she hung up.

I walked upstairs to get my watch and keys. The door to Melissa's room was open. I stood in the hallway outside her room, and I could see the photo of Janet on the nightstand. I walked into the room and picked up the picture.

I thought about the first time we met. Bobby and I were walking around the Tufts campus one night early in our senior year. We struck up a conversation with three freshman girls. I was captivated by Janet. She was obviously less impressed by me; the next few times I saw her on campus, she called me Gary.

I remembered an afternoon a few years later when she and I sailed alone in Maine's Penobscot Bay. Night fell, the moon shone on the water, and we were completely sealed off from whatever was happening elsewhere in the universe. There were no words, no sense of time, no sense of place. It could have been a thousand years ago, or next week, or now. It was something Janet used to call a "life moment"—an occurrence of special meaning and intensity that would remain in my heart forever.

Every once in a while I still drove past the Cambridge apartment we shared early in our marriage. I liked to look up at the third-floor windows and recall the times we shared when everything was new and so much seemed to lie ahead of us. At night in that apartment, we used to lie in bed and plot our future together. I thought we had everything planned.

"This isn't what we planned," I said one evening as Janet lay wasting away in a bed on the cancer ward at Mass General Hospital. "This isn't the life we planned at all."

She smiled at me, full of fatigue, wanting me to be strong for both of us. "Life is what happens while you're busy making other plans," she replied.

She died in my arms in that hospital bed a few days later, in the predawn hours of a frigid February morning. Afterward I came home and sat in Melissa's room, waiting for her to rise so I could break the news to her. When she finally opened her eyes, I tried to say the lines I'd rehearsed—about God loving Janet too much to see her suffer any longer, and Janet going to heaven where she would watch over us forever. But I couldn't get the words out.

Janet was my other half. I would love her and miss her forever.

"I didn't know if you have anything for lunch," I said. "I brought over some cold cuts. Any calls yet?"

"No," Veronica replied. "If the phone rings normally, that means it's a call to my Concord number. But if each ring is broken into two short rings, then it's a call to the Boston number that was printed in the *Globe* this morning. Two phone numbers, but the same phone. That was the quickest and easiest way to do it."

"Does the answering machine pick up for both of them?"

"Yes."

I went into the kitchen and made sandwiches. Neither one of us was hungry yet, so I placed them in the refrigerator.

A short while later there was a double ring that signified a call to the number in the newspaper. We looked at each other. Veronica pressed the record button on her answering machine, put the call on the speakerphone, then answered by saying her name.

The caller was a man with a thick Boston working-class accent. "Is this the lady in the story in the paper?"

"I am."

"Is this, like, for real? If I know the guy who did it, do I really get two hundred and fifty thousand bucks?"

"This is very real." She hesitated, then said, "Do you know something?"

"Nah. I mean, I don't know just now. I got a couple ideas. Guys I know who used to go out to the suburbs. I can ask around. I just wanted to make sure this was for real before I did that."

He ended the call without identifying himself. Veronica turned to me and said, "Nothing."

"Nothing," I agreed.

There were two hang-up calls and nothing else before lunch. After we ate I started a fire, then stretched out in front of it. I was finally beginning to feel relaxed, drifting into half-asleep mode, when I was jarred awake by another call to the Boston line. Again Veronica engaged the recorder. And again she put the call on the speakerphone so I could listen.

"This is Veronica Pace." There was no immediate reply, but someone was definitely on the other end; a radio played in the background. "Hello? Is anyone there?"

A woman's quiet voice spoke in a thick Hispanic accent, perhaps Puerto Rican. "Yes, miss. I am sorry so much for your loss."

She sounded elderly. Her sentiments seemed genuine. "Thank you," Veronica replied. "Are you calling about the reward?"

Hesitant, the woman finally answered, "Yes. My name is Rosa Mercado."

Veronica took a deep breath, forcing herself to stay calm. "What would you like me to know, Ms. Mercado?"

"I think . . . Just a moment, miss." She turned her radio off. When she spoke again, she sounded as though she were forcing back her tears. "I think this maybe was my son, Miguel."

Rosa Mercado was calling from her home in Waltham. She lived there in 1972, when Rachel Pace was murdered, and she still lived there. Her son, Miguel, was eighteen at the time of the murder, living with his mother in the home she still occupied. He worked as a busboy at the Wellesley Inn.

Rosa Mercado said, "Sometimes he bring things home I

know are not his. Things he say he buys. But I say, Miguel, a busboy—how can he afford that?"

"What sorts of things?"

"It was a long time. I don't know anymore."

Veronica wrote the woman's name and her son's name. "Has Miguel ever been in jail, Mrs. Mercado?"

"Yes, miss."

"Has he ever been in jail for hurting someone else?"

"Yes. He even hurt me once. He hit me very hard."

Veronica shuddered slightly. She dug her fingernails into her leg. "Mrs. Mercado, where is Miguel now?"

The woman began to weep softly. "Miguel is dead, miss. He broke into a house in Belmont, and he was shot."

"When did that happen?"

"In 1974." She paused. "I don't know if this helps you, miss. I am old and I am poor. I hope it is not him. I don't know, miss. I don't know."

Veronica took the woman's phone number and address. She promised to investigate the situation and inform the woman about the outcome.

She turned to me and said, "What do you think?"

"She's like a person betting money against the team she's rooting for in a football game. You want to win the money, but you'll be sad if you win the bet."

"The facts as she remembers them fit my situation. I know, I know, you don't have to tell me—so would the facts of a hundred different situations."

"What will you do next?"

"I'll wait for more calls today, and I'll check this out either tomorrow or after the weekend. It sounds like he was arrested on several occasions. All I need is one set of booking fingerprints to rule him out." She paused. "Or to rule him in."

I tossed another log into the fire. Veronica turned her television on for background noise, and we sat without speaking for the next hour.

At three o'clock I heard Ingrid's car. She parked between the barn and house and went inside to wait for Melissa and prepare dinner. I called her on the intercom to let her know where I was, and to tell her that I had set the phone to forward my calls to Veronica's phone.

I lay on the floor in front of the fireplace with a throw pillow under my head. I replayed the phone call from Rosa Mercado in my mind. I said, "Miguel Mercado's mother said he was a busboy at the Wellesley Inn."

"Yes, she did."

"Do you see any relevance in that?"

She thought for a few seconds. "Depending on his schedule, it could explain why all the break-ins occurred on the same night of the week."

"Possible," I said. "But I'm thinking of something more specific. I'm thinking about linen napkins."

"Linen napkins?"

"Charlie said that linen napkins were found at all four break-ins. A busboy at the Wellesley Inn would have access to linen napkins."

Shortly before four o'clock Veronica's phone rang: long, single rings signifying a call to her Concord number. Veronica answered it, then handed it to me.

"Was that your womanfriend?" asked Kay Wheaton.

"Yes."

"Do you think you can bear to leave her side for an hour or two?"

"Why?"

"I'd like you to come to the police station. I have a couple of graffiti artists I want you to meet."

21: WET

"Take your time," Kay Wheaton said.

I looked through the one-way glass at the six teenagers in the next room. Next to me was a lawyer who was representing one of them—the one whom Kay hoped I would pick out of the lineup, whichever one he was.

She said, "Let me know if you want them to turn to the left or to the right."

I said, "How about a line dance, or maybe the bunny hop?"

The lawyer grinned. "I really don't know. I told you—I could barely make out shapes and shadows."

"It was a full moon."

"Let's not go through that again, if you don't mind."

"Are you sure that none of them look familiar to you?"

"I didn't say that."

"Well, what *are* you saying?"

"I'm saying they *all* look familiar to me. That first one—isn't that George Lowell's kid? And that one—I think he works after school at New London Pizza." I pointed at the others one by one: "That one, that one, that one—hell, they all look familiar for one reason or another. But I can't tell you anything about the person who assaulted me and killed Richie Conover. I told you that before you brought me in here."

The lawyer grinned and scribbled some notes—most likely a verbatim transcription of my expression of futility.

The detective said, "Can you rule any of them out?"

"No. If you want me to rule someone out, show me someone in a wheelchair."

The lawyer began to laugh hysterically. Kay Wheaton called an end to the procedure and took me into a private room.

She said, "That wasn't very helpful."

"I told you before we started that I couldn't identify anyone."

"I'm not talking about that. It isn't helpful to have you show me up in front of a defendant's attorney."

"Oh." I thought about it for a few moments. "I'm sorry. I didn't realize."

She sighed. "Well, a decent identification would have been icing on the cake. But I think we'll have enough for a conviction without it."

"Are you able to tell me where things stand?"

She shrugged. "I don't see why not. The chief says you can be trusted."

"He did?"

"He did. You seem surprised."

"It's a long story."

"Do I need to hear it?" she asked.

"No, not necessarily."

She yawned. "Good, because I'm tired, and I still have a lot to do. But I can give you a quick summary."

Early that morning the detective sent one police officer to each of the three high schools in town: the public school and the two private schools. The officers returned within the hour with lists of students' names. Kay Wheaton assumed that the suspects were at least sixteen, old enough to drive; thus she focused on the upper grades. There were, Kay Wheaton told me, a total of three hundred and ninety-six boys in the eleventh and twelfth grades in the three schools in town. Fourteen of them were named Tom or Thomas.

Her plan was to focus first on identifying—and attempting to interview—everyone on the "Tommy list" who was absent that day, on the theory that an absence might be due to the injury he received courtesy of my red maple tree.

She said, "But when you're in a hurry, and in a world of limited resources, sometimes you just go where the evidence leads you. One of the names on the list almost jumped off the page at me."

"Who was that?"

"Number five."

"What kind of a name is that?"

"That isn't his name. That was his position in the lineup you saw a few minutes ago."

"The curly-haired kid in the red sweater?"

"That's the one," she replied. "He goes to Concord-Carlisle High School. His name is Thomas Mason. And his parents are . . . ?" She threw her hand forward, palm up, inviting me to finish her sentence.

I said, "Alex and Yvette Mason?"

"Bingo."

She told me that as soon as she recognized the connection, she drove over to the school.

Thomas Mason was absent.

A few questions to a helpful teacher elicited the name of the boy's girlfriend. Kay Wheaton had her summoned to the principal's office.

The detective identified herself and said, "I need to talk with Thomas Mason. Do you know where he is?"

"Is Tommy in some sorta trouble?"

"He and a friend witnessed an accident last night. I need to talk with Tommy about what he saw."

The girl shrugged. She was chewing gum, and her vacuous manner suggested that the task required all of the concentration she could muster, leaving little energy for answering the detective's questions.

She said, "He's sick. He called me and said his mother was taking him to see Dr. Silverstein."

"Perhaps I can talk with his friend. Do you know who Tommy was with last night?"

Shrug and chew, shrug and chew: The girl's efforts were so focused on those simple tasks that Kay thought she may have meditated herself onto a higher plane, like a mystic elevating himself to spiritual bliss by concentrating his mind on the contemplation of his navel.

Finally the girl said, "Tommy was with Paul Nickerson last night. He's not here today, too."

"Thank you for your help. I'll go to their homes to talk with them."

"No, no—you can't do that! He'll get in trouble."

"Who will get in trouble?"

"Paul Nickerson," the girl replied. "Paul will get in trouble. He's not really sick today. Tommy is, but Paul isn't. Paul is at his girlfriend's house. Her mother volunteers someplace every Thursday. Sometimes they go to her place together. You know."

"Sure," said Kay. "I know. Well, I certainly don't want to get anyone into trouble. If you give me the name and address of Paul's girlfriend, I won't have to go to his parents' house to look for him."

When Kay Wheaton reached her car she called in to the station and had an officer dispatched to the home of Paul Nickerson's girlfriend. "Tell him we need to talk with him about a friend who's in trouble. If he has a car there, let him drive himself to the station and just follow behind him. I'd like to take a look at his car."

Directory assistance told her that there was a Dr. Silverstein with an office in the physicians' building on the grounds of Emerson Hospital. Ten minutes later she was standing in the doctor's reception area. There were only a few patients waiting, all of them old; there was no sign of a teenager sitting with a broken hand and his mother.

She approached the receptionist. "I'm looking for my friend Yvette Mason. She told me she was bringing her son here for an appointment."

"They're not here. The doctor sent her son to the basement to get X-rays."

The detective walked briskly to the stairwell in the corridor, then bounded down four flights to the basement as quickly as she could.

There was no formal waiting area in the X-ray department, just a few chairs in the corridor. Seated there were a teenage boy and a woman whom Kay presumed to be the boy's mother. The boy's right hand was immobilized with a temporary splint;

he held it at an odd angle, and he was in obvious pain. As Kay walked toward them she heard the woman say, "Honestly, Thomas. It's always something with you." The detective kept walking until she reached the stairwell at the other end of the corridor.

Sitting across the table from me now, Kay Wheaton checked her watch and said, "Paul Nickerson was waiting here when I returned. He was shaking like Jell-O. Well, not quite. But I could tell that he was very, very nervous. I decided to use that. I took him into an interview room, sat him down, told him my name, and read him his Miranda rights. Told him he was being charged with the murder of Richie Conover. Until that moment I don't think he realized the victim had died."

"How did he react?"

"He came up a little short on the courage-and-valor end of things. When he heard the word 'murder,' the very first words out of his mouth were, 'But Tommy Mason is the one who beat up on those people. All I did was carry the spray paint.' I said, 'What people?' And he said, 'The kid who chased us down, and the old guy who ran over to us a few minutes later.' "

"He called me an *old* guy?"

Kay Wheaton smiled. "Like I said—there was a full moon last night."

"She handled that quickly," Veronica said, "and she handled it well. I'm impressed. I'd like to meet her."

"Well, if you do, just don't refer to me as your boyfriend."

"Why not?"

"It's just a joke. Nothing important."

We were sitting in the kitchen, eating the jambalaya that Ingrid made that afternoon. Veronica had waited for me; Melissa ate earlier, at our usual dinnertime, and now she was elsewhere in the house monopolizing the telephone. Perhaps this was part of a strategy to make me reconsider my decision not to give her a phone line of her own.

I said, "When I left the police station, Kay Wheaton was getting ready to interview Thomas Mason. She was going to hit him and his lawyer with what she has against him."

"What else does she have, besides the other kid's statement?"

"They have blood on the seat and door of the passenger's side of Paul Nickerson's car, which they assume will prove to be Richie Conover's blood. They have some boot prints that they've already matched up with the boots Paul Nickerson was wearing today. They hope to match some others with Thomas Mason's boots. Which reminds me—I have to bring her the shoes I was wearing last night so they can separate out which prints belong to me. And, of course, there's the matter of Thomas Mason's broken hand, which, by the way, is now encased in a fiberglass cast."

"And you still couldn't pick him out in the lineup?"

"All six of them had their right hands wrapped in towels."

She laughed. "Well, if the Mason kid's attorney indicates an interest in cutting a deal, the DA's office will send a prosecutor over to negotiate a plea. How old are these kids?"

"They're both seventeen."

"Good. That gives the police and the prosecution more leverage. Seventeen-year-olds are adults in the eyes of the criminal courts. They face adult trials, with adult penalties. More incentive to plead out."

She was a former homicide prosecutor herself, and she seemed to enjoy the diversion that thinking about this case provided. There had been no more calls to her Boston line while I was at the police station.

I said, "What do you think will happen to Thomas Mason?"

She paused for just a moment. "Do you want the short version or the long version?"

It seemed like ages since she had been this enthusiastic about anything. I liked seeing her that way. "Give me the long version."

"When the attorneys sit down together, the prosecutor will pretend to have no interest in making a deal. He'll contend that the facts point to a first-degree-murder conviction. That's an intentional homicide with premeditation, or an intentional homicide with extreme atrocity. A conviction means a mandatory life sentence, with no chance ever of parole. More jambalaya?"

"No, thanks. I'm all set."

She walked to the stove with her bowl, scooped some more jambalaya for herself, then returned to the table and continued her narrative.

"The defense attorney will laugh. He'll say something like, 'Get real. The *best* you can hope for if you take it to trial is second-degree murder.' "

I said, "An intentional homicide, but without the premeditation or atrocity."

Veronica nodded. "The prosecutor will look irritated, or bored, and he'll pretend he's agonizing over the decision, and finally he'll say, 'All right. Plead your client to second-degree murder and we can avoid a trial. Your client gets a life sentence, but he can get out on parole in fifteen years if he keeps his nose clean in prison.' "

"Will the defense attorney accept that?"

"Not a chance. He'll say, 'I told you second-degree murder was the *best* you could do in front of a jury. But I think I can get a jury to go for involuntary manslaughter.' "

I walked over to the refrigerator with my glass. "I *told* Ingrid to cut back on the cayenne. I think she's trying to torture me. Do you want more sparkling water?"

"Sure."

I filled my glass, then hers, and sat down again.

She said, "Involuntary manslaughter is a completely unintentional homicide. Someone dies because of another person's neglect or carelessness. As in the case of parents who deny their child medical treatment, and then the child dies."

I thought about that for a few seconds. "I think that would be pushing it in this case."

"I agree. And the prosecutor won't go for that. So after much posturing on both sides, one or the other will grudgingly float the notion of a plea to voluntary manslaughter. An *unintentional* homicide committed during a *voluntary* assault. You intended to hurt the person, but not to murder him."

"What kind of sentence does it carry?"

"I believe in Massachusetts the sentence is twelve-to-eighteen years. If there are no disciplinary problems in prison, he would automatically get out after twelve years. He would be eligible for parole in eight years. But if he participates in various programs, he earns good time, and then he could wind up becoming eligible for parole in about six years."

I thought about the embarrassment their son's arrest would bring to Alex and Yvette Mason. Surprisingly, the thought of their misery brought me no particular pleasure. I said, "Six years for taking a life. Huh."

"It fits the situation, Harry. Thomas Mason and Paul Nickerson came here to spray-paint your wall. Property damage. You can argue that the intent of that damage was to terrorize the victims, meaning you and me. But there was no intent to assault anyone, let alone kill anyone. If I were the prosecutor, I would go into that room with the goal of getting a plea to voluntary manslaughter. I could sell it to my boss, I could sell it to the victim's family, and I could sell it to myself. Justice would be done."

We sat there quietly, finishing our meal.

Outside, the wind picked up. A three- or four-inch powder snowfall, nothing major, had been predicted for the late night and very early morning. With any luck, it would be one of those little New England gems: There would be enough snow to put a fresh coat of winter white on the town, but not so much as to cause problems. And because it would fall overnight there would be plenty of time to clear the roads before the daytime came.

We stood side by side at the sink, rinsing dishes and putting them into the dishwasher. I said, "What do you think will happen to Paul Nickerson?"

"A lot depends on whether he's been in trouble before. I doubt that they'll charge him for anything other than the vandalism, even though under the law he could be charged as an accomplice in the homicide. With a good lawyer, an attitude of contrition, and a reasonable prosecutor, he may not have to serve a sentence. Instead he might get a suspended sentence, or outright probation. If he does get a sentence, it won't be a long one."

"Would that be justice?"

"In my opinion, yes."

We finished with the dishes and cleaned off the counters and table. I thought about the questions Father John Fitzpatrick asked in the same room six days earlier. *What will Veronica do if she succeeds? Is she merciful?*

I said, "What would be justice for the man who killed your mother?"

"I don't know."

"What will you do if you manage to identify him?"

She hesitated. "I don't know."

I pondered that for several seconds. I said, "Will you kill him?"

She said nothing. She averted her eyes and turned away from me.

I took her arm and turned her to face me. "Please listen to me. If you kill him, I won't stay with you. I won't be able to keep you in my life, or in Melissa's life."

"We're not virgins here, Harry. I've killed when I had to. You know that. And *you've* killed when you had to, I shouldn't have to remind you."

"Exactly. When we *had* to. You killed someone in the line of duty to save other people's lives. I killed someone who was trying to kill me. Neither of those circumstances applies here, Veronica."

"You're hurting my arm."

I let loose my grip. "Sorry. I didn't mean to hurt you."

"I know." She rubbed her upper arm for a few seconds. "I'm going back to my place to check the answering machine."

"Are you coming back to the house?"

"I think I should stay in the barn, just in case I get more calls about the *Globe* article. You can come over, if you'd like." She paused. "Let me try that again. I *want* you to come over."

"I haven't seen Melissa for more than a minute since breakfast yesterday. I'll come over for a little while after I talk with her. But I want to sleep in the house. I don't want her to feel alone tonight."

"I understand." She turned to leave.

"Veronica—"

She turned back to face me.

I said, "It's been a while since I asked you to move in with me—with us—into the house. That doesn't mean I don't want you to. It just means I didn't think it was doing either one of us any good for me to keep asking and for you to keep saying no."

She smiled. "You're a sweet man. I know I'm often not as nice to you as you are to me. Come over when you can."

Melissa was sitting on her bedroom floor making notes about something. The *Nightingale* album was playing in the background.

"Hi, sweetheart. What are you doing?"

She smiled when she saw me. "I decided to make tapes of all of Mom's old record albums. That way I can play them whenever I want and not worry that I'm wearing the records out. I'm writing the names of the songs to stick inside the cassette cases. I really like this album by Veronica's Aunt Marilyn."

"She came by to see me yesterday. She's coming again tomorrow afternoon."

"Great! She said she'd help me learn some things on the guitar. Why is she coming to see you? Is she a patient now?"

"No, I guess you can say she's a friend of the family."

"I like her."

"I do, too. Can I listen with you for a few minutes?"

"Sure."

I sat next to her and listened to the songs on Marilyn's only album. The lyrics were innocent and gentle, but Marilyn's sultry voice imbued them with an undercurrent of worldliness and sensuality.

On this particular night—just eight nights before the anniversary of Janet's death, and one night after I was attacked—it was perhaps no accident that Melissa was reaching into the past for a piece of her mother.

I said, "The police arrested the two boys who killed my patient."

"Who was it?"

"The one who killed him—and hit me—was Mr. Mason's son, Tommy. The other boy is named Paul Nickerson. They go to the high school."

"The spray painting looks awful."

"I know. Someone is coming tomorrow to cover the graffiti until it gets warm enough outside to paint the house."

"But that'll look so ugly, Dad."

"Not as ugly as the words that they put there."

The last song on the first side of the Mara Lee album came to an end. Melissa pressed the pause button on her tape deck, turned the record over, and began taping the second side.

I said, "Do you have any questions?"

"About what?"

"About what happened here last night. Or about the article in today's paper, and what Veronica is trying to do. Or about your mother, or the things about religion we talked about on Saturday. This is a lot for anyone to absorb all at once. I just thought you might have some questions."

She shrugged. "Uh-uh. Do you have any?"

"More than I can count, sweetheart. More than I can count."

"Did Veronica go back to her apartment?"

I nodded. "I'm going to visit with her for a little while, maybe watch *Seinfeld* with her."

"It's a rerun."

"That's all right. It's something to do. I'll be back in about an hour. If you need me, hit the intercom."

The first few scattered flakes of snow drifted down as I made my way to the barn. Veronica was in the shower. I walked into the bathroom and let her know I was there.

She said, "Jonas Cavaleri called. He wants to meet in the morning. He says he has some ideas he wants to discuss. Can you come with me, Harry?"

"Yes. I already canceled tomorrow's appointments."

"I'm glad. I gave him the name of Miguel Mercado. In the morning he'll try to locate a set of the man's fingerprints to match against the one on the Di-Gel box."

"Were there any other calls?"

"Some hang-ups on the answering machine. And the *Globe* reporter called in search of a follow-up story."

"What did you tell her?"

"I told her that a number of people called with possible

leads. I just didn't tell her that the number was one. I'll be out in a few minutes."

I went into the bedroom and turned on the television. I kicked off my shoes and lay back on the bed.

Veronica came out of the bathroom wearing a plush robe. Her hair was wrapped in a towel, and beads of shower water glistened on her body.

"You look beautiful," I said.

She laughed and removed the towel, tossing her hair back. She shut off the television.

"Don't you want to watch TV?" I asked.

"No," she replied. "I want to watch you."

She let the robe slip to the floor, and she came to me. She shivered as the air hit the water droplets on her skin. Her hand shook as she fumbled with the buttons of my shirt.

She pressed her lips against mine, softly, her tongue searching mine out and making circles around it. She used both hands to undress me.

By the dim glow of her night-light and the sound of the wind picking up, we made feverish love to one another: arms and legs entwined, bodies pushing and pulling, my hardness against her softness. Near the end, as I pounded myself into her with uncommon force, as she met my every lunge with the thrust of her hips, she called my name and told me she loved me.

Afterward I lay on my back, and she rested her head on my chest and made tiny circles on my stomach with her fingers. She said, "Do you remember what Melissa said this morning when you told her about last night? She said, 'You could have been killed, and then what would happen to me?' "

"I remember."

"Well, when you called me at my father's house last night to tell me what happened, those were the very same words that passed through my mind. I don't know what would happen to me if I lost you. And you scared me before in the kitchen when you talked about cutting me out of your life."

We lay there for a little while, and then I got dressed. "No one is going to call you this late at night. Come with me. Come into the house."

She smiled. "I'm too tired to move. You wore me out. I'll see you for breakfast, and then we'll go together to Wellesley to talk with Jonas."

It was ten o'clock when I walked back to the house through a half inch of accumulated snow. I was weary from the fatigue engendered by the events of the day, and spent from making love to Veronica. As soon as my body hit my bed I fell into a deep, dreamless sleep.

It was the soundness of my sleep that made the sudden awakening feel like such a jolt. There was a noise . . . a noise . . . a noise. I sprang to a sitting position in bed. I flipped the lamp on, blinding me for a moment, adding to my disoriented state.

I checked my clock. It was just past midnight. And the noise, I realized, was Veronica's voice on the intercom.

"Harry? Harry, are you there? Please answer me."

She sounded agitated. I reached for the intercom and pressed the button that allowed me to speak. "I'm here. What's wrong?"

"Harry—please, please come here as fast as you can. Please!"

I grabbed a robe and ran barefoot down the stairs and out of the house. I didn't stop to think about the snow on the ground or the twenty-degree weather. I ran across to the barn, my feet slipping and growing numb as I moved.

Veronica was sitting on her bed, naked, cowering against the wall. She was covered with sweat. I picked her robe off the floor and wrapped it around her. As I did she dug her fingernails into my arm.

"You're shivering," I said. "And your skin is ice-cold. Did you have a bad dream?"

She croaked, "I had a phone call. Double rings. It came in on the number that was listed in the paper." She pointed toward the answering machine. The light was flashing; she had recorded the call.

I pressed the replay button and listened.

Veronica's voice said, "Hello?"

First came the background noise: the sound that led Alfred Korvich to speculate that the caller was using a pay phone. Then came the cold, metallic voice that Kay Wheaton said was probably disguised. "Thank you for putting your number in the paper, Veronica. Now I can talk to you directly instead of talking to your boyfriend."

"Who are you?"

"Are you still making waves? I told your boyfriend that if you make waves, you get wet. I don't think he understood the significance of that remark. But I bet you do."

"Who *are* you?"

He paused for several seconds. The background sounds echoed over the phone line. Finally he said, "Do I frighten you?"

"Yes."

"The last time I frightened you, you peed all over yourself. Are you wetting yourself now?"

22: Backward

"Are you wetting yourself *now*?" he repeated, with emphasis on the final word, and then he hung up.

Veronica's face was as pale as the snow falling against her window. She was shaking, and she had the dazed, unfocused expression of a trapped animal. She said, "It's him."

I sat next to her. "Who is it? Do you know that person?"

"It's him. It's the man who killed my mother!" She held on to me and bit down on my shoulder, as if to stifle a scream.

"Shh. It's okay. How do you know that? Did you recognize his voice?"

The fear was constricting everything: It took several seconds for her to capture enough air to let the words out. "It has to be him. Don't you understand? Who else knows I wet myself?" Every other word practically exploded from her mouth. "Charlie Amory. Me. And *him*!"

I remembered now: Wellesley police chief Charlie Amory, then a patrolman who came upon the murder scene while it was fresh, made no mention of Veronica's loss of bladder control in his police report. Whoever made that phone call was likely in Rachel's bedroom on that December night more than twenty-one years earlier. Either he was one of the police officers milling about, or he was the killer.

I lowered Veronica onto her back and lay next to her, pressing against her. I pulled on the comforter and sheets that were under us, wrapping them around us.

She clung tightly to me. "He found me," she whispered. "I've been looking for *him*, and he found *me*."

She closed herself down. She didn't want to talk about what had happened. We held each other and tried to sleep, but she was too frightened and I was too worried about her for anything but a fitful sleep to come to us.

We left for Wellesley in the morning after Melissa's school bus picked her up. Veronica insisted on driving; she said it would help her stay focused. And I knew if she stayed focused she would stay in control.

For the entire time I had known her, she was always afraid of losing control. Maybe that was why she always seemed to hold part of herself in reserve, even in our most intimate moments. And who could blame her? The thought of losing control, even in a good way, probably triggered a recollection of the time she lost control and wet herself—and of the terrible circumstance that triggered it.

At the foot of the driveway I got out of the car and removed the morning *Globe* from the newspaper box. A story about Richie Conover's killing and the arrest of two suspects appeared on the second page of the Metro section.

We stopped at Snow's Pharmacy and I picked up a copy of the tabloid-sized *Boston Herald*. The article there was smaller, but there were pictures of Richie Conover and Thomas Mason. And unbeknownst to me, a *Herald* photographer had snapped a shot of the graffiti on the south side of my house.

I read the articles to Veronica as she drove. I didn't like seeing my name in stories about a homicide. I mumbled, "Been there, done that."

"Excuse me?"

"Nothing, just talking to myself. There's no follow-up in the *Globe* to the article yesterday about you. Nothing about it in the *Herald*, either."

Veronica drove to Wellesley via Lincoln and Weston. Except for a few patches of packed snow in Lincoln—the town didn't use salt on its roads—the route was clear. The overnight snowfall, perhaps three inches, provided a cosmetic cover to the dull brown grime of winter.

We arrived at the police station at around nine-fifteen. Jonas Cavaleri was standing inside the front door, reading the *Globe*. He didn't notice us at first. With his goatee and shaved head, he was an imposing sight: muscular and wide. If I were in harm's way, I would want him on my side.

He saw us and said, "I was just reading about you, Harry. Geez, between this article and the one yesterday, the two of you are having a hell of a week."

He took us into an interview room and brought coffee for Veronica, water for me. He placed the case file on the chair next to his. He said, "I've been thinking about everything, and I have an idea. Oh, by the way, I already got word back on Miguel Mercado's fingerprints. No match there, I'm afraid."

"I know," Veronica said.

"How do you know that?"

"Because Miguel Mercado is dead, and the man who killed my mother is alive."

"And how do you know *that*?"

"Because he called me last night."

"He did *what*?"

Veronica told Jonas about the man who had called, called, and called again; and about the secret knowledge he had regarding what she did the night of the murder.

Jonas sat quietly for several moments, digesting this latest information. "Goddamn, this is something." He shook his head from side to side. "I think I should tell you why I asked you to come here this morning."

He held the case file in front of him, opened it, turned it upside down, and dumped its contents on the table. He saw the startled look on our faces. "I know—you think I'm nuts. My roommate thought the same thing when I did this in our apartment the night before last. It's a little trick of mine. I'm on a case, I can't figure out what to do, so instead of looking through the file again the way I usually do, I just empty it out and kind of wade through it in whatever order comes to me. Nuts, huh?"

Veronica shrugged. "Whatever works."

"Anyways, my roommate says, 'What the hell are you doing?' So I say, 'It doesn't make sense when I look at it forwards, so I'm looking at it backwards.' And that's when it hit me. I started wondering if it's been backwards all along? Do you see what I'm saying?"

Veronica and I looked at one another, then back at Jonas. We shook our heads.

He said, "All along we've been looking at this as a break-in that turned into a murder. But what if we have it backwards? What if it was a murder that led to a break-in?" He paused, waiting for a reaction that didn't come. "Yeah, all right—I'm not explaining this real well, am I?"

He gathered the jumbled papers into a neat pile. "The killer broke into four houses on four consecutive Thursday nights. Yours was the only house where someone was home. Everyone figures he just slipped up that time. But suppose it wasn't a slipup? Suppose he knew someone was home? Where does that lead us?"

Veronica sipped her coffee. "Go on."

"He wore a ski mask. That's what you told Charlie and his partner. The only reason for wearing it was to keep his face hidden, which suggests he knew someone was home."

I said, "It was cold that night. Cold enough to snow. Cold enough for a ski mask."

"Yeah, but that's not why he wore it. I'll prove that to you in a few minutes. Hang on to that thought. For now, just take my word that he wore it to avoid being seen. Now, that doesn't necessarily mean he knew someone was in the house. We don't know that he didn't wear one at the other houses where no one was home. But still, it gives us something to think about, and it fits with a couple of other things."

Veronica said, "Such as?"

"The phone."

"What about it?"

"The police found the kitchen phone off the hook. It's doubtful the killer did it as he was running out of the house. More likely did it as he was walking from the basement to the bed-room. The only reason to do that is to keep someone from using an extension—like the bedroom phone—to dial out for help. Again, it doesn't prove he knew someone was home. And even if we assume he knew someone was home, it doesn't prove he planned to murder someone. But it's something to think about."

Veronica said, "He probably took the phone off the hook in the other houses, too."

"Well, you know, I thought of that. None of the other case files mentioned it. I called Mrs. Tinsley and asked her if she remembered if her phone was off the hook. She couldn't remember and didn't want to talk with me. But just that day I had tracked down the occupant of the second house, the one where that Asian couple lives. He lives in Arizona now. The man said he was sure the first thing he did when he discovered the burglary was go to the kitchen to call the police. He said he thought he would have remembered it if the phone had been off the hook, and he didn't think it was."

Veronica said, "The burglar had time to put the phones back on their hooks in the other houses."

"Sure. But why would he bother?"

"Maybe he's neat."

Jonas shrugged. "Well, anyways—it still gives us something to think about."

I said, "Jonas, I'm sure Veronica appreciates all the effort and thought you're putting into this case. And I don't want to sound impatient. But this has been a difficult week for both of us, and none of what you're telling us sounds very substantial."

Jonas sighed. He gathered all the items, except for two, and placed them back into the case file. He turned the items to face us. The first was an exterior shot of Veronica's house, showing the broken basement window in the rear of the house where the killer entered.

The second item was a photograph of the muddy footprint that was found on top of the basement dryer. The killer apparently had lowered himself from the window to the dryer when he broke into the basement.

Jonas said, "There's something wrong with this footprint. I didn't realize it when I first looked at it. But I realize it now, because I remember that night real well. I didn't remember it when I met you a week ago. I didn't realize then that your mother was killed on the same night I met Charlie Amory for the first time."

Veronica said, "He told us about that. He said you were fifteen."

"I was. And I know he told you. He mentioned it to me a few days ago. He wanted me to know, in case it came up in conversation with you. I never knew until he told me that there was a link between me and your mother."

"The Santa Claus outside of Filene's."

"That's right," he replied. "I was with Nicky Gibson. He was a wild kid, always getting in some kind of trouble. That fall we used to walk around town and shoplift. Once, a week or two before the night we're talking about, he grabbed a lady's handbag and we both ran like hell. He always initiated things, but I wasn't exactly innocent. You could say I fell in with bad company, except it isn't right to blame things on the company when it's you who are doing it." He paused. "Anyways, Veronica—for you and me that night changed both of our lives forever. You lost your mother. But if it wasn't for her, the police wouldn't have been called when they were, and Charlie Amory wouldn't have caught me when he did. And I would have kept hanging out with Nicky Gibson, instead of being scared into stopping it, which is what I did after that night. I started spending time with Charlie instead of Nicky, and one thing led to another, and this is where we find ourselves."

I said, "What happened to your friend?"

"He found other kids to get in trouble with. And trouble is what he got. He never straightened out. Right now he's at Walpole, doing seven-to-ten for a string of armed robberies in Newton. And that was a plea bargain. He stood to face twenty years if they took it to trial."

Veronica said, "You never would have gone that far, even if Charlie hadn't stopped you."

"I'd like to think that. But things can happen." He addressed me. "Like your situation, in today's newspaper. The kid who turned in his friend. He left home with a can of spray paint, and look at the pile of shit he wound up standing in. I don't know the same kind of thing wouldn't have happened to me. You see what I'm saying?"

"Yes," Veronica said. "I understand what you mean."

He looked at the photographs for a second. "When Nicky and I went out just after dark, there was no snow on the ground. It started to drizzle. It was still drizzling when we grabbed the money from the Salvation Army pot and Nicky knocked Santa Claus over. Which he didn't mean to do, by the way. Anyways, that happened at about five-thirty. Charlie caught me a short while later, and then he let me go, and then I walked home. I remember the rain turned over to snow before I got home, which was probably around six-thirty. Your mother died at around ten-thirty, right after the snow stopped."

I was getting ready to ask him what the point of all of this was. Just then he pushed the photo of the house exterior closer to our side of the table. He said, "This was probably taken within a half hour of the murder. What do you see?"

Veronica studied the picture without speaking.

I said, "Snow. A spigot for a hose, with no hose, of course, in the middle of December. And the broken window."

Veronica continued to look at the picture, saying nothing. Jonas said, "You see something else there, don't you, Veronica? Or maybe I should say, you see something that *isn't* there."

She looked at Jonas and nodded, then turned to me. "Footprints." She pointed to the snow near the broken window.

I said, "What footprints? *I* don't see any footprints."

She said, "No. Neither do I. That's his point. Isn't it, Jonas?"

"Exactly. If he broke in for a burglary late at night, after the snow stopped, why didn't he leave footprints in the snow outside the window?"

He pointed at the second photograph. "*This* is the footprint he left. On the dryer in the basement. In mud. Mud from the rain that turned over to snow no later than six-thirty. The killer broke in when there wasn't enough snow to cover the mud. And he was still there at ten-thirty. The way I figure it, he had to be inside your house a minimum of two hours. And since you or your mother probably would have heard him if he broke in while you were there, my guess is he was already in the house when you arrived."

Veronica shuddered: an impulsive, involuntary response to the image of her mother's killer biding his time, silently invading their space while they were in the house that evening.

Jonas said, "So you see, Harry. The ski mask was to avoid being recognized. He wouldn't still be wearing it to protect himself from the cold if he had been inside the house for several hours already."

I said, "Why bother to disguise yourself if you're planning to kill the victim?"

He shrugged. "Maybe he wasn't sure he'd be successful. Or maybe he wasn't sure he would have the nerve to go through with it. There's no way of knowing. All I know is, he probably took the ski mask off while he was waiting all that time in the house, then put it back on before he entered the bedroom."

I said, "This doesn't make any sense. Why would he wait until someone came home, if he was there to burglarize the house?"

"This is what I was trying to say at the beginning. Maybe we've always had it backwards. Maybe instead of a burglary that turned accidentally into a murder, maybe it was a murder that was made to look like a burglary."

"Are you saying he went there with the intention of killing Veronica's mother?"

"I'm saying I want to consider that possibility."

"But he only did burglaries at the other houses. Why would he suddenly turn from burglary to murder?"

Jonas looked at Veronica, trying to gauge from her expression whether she understood the point he was driving at.

Veronica turned to me. "Jonas is saying the other burglaries were committed for the sole purpose of disguising the murder. He thinks they were a setup, a prelude to his real business."

"Which means," said Jonas, "he planned it for at least three weeks, the time interval between the first break-in and the murder. It means he dropped the linen napkins to make it easy for us to link all of them together. The police assumed he was a stupid burglar who stopped what he was doing after December twentieth because he didn't want to risk getting arrested for murder. I'm saying maybe he was very smart, and stopped what he was doing because he accomplished what he set out to do."

I thought about all of this for several seconds. Finally I said, "I don't think I can buy that. It's just too farfetched."

Jonas replied, "Maybe. But I can't come up with any other explanation for why he waited for someone to come home that night if all he really wanted to do was burglarize the place. If I'm right, he went there with the intention of killing Rachel. If I'm right, he broke in while she was out of the house, then waited until both she and her daughter were asleep to catch her off guard."

I looked at the two photographs and tried to weigh the sense of what Jonas was hypothesizing. "If you're right," I said, "then we're more lost than ever."

He smiled. "No. If I'm right, then for the first time since we started, we actually have some small chance of finding what we're looking for."

"How do you figure that?"

"Because now we have a new angle to follow up on—one that was never pursued before. Now we have a question that someone may be able to answer." He looked at Veronica. "Let's start with you. Do you have any idea who might have wanted your mother dead?"

23: Seven-fourths Time

Veronica was only nine years old when her mother was murdered and so, of course, she had no useful information to give Jonas about any enemies Rachel may have had.

He said, "The first detective on the case, Joe Branson, settled pretty fast on the notion that the murder was just a random break-in gone bad. So there wasn't any investigation into your mother's situation, possible enemies, stuff like that."

Veronica said, "It's probably much too late for that now."

"Maybe. But I don't know what else to do. Meanwhile, I think it's fair to characterize the telephone calls as harassment, even though he didn't make any explicit threat. I'm going to call the Concord police and tell them what's going on, ask them to put a watch on your house for the next few days. Any objection?"

I said, "No, of course not."

"Veronica?"

She was quiet for a few seconds, then said, "Do what you think you need to do."

"I'm also going to ask them to arrange for taps on your telephone lines. If he calls again, we may be able to trace it."

As we were getting ready to leave, Jonas asked Veronica for her father's office number. He wanted to talk with Donald about Rachel, and to see if Donald knew of anyone who might have intended harm toward his late wife.

On our way home I said, "You seemed reluctant when Jonas talked about calling the Concord police."

"After my mother died, my father paid for round-the-clock protection for me. He was worried the killer might think I could identify him and might come after me. Bodyguards followed me to school and everywhere else. Friends stopped inviting me to their homes because the whole thing made people uncomfortable. Finally my Aunt Marilyn persuaded my father to drop the matter." She paused for several seconds, then said, "Whoever he is, he made me a prisoner once before. I don't want to go through it again."

A Concord police cruiser was already parked outside my house when we arrived. Veronica went inside the house. I walked over to the cruiser. The officer rolled down her window and said, "Chief wants you to call him if you don't want me to stay. Big place here. I count four entrances."

"One of them is a separate entrance to my office."

"Which one?"

"The south side."

"Where the graffiti is?"

"Yes, that one." I pointed to the barn and told her that Veronica lived there. "Are you cold?"

"Well, you know, 'neither sleet nor hail,' or something like that."

I thought, *That's for mailmen.* I said, "You can sit inside if you want to."

Veronica appeared surprised and uncomfortable when I brought the police officer into the kitchen. She took me into the den to speak privately with me. "Harry, this is just too much for me. I want to stay somewhere else for the weekend. The three of us can go to my father's house. I'm sure he and Shana won't mind. We can help them prepare for the Super Bowl party the day after tomorrow."

I shook my head. "I'm meeting with Marilyn this afternoon. And someone is coming to cover the graffiti in the morning. I'd just as soon stay here."

"Will you be angry with me if I go?"

"No, of course not. Maybe Melissa and I can join you to-morrow night."

She hesitated. "I want to take Melissa with me. She . . . she doesn't need to live like this." Veronica gestured toward the kitchen where the police officer waited.

"Well, sure, I guess."

She stood there silently for a moment, and then said, "You know, Harry, it gets wearisome always having to ask you for permission when I want to do something with Melissa."

"She's *my* daughter." I was surprised by my own stridency. "I'm sorry. I didn't mean it to sound like that."

"No, you're right. She is your daughter. And she's Janet's daughter. And I'm just a, a . . . I don't know what I am. And I know I have no right. But sometimes I just . . ." Her voice trailed off.

"What?"

"I don't know." She sighed. "Last year when you and I were separated, and yet you still let me see Melissa and spend time with her, you can't possibly know how much that meant to me. I think that's why I decided to come back to you."

"You came back to me because of Melissa?"

"No, that isn't what I mean. I came back because the man who would let that happen—who would let his daughter go off with me like that—I knew that man must really love his daugh-ter. And he must really love me."

"Well, of course I—"

She placed a finger to my lips. "Let me finish." Her voice began to quaver ever so slightly. "Lately, when I talk about Melissa with you, whenever I try to become more involved in her life, you get this look on your face, like you've moved someplace else in your mind. And I don't know how to deal with it. I know you still love Janet. I'm not trying to take her place with you. I'm not trying to take her place with Melissa. I'm just . . . I'm just trying to have my own place—with her, and with you."

"Well, *you're* the one who refuses to move in with us. *You're* the one who insists on playing it safe by staying in the barn."

"If I'm playing it safe, then how come I feel so frightened?"

She sighed. "Let's not fight over who's more committed to whom. When this is over, I promise we'll talk about it."

And I wondered: *Will this ever be over?*

Frank Cirone called around noon. His comment about my situation, which he had just read about in the Boston papers, was short and to the point. "A man shouldn't be attacked at his home. In my world, that is something we understand."

Regarding the previous day's *Globe* story about Veronica, he said, "I assume her investigation led nowhere. The article seemed like a final resort. Trying to catch water. And I'm sorry I have nothing for you, either. I asked questions. Talked to people. But it was a long time ago. And probably not done by someone who would come to the attention of my acquaintances. The police were probably right. A kid with no experience at such things fucks up one night. Maybe gets so scared he never so much as jaywalks again."

"Perhaps," I said. "More than perhaps. Probable. But the Wellesley detective who has been helping Veronica thinks it may have been an intentional premeditated murder."

I told him about the phone call Veronica received from the man she presumed to be the killer. And I recounted Jonas's tentative theory and the evidence for it, such as it was. "I told the detective that I thought it sounded farfetched."

"Indeed." He paused. "But I can tell you one thing. You and Veronica should have protection. Because if the detective is right, then that phone call to Veronica means the killer is worried about being smoked out. Which would make him dangerous."

"The police are watching my house. One of them is walking around outside right now."

"Concord police," Frank Cirone said, chuckling. "When do you think is the last time a Concord cop unholstered his gun, let alone used it?"

"Well, in this particular case, it would be *her* gun."

"You have a *woman* guarding you? Oh, brother. Or maybe I should say 'sister.' "

"I take it you're not an equal-opportunity employer."

He began to laugh. "Equal-opportunity employer. I'm gonna try to remember that one." He stopped laughing. "I'm serious about the protection. You could hire someone. I can give you names."

"I think we're all right. Like I said, I think it's an unlikely scenario. Anyway, when my daughter gets home from school, she and Veronica are going to Wellesley to spend the weekend with Veronica's father."

"And you?"

"I'm staying here tonight. I'll try to join them tomorrow. And then on Sunday her father is having his annual Super Bowl party."

"Who do you like in the game?"

"Well, I know the Cowboys are favored, but I think it would defy the law of averages to expect the Bills to lose for the fourth consecutive year."

"So you think Buffalo will at least cover the spread, which as of today is eight and a half points. Interesting."

"Well, I wouldn't want you to make any business decisions based on my thinking."

He paused for a moment. "Listen—I know this is unusual, but when you come to Wellesley tomorrow, you can stop by my house for an early dinner. Angie is visiting her sister in East Boston. Been gone all week. I hate halving recipes when I cook. I can make some pasta, and we can watch a movie before you go. I have a good setup for that."

"I'll give you a call."

"Do that," he said. "And lock your doors and windows, make sure the police stay awake, and try to keep your name out of the papers tomorrow."

Marilyn said, "I'm sorry I missed Veronica and your daughter. I thought the four of us could go slumming for the rest of the afternoon."

"You're the only person I know who goes slumming in a chinchilla coat."

"Warmth, Harry. Warmth. But tell me—how many rayons had to die to make your coat?"

"I'll drive this time," I said, directing her to my car.

"A Toyota," she said, smiling. "My, now we *are* slumming."

I headed into the center of town. I said, "Are you coming to Donald's Super Bowl party?"

"I don't do large crowds anymore, Harry. Too many eyes. Too many mouths."

I drove past the town square and headed east on Lexington Road. And as I drove, Marilyn Levine talked about the metamorphosis: the change from Mara Lee to M. L. Nightingale.

After that first suicide attempt in the Chelsea Hotel, she couldn't get back on an even keel. Her mood swings were severe and disabling. Her music career eventually washed away.

This was before the widespread use of lithium carbonate for the treatment of manic-depressive illness. So when she was depressed they plied her with antidepressant medication, which as often as not just shot her into a manic episode. And when she was manic they pumped her full of antipsychotic medication, which calmed her to the point of somnolence, and which eventually made her depressed. And so the cycle went.

By 1967, there had been three more suicide attempts and five psychiatric hospitalizations. From a friend of a friend of a friend, she learned about an ashram in India. "I thought it might help me. I knew I needed *something* to help me. They practiced Quan Yin."

"Who what?"

"Quan Yin. It's a meditation technique that some people believe can connect you directly to God. And something truly amazing happened to me there. Something that turned everything around, changed my life forever. I was meditating one day underneath a canopy. The canopy was covered with a lovely print fabric. And as I meditated and gazed at the beautiful cloth—meditated and gazed, meditated and gazed—I had what turned out to be the most important realization I have ever had. And do you know what that realization was?"

"No," I replied. "But I'd like to."

"I looked at that print fabric and I realized—my *God*, I can make a *fortune* selling this back home."

And so she did. With some capital outlay from her father,

who had made his own fortune in the garment industry, Marilyn opened a fabric import shop in Harvard Square, which led to one in New York, and then another in Haight-Ashbury. Whereas music—her first love—had sent her into an introspective tailspin, her burgeoning business career provided the structure and focus she needed to remain steady.

She discovered that she had a natural merchandising genius and a true entrepreneurial spirit. One thing led to another, and in 1969 she turned her attention to a small and floundering casual-wear company in Connecticut that was about to go belly-up. She bought it and christened it M. L. Nightingale.

"That's where Donny comes in," she told me. "I'm smart enough to know when I'm in over my head. I needed a business attorney, but I didn't know who I could trust. I trusted Rachel more than anyone I ever knew, so I figured—why not ask her husband to help me?"

We crossed the town line into Lincoln, I turned right onto Bedford Road, and Marilyn gave me a whiz-bang summary of the things Donald did that within two years made her a wealthy woman in her own right: He counseled her regarding capitalization and helped secure it; minimized her tax exposure by choosing the best corporate structure and plan; and drew up and administered contracts with suppliers, distributors, printers, unions, and plant owners.

"Donny and I developed a special bond. I called it professional intimacy. I tried to get him to leave his firm and join me full-time. I offered him twice what he could ever expect to make at that firm, even as a senior partner. He could have been my in-house counsel. Or he could have been the president of the company, with me as chairwoman of the board. We could have done it any way he wanted, but what he wanted was to stay where he was and practice law the way he had been practicing it. And I think he was a little wary of putting all of his eggs in one basket, especially when the basket had a reputation for being a little, shall we say, unsturdy."

The mood swings, which had never completely abated, began to regain strength in 1971. The same energy and focus that helped her build the company now prevented her from delegating authority and relinquishing areas of control when it would have been prudent to do so. She was always running, running, running: spending small fortunes on impromptu shopping trips in Europe, jumping in and out of highly sexualized relationships with men who were long on body parts and short on substance.

There was an overdose of over-the-counter sleeping pills in early 1972. No one, including Marilyn, could tell whether it was entirely accidental.

"I was very difficult to deal with then. Things went sour between Donny and me. I think we both needed breathing space. In June of seventy-two he asked Oliver Gray to take over his role. Oliver was a good lawyer, but I was personally uncomfortable with him. He knew about the job offer I had made to Donny, and he was constantly hinting that he would be happy to accept such an offer, and he became quite irritating in that regard."

About two miles down Bedford Road, I turned onto Sandy Pond Road and headed toward the DeCordova Museum. I said, "So you left Oliver and went back to Donald."

"I tried, but it wasn't that simple. Donny was reluctant. Finally, sometime in October I wore him down a little bit. He told me he was very busy, but he said he would reconsider things after Christmas."

"Did you tell Oliver?"

"Yes. He didn't try to argue me out of switching back. There would be no justification for him to do that. It did put a strain on our working relationship, but at least he stopped asking me about becoming my in-house counsel. Say, this is lovely. Where are we?"

"This is the DeCordova Museum," I said as I turned off Sandy Pond Road. The museum, once a private mansion, sat on top of a hill that overlooked Sandy Pond. The grounds were dotted with modernistic sculptures and mobiles. I drove up the narrow one-way road to the parking lot at the hill's crest. We stepped outside and looked at the vista: the pond below us, the hillside still covered in the previous night's white coating, the sun setting over the ridge on the other side of the pond. All was still and quiet.

She said, "Rachel's murder that December changed everything. Donny took over my legal matters again a short while later. I think he did it mostly to help keep himself busy. That was his way of dealing with his grief. But I think he also did it because he knew how devastated I was, and because he wanted to help me." She sighed deeply. "The rest, as they say, is history. I've been successful beyond my wildest expectations. I don't love it the way I loved making music, but it does satisfy me and it keeps me focused. And Donny has always looked out for my better interests, even when I didn't realize what those interests were. I guess that's why I'm here with you today, Harry."

"What do you mean?"

"He wants me to find a new psychiatrist because the old one retired. He wants you to talk me into it. I guess I came to see you Wednesday, and again today, because I've learned over the years that Donny always has my best interests in mind."

We returned to the car and followed the roadway around the museum and back down the hill. Marilyn became excited by something she saw at the base of the hill. "Harry, stop the car. I want to play that."

It was a twenty-foot-long sculpture: an array of metal rods, lined up in a row and pointing toward the sky. They were of varying lengths, randomly placed in relationship to one another. It looked like a huge xylophone set on its side, with the individual plates rearranged in no particular order.

I parked the car on the side of the road. When we reached the sculpture we found two long sticks leaning against it. Marilyn grabbed them and struck one of the metal rods. A musical tone resonated. She smiled and said, "They're like giant tuning forks."

I stepped aside and watched her work. She seemed to know instinctively which rods to strike with the sticks, in a sequence that created an eerie but tuneful conglomeration of sounds running in and out against one another. The rhythm was odd but regular, alien but engaging. She closed her eyes and swayed to the tones of the vibrating rods. In a foreign tongue she began to chant something in her rich alto voice. The tones and the words built to a crescendo, then faded slowly, until all was silent.

She opened her eyes and placed the sticks where she had found them.

I said, "That was beautiful. What was it?"

She shrugged. "I don't know. I just made it up."

"You're *kidding* me."

"No." She looked away, avoiding my incredulous stare. "It's not that big a deal."

"What do the words mean?"

She smiled. "I don't know. They were just sounds I recall from my time in India. I don't even know if I was making real words."

"Well, it really was beautiful. The rhythm was unusual. Mesmerizing."

"It was seven-fourths time. Some people find it jarring. Almost nothing written in our culture utilizes it. But I've always liked it. It alternates between three-fourths time—like a waltz—and the standard four-fourths. One after the other, measure by measure. You start out in one direction and you come back in another. Just like my life, you might say."

She reached out with her hand to caress the base of the sculpture.

"Will you play another one for me?"

"I can't, Harry. I don't want to get started down that slope. Playing takes me into the ether. And once I reach the ether, I risk dropping into the abyss. A black void that feels painful and infinite. I can't take that risk. And that's why I gave up writing music, and then gave up playing it. I gave up my dream so that I could continue to have a life."

"It doesn't have to be that way," I said. "You're worried about the depression side of your illness. If you're on the right medications to stabilize your moods, and if you're under the care of someone who knows how to monitor them, there's no reason you can't have your life and your dream at the same time."

She thought about that for a long time. Then she looked at me and said, "I don't suppose you can be my doctor, can you?"

"No, I can't. You're a close friend of Veronica and Donald. And I think you and I are going to be friends, too."

She smiled. "But I suppose you have a list of names for me to consider."

I smiled, too. "I suppose I do."

That evening I telephoned Veronica at her father's house. "Korvich is being pretty good about this," I said. "First Bonnie, and now this other fellow."

"Bonnie?"

"The first police officer, the one who was here when you and I got back this morning from Wellesley. She left at around the same time your Aunt Marilyn left, when this fellow arrived."

"So you and Bonnie are on a first-name basis," Veronica said, laughing. "No wonder you didn't object when I left for my father's house. But, seriously—are they going to keep an officer there all night?"

"That's the plan."

"Well, I'm glad. I really don't think anything is going to happen. But even so, I'm a little nervous. I had myself half-convinced that I was being followed here this afternoon. If this keeps up, I'm liable to think there are listening devices in my underwear."

"I'd pay good money for a set of those surveillance tapes."

"You're impossible." She laughed again. "I'm glad you like my Aunt Marilyn."

"I like her a lot."

"I miss you. I don't mind it when you sleep in the house and I sleep in the barn, because I know you're nearby. But this is the second time in three nights that I've stayed in Wellesley while you stayed in Concord. I don't like it when the connection is broken like that."

"I'll come out tomorrow night. I've got the graffiti to take care of in the morning, and I'm having an early dinner with a friend whose wife is out of town."

"Anyone I know?"

"No, you've never met him." That was true; Veronica hadn't met Frank Cirone. She probably wouldn't like the idea of me visiting him again, and I didn't see any reason to trouble her.

She said, "Melissa is having a grand old time. She's calling it her Super Bowl weekend adventure. She and Shana are in their bathrobes already, sitting in front of the television and eating popcorn. Shana's having a good time, too. I seldom let her do those sorts of things with me when I was a girl." She paused. "Melissa is much nicer to me than I was to my stepmother."

"Well, it's a different situation. You shouldn't be too hard on yourself for that."

"I could have done better. I could have been nicer."

"It's never too late, my love."

She was quiet for a moment, and then she said, "You've never called me that before. 'My love.' I guess we haven't been very big on terms of endearment."

"No, I guess we haven't."

"Well, maybe we should."

"Maybe."

"Well, good night."

"Yes. Good night."

Janet and I had several terms of endearment between us, some of which would never be revealed to another living soul. But as Veronica noted, she and I traveled light in that area.

As I walked around the house before retiring I realized that I missed both of them, Janet and Veronica: each in her own way. I missed them both, and I loved them both.

I no longer worried about my wife. But I was worried as hell about Veronica.

I had no idea what to expect next.

24: Quarry

As my daughter had predicted, the tarpaulin that covered the graffiti was, indeed, quite ugly. But I was glad to be rid of the visual reminder of the events of Wednesday night.

The police officer assigned to my house Saturday morning was about my age, a gregarious fellow with a take-charge personality. Unbidden, he supervised the hanging of the tarpaulin, insisting on a degree of perfection that few aspire to or attain.

Afterward I made a late-breakfast batch of pancakes for the officer and me. I learned that he, like Charlie Amory, was already a grandfather. I wondered what it was that had impelled them to begin families at such young ages. I wondered if police officers had a fatalistic attitude because of the inherent danger in their work—a belief that life could end at any time, and that they should therefore put branches on the family tree while they still had the chance.

Maybe they were simply too shortsighted or too macho to pay attention to birth control.

I spent the afternoon paying bills and catching up on my monthly professional journals. Then I packed an overnight bag and headed for Wellesley once more.

It was four o'clock when I pulled out of my driveway. I stopped at the liquor store in the center of town and bought some wine for dinner at Frank Cirone's house. A young man with a blond crew cut was ahead of me in line. He gave the clerk a hundred-dollar bill for a twelve-dollar purchase. The clerk made change without so much as a raised eyebrow.

When I returned to my car, a double-parked black SAAB was blocking me in. The driver backed up to give me room.

I stopped at the library to return a book. Then I drove a few blocks to the dry cleaner to drop off a suit. It was about four-fifteen when I headed down Thoreau Street, across Route 2, and past Walden Pond and the Lincoln town line. I cut over to Conant Road and headed south.

I was listening to a tape of *Hard Nose the Highway*, a Van Morrison album from the seventies that had a desolate, wintry feel. I wondered what it was like to write music, and I thought about watching Marilyn Levine the day before at the DeCordova Museum.

I entered Weston, a town of even greater privilege and wealth than Concord or Wellesley. I crossed Route 117 and then the commuter-line railroad track, and continued down Conant Road. I passed the estate of a prominent neurosurgeon; I had gone there once for a party. The stucco mansion loomed at the apex of a semicircular driveway, but I could barely see it through the bank of evergreens and shrubs that lined the property.

A minute later I saw a black car in my rearview mirror. I thought nothing of it at first. But as it kept pace with me for the next mile, the suspicion dawned on me that perhaps I was being followed. It wasn't close enough for me to see what the driver looked like.

The black car stayed with me, albeit a respectable and unobtrusive distance behind, as I made my way through the town. When I reached the stop sign near the center of Weston, I departed from my planned route. Instead of continuing straight through the intersection, I made a sharp right turn without signaling; the black car followed suit.

I turned off the tape deck. My autonomic nervous system kicked into overdrive: racing heart, flushed skin, perspiration pouring out of me. I thought of my daughter as an orphan. I heard the rush of blood pumping through me.

Call the police, I thought. I reached onto my dashboard for my cellular phone; I realized it was still sitting in its charger in my kitchen. *Damn.*

I surveyed the scene. I was heading toward a row of shops. I could pull over, call the police, and sit in a crowded place where the lack of privacy would protect me from harm.

Or would it? I thought about Frank Cirone's father, calmly gunned down in broad daylight in front of numerous witnesses. And if I did stop, perhaps my pursuer would just wait for another opportunity to catch up with me. At least now I knew where he was. What I needed was some way of figuring out who he was.

I thought of the neurosurgeon's estate on Conant Road, back in the direction from which I had just driven. I made a series of turns that set me northward on that road, heading back toward Lincoln.

The driver of the black car let a little more distance fall between us, and another car filled the gap. I had no doubt now that the driver of the black car was tracking me.

I was about a quarter mile south of the place I was looking for. The car directly behind me turned off of Conant Road. The black car crept a bit closer.

The road curved sharply to the left, momentarily taking me out of my pursuer's view. Almost immediately an entrance to the neurosurgeon's estate came up on my right. I turned off the road and onto the private semicircular drive. I knew that it curved back toward a second connection to Conant Road.

I continued along the driveway. Through the trees I saw the black car continue on Conant Road, parallel to my position on the driveway. He had lost track of me for a moment, and he picked up a little speed to try to find me farther down the curving country road.

At the end of the semicircle I reentered Conant Road. My detour onto the driveway, combined with the speed he picked up, now placed me thirty yards behind the car.

I crept forward slightly to get a better look. It was definitely a SAAB. The six-digit license-plate number came into focus, and I said it out loud several times, trying to burn it into my memory.

It took him less than a minute to realize I was behind him. He hit his accelerator and sped north on the narrow, serpentine two-lane road.

Like a predator impelled forward by the flight of his prey, I automatically picked up speed and set out after him. The tables had turned: The hunted was now the hunter. The pursuer had become the quarry.

The winding road wasn't safe for passing. Nevertheless he wheeled to the left to pass a car in front of him. I followed him; I reasoned that he would be the one to collide with any oncoming traffic. But there was no traffic in the southbound lane, and we both made the pass safely.

He was about a hundred yards ahead of me. He was fast approaching the commuter-train track. The crossing-signal gates were down, signaling the impending passing of a train, blocking the road. Two cars were lined up waiting for the train to pass and the gates to rise.

The black car slowed as if to stop. Suddenly the driver veered left and sped around the waiting cars. He zigzagged around the gates and crossed the track. I reached the track in time to see him accelerate on the other side. The commuter train passed from left to right, heading toward Boston. When it completed its run past me and the crossing-signal gates lifted, the black car was gone from view.

I headed for the nearest gas station to use its pay phone. I dialed the Wellesley Police Department. It was a late Saturday afternoon, and neither Jonas Cavaleri nor Charlie Amory was immediately available. I explained the situation to the dispatcher: that I had been followed by someone who was likely the murderer in an open Wellesley homicide investigation. I described the car and gave her the black SAAB's license-plate number. With some reluctance—I guess my story sounded a little preposterous—she said she would alert the Weston and Lincoln police departments to be on the lookout for the vehicle.

I asked her to tell either Jonas or Charlie to call me at my home number, which they already knew. I didn't want to confuse things by giving her Donald's phone number to pass along to them; I figured I would retrieve messages from my answering machine later that evening.

I had lost sight of the SAAB five minutes earlier, and I knew chances were slim that anyone would track him down on the road. But Frank Cirone had been able to identify me from my car license plate; I had every confidence that sometime that night or the next morning Jonas or Charlie would use the plate to identify the person who had stalked me that afternoon.

I passed through Weston and continued into Wellesley. Dusk arrived, and at a few minutes after five I parked outside the Rutgers Street house where Rachel Pace had met her end—no doubt at the hands of the man who had just eluded me.

25: The Shortest Distance

"My Angie, she went to her sister's house on Sunday, the day after you and Veronica came here. She slept Saturday night on the sofa. Said she couldn't sleep in the bedroom, knowing what happened in there."

"And that's why she's still at her sister's place?"

Frank Cirone shrugged. "Mostly that. Also on account of the hard time I gave you when I got home that day. 'They're my guests,' she says to me after you left. 'I invited them in. You want to hit somebody, hit me.' Except she knows I'd never do that. Her brother would kill me." I couldn't tell whether he was being serious. He said, "Relax. It's just a figure of speech."

He led me into the kitchen. As he prepared our dinner I described what had transpired with the black SAAB. I said, "I'm hoping we get to the end of this when the police check out the owner of the car."

"Yeah, well, something tells me you shouldn't hold your breath on that one. If a killer was following you, he could have stolen a car or switched plates. Or you might have gotten the number wrong. Good chance of that, I would think."

Dinner was shrimp and linguine in a garlic-and-pepper marinade. "This is really delicious, Frank."

"You sure you don't want some of your wine?"

"No, I'm fine, really. I brought the wine for you. Just water for me."

"Are you what they call 'recovering'?"

I laughed. "No. I just never developed a taste for drinking. My parents never drank."

He took our plates and walked to the stovetop, where the pasta sat warming in a pot on a very low flame. He scooped second helpings for both of us and returned to the table. He said, "So, anyway—Angie and me, we get into this big argument, me saying she was stupid for letting strangers *in* the house, her saying I'm rude for kicking strangers *out* of the house. And I don't know if you were ever married, or what it's like with you and Veronica, but I'll tell you—if I had a nickel for every time I win one of these arguments with Angie, I'd still be waiting on my first nickel."

He poured more wine for himself. "So finally I say, 'Angie—what the hell do I gotta do to shut you up?' And she says, 'Help the girl find out who killed her mother.' " He paused. "So you see, my offer to help out had some self-interest in it."

"It was appreciated nevertheless."

"I wish I could've found something out, but it was a long shot from the start. Anyway, Angie's coming home tomorrow. If she still can't handle sleeping in that room, we can change to another room. If that doesn't work, she'll probably make me sell the fucking house."

I remembered that the house was listed as being owned by someone else. Yet Frank Cirone clearly viewed it as being his. It was none of my business. I decided not to ask him about it.

He sipped his wine. "So, have you ever been married?"

"Yes. My wife died almost seven years ago."

"Huh. Rough. Kids?"

"One daughter. She's eleven."

"Are you gonna marry Veronica?"

"I don't know. Sometimes we seem to be heading down that road, but I don't know if we'll ever get there."

He grabbed the wine bottle and his glass, and we left the kitchen and headed toward the den. As we passed the stairwell in the front foyer, I stopped and gazed up to the second floor. I could see the open door to the master bedroom.

I said, "I'm usually not inclined to think that things or places can give off energy. But standing here and thinking about what happened in that room twenty-one years ago makes me feel angry, and very, very sad. It's as if the energy from the event is still percolating in the atmosphere."

"Christ, you're starting to sound like my wife."

"Veronica once told me about a play she read in junior high school. A Greek tragedy. A murder victim's spirit was condemned to wander in limbo until the killer was brought to justice. If Rachel Pace's spirit is wandering somewhere, then this may be the place."

In the den he directed me to a stack of videocassettes next to a projection-screen television. "I rented a bunch for the weekend. Some old classics, some newer movies. See if one appeals to you. We can watch a movie and you'll still be at Veronica's father's house by eight-thirty or nine."

My eye was drawn immediately to a cassette box with a picture of a young Warren Beatty and a young Faye Dunaway. I picked it up and said, "I was only sixteen when this movie came out. My parents didn't want me to see it because of the violence. I saw it anyway, and it scared the hell out of me. I had nightmares for a week. When I couldn't keep it to myself any longer, I told my parents what I had done and I said I wished I had listened to them. It turned into one of those ridiculous situations. 'We're really proud of you for telling us the truth, and by the way—you're grounded for a month.' "

"Did you ever see it again?"

"No."

He smiled. "It's one of my favorites." He popped the cassette into his VCR, and for the next hour and forty-five minutes we watched *Bonnie and Clyde*.

The irony wasn't lost on me: sitting with a reputed gangster, watching a classic film about crime. I had forgotten the jaunty humor that characterizes the first segment of the movie: Clyde robbing stores as a way of flirting with Bonnie, impressing her with his adventurism. But then Clyde kills a man who tries to prevent him from fleeing the scene of a robbery, and in that instant everything changes: for him, for Bonnie, and for the viewer. Because now there is no turning back.

The violence didn't trouble me during this second viewing. I guess I had become desensitized by later films, not to mention events in my own life. This time around I was more struck by the palpable sadness the movie engendered. I knew the end that lay ahead for Clyde and Bonnie. Waiting for it to unfold was like waiting to hit the ground after falling off a cliff: The closer the inevitable end came, the more distress I felt, and there was nothing that could be done to forestall it.

In the end their sidekick's father sets them up to be ambushed. Something happens right before they are riddled with bullets that I had always remembered, even though it lasts no more than a second, and even though I had only seen the movie once, more than twenty-six years earlier. I said, "This is my favorite part."

Seconds after I said that, Bonnie and Clyde went down in a hail of gunfire and the movie ended.

Frank Cirone said, "Your favorite part is watching them get blown away with machine guns?"

"No, no. Here—toss me the remote control."

I rewound the film to the moments just before the shots are fired. They stop their car to help their sidekick's father fix a flat tire on his truck. Clyde is standing outside the car. Bonnie is in the car with the door open.

I said, "The camera does a lot of quick-cutting here from one image to another. They show a close-up of Bonnie's face twice. Take a good look at the second time."

Quick-cut images, each one very brief: Another vehicle approaches slowly. Something rustles the bushes. Birds fly off in fright. The sidekick's father dives under his parked truck. Bonnie looks at Clyde, frightened: She understands what is happening. Clyde runs toward her.

The second and final close-up of Bonnie: Knowing she is about to die, she looks at Clyde with an expression of pure and total adoration.

And then they are butchered.

I said, "Did you see how she looked at him in that final moment?"

"Uh-huh. She really loved him."

"If someone were to look at me like that, I wouldn't be frightened of anything. In that last moment the love was what was most important."

I thought he probably didn't get my point. Then I realized I had no clear idea what my point was, or even if there was one. But there was something in that final moment between Bonnie and Clyde that had touched me once, and then endured in a corner of my mind.

Frank Cirone turned off the television and leaned back in his chair. "So what do you think, Harry? Can a limp pecker drive a man into a life of crime?" He was alluding to the problem with impotence that plagued Clyde.

"I don't know," I replied. "I don't know what drives a man into a life of crime."

He looked at me: a cold, emotionless stare that lasted no longer than that final close-up of Faye Dunaway. It froze me for a moment, and then the stare and the feeling passed.

He said, "I can tell you why people commit murder. It's really very simple. Sometimes it's out of emotion. Anger, revenge, jealousy, greed. And sometimes it's just business, the shortest distance between two points. Where you are, and where you want to be."

"Why do you think Bonnie and Clyde killed?"

He shrugged. "Business, I guess. They killed people who were in the way of that shortest distance."

"I think they killed because of the romance they felt."

"You think it's romantic to kill people? That's a new one on me."

"I don't mean the romance of killing. I mean the romance of being killers, together. Professional intimacy," I said, echoing the expression Marilyn used to describe her early relationship with Donald. "A connection they shared only with each other, that kept them bound together until they died."

"Yeah, well—you sure you weren't hitting that wine bottle

when I wasn't looking?" He yawned. "As far as Rachel Pace goes, the evidence won't lead you to the killer. You have to look at motivation. If your detective is right, then you're looking for someone who wanted her out of the picture. So now the question is, why? If you figure out the why, maybe that will lead you to the who."

He picked up the wine bottle. "My mouth is dry," he said. "I think I'll wet it with this." He poured wine into his glass. "What did your anonymous caller—the one you think is the murderer—what did he say about getting wet?" He lifted his glass to his lips.

"He told us not to make waves. He said people get wet when they make waves. He said that every time he called."

Frank Cirone paused, the glass not yet to his lips. "He called more than once?"

"Three nights in a row. Tuesday and Wednesday nights to my phone, last night to the phone number Veronica got and listed in the *Globe*."

He set his glass down without drinking from it. He grimaced, closed his eyes, and rubbed his forehead as if he were in pain. Then he leaned back in his chair and exhaled slowly. He smiled, then started to chuckle. His laughter built until the intensity made him begin to cough. When he was finished, he said, "Fucking unbelievable."

"What? What is it?"

"Your detective, what was his name?"

"Jonas Cavaleri," I replied.

"This Wellesley police detective, Jonas Cavaleri—you told him about all three phone calls?"

"Of course."

"That's what I figured. And that's why I'm laughing. I'm laughing because apparently I have moved to the town with the dumbest police department on earth." He paused. "You and Veronica are too involved with this to think clearly, so I can't really blame you. But there's no excuse for your detective missing the obvious."

"I don't get it. What did he miss?"

"When you told me about last night's call, I assumed the *Globe* article yesterday had flushed him out. But he called you twice before the article appeared. Now do you understand?"

It took several seconds to put the pieces together in my mind, and when I did, I couldn't believe I hadn't made the connection earlier. I said, "If he *is* the killer, then he knew Veronica was making waves as early as Tuesday, two days before she went public with the case."

"Exactly. Which narrows things down considerably. Ask yourself—who knew on Tuesday that Veronica was taking a new look into the matter of her mother's murder?"

I considered the question for several seconds. "There's Jonas, and there's Charlie Amory, the chief of police."

"No telling whether they mentioned it to anyone else. Go on."

"There's my best friend, Bobby. Maybe he mentioned it to his wife, maybe not. It wouldn't have gone any farther than that. And there's another friend, the pastor of the Catholic church in Concord."

"Now, *there's* your prime suspect. I'm kidding. Who else?"

"Veronica's father. I don't know about her stepmother."

"He's alibied up for the murder?"

"Yes."

"Keep going."

I thought for a moment. "Veronica's boss."

"Hmm. Interesting. I wonder if he mentioned it to anyone else. It wouldn't be the first time a murder was somehow related to an FBI action. Doesn't sound like that would be the case here."

"The current owners of the three other houses where the killer staged break-ins. We visited them before we came here last Saturday, so they know."

"That sounds like a good area to concentrate on," he said. "They no doubt told lots of people. Just like I'm sure Angie is telling half of East Boston right now."

He was right on that count, at least as far as Gertrude Tinsley was concerned. I wondered if there was anyone she knew whom she *hadn't* told.

I thought for a few seconds. "And, of course, there's you."

"Me?"

"And whoever you told when you were looking for information about the killing."

He considered that for a moment. "You know, you could probably make a case for me being the killer if I was the first person to buy the house from Veronica's family. Something like, killing her to get her out of the way, because I wanted the house and her husband wouldn't let me have it. So I kill her not because I have something against her, but because I want to influence what her husband does. I kill her and her husband decides he doesn't want to live here anymore, and I step in with an offer." He laughed. "Hey, the house ain't *that* great. And we didn't move in until twenty years after the murder."

"I know."

"As far as me talking to other people and word getting out that Veronica was looking into the case, that didn't happen. When I asked questions, I told people that an unsolved murder once occurred in the house. I told them I was interested in the case because it's my house now, but I never mentioned Veronica at all."

I glanced at my watch. "I need to head over to Veronica's father's house in a few minutes."

"You should think about all of this. Discuss it with Veronica. I'll think about it, too. If Veronica is right that it was the murderer who called her last night, then it's someone who knew what was happening at least since Tuesday. And if your detective is right about the murder being planned—and idiot that he is, we shouldn't jump too fast to that thought—if it was planned, then you have two angles. Try to figure who knew about Veronica's investigation before she went public, and who among those people may have wanted her mother out of the way twenty-one years ago."

He led me to the foyer and got my coat out of the closet. I glanced once more at the bedroom door at the top of the stairs. "May I see the room again?"

He winced, ever so slightly, then said, "If you want."

I walked up the stairs. He followed behind me. I stood outside the open doorway and looked into the room. The bed was made and everything was in order, as if no one had been living in it. Through the open door of a guest bedroom, I saw an unmade bed with a shirt and pair of pants strewn across it.

Frank Cirone saw me look into the guest room. He said, "I been sleeping in there since Angie left. She's not the only one who feels strange sleeping in the master bedroom. I can eat lunch while I look at the spot where my father was executed, but sleeping in that room is hard."

It was a side of him that he likely let few people see: the vulnerability and anxiety of a normal person in an abnormal circumstance.

I stepped into the bedroom. I looked at the wall where once were splattered droplets of Rachel Pace's blood. I stared at the spot on the floor where her crumpled, inert form lay after being slaughtered. I looked at the opposite corner, where a little girl once shook with fear in a room that smelled of urine and death.

The pain that little girl felt stayed with her, throughout and beyond childhood. It affected her in a hundred different ways at every juncture of her life, ways that often went unnoticed or were not understood. The pain affected her still. And because I loved her, it also affected me.

I sensed Rachel's terror, and I sensed Veronica's misery. I walked over to the corner, knelt, and touched the spot where Veronica had cowered in fear. It was as if I were trying to reach back across time to comfort and help her.

Images and ideas ran through my mind without being summoned consciously by me. Bonnie and Clyde. Professional intimacy. Killing her to influence what her husband does. Father John Fitzpatrick. Showeth no mercy. Gertrude Tinsley. The shortest distance between two points. Bobby Beck. And back to Bonnie and Clyde.

And back to Bonnie and Clyde.

Suddenly the pieces clicked.

I stood slowly. Unsteady on my feet, I leaned against the wall for support. I turned to face Frank Cirone. He was still in the hallway looking into the room through the open door.

Our eyes met. "What is it, Harry? You look like you saw a ghost. . . . Harry? Hey, man—are you okay?"

It took several seconds to turn the thoughts into words. But when the words came, they were short and simple. "I think I know," I said. "I think I know who killed Rachel Pace."

26: Evidence

All I had was a suspicion: a tentative conclusion derived from the stringing together of bits of data scattered across time. Looking at it objectively, I had to admit that it was highly speculative; I had no idea if it would really hold water.

If my hunch proved correct, it would bring great pain to people I cared about. And so I decided not to share my suspicion with anyone until I had more evidence.

A match between my suspect's name and the owner of the black SAAB would be nice.

A fingerprint to compare with the one Rachel's killer left would be even nicer.

I hoped to have one or both by the end of the Super Bowl party.

Until then, I would tell no one what I suspected: not Frank Cirone, who asked me directly, or Veronica, Donald, or the Wellesley police.

Sunday brought unseasonably warm weather. After breakfast Donald asked me to join him in his study. It was a custom-designed room added onto the rear of the house. A picture window spanned the width of the room and offered a panoramic view of the snow melting on the grassy expanse that led to the Charles River.

He said, "I received a visit from someone you know. Detective Cavaleri of the Wellesley police. He wanted to learn more about my first wife. He believes that Rachel's murder may have been intentional. And he told me he informed you and my daughter about that."

"Yes, he did."

"What do you think?"

"I think it's just conjecture at this point."

"And what does my daughter think?"

"I think she sees it the same way. Didn't you discuss it with her?"

"No. We haven't talked about her mother's murder since she came here Wednesday night to tell us about the *Globe* article that was being published the next day. I assume she would have told me if the article had produced new leads."

Veronica obviously hadn't told her father about the threatening phone call she received on Thursday night, the one that impelled her to seek refuge at his home.

Donald said, "Moving on to something more pleasant—Marilyn called me yesterday. She made an appointment with the doctor you referred her to. I appreciate your help on this, Harry."

"I was glad to do it. I enjoyed spending time with her."

"That's understandable." He gazed outside and sighed. "She's a remarkable person. Truly remarkable."

Something crystallized in my thoughts when he said that, and I don't know why for sure. Perhaps it was the wistful look in his eye, or the sadness in his voice. But the thought came to me, and I spoke the words without taking the time to weigh the reasonableness of doing so.

I said, "It was Marilyn, wasn't it?"

"Pardon?"

"In 1972. The woman you were involved with. The one you told Detective Branson about. That was Marilyn."

He stood and walked slowly to the window. He looked out at the river. With his back toward me he said, "Did she tell you?"

"She told me how important you were in her life. She talked about how well you worked together. She called it professional intimacy. But it wasn't so much what *she* said. I think it was something *you* said."

He turned around. "Something *I* said?"

"The night of the murder, your daughter went home with Marilyn until you could come for her. And yet there was no mention of that in the police report. And I wondered why. It was a brutal crime, the perpetrator was still at large, and a nine-year-old girl was the only witness. Why would the police let her go off with someone, yet not document where she had gone? But then you said something when we spoke in the library upstairs after dinner on Tuesday night."

"What did I say?"

"You asked me if the police report contained the name of the woman you had the affair with. I told you that Branson kept her name out of the report, and you replied, 'Branson promised me that. I'm glad he was a man of honor.' The way I see it, he bent over backward to keep her name out, including taking out whatever reference was already there about Veronica going to her house after the murder."

Donald walked back to his chair and sat down.

I said, "When Branson interviewed you the day after the murder, you told him about an indiscretion with a *former* client. You said you had ended the relationship."

"I ended the sexual relationship. And she *was* a former client at that time. I had passed her matters over to Oliver Gray."

"Marilyn told me she was unhappy about that."

He nodded. "She kept asking me to reconsider. She was certain we could continue to have—what was that expression, professional intimacy?—we could have professional intimacy without the sexual intimacy. After Rachel died, I started representing her again. Not because of the sexual aspect. That never happened again. I took her case back because I thought that was what Rachel would have wanted me to do." He paused for several seconds. "It's difficult for me to talk about this. Generally, I try not to dwell on what happened in 1972."

"Does Shana know about your affair with Marilyn?"

"No. It was over long before I met Shana. There was never any reason to raise the matter for her consideration. Needless to say, Veronica never knew, either. I would prefer to keep it that way with both of them, my wife and my daughter."

"Does Oliver know about it?"

"I'm certain he doesn't. It was a very brief affair. Two nights, I believe. Actually, two afternoons would be a more accurate statement. I told no one, including Oliver. I can't imagine Marilyn telling him. They didn't have a close relationship."

"Last week in your office, you said he took Rachel's death very hard."

Donald nodded. "He was quite distraught that night. And afterward he was very concerned about Veronica. He always asked me about her, how she was doing, whether she would be able to forget the terrible thing that happened."

"How did Rachel and Oliver get along?"

He thought for a moment. "I don't recall. It was, after all, a long time ago."

"Did she ever complain about him? Did he ever say anything negative about her?"

"Not that I recall. Why are you asking me these questions? Why are you so interested in him?"

I shrugged. "No reason, really. Just idle curiosity, brought on by my conversation yesterday with Marilyn."

In due time, I expected to give him a more truthful answer. *I'm asking these questions because I believe Oliver Gray killed Rachel.*

Shana's walk-in closet was larger than some third-world countries, and Veronica and Melissa were in there with her for quite a while that morning, helping her choose what to wear to the party. Guests were expected to begin arriving around five o'clock; kickoff was set for some time after six.

I checked my answering machine frequently. Around eleven o'clock I retrieved a message from Jonas, and I called him back immediately.

He said, "Do you know someone in Chelsea named Dolores Hurwitz?"

"I don't think I know *anyone* in Chelsea."

"So you don't know her."

"No. I've never heard the name."

"I didn't think so. Well, according to the RMV records, that's who the license-plate number of that SAAB is registered to. Only you must have got it wrong, because the records say her car is a Dodge minivan."

"Shit!"

"Yeah, my sentiments exactly."

Natalie Cole sang the National Anthem and Joe Namath performed the coin toss. A wit in the corner of the room said, "Good thing they didn't get their assignments reversed," and Super Bowl XXVIII was under way.

In a party room that measured at least sixty feet square—with a state-of-the-art projection-television system, stereo sound, and a king's-court assortment of hot and cold buffet items—the throng gathered for Donald and Shana's annual Super Bowl party. About a hundred people milled about, with additional others drifting in and out of the room from other parts of the house. At least a half-dozen caterer's assistants walked around offering hors d'oeuvres and picking up used plates and glasses as soon as they were placed down.

The Boston Globe article about Veronica's hunt for her mother's killer was muting the tone of the party. Every time she waded into a knot of people, the crowd pulled back, and her passage through was followed by whispers and knowing gestures. Veronica picked up on that early in the pregame activities, and now she was elsewhere in the house, making herself scarce. Melissa was with her; she hated watching football on TV, anyway.

Dallas returned the opening kickoff to midfield, then took an early lead with a field goal. But on their first possession, the Bills tied the score on a fifty-four-yard field goal, the longest in Super Bowl history.

I was sitting alone on a two-seater, sipping sparkling water, when an attractive woman my age sat next to me. She was thin and firm, yet busty: the apparent beneficiary of a carefully designed diet-and-exercise program. I was guessing free weights, and she looked like the sort who had the time and money for a personal trainer. Her glass was nearly drained of its amber-colored beverage; the alcohol had put color in her cheeks and a somewhat overly friendly manner in her approach. I thought I saw her glance at my ringless left hand.

She said, "Who do you like?"

"I like Dallas's chances. But I *prefer* the Bills to win. And you?"

"Oh, I'm a Cowboys fan from way back. My late husband hailed from Fort Worth. Watching contact sports used to arouse him, especially when his team won. So with the Cowboys, if you include the play-offs, I knew I could usually count on twelve to fifteen stimulating nights a year."

"That's not much."

"Well, eventually I persuaded him to become a basketball fan. They play eighty-two games a year, and another ten or more play-off games. I think that's what killed him."

I laughed at that, and she appreciated my reaction. She looked at my glass. "Sparkling water?"

"Yes."

"I may not leave with the person who brought me, and I'm well on my way toward needing a designated driver. Are you currently undesignated?"

"I'm afraid not. I'm designated, with child."

She sighed. "At least I'm refining my craft. It only took me ninety seconds to establish your unavailability. It's a pity," she said as she jutted her breasts slightly toward me.

"Indeed," I replied. "More so for me than for you."

She accepted that gracefully, and moved on.

I spent more time looking around the room than I did looking at the television screen, so intent was I on locating someone. I didn't see him until late in the first quarter. Actually, I heard him before I saw him. As Dallas was driving toward what eventually became their second field goal, a voice boomed somewhere behind me, calling out the last name of the Cowboys' quarterback, Troy Aikman.

It was Oliver Gray. And instead of pronouncing Aikman's name as it is supposed to be pronounced—with a long *A*, rhyming it with *brakeman*—he gave the first syllable a long *I*, making it sound like Eichmann, as in Adolf Eichmann.

Our eyes met. He smiled at me. I had no doubt that his mispronunciation was intentional and meant for me. I supposed it was his idea of a joke.

Early in the second quarter, Thurman Thomas put Buffalo ahead with a four-yard touchdown run. And on the final play of the half—after a drive that began with an interception of an Aikman pass deep in Bills territory—another field goal put Buffalo up by a touchdown, 13–6.

I hovered on the edge of the crowd during halftime, keeping Oliver Gray locked in my sight, but maintaining my distance. I knew what I wanted: the glass he was holding, a glass filled and refilled and then refilled again with Scotch, a glass with the perfect nonporous surface to take and hold a fingerprint image.

But he didn't give it up. Every once in a while he placed it on a table, but always in front of himself, and never to stay down.

He was glad-handing some people near one of the food tables. I crept closer. I thought I heard him say something about the Jews, but then I glanced at the television, saw O. J. Simpson standing outside the Bills' locker room with a microphone, and I realized Oliver was talking about The Juice. I made a mental note to laugh about that later.

"I thought you said you were designated," I heard a woman say. It was my companion from the early minutes of the game, come around to the corner where I was standing. Her speech was mildly slurred. "Where's your denistrator—I mean, your designator?"

I kept my eyes on Oliver Gray. "My designator is somewhere in the house."

She stepped toward me, a bit unsteady on her feet. "Is it me? Am I coming on too strong? I just don't know how to do this anymore." Tears welled up in her eyes. "You look like my husband. He died three years ago. I'm so lonely. You have no idea."

"As it so happens, I *do* have an idea how you feel. My wife died seven years ago. It took me five years after that to find someone. Actually, it took me five years just to be open to the idea of finding someone."

"And is she your designator?"

"Yes, although I can't say I've ever used that term before—for her, or for anyone else."

She smiled, a sad smile. "Well, I guess that means you'll have something to remember me by. If you ever hear that word again, you'll think of me."

"Yes, I suppose I will."

"But then again, it isn't a word one comes across very often."

"To tell you the truth, I'm going to have to look it up in the dictionary to see if it even exists."

"And if it doesn't," she said, "then it would be like a secret between us. A bond that no one else shares."

"My name is Harry Kline." I extended my hand, and she shook it. "I'm the boyfriend of our host's daughter."

"I'm Ursula James."

"What brings you here, Ursula? Are you one of Shana's friends?"

"No, I'm just someone's blind date. He wanted an attractive escort, for appearance's sake. These things happen to me. For the moment he seems to have forgotten me. If he remembers me at the end of the evening, I will probably sleep with him. That would be very much like me. I sleep with everyone, and so I will probably sleep with him. Because I am so weary."

I wondered if she would remember me or what she said to me after she sobered up. It was the sort of conversation one could only have in a quiet room, or in a room like this one—a room so packed with people and noise that two people could talk intimately without concern that others would hear.

She said, "I can't believe I'm telling you all of this. That is very much *not* like me. You should be a psychiatrist."

"Actually, I am a psychiatrist."

She stared blankly at me for a few seconds, and then she laughed softly. "Well, now—do you have any advice for me?"

Perhaps it was a stupid thing to say, but it was the only thing I could think of. I pointed at Oliver Gray and said, "Do you see that man standing near the bar? My advice to you is to cross him off your list of potential designees."

She looked at him and said, "Oh, that's just wonderful." She faced me. "He's the one who brought me here." She sighed and looked at her empty glass. "I think I need a refill." She headed toward the bar in the far corner of the room.

The Bills began the second half with the ball and a seven-point lead. Fifty-five seconds later the score was tied: Thurman Thomas fumbled the ball, and a Dallas defensive back ran the ball forty-six yards for a score. No one cheered more loudly than Oliver Gray; I supposed he had never in his life rooted for an underdog.

With that play, the game's entire momentum changed. The Cowboys' offense controlled the line of scrimmage, and Emmett Smith began to rack up ground yardage. He put Dallas ahead for good in the third quarter with a twenty-one-yard touchdown rush. And in the final quarter he salted the game away on a fourth-and-goal run from the one-foot mark.

Donald and Shana were standing near the party room entrance, saying good-bye to people as the crowd began to thin out. Veronica and my daughter were still nowhere to be seen.

Oliver Gray was standing by the fireplace, yawning and checking his watch. Ursula James had rejoined him, looking sullen and under the influence. Oliver's tumbler was empty. One of the servers was hovering near him, loading empty glasses onto a tray.

Oliver put his glass on the fireplace mantel.

He turned toward the projection-screen TV to catch the final minutes of the game.

The server was only a few steps away from the fireplace; she walked slowly toward it to scoop up Oliver's glass. I walked briskly toward the same target, hoping to close the distance before she got there, and hoping to find a way to grab the tumbler without calling attention to myself.

It's a fundamental law of physics: Two objects cannot occupy the same space at the same time. I was faster, but the server was closer to the fireplace. She was also uncommonly wide, effectively blocking me from slipping past her. I was still a few feet away when the woman snatched Oliver's glass and placed it on her tray.

Thwack! I heard it and felt it in the same instant: a hard, jarring slap on my back. I stumbled two steps forward, steadied myself, and turned around.

Oliver Gray leered at me. He grabbed my arm and held on to it. "Hey, Harry—how do you like the job my boy Eichmann is doing?"

I looked at the hand clutching my arm. "Let go of me, you moron."

He held on to me tightly. His eyes were red, his face was flushed, and the fumes of metabolizing alcohol swirled around him. "Let me guess," he said. "I bet you just dropped a bundle on the Bills. I would've thought you'd be more careful with the dollar than that."

I tried to shake him loose, to no avail. His hand was powerful, vise-like. It was easy to imagine it being an instrument of death.

I couldn't pull away from him. I decided to push into him. I leaned forward and pressed my hands on his chest. "Get the fuck *off* of me," I said, and I shoved him as hard as I could.

He tumbled backward, releasing his grip on me. He fell onto a food table and sent dishes crashing to the ground. Then he pitched forward and hit the floor, facedown.

Several people gasped. Someone turned the television sound off. Suddenly Donald was at my side. "Harry, what on earth are you—"

I leaned over Oliver's prone figure. "His name is Aikman," I hissed, "not Eichmann. Aikman is a quarterback. Eichmann was a Nazi. Eichmann designed the death camps. He killed Jews. But you already know that, don't you?"

"Enough!" a woman said. Shana Pace was standing directly next to me. "Please, Harry. This is my home. Leave him be." She touched me lightly on the shoulder. "Please."

I stepped away from Oliver. He pulled himself onto his hands and knees, and then he slowly stood. In a harsh whisper he said, "Some other time, you son of a bitch. Some other time."

"Don't make waves," I said.

He walked away quickly, with Ursula James trailing him.

I thought about Rachel's murder, and the frightened girl who witnessed it, and the killer who said to the girl, "Until we meet again." And for a moment I wanted to kill him right there. But all I knew for sure was that he was a bigot. I had nothing to prove, even to myself, that he was anything worse than that. I had nothing to prove. . . .

The glass! I looked at the mantel. Oliver's glass was gone. I scanned the room. The heavyset server was walking out of the room with a tray of dirty plates and glasses. I was about to run after her when Donald grabbed me by the arm.

He said, "Are you out of your mind? What the hell was that all about?"

"I can't talk. I'm sorry."

I caught up with the server as she was walking into the kitchen. There were several small plates, four coffee cups, and three glasses. One of the glasses was still half-filled. I pointed to the two empty glasses. "Did they come from the mantel?"

"The what?"

"The mantel. The ledge on top of the fireplace."

She shrugged. "I just pick 'em up, boy. I don't catalog 'em."

"Allow me." I took the tray from her. I placed it on a counter and started rummaging through the kitchen cabinets and drawers. Finally I found a box of paper bags. I took two, and in each bag I placed one of the empty glasses. I rolled the bags closed and sealed them with tape.

The heavyset woman and two coworkers were standing there with mouths open. "I declare," said one. "You rich folk are mighty, mighty strange."

I walked upstairs and placed the paper bags into my overnight suitcase. Then I grabbed my cellular phone and walked outside.

I dialed a local Wellesley number. A familiar voice answered on the third ring.

I said, "This is Harry Kline." And then I uttered the words that I never thought I would utter to the man they called Frank the Blade. "I'm calling to ask for a favor."

27: The Favor

When Frank Cirone offered the previous week to look into Rachel's murder, I asked him what I would owe him if I accepted his offer. He laughed and said I wouldn't owe him anything, since I hadn't asked for anything. *If you* ask *for a favor, and I give it,* then *you owe me.*

And so on Monday morning I gave him the two beverage glasses from the Super Bowl party. I gave him a copy of the fingerprint from Rachel's killer, taken from the Wellesley police files that Charlie Amory had copied for Veronica. And I asked Frank to arrange for a comparison between the murderer's print and the ones on the glasses.

We were in the same place where we met a week earlier: a second-story room above a dry-cleaning store in Boston's North End. He preferred conducting business away from his new home; he didn't want his affairs to follow him into Wellesley. I remembered that he had even arranged for someone else's name to be on the deed to his house.

He glanced at the paper bags but didn't open them. "What makes you think I can do what you're asking?"

"You were able to access license-plate records when you wanted to identify me that first time I came to your house. What I'm asking now doesn't involve gaining access to restricted information. It just requires somebody who can lift and read fingerprints. I'm assuming you know someone who can do that."

He wrote something on a piece of paper. He pressed a buzzer and a man came into the room. It was the same man who had driven me to Frank's office a week earlier. Frank handed him the note and the two paper bags, and the man left.

He said, "We'll know within the hour. Perhaps you want to know what sort of obligation I see you as having in return for the favor."

"I guess so."

"You didn't ask before giving me the bags. So you're either very trusting, foolish, or desperate."

"Or clinically insane."

"Huh. That's your field of expertise, not mine. So. Let's think about this. There are lots of people who know how to compare fingerprints. You don't know any. I do. But you're not asking for something illegal."

"No."

"It isn't expensive. It doesn't require much effort or money. And there's no risk to me—physical, financial, or otherwise. You're merely asking me to do something for you that you don't know how to do, but that I can get done quickly."

"That's right," I said.

"Then whatever I ask you to do should be in that same category. Something legal that doesn't cost you anything or take much of your time. Something you can do that I can't. Something you can do without creating any sort of risk for yourself." He paused. "I can probably come up with something. I'll let you know."

From somewhere else in the building I heard two men arguing in Italian. Frank Cirone excused himself and left the room. Almost immediately the arguing ceased. He returned to his chair behind the desk.

He said, "You could have gone to the police. Instead, you came to me. And I'm thinking, there can only be three possible reasons. One, you think they'll fuck up the job. But this is pretty basic, comparing fingerprints, so that doesn't make sense. Two, the whole thing is so farfetched, you want to be sure before you go to the police, you don't want to be the boy who cried wolf. But I don't think you'd put pride ahead of finding your girlfriend's killer. So that brings us to number three."

"And what do you think that is?"

"You want to preserve your options. You go to the police and the prints match, whatever happens is out of your hands. You come to me, you keep your options open. I don't know what you think those options are. You don't strike me as the vigilante type. But at least this way you keep them open for now."

I shrugged. "I don't know, Frank. I really didn't analyze what I was doing when I came to you for help. But what you say makes sense, I guess."

We exchanged small talk for a little while. A week earlier Lorena Bobbit had been found not guilty by reason of insanity for cutting off her husband's penis. We got a lot of mileage out of that one. And a few days later Michael Jackson agreed to pay millions of dollars in a settlement with a prepubescent boy who claimed to have had close encounters with the King of Pop's erection.

Frank said, "The kid says he can identify Michael Jackson's dick. It would be pretty easy to identify John Bobbit's dick. It's removable. Interesting concept, a removable penis. You could lend it to a friend if you weren't using it. Or you could leave it at home if you think it's gonna get you into trouble."

The phone rang. Frank answered it. "Cirone . . . How much longer? . . . Let me know." He hung the phone up and said, "The prints on the first glass don't match up with the killer's fingerprint. We'll have an answer on the other one in a few minutes."

I stood and began to pace the length of the room. I was suddenly conscious of the heat from the dry-cleaning shop downstairs as it sifted up through the floorboards. It sucked the energy from me, and I felt dizzy and weak.

"You look nervous, Harry. What makes you more nervous—the thought that you'll get a match, or the thought that you *won't* get a match?"

"I don't know. Without a match, we're back where we began. Worse, in some ways—because now we've smoked the killer out, and there's no predicting whether he'll leave us in peace. But if it's a match, then I don't know what to do about it. If I take it to the Wellesley police, they'll tell Veronica, and I don't trust her not to kill the guy. And I have a problem with that."

"Why? Because you think it's wrong, or because you think she'll get caught?"

"Definitely the latter. Probably the former."

"You haven't told me the name of the person you suspect. Does he have a record of violent crime?"

"I doubt it. He's a successful lawyer in a big firm."

"Criminal?"

"No. Corporate."

"No need to be violent, then. He has so many other ways of working his will on others." He leaned back in his chair. "Tell me about this fingerprint. The one the Wellesley police already have. It was found at the murder scene, in my home, right?"

"No, it wasn't." I told him about the print: how it was found at another break-in sight, and that the police believed all four break-ins were committed by one person. I told him the details of the connections between the break-ins as they had been given to me by Charlie Amory ten days earlier: the linen napkins, the footprints, the Di-Gel tablet and box.

Frank Cirone considered all of that. "Let me tell you two things. First, I think you're right. I think if the prints on the second glass match up, then you have your killer. Second, this is what to expect. If you go to the police, you'll probably—but not definitely—get the district attorney to prosecute. And if he prosecutes, you will *not* get this guy convicted. This man will have a good lawyer. And a good lawyer will come up with so much reasonable doubt, he'll wish he could save some to use on ten other cases. With a good lawyer, even *I* could beat this case."

His words gave me pause. I hadn't focused on that aspect of things. Nor did I have the direct experience that Frank Cirone probably had. I stopped pacing and stood in the middle of the room.

He said, "I'm trying to figure out if you're going to ask me to . . . resolve this situation for you. That would be a large favor, indeed."

Resolve this situation. I had no doubt what he was alluding to. "No," I replied. "I won't ask for that kind of help. I can't afford that much indebtedness. I won't even tell you the man's name."

The phone rang. Frank said, "Sit down, Harry." He picked up the phone.

I sat across from him and tried to read the news from the expression on his face. I couldn't do it.

Frank listened to his caller. "Uh-huh . . . Uh-huh . . . Another print wouldn't be useful, then . . . You're certain . . . Okay."

He hung up the phone. He looked at me. He folded his hands on the desk and leaned forward.

"May God help you, Harry." And then he whispered, "You have your killer."

28: The Meeting

I called from my cellular phone as I drove away from Frank Cirone's office. "I owe you an apology," I said. "I'd like to take you to lunch."

"I don't know about that," Oliver Gray said. "Has your sanity returned?"

"Listen—I don't want there to be a problem between us. If there's a problem between us, then I have a problem with Donald. And if I have a problem with Donald, I have a problem with Veronica."

"You do connive, don't you?"

"Look at it any way you want to, but I'm serious about this. I want to reach an understanding."

He hesitated. "Where do you want to meet?"

"Do you know the Seaside, over in Faneuil Hall Market Place?"

"What time?"

I checked my watch. "How about noon, an hour from now?"

"Noon it is, then. Good-bye."

I knew I had plenty of time to drive to Faneuil Hall, park, and get to the restaurant in time for its eleven-thirty opening. And that was good, because I wanted to make certain I got a window seat.

I wanted to be sure I would see Oliver Gray approaching.

* * *

269

Faneuil Hall Market Place consists of four buildings. There is the hall itself, where Sam Adams and his cohorts plotted the Revolution.

Behind the hall stretches Quincy Market, a block-long single-story building filled with food stalls and artisans' carts.

North Market and South Market run parallel to Quincy Market, on either side of it: two-story buildings with restaurants and upscale specialty stores.

The Seaside was at the eastern end of South Market. My second-story window seat overlooked the cobblestone walkway between South Market and Quincy Market.

My plan was either simple, stupid, or both. Frank Cirone had persuaded me that the fingerprint match by itself would be less-than-compelling proof to a district attorney. I had my microcassette dictating recorder in my pocket. I intended to let it run while I confronted Oliver with my suspicions. I hoped I would get him to say something incriminating. Then I would present the tape to Jonas Cavaleri, tell him what I knew about the fingerprint match, and hope it would be enough to put Oliver under investigation.

A Latino man at a nearby table kept checking his watch as if he, too, were waiting for someone. Like me, he nursed a beverage while he waited.

My stomach was in knots. Sweat poured into every crevice of my body. I took my sport jacket off and draped it over the back of my chair.

I didn't know if I could pull this off. And it wasn't what I really wanted to do, anyway. What I really wanted was to pound him to death with my own fists, just as he had done to the mother of the woman I loved. I wanted him to die: with great pain and suffering, and very slowly.

I remembered a moment from my childhood. My parents and I were watching a news account of Adolf Eichmann's capture by the Israelis. I was about nine years old: too young to comprehend the incomprehensible. I knew something of the Holocaust. I knew my father once had a cousin his age who was no more. I heard the news reporter say something about the world's most infamous living war criminal.

My father said, "He deserves a slow death—by hanging."

"But, dear," my mother replied, "hanging is a very quick death."

"Only when they hang you by the *neck*."

Like Eichmann, Rachel Pace's killer had eluded justice for many years. I was certain Oliver Gray was that person. I could only speculate about the motivation behind the murder. But it was speculation about motive that had caused me to settle on him as a suspect.

Frank Cirone had suggested that I focus on motive the night we watched *Bonnie and Clyde* together. He said, *You're looking for someone who wanted her out of the picture. So now the question is, why? If you figure out the why, maybe that will lead you to the who.*

And when I went upstairs afterward for another look at the room where Rachel Pace met her end, I was still thinking of Bonnie and Clyde and the strange things some people will do in the name of love.

And the words jumped into my head: *When it comes to love, there's no telling what some people will do.* That's what Bobby had said to me several days earlier when he told me about another couple he called Bonnie and Clyde: the couple who conspired to murder a woman merely to drive that woman's daughter mad with grief. And in that instant it came to me. . . .

Oliver Gray was approaching the Seaside entrance. A wave of revulsion swept over me. And I felt sick to my stomach— because of what I knew he had done, and because of what I was thinking: *I want to kill you.*

I was shaking with nervous energy and nausea by the time he reached the table. I excused myself immediately and headed for the men's room.

I vomited into one of the toilets.

I was standing at the sink, dousing my face with cold water, when Oliver Gray walked into the room. He said, "Are you all right?"

"I think so."

"You left this in your sport jacket. Too valuable to leave unattended."

I turned around and looked at him. He had my tape recorder in his hand. He held it out toward me. I reached for it.

Suddenly his other hand flashed forward. His open palm smacked against the side of my head. I fell against the wall. He lunged at me. He pinned me against the wall. He punched me full force in the crotch. I crumpled to the floor, clutching myself, writhing.

He smashed the recorder against the wall, then threw it in the trash.

He snarled, "Last night you told me not to make waves. Do you think I'm an idiot? Did you think I wouldn't know what that meant?"

I closed my eyes for a moment, waiting for the pain in my groin to pass. When I opened them, I was staring down the black metal barrel of a handgun.

"Stand up," he commanded.

"I can't."

"Stand *up*, goddammit!"

Still training the pistol on me, he reached out with one hand and jerked me into a standing position. His strength was impressive. Rachel Pace had been no match for him then. In my weakened condition, I was no match for him now. I grabbed the sink for support.

He backed away a few feet. "I asked you, do you think I'm an idiot?"

"No," I gasped. "You got away with murder for twenty years. You're no idiot."

"How did you figure it out?"

"Bonnie and Clyde."

"What the hell are you talking about?"

"What's the difference?"

"That's what I like about you psychiatrists. You always answer a question with a question." He grabbed a paper towel and mopped the sweat on his brow. "But you don't have any proof that you're right, do you?" It was more a taunt than a serious question.

I motioned toward the gun. "I'd say that's proof I'm right, wouldn't you?"

"Fuck you! I mean proof you can actually use. If you did, you wouldn't be here with a tape recorder, and I would already be in custody. Who else knows?"

No one, I realized. I hadn't told Frank Cirone my suspect's name. "Everyone," I said.

"Well, I'll have to take my chances that you're bullshitting me." He drew the pistol upward, taking aim at my head. "A hundred people saw you assault me last night. Today you lured me here on the pretext of apologizing. You followed me into the bathroom and assaulted me again. I pulled out my gun— which I'm licensed to carry, by the way—and in the struggle it discharged, killing you instantly. Oh, why the fuck am I explaining this to you? You're history."

He grabbed the pistol with both hands. He took one step closer.

The men's-room door swung open and two men rushed in with guns drawn. The first was a Latino man, perhaps the one who had been waiting at the table next to mine. The second man had a blond crew cut and looked vaguely familiar.

Oliver swung around in the direction of the commotion— just in time to take a bullet in the chest from the Latino man.

The second man pushed me into the toilet stall. "Hands against the wall!" he yelled.

I did as he commanded. I felt the cold steel of his gun barrel against the back of my neck. I felt his hands going through my pockets, taking my wallet.

He leaned against me, hard, and hissed in my ear. "You don't *know* us. You don't *see* us. You just stay there and keep your fucking mouth *shut.*"

He stepped away and closed the stall door. I heard him say to the Latino man, "Let's be sure about this one."

A second shot rang out. The explosion reverberated off the tile and porcelain.

The men's-room door opened and shut, and there was only the sound of my own shallow breathing.

I rushed out of the stall and over to Oliver. He lay prone:

massive chest bleeding, a small circular blood-red indentation
in the center of his forehead.

His gun was still in his hand.

Unblinking eyes stared motionless at the buzzing fluores-
cent overhead light.

Even if I wanted to save him, I couldn't.

29: The Inquiry

Bobby Beck and I sat alone inside the manager's office at the Seaside restaurant. He said, "Who's that little fat guy in the hall outside? Keeps walking around saying, 'This is terrific, just fucking terrific.' "

"He's the manager. He's unhappy that the police won't let him resume seating people until all of the employees have been questioned."

Bobby looked at my head. "I don't see any marks, other than a trace of the bruise you got last Wednesday when your patient was murdered."

"He wasn't murdered. He was manslaughtered."

"Whatever. Like I said, no visible marks."

"My crotch is still numb. Should we check for bruising there?"

"You can do that on your own. Or maybe I'll send the manager in to help you. Give him something to do while he counts the money he's losing."

Somewhere in the building a police radio kept clicking on and off, a dispatcher calling out numbers and locations in a private code that presumably made sense to the members of the police force.

Bobby said, "So how come you call me every time something like this happens? Last year when you killed that guy, and now."

I shrugged. "Because I know you'll drop whatever you're doing and come help."

"Well, I guess you got that right. In case it comes up in conversation, it's about a three-minute run from my office to Faneuil Hall."

The office door opened. Donald Pace walked in. "Jesus, Harry—what the hell is going on? Is it true what they said about Oliver?" He looked at Bobby with an expression of uncertainty.

The two had never met. I introduced them to one another. "He's dead, Donald. We were robbed at gunpoint by two men. Why they killed him and left me standing, I'll never know."

The door opened again. A uniformed police officer—the first one on the scene, who took my narrative statement about what had happened—stepped into the room with a silver-haired man of Asian extraction. The officer pointed at me. "That's the other robbery victim, detective. The doctor I was telling you about."

The police officer left. The silver-haired man said to me, "I'm Detective Katari, Dr. Kline. And these men are . . ."

"My friend, and my girlfriend's father."

Katari arched his eyebrows. "Girlfriend? Unusual expression for someone of your obvious maturity."

"I've been told that before."

"My name is Donald Pace, detective. I'm also . . . I was also a law partner to the man who was murdered."

"I'm Bobby Beck, from Carlton Trenam & Honigman. I'm sure you don't mind if Mr. Pace and I sit in while you question Dr. Kline."

Katari let out a slow, weary sigh. "You guys gonna bust my balls? Your friend here is a victim. I just need to ask him what happened. No need for him to get lawyered up."

I said, "I'll tell you anything you want to know, detective. I'm just not certain I have anything useful to say."

"You and the deceased met here for lunch."

"Yes."

"You do that often?"

"This was the first time. I don't like the man. Didn't like

him, I guess I should say. We were both at a party yesterday at Mr. Pace's house—"

"A Super Bowl party?"

"Yes."

"The Bills fucked me again," said Katari. "They didn't even cover the spread. So, go on."

"Mr. Gray made what I considered to be some anti-Semitic remarks. This wasn't the first time. We had some words, a little bit of shoving—"

Bobby jumped into the conversation. "Maybe you and I should talk about this first, Harry."

"It's all right, Bobby. Like the man said—I'm a victim here. Anyway, detective, I felt bad about it afterward. I believed I had embarrassed our host, Mr. Pace. So I called Mr. Gray this morning and invited him to lunch, and he accepted very graciously."

"Did the two of you argue again today?"

"Not at all. We didn't even have time. I got here first. I wasn't feeling well. I went to the men's room immediately after Mr. Gray arrived. He came after me a few minutes later to see if I was feeling all right. And then, as I already told the police officer, two men came in and robbed us at gunpoint. One of them pushed me into the toilet stall and made me look at the wall. The other one shot Mr. Gray twice. Then they left."

I gave him descriptions of the men, but they were vague and probably not very helpful.

"You ever see them before?"

"I think I saw one of them, the Hispanic-looking man, in the restaurant while I was waiting for Mr. Gray. The other one looked familiar, but not in a specific way. Lots of people look familiar the first time you see them."

"What I can't figure out is, if they killed the other guy, why are you still alive?"

"Maybe the fellow who robbed me has a gentler nature."

Katari shook his head. "I don't think so. You said the Hispanic man shot the deceased twice, but that's not how it happened."

"I definitely heard two shots. And he was bleeding in the chest and the head."

The detective nodded. "Yes, but they appear to be from two guns of different calibers. The man who robbed you must have caused the second wound. Probably the one to the head as the victim lay on the floor. The coup de grâce, as they say. Cold-blooded killer. But he didn't kill you, best as I can tell."

I said, "Mr. Gray apparently tried to defend himself with his own gun. Perhaps he provoked them. Like I said, I was in the toilet stall. I didn't see what happened to him. As for me, I've never considered owning a gun."

"Yeah, well, you know what they say. Guns don't kill people. Postal workers kill people."

The detective finished questioning me, then stood to leave and reinspect the murder scene. He said, "I'll meet you at the police station in a little while. One of my men will drive you. I want you to look at some photos, see if you can ID anybody."

Bobby got up to leave a few minutes later. "You need anything else right now, pal of mine?"

"How about some money?"

"Money?"

"They took my wallet, remember? How the hell am I going to get my car out of the parking garage?"

"You still have your car keys?"

"Yes."

Bobby took out his wallet, peeled off two twenty-dollar bills, and left.

When Donald and I were alone I said, "Do you know where Veronica is?"

"She should be back in Concord. She left right after you did. She said she was dropping Melissa off at school, then going home."

"I don't have time to explain this now, Donald. But I want you to call Marilyn Levine, and I want you and her to go to Concord and wait for me. I need to talk with the two of you and your daughter about something very important."

He furrowed his brow. "Is there something you want to tell me now?"

"Frankly, I really don't *want* to tell you at all. But you have a right to know. You all do—you, Marilyn, and Veronica. I'll get there as soon as I can."

A police officer took me to the area police station on Warren Avenue. I spent an hour in a fruitless visual tour of books full of two-by-three photographs of unhappy-looking men. Then another officer drove me back to the parking garage across from Faneuil Hall Market Place.

I unlocked my car and started the engine. I put the car into reverse, but I couldn't depress the accelerator pedal. It felt as though something were wedged underneath. I turned off the engine. I stuck my hand down, dislodged an object that was stuck underneath the pedal, and brought it up to take a look at it.

It was my wallet.

30: Explanations

I arrived home around four o'clock. Donald and Marilyn were already there. Donald had told Veronica and Marilyn the story of Oliver's murder—the story as he understood it, based on the account he heard me give to the Boston police detective.

My part-time housekeeper, Ingrid, agreed to take Melissa to Papa Gino's for dinner. I sat down with the others in the den to tell them what really had happened—that is, *most* of what really had happened.

Veronica sat next to me on the sofa. Donald and Marilyn sat across from us on the Queen Anne chairs.

The phone rang. Frank Cirone was on the other end. "Harry, I just heard what happened. Are you all right?"

"Yes, I am. Thanks."

"A pity what happened to your friend."

"Yes, a pity."

"Was he your friend?"

"What do you mean?"

"Was his death something that causes you grief? Because if it was, then I'm sorry for your grief."

"And if it wasn't?"

"Then any loss of life, no matter how necessary, is still regrettable. I'm home now. Call me later if you want to talk."

I brought a glass of water and two Tylenol tablets with me. "My head hurts where he smacked me."

"Which one hit you?" asked Donald. "The one who robbed you, or the one who shot Oliver?"

"Neither."

"Neither?"

"No." I paused. "Oliver hit me."

"Oliver? Why in the world did he do that?"

"Because he was getting ready to kill me."

For a few seconds no one said anything. Then Donald frowned and said, "That's ridiculous. Why would he want to do something like that?"

"To keep me from talking about something I knew. Something he managed to keep secret for many years. Something he wanted to keep secret forever."

"Aha!" said Marilyn. "I *knew* it. Oliver was gay, wasn't he? Did he tell you that?"

I shook my head. "That's not what this is all about. That's not the secret I discovered." I looked at Donald, and then Marilyn. "This won't be an easy thing for you to hear. It won't be easy for you to live with."

I turned to Veronica. "I love you," I said. "When you're happy, I'm happy. When you hurt, I hurt. And I ache for what happened to your mother, and for what happened to you." I reached my hand out, and she placed hers in mine. "I discovered Oliver Gray's darkest secret. He was the one in your parents' bedroom that night. The one you tried to shoot, but couldn't." I paused. "Oliver Gray killed your mother, darling, and I'm so very, very sorry."

Quietly, she said, "Are you certain?"

"Yes. I'm certain. He admitted it right before he tried to kill me."

"How did you know?"

"The fingerprint. It was his. I had someone match it to the fingerprints from the glass he used at your father's party."

"Jonas matched them?"

"No."

"Who, then? Charlie Amory? Alfred Korvich?"

"No. Someone else. Someone did me a favor. I can't tell you who."

Donald interrupted. "What are you talking about? Why would Oliver do something like that? Why would you even suspect him?"

"I can give you a guess. I think it's a good one, but it's just a guess." I turned to Marilyn. "Oliver killed your friend Rachel because he didn't want to lose you."

"Didn't want . . ." She looked perplexed. "Tell me what you mean."

"At one point Donald gave your legal work to Oliver because of a temporary impasse in your working relationship." I glanced at Donald. I was being elliptical; there was no need for Veronica to know about the affair her father had with her mother's best friend. "But you didn't want to stay with Oliver. You finally convinced Donald to consider taking you back. You told Oliver you had done that. But he wanted to be your lawyer. You told me he wanted you to make the same offer you had made to Donald—the astronomical salary for going in-house with your company."

I turned to Donald. "Oliver wanted you out of the picture. But he couldn't move against you directly. Maybe he was frightened of you, or maybe he genuinely liked you. I don't know. But I think he killed Rachel because he believed you would be too crushed to do anything but grieve. And you *were* crushed. But you drowned your grief in work."

Donald said, "I still can't believe this."

"Oliver knew you were out of town on a business trip. You came back that night, Thursday, but you weren't due back until Friday. He broke in while no one was home and waited, just like Jonas Cavaleri said."

I thought of Frank Cirone's tongue-in-cheek fairy tale about killing Rachel himself in order to get Donald to sell the house. *So I kill her not because I have something against her, but because I want to influence what her husband does.*

Veronica said, "But this doesn't make sense. The killer made his first phone call to you on Tuesday night. But the article about the case appeared in the Thursday paper. How would he have known I was trying to find my mother's murderer?"

"Your father probably mentioned it." I turned to Donald. His face turned ashen. "You often confided in him. You mistook the questions he used to ask as an expression of concern about Rachel and Veronica, when he was probably only trying to ascertain whether you suspected what he had done. And when you found out Veronica was looking into the murder, you were worried and upset. You probably mentioned it to him."

Donald looked away. "I think I may have."

Veronica said, "It *still* doesn't make sense. I didn't tell my father what I was doing until Wednesday night, after the killer made his second call to you."

"Yes. But your father already knew."

She closed her eyes for a moment. "I asked you not to tell him."

"I didn't." I described the chain of events: Gertrude Tinsley calling the governor's office, the governor's chief of staff calling Donald, Donald asking me about it. "Your father knew. He asked me not to tell you that he knew. I kept his secret, just as I had kept yours."

No one spoke for a few minutes. Finally Veronica said, "Why won't you tell me who matched the fingerprints? Was it who I think it was? Was it that mafioso who lives in the house I grew up in?"

"I don't want to talk about that right now."

"You don't know him. You don't know if you can trust him."

"I trust him on this."

"So it *was* him. And you think what he told you is proof that Oliver Gray killed my mother?" She was incredulous.

She had more reason than anyone I ever knew to be angry about the course of events in her life. I didn't mind her letting some of it out on me.

She walked over to the phone and dialed a number. She identified herself to whoever answered and asked to speak with Timothy Connolly. While she was on hold she said to us, "He's a Boston detective. You met him, Harry. Remember? When we were working on that serial-murder case a couple of years ago?"

"I remember."

She said, "All homicide victims are routinely fingerprinted

by the medical examiner. . . . Yes, hello, Tim . . . Yes, it has been a long time . . . Tim, I need a favor. A man named Oliver Gray was murdered in Boston this afternoon. I need a copy of his fingerprint card . . . No, I won't go out with you, Tim . . . Yes, I'm still with that same guy . . . Yes, he's treating me all right." She looked at me and smiled. "More than all right."

She finished her call with the Boston detective and sat down next to me again. "I almost lost you today. The second time in less than a week. It scares the hell out of me. If those men hadn't come in to rob you and Oliver, you would be dead."

Marilyn said, "The following sentence probably has never been uttered before in the history of mankind, and probably will never be heard again. Harry, you're very lucky to have been robbed at gunpoint in a toilet stall this afternoon. Those men saved your life."

Donald said, "It's amazing that they picked that particular moment. I wonder who they were. Who killed Oliver Gray?"

"I don't know who they are," I said, and that was the truth.

But I had a damn good idea who they were working for.

I drove alone to Wellesley that evening, along the same route I took two nights earlier to Frank Cirone's house.

The last time I drove that route, I was trailed part of the way by a black SAAB. I thought then that the driver was a killer, and I was right. But he was not the man who killed Rachel Pace.

On my way to see Frank two nights earlier, I stopped in the liquor store. Another customer paid for a small purchase with a hundred-dollar bill. That customer sported a blond crew cut. I only saw him from behind. I couldn't prove he was the same man who took—and returned—my wallet. But just because you can't prove something, that doesn't mean it isn't true.

The driver of the SAAB—the one who blocked me by double-parking, then backed up to let me out—was, I assumed, the Latino man.

They were killers, but they meant me no harm. Quite the opposite: They were there to protect me—that night, and this afternoon in the men's room at the Seaside restaurant.

I knew only one person who would arrange something like that. And I thought of a way to check out that supposition.

I called directory assistance on my cellular phone, and I asked for the number of the man whose name appeared on the deed to Frank Cirone's house. There was a listing for an Alan Hurwitz in Chelsea, just as Angie said there was when she offered to look it up for us the day Veronica and I met her.

I dialed the number. A woman answered. I said, "Dolores?"

"No."

Shit, I thought.

She said, "Dolores and Al went out. You want I should take a message?"

"No, that's quite all right. I'll call some other time."

"Your hired hands took the license plates from the Hurwitzes' minivan and put it on the SAAB, just in case something happened and they were spotted. If that occurred, your friend Al could always say the plates were stolen."

"That's quite a story you're telling," said Frank Cirone. "You should write a book."

"They were very good at what they did. Improvising when the game plan changed. Taking my wallet was brilliant. It not only convinced the police that the murder had nothing to do with me, it also convinced me. And leaving it in my car was equally brilliant. It was a message to me. A warning not to try too hard to identify them. The only problem is, they assumed I would get that message *before* I looked at police photos."

He raised his eyebrows. "And was looking at the photos a productive endeavor?"

"No," I replied. "Not productive at all."

Frank Cirone drummed his fingers on his kitchen table: thinking, thinking, thinking. He said, "I don't suppose you're willing to entertain a denial."

"You probably had someone tailing Veronica, too. She wondered if she was being followed to her father's house Friday night, then dismissed the idea, thought she was being paranoid."

"Let's suppose, just for the sake of argument, that there's some validity to what you think. Would that trouble you?"

"Yes. It would mean I'm in way too deep. Much too beholden to you. It would mean we can't be friends."

"But you didn't ask. You would only be beholden if you asked."

"That's not my world, Frank. People are beholden. We're all beholden. I don't even know what the fuck I mean by that, but I'm sure I'm right."

He paused. "You've had a rough day."

"I've had a lot of rough days. We all have."

"Yes. We all have. This is a common denominator."

I stood and reached for my coat. "Frank, I like you. And I'm deeply appreciative for everything you've done. But I don't think we should see each other again."

He smiled, a knowing and sad smile. "You're breaking up with me?"

"I'm in love with Veronica. I want to spend the rest of my life with her, if she'll have me. And you know who she is and what she does. I can't have both of you in my life. I can't do that to her."

He stood. He offered his hand. I shook it. He held it and said, "That favor you owe me—the nonillegal, noncostly, nonrisky one we spoke of this morning. Let's say you just discharged it by talking with me the way you did. Let's say the books are balanced."

I walked outside, stepped into my car, and drove home to my woman and my child.

31: Wingless Angels

On Tuesday morning Richie Conover was laid to rest. I didn't go to the burial, but I attended the service at the funeral home. His parents were inconsolable: His mother sat in stupor-like silence; his father wailed so hard it was like a knife cutting into my heart. Richie's sister was all smiles as she glad-handed the other mourners, welcomed them, thanked them for their thoughtfulness.

All three reactions surprised me. They shouldn't have. I've had ample opportunity to learn over the years that grieving is the most private and personal thing one ever does.

That same morning Veronica obtained Oliver Gray's fingerprints from the Boston police and matched them to the one the killer left in 1972. She called her father with the news, and he told Marilyn Levine.

Marilyn called me that afternoon. She had been crying. "You shouldn't have told me about Oliver Gray, because now I wonder about my own role in Rachel's death. Donald never would have slept with me if I hadn't initiated it. If I hadn't slept with Donald, he wouldn't have handed me over to Oliver. And if he never handed me over to Oliver . . . Well, you can see where that progression leads."

"Yes. And I'm sorry. What will you do?"

"I don't know. If Donald doesn't want to be my lawyer anymore, I won't fight him on that. I just hope he'll still want to be my friend."

"I'm sure he will."

She sighed. "If he doesn't, I guess that will give me something to talk over with my new psychiatrist." She paused. "I met with her today, by the way. I liked her. The nightingale thanks you for that, Harry."

"The nightingale is entirely welcome."

On Wednesday morning I spoke with Dr. Greta Anselm, the director of the Veterans Administration Hospital in Bedford. She wanted me to go there two mornings per week to do some teaching and supervision. I told her that I would.

She said, "I'm sorry it took me so long to get back to you about this. There was a death in the family. It took me off course."

"Yes," I said. "I know the feeling."

Alfred Korvich called that afternoon to tell me that Tommy Mason was going to plead guilty to voluntary manslaughter for killing Richie Conover. "Probably won't spend more than three years in prison," he said.

"What about the other kid, Paul Nickerson?"

"He'll plead guilty to malicious destruction of property, get some sort of fine or community-service requirement. The district attorney also wants a guilty plea to involuntary manslaughter, with a period of probation. That may or may not happen."

"Your detective did a good job."

"Yeah, she did. Which reminds me—I read about you in the *Globe* again yesterday. The murder you witnessed in Boston. You're one lucky son of a bitch that you weren't killed."

"I know," I replied, because I was, indeed, almost killed— although not by the men who shot Oliver Gray.

"It sounds like the Boston police are going nowhere with the case. You couldn't pick their pictures out?"

"No. I was too frightened to get a good look at them."

"Well, not every murder gets solved."

"No," I agreed, "not every one."

I planned on telling no one—not even Veronica or Bobby— what I knew about Frank Cirone's involvement in ordering the killers to protect me. The Boston police would never clear the murder of Oliver Gray.

And the Wellesley police would never clear the murder of Rachel Pace. The four of us—Veronica, Donald, Marilyn, and I—had agreed to keep our knowledge amongst ourselves. Oliver's parents were old and infirm; no purpose would be served in dragging his name down. It was self-interest, too: None of us wanted to deal with the scrutiny that would likely come our way if we revealed what we knew. And I knew that Frank Cirone wasn't likely to tell anyone, either.

Veronica and I told Melissa that we had learned the identity of Rachel's killer. We told her that he was dead: killed a number of years later while trying to murder someone else. She was satisfied with that explanation. I doubted she and Charlie Amory or Jonas Cavaleri would ever be in a position to compare notes and realize they had been told different stories.

Police chief Alfred Korvich said, "That's two times in six days that someone in your presence got killed. You're dangerous company. If it's all the same to you, Harry—when you want to talk with me, use the phone."

Never having purchased a Yahrzeit candle before, I was surprised to learn that they were available in the international foods aisle of the local Stop & Shop. I bought one on Thursday morning to light the next day in memory of Janet's death. It was a plain-looking uncolored hard-wax candle, with visible air bubbles, in a cheap glass. It was smaller than I thought it would be.

"What's the deal with this ugly candle?" I asked Bobby. "Why can't I just light a normal candle?"

"Well, you can. But the candle you bought has received the appropriate blessing when it was manufactured. And it's certain to last the entire twenty-four hours. Don't forget to light it this evening, Harry. The Jewish day starts at sunset."

"I know. But tomorrow isn't the Hebrew-calendar anniversary of her death. It's the regular calendar anniversary. She died on February fourth, and tomorrow is February fourth."

"It doesn't seem like seven years."

"I don't know," I said. "Sometimes it feels like a million years ago. Other times it feels like yesterday. I miss her."

"I know, pal of mine. I miss her, too."

I lit the candle that evening, just after sunset. Then I joined Melissa and Veronica for the dinner Ingrid had prepared.

Midway through the meal, Veronica said, "You seem very pensive tonight. Is something wrong?"

If Veronica wants to be with you, she'll have to make space in her life for the memory of this woman. . . .

"I was thinking about Janet," I replied. "Tomorrow is the seventh anniversary of her death."

"Oh."

None of us spoke for several moments.

"I'm going to visit her grave tomorrow. Melissa, I'd like you to stay home from school and come with me."

"Okay, Dad."

I turned to Veronica. "And I'd like you to come with me, too. With Melissa and me."

She averted my gaze and shook her head slowly. "I don't think I can, Harry. Please don't pressure me into going."

"I won't."

The three of us finished our meal in silence.

Six inches of snow fell overnight.

* * *

JANET ROSE KLINE

AUGUST 3, 1954—FEBRUARY 4, 1987

BELOVED DAUGHTER, WIFE, AND MOTHER

"EVEN THOUGH WE ARE APART

YOU WILL STAY HERE IN MY HEART"

* * *

Melissa and I stood before Janet's grave on the side of a low hill in Sleepy Hollow Cemetery. She lay a mile from our house, and less than a hundred yards from Authors Ridge—the steep rise that holds the graves of Emerson, Alcott, and Thoreau.

I came here often in the year after her death. Now I came three times a year, all in warm-weather months: her birthday, the day before Mother's Day, and our anniversary. And so it had been several years since I visited her grave in midwinter, at the same point in the seasons as were her death and burial.

It was as I said to Bobby the day before: Sometimes it seemed like only yesterday. This was one of those times. The snow and the winter chill mimicked the feel of the day we laid her to rest, when I threw a cup of dirt into the open grave, when I recited for the first and only time the Kaddish—the Hebrew prayer for the dead.

I pulled a paper from my pocket. On it was an English phonetic transcription of that prayer; the day had long passed when I could make a go of it in Hebrew. I stared at the words, but they were just words. I had no idea what they meant. I put the paper back in my pocket.

I remembered a visit we made nearly two years earlier, the day before Mother's Day. I told Melissa then that eventually I would be buried next to her mother.

"Even if you get married again?"

"I'm not getting married again."

"Will I be buried with you and Mommy?"

"No, sweetheart. When it's time for you to be buried—a long, long, long time from now—you'll be buried with your husband."

"But if you don't get married, I won't either. I'll stay with you so you won't be lonely."

"I won't be lonely. I'll always carry you in my heart, no matter where you are."

"Do you still carry Mommy in your heart?"

"Yes, I do."

"I do, too." She rolled her hand into a fist and held it up for me to see. "My heart is only this big, but it has room inside to carry both of you. I think you can still love someone after they're not alive anymore."

The words were true then. They were still true.

I reached out and brushed the snow from the top of Janet's tombstone. I said, "You were only four when she died."

"Uh-huh."

"I used to worry that you were too young to remember her, and how much she loved you."

She thought about that. "I remember she showed me how to make snow angels in the field next to our house."

A male cardinal flew by, his body like a scarlet arrow against the snow. His two-tone chirp resonated in the quiet wooded cemetery.

"Dad, why wouldn't Veronica come with us?"

I sighed. "Well, that's a hard one to explain. I guess she just needs some time before she can do that. She misses her own mother. Maybe that gets in the way."

"Are you mad she didn't come?"

"No, sweetheart. It just makes me sad. And I wish . . ." My voice trailed off.

"What, Dad?"

It was an odd thought, one I couldn't recall having before. "I just wish she could have known your mother."

"Maybe they'll meet in heaven. Father John says that everyone gets connected to God in heaven, and that through God they get connected to everyone else. That means I would get to see Mom again. Veronica would know her, and I would know Veronica's mother."

If only I could believe, I thought. *If only.*

She said, "Should we say a prayer or something?"

I took the paper from my pocket once more and read out loud. *"Yis-ga-dal v'yis-da-dash sh'may rabo. B'ol-mo dee-v'ro chir-u-say . . ."*

It was no use. The words wouldn't come. "I can't remember how to pray," I said. "I can't remember." And then I cried.

Melissa turned to face me; she was crying, too. But then she looked beyond me and smiled.

Veronica stood nearby, shivering in the snow. I wondered how long she had been there. She said, "I changed my mind. I realized you would be here for me if the situation were reversed."

"I'm glad you're here."

"I know a prayer." She took a step toward us, then closed her eyes and bowed her head. "Eternal rest grant unto her, Lord, and let perpetual light shine upon her. May her soul, and the souls of all the faithful departed, through the mercy of God, rest in peace. Amen."

"Amen," I replied. "Thank you."

Melissa said, "That was pretty. My mother would've liked you." She hesitated. "Do you think you would've liked her?"

Veronica pondered that. "I don't know, honey. I might be too jealous of her place in your father's heart . . . and in yours."

Melissa thought for a moment. Then she took Veronica by the hand and drew her close to the tombstone. "Mom, this is Veronica. She lost her mother, too. She lives with us now, sort of. I hope that's okay with you." She paused, a long pause, and then she said, "I love her, Mom."

With that, Veronica's dam broke. Tears flowed down her cheeks. She buried her face against my chest and sobbed. Melissa grabbed on to her from behind. I held both of them and said to myself: *Dear God, please watch over the ones I love.*

We walked home from Sleepy Hollow Cemetery, past the colonial homes that lined Monument Street. Snow began to fall once more. When we reached the house Melissa broke away from us and ran toward the field. "Come with me, Veronica," she called.

"I'll be right there, honey. I want to talk with your father for a minute." When Melissa was out of earshot, Veronica said, "We need to talk about the money I owe you."

"What money?"

"The quarter of a million dollars for finding my mother's killer."

"This is a joke, right?"

"Do I look like I'm joking? I'm dead serious."

"Forget the money. All I want is you. For the hundredth time, will you move in with me?"

"I'm not ready for that yet, Harry. Maybe I will be soon. But I'm not ready to move into Janet's house yet."

"Well, I can't take your money."

"But you have to take it. You can do whatever you want with it, but you have to take it. This is part of the bargain I made with God."

I looked at her, and for a moment I saw her not as she was, but rather as a child: as a nine-year-old girl, crying in her Rutgers Street bedroom, trying to strike a magical bargain with God to get back that which had been taken from her.

Perhaps she would be whole again in heaven. But short of that, nothing would ever put things completely right for her. Nothing on this earth would ever put things completely right for any of us.

"I have an idea," I said. "You give me the quarter million. I put it in trust for Melissa. In return for the money, I sell you half the house—"

"But that's not enough. Your house is worth more than a half-million dollars."

"Let's worry about details later. The key point is, I sell you half the house. Your name goes on the deed right next to mine. That makes this your house, too. And then you move in."

She tilted her head and looked at me, as if by looking from a slightly different angle she might understand better what I was trying to say. "Well, you certainly seem to have everything figured out. Is that all, or is there more?"

"One more thing," I said. "You move in, and then you stay with me for the rest of our lives."

She was silent for several moments. "Let me sleep on it. I'll give you an answer in the morning."

"Where are you going to sleep?"

She smiled at me, and then the smile turned into laughter. "Wherever you're sleeping."

She ran into the field and caught up with my daughter. Melissa took Veronica by the hand and pulled her down into the snow. They disappeared from my view.

I could no longer see them. But up in heaven, I thought, God was once again looking down on two snow angels.

*Don't miss
the first two Harry Kline novels
by Philip Luber!*

FORGIVE US OUR SINS

Success turns to horror when psychiatrist/author
Harry Kline's latest book touches off a massacre
by a deranged Vietnam veteran. The slaughter
propels Harry's book onto the bestseller list—
even as it sets in motion a relentless nightmare
that will drag Harry, and those closest to him,
into the depths of terror.

DELIVER US FROM EVIL

A prominent Concord, Massachusetts, man has
been cut down in a hit-and-run accident. The
murder investigation zeroes in on one of
Harry's patients, and then on Harry's lover.
Who is the killer? And was the hit-and-run
really an accident—or something more sinister?

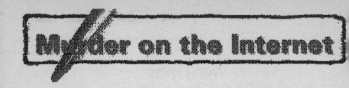